SEX IN THE HOOD 2

Also by White Chocolate

Sex in the Hood

SEX IN THE HOOD 2

White Chocolate

www.urbanbooks.net

Urban Books, LLC
10 Brennan Place
Deer Park, NY 11729

©copyright 2006 White Chocolate

All rights reserved. No part of this book may be
reproduced in any form or by any means without
prior consent of the Publisher, excepting brief
quotes used in reviews.

ISBN 1-893196-55-0

First Printing August 2006
Printed in the United States of America

10 9 8 7 6 5 4 3 2 1

*This is a work of fiction. Any references or similarities to
actual events, real people, living, or dead, or to real locales
are intended to give the novel a sense of reality. Any
similarity in other names, characters, places, and incidents
is entirely coincidental.*

Submit Wholesale Orders to:
Kensington Publishing Corp.
C/O Penguin Group (USA) Inc.
Attention: Order Processing
405 Murray Hill Parkway
East Rutherford, NJ 07073-2316
Phone: 1-800-526-0275
Fax: 1-800-227-9604

Acknowledgements

Thank you, God, for blessing me so abundantly.

I will always express the most gracious gratitude for literary phenom Carl Weber.

Arvita and Roy at Urban Books—I appreciate your love and literary labor.

And to the readers—thank you for indulging the passion on these pages. I hope you enjoy reading about the lives and loves of Duke, Knight and The Queen as much as I did while writing!

Peace and love to all.

Chapter 1

The Queen shivered with a "powergasm" as she surveyed the hundreds of women and Studs who were fucking and sucking on every plush surface of The Playroom. "Damn, I love my job." The words floated over her hot, parted lips and blended with the blasting sound of her own voice singing nasty lyrics over the funky electric beat of the *Dick Chicks Party Mix,* which she had recorded with the Bang Squad as the signature hip-hop album for all Babylon sex parties from New York to Los Angeles.

"Couldn't be nothin' sexier than this on the whole planet right now." She loved the way the relentless beat synchronized with her excited heartbeat and the rhythm of so much fucking around her. "And all hail The Queen up in this mug."

All around the huge industrial loft of this converted warehouse building overlooking the Detroit River, nude bodies writhed on rows of giant beds draped with white mosquito netting that glowed red and purple under the star-shaped neon lights dangling from the ceiling, and cast colorful hues over the tangle of legs, asses, and titties on white polar bear rugs surrounding the beds.

"Yeah, lick those pussies," The Queen said, glancing to her right. In the soft pink haze, a dozen Studs knelt before as many women who were lying spread-eagled on the edge of a long, low couch. "Love that shit."

The lyrics, which she had written, were a musical tribute to what she watched and craved:

> Wrap them lips around my clit
> So I get hit wit' some legit shit
> That makes me cum, oh yum, yum, yum
> Give me some tongue, we young
> It's fun to suck my honey bun
> Take a nibble make it dribble
> Wit' cream so I scream . . .

The Queen moaned, squeezing her pussy muscles to make her clit throb. Damn, the black satin of her thong was marinating in hot cream, but Knight would suck it dry later on. For now, she was loving the way the wet sling of fabric massaged her pussy as she swayed slightly with the beat of the music.

"Love it," she whispered as female clients and Studs twisted into "fucknastics" on the leopard-print benches and Cleopatra-style chaises.

Against the exposed brick walls sat giant framed mirrors, which rested on the floor and angled slightly upward, and reflected a multidimensional freak frenzy. Oversized swings hanging from the exposed beams and pipes of the high ceiling allowed couples to fuck face-to-face as they swung back and forth.

A half-dozen oversized fireplaces cast a soft orange glow over the rainbow of bodies as women and Studs stood kissing, smoking blunts, toasting martini glasses, and nasty-dancing beside glowing flames.

"Oooh, pound that pussy!" a sista shrieked from just a few feet away. On a huge white mink pillow, the woman convulsed with orgasm as a Stud named Antoine jackhammered her so hard, you could see his dick making an imprint from the inside out on the smooth, nutmeg-brown skin between her belly button and the black puff of her pussy hair. The woman's long red fingernails scraped against the creaminess of her titties. She pinched her nipples as skillfully as Antoine's long fingers held her ankles over the rippling muscles of his glistening, rock-hard shoulders.

"Damn," The Queen whispered.

Antoine was gorgeous, but nobody could compare to her beautiful African god named Knight. The image of his sculpted, black velvet face and sparkling onyx, genie eyes superimposed itself like a hologram over her every thought, vision, and dream. Still, that didn't stop her from indulging in all the eye candy that she served up to fiending females for big fees on a daily basis. If she weren't so happy in love, she would definitely get a taste of some of that creamy milk chocolate called Antoine.

He glanced up at her, and the lust in his brown eyes made her shiver. He was a big piece of candy, starting with those cheeks and lips that were Twizzler-colored from fucking, down to a perfect dick that didn't quit.

SEX IN THE HOOD 2

She'd seen his long, fat, big-headed hose in "sexercise" class, but everybody knew Knight would kill a muthafucka who even *thought about* competing with his lead pipe. The last one who tried—well, nobody even remembered his name, since he had disappeared. Never came out how Knight found out. But Knight knew everything.

Antoine is up to somethin', whispered Celeste, the name The Queen gave to her all-knowing inner voice. (Knight called his *Intuition.*) But The Queen also believed that female intuition rose up from the mind-body connection between her brain and her sex organs—that's what her mother had told her as a little girl—and that's why her pussy was also named Celeste.

So The Queen's little voice inside spoke straight from the lips down below, and Celeste was never wrong. *That was just too bold the way Antoine looked at you.* The Queen cast a "don't-even-try-it" look down at the Stud and mouthed to him, "Fuck on."

Antoine smiled, flipped his long braids over his shoulder, and banged that booty even harder.

The chrome points of her stiletto heels and her long legs in black leather pants made her feel a mile tall, which intensified her sense of being the baddest bitch in charge of the most erotic enterprise ever heard of in D-town and beyond. And nobody but the right folks would hear about it. Nobody would know who she was, where she came from, or where she was going, even though her sexy rhymes with the Bang Squad were blazin' up the music charts and every hip-hop media outlet wanted to know who The Queen was. But they would never find out who she used to be, who she was now, or how she planned to rule this sexy underworld forever.

Victoria who? Rich prep-school white girl, who? A fugitive wanted by who?

The Queen smiled as she remembered how much life had changed over the past year. Then, she had been desperate to escape her "Alice in Ghettoland" nightmare after Daddy died and left her with nothing but Feds on her tail.

She was horny, terrified, and condemned to live in Grandma Green's raggedy shack in the hood—until the riches

3

of Babylon became her salvation. Because the baddest gangsta in the hood swept her into his Porsche, his bed, and his erotic enterprise. He was Duke, she was his Duchess, and in a week's time his ghetto reversal of "My Fair Lady" morphed her from a white, prep school virgin into a black, diva nympho.

Just in time for big brother Knight to come blazing back to Babylon after years in lock-up. Bigger, badder, and blacker than Duke, Knight literally pulled her, butt-naked, right off Duke's limp dick, as Babylon magically fell under his command.

I'm The Queen now. Black, blingin', and bold as hell. Rulin' with my Knight . . . to the Infinity. The Queen turned as her assistant, CoCo, approached.

The five-foot, three-inch, cinnamon-hued nymph wore a white leather mini-dress and pointed thigh-high boots that were as sharp as her business-minded brain. Her fluffy black bob-style haircut, curled up in a sassy swoop on the ends, gave off the scent of coconut shampoo.

"Queen," CoCo said close to her boss' ear, "these bitches don't play. They all paid up. Three hundred *K*, plus the fee." CoCo tapped her pink rhinestone-covered ink pen on the white papers on her clear pink clipboard. A red light flashed at the top of her pink rhinestone-covered cell phone, whose holster hooked to the top of the clipboard. "We got the full half-mil tonight." CoCo's sharp eyes, framed by black awnings of fake lashes, scanned her list of names and payments. Pink circles on her cheeks highlighted her round face not because she wore blush, but because the excitement of her job gave her a natural glow. Chanel-set diamonds sparkled in the big gold hoop earrings Jamal had given her tonight.

"Check wit' Mikki at HQ," The Queen ordered. "See if everybody over there paid up."

"It's done." CoCo shot a look at the two B'Amazons and two Barriors at her sides.

The Queen glimpsed all the bodyguards positioned throughout The Playroom, which was the entire top floor of this building known as The Playhouse. Every black female soldier with the strength of an Amazon goddess—known as B'Amazons—and every male warrior—known as Barriors— wore a ninja black uniform.

The ones at the door were making sure the line of women still entering each wore a pink wristband and a health card; when scanned through a small black machine, a computer chip inside confirmed that the client had been checked downstairs at the clinic for pregnancy, major health problems, and all sexually transmitted diseases, including, of course, HIV.

They didn't want any pregnant women up here risking their baby's safety with wild sex. Other health problems they needed to avoid included weak hearts and neurological problems—one ground-shaking orgasm and a bitch could fall out or drop dead. And Babylon didn't need any ambulances pulling up to the pussy party.

Near the entrance, another door led to the locker-room. There, Lee Lee Wilson glanced up and winked at The Queen. The chief B'Amazon was gorgeous tonight, with her wild mane of curly black hair that was highlighted with maroon streaks around her dark, slanted eyes, button nose, and full cheeks. Hip and sexy, Lee Lee had a sort of *Bride of Frankenstein* look, but her glamour didn't stop her from being tough as she oversaw the B'Amazons, checking in every woman's purse and giving her a key to a locker for her clothes. The B'Amazons also waved each woman's nude body with a metal detector; no weapons, phones, cameras, recording devices or other electronics were allowed in the party, for privacy and security reasons. If anything went wrong, a deafening alarm would ring. That would put all Barriors and B'Amazons on red alert lockdown until the culprit was caught and dealt with accordingly.

"I just did a security check," CoCo said. "Lee Lee handled one little disturbance with a chick who wanted to bring her cell phone into the party. Turns out it had a built-in camera. She wanted a picture of herself fuckin' Flame 'cause she heard the legend. We took it, an' she changin' right now."

"Keep an eye on her," The Queen said.

5

"It's done, Queen."

CoCo turned to the four bodyguards with the money. Each held a small gold treasure chest, which they inserted into large Coach leather bags that hung diagonally over their shoulders and chests. All of them rested one hand on the bag, the hand on the opposite side, gripping the black metal shafts of gunpower strapped to their solid-muscle thighs.

"We on schedule," CoCo said, meaning that the money would be delivered as planned to the vault down on the third floor.

"You always on point, girl." The Queen stroked CoCo's bare shoulder.

Trust was hard to come by in this business, but CoCo and The Queen were tight; they had history.

What a pleasant shock it was for The Queen to see CoCo at Babylon's HQ, about a year ago when Knight took charge, asking if she could work for her. The 26-year-old had said that the Feds had questioned her about Dan Winston's work—and The Queen's whereabouts. But rather than snitch on the family that had saved her life, CoCo's loyalty had taken her straight to The Queen's side—literally and lustfully.

CoCo's eyes locked to the right. "That Stud wit' an attitude, Flame, he cuttin' a look that ain't right; we betta check that shit."

The Queen loved the way CoCo's maroon-glossed lips looked so soft and sparkly in contrast to the hard tone of the words shooting up out of her mouth. "I'm 'bout to splash Flame's ass with some ice water. Make that muthafucka show some respect."

CoCo burst out laughing.

"What, girl?" The Queen asked playfully.

"If your daddy could see you now . . . you did a 180 into your dark side, and you all the way there now, like you could do a TV show called *Extreme Black Makeovers*." CoCo laughed.

The Queen did too.

"Sometimes I forget you little Victoria wit' the preppy school uniform and proper English."

SEX IN THE HOOD 2

"Love it," The Queen said. "Remember all those blue-suited business people in Daddy's office? If I saw 'em now, I could say real prim and proper, 'Hi, I'm The Queen. My product is pussy and dick. My service?—all the orgasms you could never even imagine, in a secure, confidential, and medically safe environment."

CoCo laughed as she and the moneybags went to make a deposit in the vault on the third floor.

The Queen felt a sly smile raise the corners of her mouth as she scanned the bare asses, the flailing legs, the titties of every size, the spread-open pussies, and the perfectly manicured toes pointing up over the Studs' shoulders. These beautiful body parts belonged to some of the most powerful businesswomen in America.

"Girl," a naked sista shouted into The Queen's ear, "I been dreamin' of this since the day my law degree started turnin' every man I meet into an intimidated, domineering, or social climbing prick. Dicks for hire!—Now this is a way for a sophisticated sista to get her freak on, no strings attached."

The woman, whose face was well-known as a legal analyst on Global TV News Network, kissed The Queen's cheek. "You need to do this from coast to coast; I'll help spread the word."

The Queen loved the raw, wild pleasure in the eyes of every woman in this room. Including this famous face.

The well-known anchor, Trina Michaels, now wore a birthday suit instead of her usual TV business attire, a sheen of sweat highlighting her sleek, toned body. One of her nipples, which pointed out from big, perky boobs like chocolate kisses, brushed The Queen's bare arm.

Damn, Celeste is soakin' wet. Can't wait to slide down on Knight's lead pipe and ride into morning. The Queen wondered how many other women in the room named their pussies and let them come to life to the point that they had conversations with all that woman power between their legs. *Probably none.*

So, did this TV chick name her waxed-bald pussy? Clearly if she took the time to get it professionally groomed, she had a special relationship with that pretty blooming brown and pink flower, aerobicized thighs framing it just right.

7

"Just don't call me when my network does a story about the latest craze," Trina said. "I can hear it now: 'A new epidemic strikes women across America—a rabid addiction to sex from the hood.' " Trina laughed. "I'm not tryin' to get featured on my own show as the legal chick who broke the law by soliciting for prostitution!"

The Queen smiled. "Here at Babylon, we provide a service that clearly"—She waved her right hand over the crowd—"is making the world a better place by giving pleasure to those who crave it. And this is much safer than picking up a random dude in the bar. Here, you know our Studs are clean, it's supervised; the perfect hook-up."

"Fantastic!" Trina exclaimed. "And as fucked up as our economy is, you're giving our fine brothas from the neighborhood some phenomenal employment opportunities."

The Queen smiled as dozens of naked Studs walked around with platters of martinis, champagne flutes, and raw oysters. Others carried trays offering silver bowls to collect used condoms and neatly rolled, warm, white washcloths to clean up after sex. All in a day's work.

The girls from the hood were cashing in too. Right now, a hundred of Babylon's best Sluts were enjoying the same employment boom at Babylon HQ. A major rap group was holding its concert after-party in The Garage and on the Club balcony. They were "orgifying" the very place where, one year ago tonight, The Queen had connected face-to-face with her soul mate and said goodbye to the man who'd saved Alice from Ghettoland.

Just like two Studs were about to save Trina from conversation and help her escape into sexual abandon.

The Queen scanned Trina's beautiful body and the enormous hard-ons of the Studs who were taking her pampered hands. "This is my purpose in life—to help you and everybody pursue their pleasure. No shame, no worries, no double-standard bullshit—just wild, free fucking."

Trina ran her fingertips over the chiseled, caramel- and charcoal-hued chests of the Studs. "It ain't free at all." She tugged on the silver hoops in the caramel dude's nipples.

"No, baby, but you get what you pay for," The Queen said, giving a subtle nod to the Studs, who immediately led Trina to a nearby giant bed.

"It's all for you, baby," The Queen whispered as the darker Stud with waist-length braids laid back, his cock pointing up like Cupid's arrow.

Trina stood over him, squatted, and speared herself down on it. His dick disappeared between the two arcs of her pretty little ass.

For a split second, The Queen wondered if the TV star had any clue that her hostess tonight was the fugitive whose face had appeared many times on GNN. Trina had even done an in-depth report on the mysterious suicide scandal of Dan Winston and the ensuing federal investigation, and the disappearance of his bi-racial daughter in Detroit's worst ghetto.

I am not that scared, sheltered little girl anymore. I'm a bad-ass bitch who's runnin' things now . . . with the finest man, who loves me more than oxygen. Couldn't be happier. In a few hours, The Queen would be with her own African god, soul mate, helping him relax from all the pressure he was under, by doing what all these people were doing—fucking.

In the center of the room, women ate doggie-style from a live buffet—a lavish spread of tropical fruits, exotic cheeses, gooey desserts, and first-class seafood—served on top of four naked Studs. The men lay on a long, Japanese style table surrounded by dozens of women sitting on purple velvet pillows.

These businesswomen were loving The Playroom tonight as much as the 'round-the-way girls had enjoyed it last night—hundreds had celebrated a bachelorette party—and both groups paid big dollars for big dicks all night long, without batting an eyelash. Everybody was medically clean, using condoms, and loving the product of The Queen's marketing genius.

My erotic empire in full effect. Duke created a monster Madame in me, and Knight's giving me free reign. Now I just gotta keep some of these muthafuckas in check 'cause they

9

can't deal with a woman in charge—like Flame. The Queen's pussy creamed at the sight of that star Stud's bare, rippling, licorice-black shoulders as he gyrated his body to the beat of his wild licking. His elbow shot back and forward like a piston; that bitch was getting a royal finger-fuck and licking. No wonder her skinny brown legs were spasming at each side of Flame's tapered waist—she was shaking like a rag doll in a dog's mouth. The way Flame was licking her milk like he was a little puppy, the poor bitch couldn't help it.

That was all the lip service The Queen needed out of that crazy-ass dude who used to be one of Duke's boys. And rumor had it that Flame used to be fucking Milan when she oversaw the Sex Squad. Now he was having a hard time adjusting to the new chain of command. Ever since Knight had put The Queen in charge, Flame had all but opened up his own complaint department at Babylon. The 20-year veteran of sex for sale was mad about his apartment; he wanted a bigger one. He was angry about his workload; the star of the Sex Squad wanted the same pay, but for part-time work, like he was negotiating a damn corporate retirement pension. And he was demanding a "no pussy eating" clause in his contract, after he caught a little infection from some bitch who'd somehow gotten a clean bill of health at the mandatory clinic here at The Playhouse.

Prima donna muthafucka—he mighta been Duke's boy back in the day, but it's a new day at Babylon. So he better just do his job, or he'll have to answer to Knight in a minute. The Queen wasn't thinking about anything right now except the scheme in Flame's gray eyes, and the nod from CoCo that meant the money was safe and sound.

"Send me Ping and Pong," The Queen said. She nodded at the Barriors and B'Amazons, including Lee Lee, who had transported the cash.

As paranoid as Knight had become lately, because of all this money and fools tryin' to jockey for his power, he still trusted the six people around her right now with their lives and their bank. Their job, after the party, would be to take the money to the main vault at Babylon HQ, where it could be processed into the overseas accounts.

"I'll be in the Champagne Room," The Queen said with her steely-cold business voice. It contrasted with the sexy-sultry tone of minutes ago, as her voice reflected what Knight called the yin and the yang of this erotic enterprise. The ancient Chinese philosophy said that everything had both bad and good, negative and positive, dark and light. And she was about to deal with the ugly side. All the electrifying fucking around her, and the millions she made from it, was the yang, the positive energy, and a direct result of her brilliant business plan to expand Babylon to the untapped women's market.

This 100 women-strong national sorority party was a taste of things to come, for sure. Every women's convention coming to Detroit, and the cities where she and Knight were running Babylon, were getting a tour from a visitors and convention bureau of a different sort, offering the kind of extracurricular diversion that was usually reserved for their husbands, boyfriends, fathers, and brothers.

Like Daddy always said, "Get rich in a niche." So now it's the ladies' turn. The Queen scanned the throng of bodies for the organizer, a high-powered CEO from Chicago, who had orchestrated this night. There she was, kneeling on a window ledge, her hands gripping the sheer white drapes like a rope, as a Stud gripped her hips and drilled her so hard, her close-cropped head snapped back with every thrust.

"You should win a businesswoman of the year award," a white female voice shouted into her ear. "We finally get to enjoy the oldest profession in the world, and hey, this brings new meaning to the term, 'diversity training.' "

The suntanned woman, with a milky white butt where her bikini bottoms must have been, slinked past, holding hands with a dark chocolate Stud.

"This is for you, Queen," the woman shrieked as the Stud lifted her up and slammed her blond-haired pussy down on his huge dick. Her blue eyes closed, her pampered face crinkled in pleasure, she was no teenager; none of these women were, not with that kind of bank and career success.

11

Professional women with lots of money and hungry pussies, and married, single, dating, whatever, these doctors, lawyers, and executives had ridiculous amounts of disposable income, and Babylon was poised to be their receptacle.

The Queen's pussy pulsated as the Stud's long fingers wrapped around the woman's thighs, and he yanked her up and down, pounding up into a place that was previously uncharted territory for Babylon.

As the couple fucked, The Queen looked past them to the buffet. The serving platters were gorgeous, naked men whose chests, thighs, and open palms served up decadent mounds of grapes, pineapple chunks, shrimp, scallops, and wedges of brie. All around them, naked women perched on the pillows, chatting and nibbling with abandon. A few women dared to eat with their mouths . . . directly off the Studs!

A black woman, someone The Queen had seen in an important national news magazine, licked a gooey slick of butterscotch that was running down from the cakes and pies piled onto a peachy-skinned Stud. The woman's tongue slithered over his hip and toward his groin, where she slurped in a bite-sized piece of fudge. A Hispanic woman, who also looked familiar, crept up and ate doggy-style right beside her.

I am brilliant. These high-powered women have needed some good dick for a long time. Now I'm fulfilling an important role in the world by providing it. And gettin' mine at least twice a day with the sexiest man alive, because I am Queen of the Knight. The Queen focused on the fucking couple before her.

The woman's eyes opened, and she smiled.

Damn, my pussy is hot. But this was business.

Pleasure would come later. Because Knight knew his job description as King of Babylon and as The Queen's soul mate meant he had to fuck her good after every event. And he would tonight, later, on the boat.

Now, for the yin—the negative shit that she had to deal with in this unique line of work.

Flame made it easy, because no sooner did The Queen turn to glance at him, when he stood up, wiped his mouth with the back of his hand, and made a face like he was disgusted. His client crouched on the couch and sobbed into her hands.

The Queen nodded to one of the Studs sipping an energy drink beside the giant fireplace. With a subtle point of her index finger, he walked over to the crying chick, pulled her into his arms, and carried her to a plush window seat overlooking the river. He rocked her in his lap then turned her toward him. Her long, brown hair tossed down her back, her tiny ass slid down over his big dick, and he bounced her troubles away.

That's exactly what The Queen was about to do with Flame. "Get the fuck in the Champagne Room wit' me," she said with a hard, grinding tone in his ear.

"Bitch, you crazy."

"Get the fuck in the room . . . unless you'd rather talk to Knight."

Johnny "Flame" Watts flashed his famous, smoky-gray bedroom eyes. His black-as-licorice linebacker body stiffened. Then he turned and walked butt naked toward a red door to their right. Even though he was pushing 40, his body was perfect—hard, cut, not an ounce of fat.

The Queen drew power from the fact that Knight's two most trusted Barriors, Ping and Pong, followed right behind her. In their black ninja uniforms, guns strapped to their bulging thighs, the two brothers had supersonic speed, black belts in karate, and sharpshooter skills. The Queen had seen them in action, both at pussy parties and when festivities at The Garage got too wild, and they were always right on point. Never missed a shot.

"Y'all's goatees look hot," The Queen said, admiring the way black hair formed perfectly groomed mustaches and skinny strips of hair beside their dark berry mouths to points at their chins.

Just a year apart, Ping's and Pong's oatmeal-hued complexion, shoulder-length braids, and small, all-seeing eyes made them look like identical twins. And their earpieces assured her that they could be summoned in a split second if she needed their brawn to beat down this unruly Stud named Flame.

Now, as The Queen and Flame went through the red door and closed it, Ping and Pong stayed outside. They'd be on her in a flash, if necessary; plus the closed-circuit TV would allow Paul and Gerard, co-directors of Babylon security, to watch and listen to their every word and movement. The champagne fountain in the middle of the room gurgled as Flame stood near white couches and cube-shaped chairs that glowed pink under red lights.

A flat-screen TV on the wall blasted a bank robbery story on the 11 o'clock news. "In other news tonight," the anchor said, "Federal agents are still searching for fugitive Victoria Winston. It's been one year since the 18-year-old disappeared after her father's mysterious suicide. New information in the case of embezzlement and money laundering against her father has investigators desperate to find the teen; now it's believed that she helped her father launder money for a powerful crime family—"

The Queen snatched up the remote from the glass coffee table. "Turn that shit off!" Her picture, so different from the woman she was now, flashed on the screen. That girl with the innocent smile and the starched white-collared school uniform and pearl earrings was someone else. Victoria Winston had stepped into the hood as a terrified, virginal, white girl, but sex with two Mandingo warrior studs, a crash course in "streetology," and the discovery of her racial roots had transformed her into a sexy black diva running a multi-million-dollar urban empire with the sexiest man on the planet.

"Stupid bitch!" Flame's deep laughter assaulted her ears as he doubled over with hysterics. "You can run, but you cain't hide."

She stepped close to him. "You can talk, but call me a bitch one more time and you won't be able to walk."

"Listen, quit your corny-ass rhymin' on me."

His legendary dick was still semi-hard, forming a perfect black arc from a close-cropped frame of black hair between the

V of his groin muscles and the iron-hard bulges of his thighs. His dick reminded her of the triangle-shaped head of a python lying still before pouncing on its prey.

"Listen, the only reason you got a record deal was 'cause Knight told the Bang Squad to do it; ain't 'cause you can sing."

"You seem to have forgotten that I'm your boss." The Queen's black leather pants made a crinkling noise as she strode angrily toward him. "This is your job, and it ain't shit for you outside o' Babylon."

Flame smiled at the TV. "One phone call and your wannabe-ghetto ass would be on lockdown with Uncle Sam. Think you tough now that you found your black side, but you ain't never been and won't never be nothin' but a prissy, white bitch who got turned out by some 'soul brotha' sex in the hood."

A mirror over the couch behind him, caught The Queen's attention. She glimpsed the expression that she was casting down on him. Her straight, black hair hung down her back and over her forehead in bangs that hit just above her perfectly arched black eyebrows. Big gold hoop earrings tickled her cheeks, which were suntanned deep bronze. Her high, Indian-priestess cheekbones glowed as naturally red as her full, puckering lips.

Damn. I look tough as hell, and so sexy. I'd lick my own pussy if I could reach her . . . because I love my life.

That passion sparkled with power in her silver-blue eyes, which were ringed by thick, black lashes and Cleopatra-style liner extending from the corners. Her little round nose crinkled as Flame's words tried to penetrate her thoughts, but she wasn't hearin' it. Her mouth watered at the sight of her blue-and-gold striped haltertop, which squeezed her creamy titties together to look like the crack of her ass on her chest. She loved the way her newest tattoo played up the phrase *Cleopatra of the Nile* by announcing, in cobalt blue script-style letters that rolled up and over the hills of her chest, with two words on each breast—*Cleopatra of the Knight.*

And her low-cut pants offered a succulent slice of smooth stomach and showed off the sparkling diamond in her pierced belly button. Black leather hugged her hips just low enough to flaunt her first tattoo—QUEEN OF THE KNIGHT—in Gothic script across her lower back.

Yeah, this was the woman The Queen wanted to become. The woman who wasn't scared anymore. Not scared of the mixed-race sex power that killed her mother, not scared of her black side, not scared of punk-ass thug wannabes like Flame here, trying to flex with his bad-boy talk.

She glared into his eyes. "It's your decision." Her fingertips danced over the choker Knight had given her last night for their first anniversary. The diamonds scratched the back of her index finger as she underlined the thick gold block letters and said, "Read this—*Queen*—whether Duke or Knight is beside me. So you can do your job without the prima donna-bitch routine, or leave Babylon—"

"I ain't eatin' no more pussy." He plopped down on the couch and crossed his arms. "That bitch out there stank!"

"Babylon allows dental dams if both parties agree—"

"Listen, ain't no bitch gonna pay for me to lick her pussy through some plastic." His gray eyes flashed with rage as he glared up at her.

"You're one of the highest paid Studs at Babylon. You can retire at 40 and you'll be well taken care of."

"I came to Babylon when Prince, Duke, and Knight was a team. And when Knight was down for a while, Duke was handlin' it just fine. Even Milan with her twisted ass was takin' care of bidness, but you—"

"I'm in charge, period."

"Wish Duke was back."

"Duke could be dead for all we know, so get back to reality. And get back to work."

Flame shot to his feet. His nose touched The Queen's nose, and his pussy breath steamed her lips. And his eyes burned with hostility as he glared into hers.

"Step the fuck off!" The Queen pressed her fingertips into his shoulders.

Flame grabbed her wrists. "I'm gon' step the fuck in." He twisted her around, bent her over, and grabbed her pants just over her ass.

The Queen yanked her wrists, twisting them like Lee Lee had taught her in self-defense classes at the Babylon gym, but his grip was too tight. She stabbed her heels into his bare shins.

"Bitch!" His fingertips scraped the soft skin at the base of her back, stinging her. "I'm gon' cum all over that tattoo. See if you call yourself The Queen after I beat this shit up." He dug under the waistband of her pants.

"Stop!" she screamed. In an instant, she realized just how quickly shit could turn on her. *Did Ping and Pong not hear me outside the door with that music blasting? Damn! I should've had them come inside.* She had all the power, in the business sense of the word, but Flame was still a man with strong muscles and a pleasure stick that he could turn into a weapon against any woman he chose.

Panic jolted The Queen's every cell. *This is some dangerous shit I'm into right now. Flame could rape me, kill me right now.* But she loved it. And Knight would never let anything happen to her. "Let me go, or you'll be swimmin' in the Detroit River," The Queen said with a deep, cool voice.

He laughed. "Who gon' stop me?"

That soft voice inside her head, Celeste, spoke from the core of her woman power, *Knight will stop you, muthafucka. Knight won't let you harm a single hair on The Queen's head.*

And then she heard his beautiful, bad-ass voice inside her head. *I got your back, Baby Girl . . . always.*

The Queen's eyes widened, not from fear, but from complete faith. Knight had always said they were so deeply connected, soul to soul, that one day they'd communicate without talking or even being in the same room. And now it was happening. Her muscles suddenly relaxed. She was safe. She knew intuitively that Knight was on it.

Flame pulled harder on her waistband. It yanked up into her gut, making an animal grunt escape her mouth. He leaned down to her ear and, with his pussy breath, said, "I'll be doin'

Duke a favor for you turnin' on him. He saved you, and you fucked him by fuckin' his brother—slut-ass bitch, you 'bout to get your due."

Chapter 2

In the sleek, silver surveillance room that felt like the cockpit of a space ship, Knight Johnson watched Flame on the closed-circuit TV security system. That nigga was about to get zapped for forgetting his place in the new Babylon, for speaking Li'l Tut's name, and for daring to touch The Queen.

Knight had to crack down on all renegade muthafuckas who interfered with the smooth operations of Babylon, both inside and out, coast to coast. *'Cause I'm a visionary with thirty days to Manifest Destiny as the boldest king of the universe, and nobody, nothing will stop me. Not Li'l Tut, not the gold-diggin' bitches, not the scheming gangstas, not my health, and not this testosterone-crazed fool.*

A cold fist of pressure clenched Knight's chest as he sat still as a statue in his high-backed, black leather chair at the wide silver console.

"You think Knight gon' save yo' mixed-up ass?" Flame growled at The Queen. He bent her over. His huge dick swung up, ready to stab.

"Now!" Knight commanded into the microphone on the console before him. The deep bass of his voice crackled on the line. He imagined his words shooting like lightning into the earpieces of Ping and Pong.

In a flash, the two enormous men burst into the Champagne Room. With braids bouncing and huge, ninja-black bodies moving as gracefully as quarterbacks, Ping and Pong each hooked a giant hand under Flame's armpits then slammed him up against the wall.

"Yeah, corral that buckwild muthafucka!" Knight said coolly. "Gerard, gimme a close-up on The Queen."

All around her face, pornographic video images danced on dozens of screens covering the large, circular room, where Knight's two security directors, Paul and Gerard, worked knobs and computer mouses to click onto close-ups and wide shots of people fucking at the party. A half-dozen more Barriors and B'Amazons, sitting around the circular console in chairs like Knight's, studied screens that showed nearly every space inside and outside of the ten-story building.

Knight kept one eye on Flame and another eye on the monitor zooming in on The Queen. *I gotcha back, Baby Girl.*

As if she had heard him, she looked into the camera hidden above the mirror, her blue blow-torch eyes burning straight through him with erotic power.

His skin danced with tiny flames of love and lust that threatened to explode the pipe bomb between his legs. Yeah, Shane was about to blow from just looking at her deep-bronze face, the *Cleopatra of the Knight* tattoo curving over her swollen C-cups, and those two juicy bubbles of her ass under that baby-soft black leather.

Knight let one hand fall to the heat blast in his lap. All that was for her, and tonight he'd make it official for life—with a diamond engagement ring.

"Don't that crazy *MF* see they guns?" Paul exclaimed as Flame kicked each of the Barriors' chests. "He seen too many Jackie Chan flicks."

"Dang! He strong," Gerard said; "must be on somethin'.'"

Flame broke free. He screamed, "Bitch!" and charged The Queen.

With a shocked expression, she spun to face him, and the screen went black.

That pressure-fist of stress squeezed Knight's chest. "Get her back," he ordered Gerard.

The slim, freckled dude with an auburn "twist" hairstyle, turned knobs and pushed buttons. "Queen on c-c-c-amera three," Gerard squeaked.

She appeared, eyes glowing with terror, chest rising and falling with panicky breaths. Ping and Pong slammed Flame into the wall. He slid down and crumpled to the floor.

Knight spoke into the mic, "Send that muthafucka south of the border," then stood slowly.

He wore black jeans, cowboy boots with silver tips on the pointed toes, a big silver belt buckle that said *KNIGHT*, a brown suede leather jacket with fringe, and a matching cowboy hat. As his 6 foot, 7 inches of brawn rose up, he felt pumped with all the cowboy machismo he'd loved watching on all those western movies he'd studied as a boy. He even stood with his knees slightly bowed and his huge hands at his sides, like he could double-draw and blow away ten outlaws at once.

He took one step toward Gerard. "Why the fuck did that monitor just black out?" Knight's words electrified the cool air.

The men and women in the room froze.

"I-I-I-I'm sorry, B-b-b-boss Knight." Gerard's eyes grew huge. His bushy eyebrows raised up, making stress lines on his forehead. "S-s-s-so s-s-sorry—"

"Sorry don't do CPR if some shit goes down. Sorry don't excuse the fact that you were supposed to test every monitor in Babylon before the parties tonight. Did you?"

Gerard's lips flapped well before any sound came out. "N-n-n-na, b-b-boss," Gerard said. "I was so busy riggin' Hummer One wit' the new n-n-navigation system—"

Knight's eyes were as lethal as six-shooters. He blasted a disgusted glare at the man who'd helped him secretly slip back into Babylon and take over a year ago. "Now," Knight lowered his voice to reverberate a new work ethic into this muthafucka. "If I find out you were having your sex-addicted dick sucked instead of handling our top priority here at Cairo . . ." Knight paused then yelled, "Security!"

Gerard jumped, his lips trembling.

"Then you'll get jacked so bad, even your dick will be in a mummy wrap. Then you'll be able to concentrate."

Paul, who sat on the other side of Gerard, ran a hand over his thick black beard and exhaled. He turned to Knight. "Boss Knight, man, I can vouch for Gerard." Paul's narrow, dark eyes glowed with concern. "He's been workin' his tail off, getting ready for tonight and The Games."

Knight shot him a hard look. "Nobody works as hard as I do. And if the greatest among us can be a servant to all, then the servants need to strive to be the greatest they can be too." Knight loved the way his words sounded so clear and clean, thanks to his crash course on the King's English while in prison. "That means you, Gerard!"

Gerard shuddered.

Paul shook his head. "All due respect, Boss Knight, but don't nobody else have yo' superhuman powers. The rest of us need sleep. We make mistakes—"

"'Don't nobody else'?—that's a double negative. Say, 'nobody else.' "

Paul stood, making his chair shoot back and bump the console beside a B'Amazon. "I'll be straight wit' you, Boss Knight—no doubt, you're king of Babylon, but a lotta folks feel like you done got too righteous . . . power-trippin'."

Knight respected Paul's courage to speak up. His childhood buddy had always called Knight out on himself, like when he'd cornered the snow-shoveling market in the neighborhood by offering to provide stud service for the ladies, married or not, after he'd cleared their walks and driveways. Back then, Paul told Knight that his business tactics would unfairly crush the competition, and they did. So Knight recruited Paul into business, taking a cut of his earnings every time Knight hooked him up with a horny lady who needed help during a snowstorm.

"My power-trippin' has always been a good thing for you."

Paul shook his head. "You goin' overboard, Boss Knight. Folks say you paranoid, moody, unpredictable. That's why we're on red alert half the time. Folks be tryin' to strike back, make it like it was under Duke—relaxed, without all these new rules."

The tension in the room felt like a vise around Knight's chest. Hearing them speak of Li'l Tut with longing in their voices created a tight sensation in his throat. But he would not allow these inferior-minded followers who lacked his discipline and vision to block his noble mission. So he imagined his eyes were like flamethrowers, casting fiery stares down on Paul and Gerard that would singe them into submission.

This situation required Knight's big brother's unwritten rules of domination. The Prince Code said, *Say as few words as possible. Less is more.*

So he said nothing. He just let them know, with his eyes, that their asses were on probation right now. One more wrong move and they would be royally fucked up.

Knight turned his back to them then did a 360 glance around the room to check on every monitor. *Gotta keep an eye on everything my damn self. Can't trust these sneaky mutha-fuckas who might be scheming with Li'l Tut or Moreno to take what's mine.* The dizzying array of pictures and the enormity of all he had to keep in check made his chest squeeze harder. He struggled to inhale against the pressure. Especially when he looked at the red metal panel that controlled the emergency mechanisms that would turn this ten-story building into a fortress, complete with a flaming moat and rooftop snipers. *We ready to rock.*

Knight coughed. One more month couldn't pass soon enough, so he could Houdini himself and The Queen into a new life. Like magic, they would vanish, and there'd be so much smoke and confusion, nobody would notice until they were already relaxing on a Caribbean island. Had to keep his plan under wraps from The Queen, too, because her nymphomaniacal, sweet self was loving every pussy-throbbing second of their orgasmic lifestyle here in Babylon. Knight's dick would stay as hard and heavy as lead. *Shane can lay a lifetime of pipe inside my Queen to make up for any thrills she thinks she's missing away from here.*

Yeah, his top-secret plan, called "Manifest Destiny," gave him one month from right now to bank $50 million. *Five parties a week like this in ten cities across America, then The Games, and the sale of Babylon to Jamal, and it was a done deal—if all this bullshit don't kill me first.*

Knight's heart hammered so hard, he felt the rope-like veins in his neck bulge to the same fast beat as the Bang Squad's funky bass from the party on The Playroom floor above. These physical symptoms made Knight believe that his body was responding to the growing pains that Babylon was experience-ing, thanks to the combined brilliance and business savvy of himself and The Queen.

WHITE CHOCOLATE

Over the past year, they'd expanded their erotic empire to cities across the country. They were raking in huge bank, controlling thousands of Sluts and Studs. Plus they were collecting even more dough from the personal protection services and security details that the Barriors and B'Amazons were providing for musicians, athletes, and politicians, as well as sporting events, concerts, and rallies.

He scanned the video screens that showed Babylon parties—Chicago, Miami, Los Angeles, New York, Atlanta, and Las Vegas. They also showed the outside of this building, a ten-story tower of sandblasted brick and tall, multi-paned windows. In front, the building faced a street and many abandoned buildings here in the uninhabited warehouse district. A wooden bridge for cars rose over the ten-foot-wide stream that formed a horseshoe of water around the building's expansive lawn, the circular driveway that was now crammed with limos, and the patios. The horseshoe-shaped stream created a security moat, because its ends flowed into the river, where boats bobbed in Babylon's private marina.

Still more cameras also provided video for entryways, hallways, and the vault on the third floor. Another bank of monitors provided 24-hour surveillance for the tropical-style swimming pool and Jacuzzis, the auditorium, and the game rooms. Some important zones, like the tunnels, were deliberately not wired with cameras—no evidence, no knowledge, no problem.

Other screens showed Babylon's headquarters, about two miles from here. The building was similar, but it stood in the middle of the hood. Next door was the Cape Cod-style house, where the Johnson brothers had grown up. The vacant lots, broken glass, and abandoned cars were cleaned up on Babylon Street, where soldiers patrolled the sidewalks to keep children, grandmothers and everybody else safe.

Right now, a VIP rap concert afterparty was rocking HQ. Cameras showed the apartments, the Penthouse that Knight shared with The Queen, the corporate offices, and the gym. Other video screens showed the entire first floor, called The Garage. The football field-sized, three-story room was wall-to-

24

wall sex. Every dick and pussy in there represented thousands of dollars. Bank that could only be trusted with Big Moe.

Knight dialed his top lieutenant. "Still rainin' hard?"

Big Moe answered with his soft Jamaican lilt, "Yeah, mon, some shade cleaned out wit' my special sunshine." That meant he'd had some problems but wielded the appropriate influence to check the niggas.

Big. Moe's deep laughter made Knight smile. Didn't even need the details. He just knew the problem was fixed.

"Twenty-five *O* an' comin'," Big Moe said.

Knight had projected a two hundred thousand dollar profit at that party, so the prosperity gods were smiling down with an extra fifty grand. But the bigger Babylon got, the longer the list of suspects grew.

As he hung up, Knight's chest clenched as his mind ticked down a list of muthafuckas who were scheming to usurp power as boldly as he'd taken this exotic underworld from Li'l Tut a year ago. *I know that was him who called me.* Right now, tiny needles of pain assaulted his heart, as they had since earlier today when that sinister voice had shot through his phone.

Knight inhaled as deeply as when he meditated every morning and night. All that fresh oxygen expanded his muscular belly, filled his lungs, and amped his brain to superhuman intelligence and intuition. This power resulted from all the reading, studying, and meditation he had done in prison to tap into the infinite powers in his mind, body, and spirit. Now he could use those powers to build his Babylonian dynasty with his Queen.

Knight rested a giant hand on his crotch, discreetly massaging Shane as he watched The Queen return to the party. Their combined sex power was another secret to their success in expanding Babylon nationwide. With tantric sex visualizations, they practiced tuning into each other's thoughts, so that they could communicate without words. They also concentrated on mental pictures of their dreams as they reached orgasm. That allowed the most powerful energy in their bodies—sex—to fuel their dreams into reality.

That was all part of a year-long training for The Queen to become as big and bad as Knight, even though she didn't always know when he was putting her through a drill. Like tonight, this bullshit with Flame was a test for her, to see how she'd handle it, to test her trust and her toughness.

On the screen, she walked through the party with a new expression. Her eyes were hard; her chest was still rising and falling from her brush with terror.

Good. He'd scared some reality into her for a hot minute. Because even though The Queen had toughened up over the past twelve months, her sheltered upbringing had blessed *and* cursed her with naïveté. It was a blessing in that she was oblivious to the real danger of her life here in Babylon; a curse, because it might be too easy for a bitch or a nigga to get over on her. So a few split seconds of the gritty low-down with Flame's animal instincts would get her primed to happily accept Manifest Destiny when the time was right.

She's feelin' it now; she knows this ain't no joke. Knight's insides melted. Heart pounded. If anything ever happened to her, he would have no reason to live. Not for the millions they were making together, not for the fulfillment of providing jobs and security in his neighborhood, and not for the satisfaction of using his money to feed a village of hungry, AIDS- and war-orphaned children in Africa.

After tasting the sweetest love with a woman who was truly his other half, the death of her would be the end of him. Anxiety stabbed his heart then radiated throughout his whole chest. The pounding pulse in his ears, and its irregular rhythm, let him know something was very wrong. Those little bouts of something—the tight chest, the dizziness, the pounding heart—would come and go in terrifying episodes that lasted for thirty seconds or thirty minutes. His doctor said it was anxiety attacks. But there was no way a six-foot, seven-inch survivor of D-town's meanest streets and now king of Babylon was having punk-ass anxiety attacks.

No, something was wrong. And it had gone wrong in jail, when the doctors had injected him with what they called a flu shot, despite his objections.

26

A flu shot, my ass. The oppressors poisoned me.

Knight was countering its effects every day with meditation, exercise, and a healthy diet. But he needed to step up his visualizations of himself in perfect health, and never let The Queen know about this heart crisis that he feared could kill him at any moment. No, he had to cure it before she ever knew. And in the meantime, his every thought focused on protecting his Queen and preparing Babylon for their dramatic exit. *Soon I'll put her through the ultimate test.*

The phone vibrated on his waistband—*Reba* flashed across the blue screen.

"I told you not to call me," Knight said, watching The Queen.

"Oh, Daddy, you know you missed this good pussy while you was down."

Reba's high-pitched, little-girl voice always made him think she'd just eaten some cotton candy or put away her Barbie dolls.

"You gotta make up for what you lost. An' I know 'miss white chocolate' ain't gettin' down like you know this ebony sista can."

Knight glanced at three couples fucking on top of a Hummer in The Garage. "Reba, you're the lead dancer at the Bang Squad's afterparty—why the hell aren't you working?"

"Came up to my apartment to call you."

"We don't pay you to play on the phone. Get your ass downstairs to work. And one more call like this, we won't need your services anymore at Babylon."

"I'm one of y'all's best Sluts," Reba said. "Shoot, I'll go to Vegas, make my own fortune, 'steada bein' a trampoline for every rapper that hit D-town."

"Those were Willie Mae's last words," Knight said, "before she ended up working five-dollar johns on Eight Mile—that'll be you, if you keep forgetting where I stand."

"But where The Queen stand?" Reba snapped. "I seen her standin' on top of a fat dick this mornin'. She was doin' sexercise wit' Antoine an' his fine ass—an' I ain't just talkin' about sit-ups."

27

Knight took a deep breath to flush out the image of his Queen fucking anybody but him. He knew for a fact she hadn't . . . because he knew her every move, her every spoken word, and every word spoken to her. He knew with technological sureness that she had never, not once in a year, even talked about flirting or fucking with someone else. But the image of Antoine and Queen tonight at the party—and of her squatting down on that Stud's chocolate dick—made Knight's heart pound with pain. Felt like all the little muscle fibers were sharp needles poking into each other.

"My pussy drippin' right now, Knight," Reba whispered. "Just yo' voice make me wanna cum all ova yo' face."

"This is our last conversation," Knight said. His ears tuned out, and he focused his attention on The Queen.

He handed the phone to Gerard and said, "Truce, my brotha—let me share some of the wealth of Babylon." As far as Knight was concerned, Gerard was through, but he'd keep him on board so he could keep tabs on him and put Paul in charge of security.

Gerard said playfully as he took the phone. "Man, I'm married."

"Reba's clean as a whistle," Knight said. "Since her sister died of HIV, she's vigilant about safe sex."

Gerard smiled as he pressed the phone to his ear, his eyes glazing with lust when he was supposed to be watching the monitors.

Yeah, Paul's in charge. Gerard is oblivious to his work when his dick gets hard. Knight watched The Queen, who was having a serious conversation with the woman Flame had dissed. The woman was smiling, thanks to the Stud who picked up the slack and was holding her hand, but was still going off about something.

Gerard groaned, "Yeah, the Jacuzzi, when I get off at three tonight. Yeah, baby, I can hook you up at the mall tomorrow. Big Daddy rollin' like that."

Knight thought Gerard was a ridiculous, unprofessional muthafucka. Five minutes ago he was being reprimanded for slacking on the job; now he thought everything was cool since

Knight passed some pussy off to him. Just like everybody else, Gerard didn't need to have a clue about what Knight was planning.

Paul was watching the monitors, but his eyes were moving back and forth in a way that showed he was trying to figure out what Knight would say or do next. *Scratch that, muthafucka*, because Knight was master of The Prince Code— *Be unpredictable.*

And Gerard was too dumb to know that, looking all pussy-whipped. "Knight, man, you literally got pussy comin' outta your ears, and, your boy here, I'm all ears anytime. Thanks, man."

"Dig that," Knight said with a cool nod as he took his phone back. "He who giveth, receiveth the kingdom."

"Say it any way you like." Gerard scanned the monitors. "I'll receive a kingdom of pussy all day long. 'Specially from Reba— she act like she in heat twenty-four/seven."

"She's in heat for 'benjamin,' just like all of them are," Knight said as two white women with business-style haircuts sauntered over to the buffet, knelt with their hands behind their backs, and plucked shrimp off the bare body of a Stud.

As the women stood, chewed and burst into laughter, the diamond wedding rocks on their left hands sparkled in the pink and purple light. The Queen's necklace glistened too.

"Paul, I'll have her collar tomorrow so you can do a sound check an' upgrade the lo-jack chip," Knight said. Yeah, he trusted his lady. But he needed to keep her on 'round-the-clock radar for her own protection. If anything ever happened, he'd be able to find her in a heartbeat. And she never needed to know.

"Sure thing, bossman," Paul said.

Gerard punched several green buttons and studied the screens. "All your admirers, they jus' jealous you might kill they ghetto girl dreams an' marry 'miss suburbia' instead; you the most eligible bachelor, so you gotta take the heat."

The heat of the cell phone on Knight's palm made his heartbeat quicken. Heat was a bad word these days.

"Seems like every woman I meet is in heat," Knight said, "degrading themselves as they dig for some gold key to my heart."

"It ain't that deep, brotha," Gerard said. "'Scuse me." He punched a red button then shouted into a microphone. "Where the fuck the Barriors on Door Two?" He frantically scanned the screens. "Y'all tryin' to let any damn fool walk up in here wit' all these executive pussies gettin' they freak on?"

Three Barriors appeared on camera, in front of Door Two, a fire exit leading to the patio facing the river and marina.

Intuition spoke, loudly and clearly, in Knight's mind. *They're scheming.* They used to be Li'l Tut's boys and were pissed when Knight took charge.

"We here," one said. "We was just checkin' somethin' out."

"What?" Gerard demanded. "You s'posed to call it in then check it out . . . in case somethin' go down."

"Wasn't nothin'," the Barrior said.

"They out," Gerard said. "Some heat coulda come creepin' through while they messin' around. Probably suckin' each other's dicks. They out like a mug."

"Not yet," Knight said. "Have them followed 'round the clock. Get me their phone and computer records. Search their apartments. The Fed is sniffing hard for The Queen and Babylon in general. And Duke's at large. We need to know what we're dealing with."

"Over and out, boss," Gerard said.

Knight's phone vibrated once more. His chest tightened. He stared at The Queen as if his eyes could protect her from the violent words recorded inside this tiny device that he refastened to the clip on his belt. He had to save her from those vile threats hissed from the mouth of someone who once loved them both.

Manifest Destiny will save us both. We'll steal away to our own secret heaven before anybody tries to send us to hell. That was all Knight knew for sure. Didn't know how long he'd live. Or how long his empire could evade the heat's radar. Or how long The Queen could defy the FBI by living the glamorous life at Babylon. Or how long it would take his bad-ass brother, Li'l

Tut, to resurface and come back to stake his claim on his Duchess and Babylon.

Despite Knight's careful planning, any of the above factors could topple the kingdom in a heartbeat, literally, if Knight's condition were as serious as he feared.

"Show me the back," Knight said.

Gerard zoomed in on the delivery dock leading down to the marina. Ping and Pong prodded Flame into the back of a white van marked *Feast for Your Eyes*, Babylon's own catering company, which provided food for all its events.

Damn, his phone was blowing up. He glanced down. PRIVATE CALLER flashed on the display; that's what it read when the threat came in. Knight's heart pounded. He had the power. He was unstoppable. But in order to stop this fool, he'd have to wield the ultimate power. And he didn't want to do that to his little brother, no matter what a hot-headed punk Li'l Tut had become.

Knight flipped the phone open. Sirens blared into his ear.

Then a male voice quaked, "We gotta talk."

"Who is this?"

"It's the beginnin' of the end, muthafucka."

Knight grabbed his BlackBerry from the console. He text messaged "yellow" to the four Barriors, whose job was to watch The Queen at all times, in The Playroom.

On the monitor, she was holding hands with that TV analyst who looked like she wanted The Queen to lick her pussy right there in the middle of the party. But The Queen never mixed business with pleasure. And she never ate pussy unless Knight could watch, in person, and fuck her while she feasted.

Four stars flashed across Knight's text screen, one at a time. That meant each Barrior got the message and would respond accordingly. No telling where this joker was calling from.

"You decide," Li'l Tut said. "Give me what's mine, an' e'rybody be cool. Keep fuckin' me an' my Duchess, an' dawn gon' shine on Babylon. Knight gon' be all over an' done wit'."

Knight's heart ached. Seizing control of Babylon was a business decision, so he could take care of Mama and provide jobs for thousands of young black men and women. "Li'l Tut, let's meet—"

"Midnight. On the boat."

Knight glanced at his silver Cartier watch which he had bought in New York with The Queen. She wore a matching one—only hers had a pink alligator band and a mother of pearl face surrounded by diamonds. Both had their favorite saying engraved on the back: LOVE YOU TO THE INFINITY. A watch, they both agreed, was the intimate symbol of time, of love, of life. Every day, they made sure their watches ticked identically, right down to the second hands.

Now, Knight's watch said 11:45 p.m. He and The Queen had planned to make love tonight on the boat, after the party, which wouldn't end until three. "Check, baby bro'. See you in a quarter."

Knight slipped his phone back onto his belt then turned to Paul. "I'm makin' a run for a hot minute. I put out a yellow. Any trouble . . . handle it then call me."

Paul nodded. "Over and out, boss Knight."

Knight strode into the back hallway then took the steps, two at a time, up to the next level. In the ammo room, he packed another Glock in his waistband and a fourth one in his boot. That, on top of the one in the holster under his brown leather jacket. His head spun. The dizzy feeling again . . . and his chest . . . so tight . . . hard to suck down air.

He grasped the back of a sleek metal stool at the counter where the ammo manager cleaned, inspected and loaded weapons. Knight leaned over it. A revolver, its chamber open and empty, laid facing Knight's eyes. Weak, he stared down the barrel into an infinite black hole. *No. I am a warrior. My goddess and I will make our escape and live long and happily. This is just stress . . . my body is strong.*

Knight stood up straight and took a deep breath. "Mind over matter," he whispered as he hurried down the back staircase to meet Li'l Tut. "Mind over matter."

Chapter 3

Duke peered from the cabin door of the 50-foot Sea Ray. He and his two brothers had bought the top-of-the-line boat, which they christened *Babylon Beauty* across the bow, just before Prince died. Right here on deck, they'd spoken their most intense words of bonding, three black powerbrokers, between the black of the sky and the river.

So now, on this warm Indian summer night in September, on that patch of gray-carpeted plexiglass, and on those gray leather bucket seats, was the best place for Duke to let Knight know. *It's my birthday, and I'm 'bout to get back in the captain's chair. I'm a year older, a year wiser, and I'm takin' Babylon back. Got my team ready for a hostile takeover. And I'll fight to the death to get my Duchess back too.*

Duke stared up at The Playhouse, the building on the river that he was getting ready to buy when he lost everything. Now Knight had transformed it into "party central." The outside—red brick stretching up to the sky for ten stories—gave no clue of the carnal indulgence inside, except at the edge of the rooftop terrace, every once in a while, some women and Studs danced and sipped champagne.

Lights flickered on the third floor. That meant the Barriors and B'Amazons were delivering all that loot to the vault, which would be transported later to HQ on Babylon Street.

Duke smiled. His inside sympathizers had dollar signs in their eyes and loyalty in their hearts, and were ready to help him make the heist of the century. *One month to The Games, an' I'm gon' win the gold.* Then he could have what was up behind those steamy windows of the top floor.

My Duchess was up there in The Playroom. Maybe one of those silhouettes moving in the dim purple and pink light was her.

Timbo throbbed. His was the first dick to give that rich girl from the suburbs a taste of sex in the hood. He had turned her out and gotten her hooked on that pulsating firehose in his pants. Made her love the wild abandon of Babylon and gave

33

her an all-you-can-eat selection of fresh pussy. She was a freak, and Duke needed to tap into her power to take charge.

He stared hard at the top floor, imagining her coming to a window and blowing a kiss down at him. His gaze lowered to the middle windows. "All that money just sittin' there," he groaned.

On the ground floor, the only activity took place a few minutes ago, when the huge delivering doors opened, and Ping and Pong took Flame away in that white catering truck.

I'll get back wit' my boy later. I'll need him. But why the catering truck?

That was another of Knight's entrepreneurial endeavors. He wanted to own shit himself, instead of paying other folks, because he always wanted to make all the money himself.

Always so smart, that muthafucka.

Knight even had a better way to get more money, when they were young teens, when they went door to door offering their services to shovel snow.

"If it's a lady by herself, tell her you can lay pipe too," Knight told him.

At first Duke had said, "No way am I gonna do plumbing after busting my ass to clear the driveway and sidewalk of all that heavy white stuff."

But he tried it, and the $50 bill in his palm was all the convincing he needed. And so Babylon was born.

Now, Duke's laughter echoed up into the black night. Detroit's skyline—its crown jewel the shimmery towers of the General Motors world headquarters—sparkled along with the Ambassador Bridge, which looked like lighted pearls strung over to Canada. There, the green and purple lights of the Windsor Casino and all those floodlights, like it was a glamorous premiere party in Hollywood, lit up the night. All to let the world know that Duke was back and—

The deep rumble of a cigarette boat sliced past on the water, causing a sudden wake that rocked *Babylon Beauty*.

Duke gripped the doorway to steady himself. "Damn, muthafucka!" he shouted. The boat sped away so quickly, it left only the white fishtail pattern in the water. "Slow the fuck down!" Duke grabbed the wide dashboard to steady himself.

Whoosh! Another boat whizzed past, and the force knocked Duke into the captain's chair.

"Cain't even stand up right in this mug," he exclaimed.

Suddenly, female laughter from a pleasure boat made him grind his teeth. He could feel his jaw muscle flex hard as he watched three lovey-dovey couples smile and cuddle on a sleek blue cabin cruiser. The soft tinkle of jazz, the champagne glasses in their hands, and the black urban professional look about them set off something inside Duke.

Duke glared at one clean-cut guy on the boat, who wore a pink polo shirt, plaid shorts, and gold-rimmed glasses. "Preppy-ass muthafuckas. Act like you ain't neva seen the hood." Duke gripped the steering wheel. Even his fingers were trembling. Just like the rest of his body, from head to toe. All 6-6 of his once mighty brawn was shaking in his black Timberlands, because he was about to do something he'd never done—stand up to his bigger, blacker, badder brother, Knight.

So where the fuck is he? Duke snatched his cell phone from his waistband. His fingers touched the warm metal butt of his gun. He was ready to rumble, if necessary. He held up the phone. The tiny blue display said 11:58. "Oh, shit."

Knight stepped out of the doors leading to the back patio, which was softly lit by tropical-style torches. They cast a fiery glow around Knight's six foot, seven inches of power.

That made Duke's leg muscles feel as wobbly as the Ramen noodles that kept him alive for much of the past year, that is, when he ate at all during that 365-day hiatus into hell. At least now, his stomach was full of Mama's best pork chops and potatoes. She promised not to tell anybody—especially Knight—he was living in the room over her garage.

*

Suddenly Duke's mind reeled with a wicked flashback to that night a year ago in the elevator, when he was going to his birthday party at Babylon HQ.

Lookin' finer than ever, Duchess said, "That fuck was the best ever."

But we hadn't fucked.

Knight had somehow gotten up in the guarded bedroom and laid some of that magic pipe of his that she said felt longer, thicker and better. Duke didn't figure it out until the party, as he and Duchess were gettin' their freak on with all those strippers.

The conspiracy to usurp his power had played out as Knight walked in. Seemed like everybody knew except the birthday boy. Knight had looked like some "wild west" muthafucka in all that distressed brown leather—pants, boots, hat, long coat. Then he said he's the new sheriff in town, stole my Duchess right off my damn dick, and took over Babylon. Left me standin' there wit' my limp dick in my hand. And didn't nobody stop him. Including my punk ass.

*

No wonder Knight looked just as ominous and powerful tonight, striding down the dock like a black cowboy, his big silver belt buckle shimmering with diamond block letters which spelled out *KNIGHT* giving just a hint of that "wild west" machismo.

Duke hated the way Knight walked. *Like he own the whole muthafuckin' planet!* Every step of his long legs and boots radiated with cockiness, confidence, and stealth precision, like he never took one stride without analyzing its impact first.

Duke laid his fingers over the metal bulge under his baggy white T- and jeans. *Analyze this, muthafucka.*

But how would Duke stand up to Knight when his insides felt as choppy as the black water lapping at the sides of the boat? How would he stand strong when his body was thinner, weaker, and scarred, inside and out, from twelve months in hell? When a brotha has no money, no home, no mercy, he'll do whatever he can to get his hustle on, even if every hustle went up in smoke, to ease the pain of losing everything. *But I quit that shit, an' now I'm back where I belong.*

Knight's boots thudded on the wooden planks.

Duke's pulse hammered in his ears. He forced himself to focus on the best image of his life—him, sitting in his golden throne at his birthday party last year, with Duchess on his lap. He had been ruling the empire with his goddess at his side. He had everything. Now, he forced his eyes to cast that image over the sight of Knight as he walked the thirty yards to the marina.

The image faded as Knight came into closer focus.

That muthafucka's face is glowing like the sun! Like he's in love. Like he got the juice and the bank to do any- and everything he damn well pleased.

Duke's muscles trembled harder. He bit the inside of his lip to stop the mile-long barrage of verbal bullets that were cocked to shoot and kill. He ground his teeth. The words ricocheted back down into his chest, making his heart pound harder.

No doubt Knight had half an army of Barriors lurking in the shadows, plus his own ammo strapped on every limb.

Duke concentrated on his vision, so the sight of Knight didn't push all his mad buttons, but when Knight stopped on the dock, right at the stern, Duke felt a tornado ripping through his mind. Could hardly think of a sentence to speak. Could hardly see straight.

Because the way Knight stared down at him, the way his bright, black eyes glowed with brotherly love and affection for a split second but turned instantly to disgust, revealed that Knight knew. His bigger, badder, more brilliant brother knew exactly where little Duke had been and what unspeakable things he'd been doing for the past twelve months.

That stare was so potent, Duke wanted to cower in self-disgust like a beat-down dog. *I hate what I did!* Duke's throat swelled with tears. He'd rather die before letting them fall. His tongue felt thick and slimy, his eyes burned as he stared at his brother's clean-cut face, with its perfectly healthy, dark-chocolate complexion and "good-living" fullness to his cheeks. No chance folks would confuse the two of them now. Not the way Duke's skin was looking these days.

He ground his teeth so loudly, he could hear a cracking sound in his ears. Because the mirror image before him was like looking at a reflection of how he used to be. Now he rarely even looked in the mirror. Even though he'd quit that shit and was living clean, his face, eyes, and body hadn't caught up with him yet.

And the disgust in Knight's eyes pulled the trigger on all those wicked words cocked on Duke's tongue. "It's your fault, muthafucka!" Duke shouted. He shot up from the captain's chair. His boots thudded on the floor as boats roared in the background. "You gon' give me back what's mine! I hate your ass, muthafucka! I hate your ass!"

A boat zoomed past, causing a wake. The waves slapped the side of *Babylon Beauty,* causing Duke to wobble.

Knight stood perfectly still, his big hand on his waist, his eyes radiating pity and disgust.

"I want Babylon!" Duke screamed. His lips felt wet; little bits of spit sprayed into the night as he yelled. "I want Duchess! An' I'm gon' take it!" He knew he was ruining his moment; hysterics would get him nowhere, especially with always calm-ass Knight. He was acting like a whacked-out crackhead but couldn't stop it. The chemicals, the craziness—that's what was talking.

"You ain't gon' keep me down!" Duke screamed. His head spun so hard, his vision blurred with silvery lights, like just before those horrible migraine headaches came. His tongue felt like it was moving with a mind of its own, and his muscles trembled so hard, felt like a convulsion would knock him down any second.

Knight just stood there, watching him self-destruct.

"You ain't gon' play me like a punk no more!" Duke screamed. His hand slipped into his waistband. He pulled out his gun and aimed it at Knight. His finger spasmed on the hard metal trigger.

Ka-pow! Pow! Pow! The shots echoed off the black eternity of water and sky. Coldness . . . darkness . . . numbness.

Chapter 4

Her hot, hungry pussy was poised over Knight's giant dick—this was the moment in life that The Queen loved. This intense anticipation of being just an inch away from fucking scored a close second place to the actual orgasm, and the shit was so good with Knight, he could make her cum with one stroke.

But right now, in the candlelit master suite of the yacht, she wasn't thinking about the sneaky way he had first hooked her on his magic pipe by taking the pussy a year ago. She was focused on the now as she squatted above his massive lead rod, ready to fit herself on it with the perfect grip, then slide down and ride.

She loved to look into his onyx eyes, and watch the way all those dark jewel tones of jade and topaz sparkled with enchantment as her pussy sucked him inside to stroke her soul. She could feel the love and lust burning in her gaze as she stared into his eyes.

But his mind was a million miles away. His thoughts had heisted the precious jewels, leaving only blank window displays. He was always thinking about Babylon and money and safety and security and other cities and whether Duke was about to commando into D-town to try and take Babylon back.

I gotta work some magic on my baby; make him forget about everything but us.

All that sexercise she was getting at the Babylon gym had strengthened her quadriceps to the point that she could pump down on him for hours if she wanted to without getting tired or feeling that burn in her muscles that once forced her to stop when she was on top. No, tonight she would do all the work to soothe his mind, body and spirit with supersonic sex and lobotomizing lovemaking.

"Knight, baby," The Queen whispered as she squatted over him, "you stressin'; don't be thinkin' business when you gettin' booty."

Knight laced his fingers with hers. He was lying on the king-sized bed on the white, 500-thread-count Egyptian sheets.

The yacht rocked gently, the silence between R. Kelly's best love songs allowing them to hear the soft slosh of water against the hull. Knight squeezed tight; his fingers were so long they covered the backs of her hands and reached the tops of her wrists. "That was a close call tonight with Flame," Knight said. "Got me thinking about—"

"Oh, man," she groaned. The Queen didn't want to hear anything about thinking. She wanted to hear the sloshy, slurpy sounds of fucking, the moans and groans and skin-slapping of lovemaking, and the supernatural sizzle that always lit up the air when these two halves of one powerful soul united in body.

She gently sat on his rock-hard stomach, leaning forward and "pooting" her ass back as if she were sitting on his motorcycle, her steamy, wet pussy creaming all over his hot stomach.

"Oooh, Baby Girl," he said playfully, "you sure know how to change a man's train of thought."

She ground her hips just enough to make her cherry-sized clit slip into his innie belly button. The sensation sent an erotic ripple up through her core that exploded on her skin. Her nipples hardened, lips parted, and her eyes burned down lustfully at him.

Shane's giant head whipped up against the soft curve of her bare ass.

She leaned down to kiss him. "MMMMmmm." God couldn't have made a more perfect fit for two pairs of lips. Especially when his slightly opened mouth touched ever so slightly her parted lips, and they just held steady for a second, a minute, or an hour. They'd done that once. Just breathing in and out, inhaling the air that had circulated in each other's bodies, keeping their brains thinking and their hearts beating.

She loved the way his lips were always so hot and soft, so inviting, so nurturing; even a quick peck promised a lifetime of love.

Right now, though, Knight pulled back. Her lips felt cold and abandoned as his beautiful genie eyes sparkled up at her. Something in them glinted like he'd seen something bad and couldn't shake it from his mind's eye.

"Knight, baby, what's wrong?" She ran her fingertips with a feather-soft touch over the sculpted planes of his gorgeous face. The high cheekbones, the strong Indian chief nose, the full lips and square jaw. All baby-soft, clean-shaven, and delicious as the rest of his muscular body. "This is our one-year anniversary. We should be celebrating."

But Knight's laptop full of work, plus his four guns on the dresser, and the way he kept looking toward the bedroom door here on the yacht, let her know something was wrong.

"Baby, you been so paranoid lately," she said softly. "Like, we were s'posed to take a ride on the Sea Ray tonight; then you all of a sudden switched it to the yacht—"

"More luxurious accommodations for my Queen," Knight said, kissing her forehead.

"That sounds real nice, but you ain't bein' straight up."

"Baby Girl," Knight whispered, staring intensely up into her eyes, "you know I love you to the infinity."

The Queen's insides melted. His voice was so deep, it reminded her of that rapper Tone Loc, the one her punk-ass ex-boyfriend, Brian, was always trying to lip synch, but ended up sounding horribly off-key. Knight was the real deal, the most masculine, sexy voice she could ever imagine, rapping the sweetest stuff any woman could dream about.

"Yeah," she cooed. "Say it again."

"I love you to the infinity."

She closed her eyes, letting his deep voice vibrate through her chest, then come to rest in her heart. She inhaled the delicious scent of him, his Black Cashmere cologne, and the gardenia-scented candles glowing around the cabin.

"Baby Girl?" His expression was different than any she'd seen on his face.

She drew her eyebrows together and asked, "You didn't meditate today, did you? You got your karma all twisted around. And you look pale."

Knight touched his fingertips to her jaw. He gently drew her down for another kiss, but she pulled away.

"What's wrong, Knight? You know if something happens to you, I'll just die."

Knight shook his head, but his gaze softened as if he loved hearing this declaration of her love. Then, with a tone half-playful, half-somber, he asked, "So if I dropped dead right now, what would you do?"

The Queen tapped her fingertip to his nose and said matter-of-factly: "I'd strap myself to your big fine ass, drag us out that door to the water"—She pointed to the French doors leading to the boat's sports deck, which had an open area for scuba diving, swimming, and getting onto jet skis—"and I'd slide us both into that black infinity forever."

Knight covered her cheeks with feather-soft kisses.

His comfort felt so good, it made her lips part. A soft moan escaped up from her soul. Because this tenderness was love. She sang that Mariah Carey song that says, "I can't liiiiiiive . . . if livin' is without you—"

He pressed his hot cheek to hers; she put her hand on the back of his satin-smooth head and stroked softly. "Baby Girl, I think you played Juliet in the school play one too many times. And this Romeo ain't goin' nowhere. I'm yours for life."

"Life," The Queen whispered. "You *are* my life."

"My Queen." His hot breath tickled her ear. "We have what every other man and woman on the planet dreams about. And I'll fight to the death to make you always feel like my Queen—"

She pressed a finger to his full lips. "SSSsshhh. Let's celebrate." His face was so beautiful, and the emotion radiating from it was so intense, she felt dizzy. Without him, she had no one. Two dead parents. A brother who had disappeared when they got split up a year ago after Daddy died. And her look-alike, older sister, Melanie, who had chosen a convent instead of life in the hood with Gramma Green.

He's trying to tell you something serious, Celeste said, *something that will change your life.*

*

42

SEX IN THE HOOD 2

Her heart pounded with that same panicky feeling when she'd lost all the people who were supposed to love her, in the space of a day. Daddy killed himself. The media exploded with scandal over him, his three kids and their young, beautiful, black mother who had died from a sex overdose years ago.

Lawyers said sweet, virginal Victoria would have to live with her sickly, black grandmother in Detroit's worst ghetto. Her brother and sister said, "Hell no and booked," and when she asked the parents of her white boyfriend and her best girlfriend if she could live in their mansions for awhile, they all scolded her for deceiving them about her racial background.

She could still see the animalistic violence in Brian's blue eyes as he'd tried to rape her in his mansion while his parents, down in the kitchen, read about her blackness in the newspaper. *Racist punk.* Always blasting rap music in his Porsche and Range Rover, watching movies like *Boyz in the Hood* and *New Jack City*, and saying, "Yo, dawg," to his friends at their prestigious private school. But the second he'd found out that the exotic Native American looks that he loved about his girlfriend reflected a much darker heritage, he became a violent hater.

"Lillywhite" Tiffany and her parents had been no better. After all those years of growing up and going to school together and spending countless sleepovers and family vacations with each other, they had straight-up cut her off once black came to the surface.

If I ever see either of them again, I'ma show 'em how I really feel. Hood style.

Suddenly her whole body burned with the anger and betrayal and disappointment and sadness that she had stuffed down for the past year. Everyone she had known and loved had abandoned her, tossing her out like a pretty doll that had suddenly been ruined by a big, ugly smudge of dirt. Worthless. Disgusting. Black.

*

Here at Babylon, and in Knight's bed, she had found amazing love that she thought could make up for all the pain she'd endured.

43

But what if he's about to toss me out too?

The Queen shook her head, to exorcise those emotional demons from her past. Why did she have this sudden terror of rejection? Had he discovered something awful about her, and now it was time to trade her in for a blacker model? He was always talking about The Prince Code, how Number One was Trust no one. Should she not trust him, and did he not trust her? Was one of those scheming bitches who were always putting their panties in his pocket or blowing up his phone or sticking their titties in his face actually succeeding in stealing her man? Could that be why, despite all his deep declarations of loving her forever, she was getting the same vibe that he was about to cut her off?

Everybody turns on you eventually. Love doesn't last. And it's only a matter of time before you get the boot so they can move on to someone new. But my Knight too?

The Queen had often wondered, if he could come in and do his little brother like that—steal his woman and take all of Babylon under his control with a secret conspiracy—then apply that same ruthlessness to the woman in his life.

And with the long line of pussy constantly trying to hook his gorgeous, brilliant, millionaire ass with their conniving any-means-necessary ways, maybe this conversation was just inevitable.

Perhaps it was time for Alice to pop a little pink pill marked *Reality* to end this Ghettoland fantasy that she was loving so much. But the white Wonderland that she'd wished for a year ago no longer appealed to her. She had faded to black and dropped off the world's radar by slipping into an urban underworld. *And I love it.*

Yet in her mind she could hear Daddy warning in his deep but gentle voice. "If something seems too good to be true, then you can be sure that it is."

The Queen slid off Knight's stomach, stood beside the bed, and turned on the lamp on the nightstand. The spacious, plush room that she had decorated in soft beiges and turquoise, and with an Egyptian theme, suddenly felt too hot, too small, and too vulnerable, as if its high-tech devices, lifejackets, and state-of-the-art design were too meager to weather the sudden, unexpected fury of nature that could sink this yacht called *Miss Infinity* at any moment.

The fury of Fate was what ripped away little Victoria's mother when she was just six years old. That same ferocious Fate had stolen her charmed life just a year ago. And perhaps, if these things ran in cycles of three, then Fate was back to rip the love of a lifetime from her arms.

"If you're about to break up with me," The Queen said, glaring down at Knight as he shifted to sit on the edge of the bed, "then I might as well go jump in the Detroit River. My life here with you is everything, Knight Johnson. And—"

"Baby Girl!" his voice bellowed like the fog horn on a passing tanker ship. He reached for her hands. "How'd you jump from *A* to cra-*Zy* with one glance?"

She snatched her hands back and squeezed the tears from her eyes. "Don't call me crazy! If you went through what I—"

Knight shook his head. "Baby Girl, stop. You're still hurting; you're afraid to trust even now."

*

She crossed her arms. Her mind fast-forwarded through all her options if she were to leave right now. Her plan to attend the University of Michigan—she would've been a sophomore now—was a joke. One flash of her social security number in their computer system and the Feds would eat her for lunch.

Her lifestyle, her money, it was all through Babylon. Plus, this wasn't the kind of work where you finish your contract and move on to the next company. Who knew what had happened to that ho, Janelle, last year who dared scheme against Duke?

And Milan. Duke made his own baby momma, wicked as she was, marry his back-stabbing boy, Beamer. Then when Duke disappeared and Knight took charge, Knight sent the two of them off to some brothel in Mexico—that's how much juice they got in Babylon. Duke's children, however, little Zeus and Hercules, plus his three other kids, were on the East Coast at a boarding school that Knight financed, to keep his blood safe while they got educations far away from Duke's drama.

Plus, The Queen realized, she knew way too much. She knew about the money, the Caribbean accounts, the laundering through the catering company and the security business. Her mind was a virtual file cabinet of the men and women who worked as prostitutes and gigolos for Babylon. And worse, she had a mental Rolodex of all the folks who solicited their services, from city officials to business people to celebrities to just plain married muthafuckas tryin' to get some extra booty.

*

"My queen," Knight whispered, grasping her trembling shoulders, "I see a hurricane tearin' you up inside. C'mon, Tinkerbell, sprinkle some of your magic pixie dust on those worries." He pulled her closed.

Oh my God. She nestled into the soft spot at the core of his being, his solar plexus, where the round curves of his pecs came together to form a little indention that was a perfect fit for her hot cheek. But the better place was his neck. *Yeah, his neck is my Nirvana.*

First, she stared in awe at the skin that was so smooth and dark that an iridescent shimmer seemed to dance over it, like his body had a natural glimmer. His super-dark color mesmerized and intrigued her; it was so exotic and foreign to her father's beige pinkness and even Mommy's caramel brown complexion.

"Are you alive?" she giggled into his neck. "How come I can never feel your pulse in your neck?"

Knight stiffened. "My resting heart rate is slow, almost silent, because I'm so in shape; my heart is conditioned to stay on reserve—"

"It scares the hell outta me," The Queen said softly. "My big strong warrior should have a heartbeat that pounds like a Bang Squad song."

Knight let out a low, sexy laugh as he ran his fingertips over her nipples.

SEX IN THE HOOD 2

They immediately stood at attention and sent an electric jolt down to juice her pussy.

"It will be bangin' in a minute."

The Queen nestled her face deeper into his neck. "MMmmmm . . . this is where I belong. Nowhere else. Ever."

Knight kissed the top of her head. "That's my Baby Girl. And to prove it," he whispered, his eyes sparkling down on her like black diamonds as he reached behind his back, "I have this for you."

He took her left hand. Whatever he was about to slip on her ring finger, she couldn't see it. He blocked it under his fingertips as it slid on. Then, in one smooth move, he bent down on one knee. Shane was a beautiful black arc, semi-hard, pointing down at her toenails, whose polish made them look like Red Hot candies.

The Queen couldn't help marveling at his penis. No matter how many times she'd seen it and felt it in her mouth, in her pussy, in her hand, its beauty always took her breath away. In fact the head reminded her of Darth Vader's shiny black helmet. Shane was as long and hard and indomitable as a light saber that pulsed up inside her with intergalactic stealth. The shaft was like three cylinders of magically expanding flesh fused under satin-soft skin.

Even though she'd been fucking and making love for a year now, it still tripped her out that such a bizarre-looking organ could create indescribable pleasure inside her. And it was even more mind-blowing that it was connected to this man, whose intelligence and coolness and power made her shiver.

Inch by inch, she raised her gaze up over his nude body that was like a museum-quality, ebony statue—as perfectly sculpted and elegant as Michaelangelo's *David*.

"The Queen . . . my queen," Knight said with a deep, quaking voice. He pulled back his hand to reveal the ring. "Be my partner in life, here on earth and in eternity, as my wife."

The sound that came up out of The Queen's soul was a blend of a shriek, a cry, a sob, and a purr. He held his open palms under her hand, framing her caramel fingers with his huge, dark hands.

47

"I feel dizzy," she said, sinking back onto the soft bed, where the silky gold spread caressed her bare ass. She sat upright, facing him. But he was still so tall, just kneeling, that she had to look up into his eyes, their onyx sparkle even more brilliant than the incredible diamond on her finger. She gasped. "Oh my God, Knight, always look at me like that."

He leaned close with parted lips. She leaned forward with an open mouth. And like two, one-of-a kind puzzle pieces, their lips locked with perfect precision. Intense heat fused them together. And the power of that union sent electric jolts through her every cell that ricocheted back to make pink and purple bolts of lightning behind her closed eyelids.

"Promise you'll always kiss me like this."

"Promise you'll always look at me the way you're looking at me now," Knight said. "Promise me."

"I promise," she purred. "Promise me you'll always see that we can be, you and me, into eternity, for all to see. Never flee, but always be free to be in unity. Fly high with me; cry, sigh, lie with me; die with me as our souls float into infinity."

"Let's go to the studio tomorrow," Knight said. "Have Jamal lay a soft beat with that. So we can play it at the wedding."

The Queen shrieked. "Oooh, the wedding! I love it!" She held up her hand. Her eyes bugged at the breathtaking diamond. It was shaped like a heart, just like the one she had seen advertised by the world-famous jeweler Harry Winston in the *Town & Country* magazines that Daddy kept in the dark-paneled lobby of his offices. But this ring was even more spectacular.

As her mind fast-forwarded to what this meant, her brain felt like a giant stick of butter that melted down to her soul and dripped into a hot puddle around her pussy. "Knight," she purred, "I've always wanted a heart-shaped diamond. And this is beyond bling."

Knight smiled. "I know it sounds corny as hell. But when I saw it, I said, 'That's perfect for The Queen of my heart.' "

"You're right," she said; "it is corny as hell, but I love it. Love it!" She studied the sparkling stone. It was about three carats secured in platinum prongs on a platinum band, whose sides glistened with tiny rectangular baguettes.

"There's more." Knight took her hand and turned it over. In her sweaty palm, he placed a platinum band. "Put this on me," he said softly, "to show the world that I'm yours forever. Read the inside." His stare penetrated her eyes so deeply that it raised the tiny hairs on the back of her neck.

She picked it up. THE QUEEN'S KINGHT was inscribed in the metal. She slid it onto his ring finger. "So now are we married?" She stared into his loving eyes.

Knight smiled. His big, white teeth contrasted against his full, dark lips. They were the same as what Duke had called "sucka" lips, because all the females said his mouth looked so juicy, they just wanted to suck on his lips all day long. And since Knight was a bigger, badder, blacker version of gorgeous Duke, The Queen had always secretly agreed with the females that Knight had the same beautiful "sucka" lips.

Now, she stared, trance-like, at his mouth.

"We're married as far as I'm concerned," Knight said, "but here's what I propose."

The perfectly curious and attentive expression on The Queen's face gave no hint of the tornado of thoughts ripping through her brain. *Marriage means I'm here to stay. Forever. And I'm only nineteen!*

But did Alice want to stay in Ghettoland, even as The Queen of Hearts, forever? Did she ever want to pop a "back to white" pill and return to her previous life? Was it possible to take the chocolate out of the milk once it had been stirred up, sipped, and savored?

Hell no! The Queen loved every taste, every sip, every decadent sensation of her life as it was right then. With this gorgeous Mandingo warrior who was pledging the most tender love forever.

*

It didn't matter that a year ago, the first night that she had arrived at Babylon and made love with Duke, she had vowed to stay in this ghetto underworld only long enough to get her Ph.D. in street smarts. Then she would go to college where she belonged, get a master's in business administration, and with her MBA and Ghetto-ology degrees, dominate the real business world.

All her training in Daddy's office, and her desire to make a big impact on the world, would allow her to become a *femme fatale* as a female entrepreneur. Back then, she had started off scared, sheltered, and determined to remain a virgin so she wouldn't get pregnant, catch a disease or kill someone with the mix-race sex powers that she'd inherited from her mother.

But Duke turned her out the first time, Knight took over from there, and now she couldn't imagine life without the mind-blowing sex and love and power and adventure that she enjoyed here every day. As The Queen. Hidden far away from the Feds who were looking for her after crucifying her daddy. So she had decided to become the baddest *femme fatale* in Babylon, helping Knight grow it bigger and better every day. Now, her eyes sparkled at him as he described his plan for their wedding and future.

*

"First," he said, "we get married on the sexiest day in Babylon. The day of The Games."

"Love it!" The Queen exclaimed. "That's in a month!"

"Four weeks from tonight," Knight said. "First we have a wedding ceremony on the rooftop terrace at The Playhouse. All our guests will be under a white tent overlooking the river, and we'll have a reception on the patio."

The Queen nodded. "Everybody will already be in town for The Games."

"You got it, Tinkerbell. And The Games will actually be our reception, but even more of a celebration because everybody'll be watching the competition. Then we take a boat ride away to paradise and it's all over."

The Queen's face drooped into a sad expression. "Love it," she whispered.

"You don't sound like it," Knight said, tapping a fingertip under her chin to raise her face. "Tinkerbell looks like she lost her pixie dust."

SEX IN THE HOOD 2

"My parents are dead," she said, her insides aching that they would not see her on the day that she dreamed about as a little girl. Bridal day dress-up was always fun in Mommy's closet, with all her gowns and sparkly shoes and pretty scarves that little Victoria would use as a veil.

Knight sat on the bed and scooped her onto his lap. Shane pressed against her hip. And the heat of his lap against the bottoms of her thighs, along with the firm warmth of his chest against her left arm, inspired her to nestle her cheek into his solar plexus and close her eyes.

"Your parents are watching," Knight said, his deep voice vibrating through her ear down to her soul. "This is all predestined—you know that, Baby Girl. Everything that's happened to you was Fate's purpose. To bring you to me. And help us do great things together."

She smiled and said in a sultry tone, "To help folks get their freak on."

"And 'The Talented Tenth' that W.E.B. DuBois wrote about, it's our responsibility to uplift the masses of black folk whose minds are still poisoned by the toxic words of Willie Lynch," Knight's voice was so potent and passionate, it made all the tiny blond hairs on The Queen's body stand on end. "DuBois was as light as you, my Queen, before you turned caramel-bronze-brown in the tanning booth. But it's not about pigment, it's about power and politics."

The Queen nestled her cheek deeper into the valley of muscle at the center of his chest. She inhaled the delicious scent of his natural, masculine musk mixed with Black Cashmere cologne. "Okay, Prophet Knight, you're gettin' a little too deep for The Queen right now. I been lookin' at pussies and dicks all night—"

"To build our empire and secure our future," he said. "I couldn't do it without your brilliant business mind, Miss Female Marketing Genius. Them chicks tonight, boy, they looked like they were in Nirvana and never wanted to leave."

The Queen smiled. "Daddy always said, 'Get rich in a niche. Figure out what nobody's doing, and do it as bold and

51

beautifully as you can.' And nobody was providing dick to the professional ladies."

Knight's deep laughter boomed into her ear. "We'll see if that TV anchor, Trina Michaels, can make a sentence when that prim and proper "oreo" sista gets back to work. I swear I saw her eyes cross while she was samplin' our sex from the hood."

The Queen stiffened. "She made a joke about doing a report about our product. I let her know that shit was not welcome. At all." As The Queen heard the confidence in her own voice, and felt the strength surge in her body as she thought about anybody trying to expose or double cross Babylon, something deep down in her gut cramped.

How could she be so strong and confident in business, but just minutes ago, her mind had slipped into an abyss of fear, insecurity and doom? How could she have been so quick to think it was all over? In one ominous moment, she had reeled herself into either suicide or exile from Babylon—as had happened to Duke if he were still alive.

And suddenly, Knight's words echoed back into her thoughts. "You said a boat ride away . . . and it's all over. What do you mean, 'over'?"

"The wedding day," Knight said. "Life as we knew it before marriage—that's over. And we start our new life on our honeymoon."

The Queen pulled her cheek away. It felt cold as she turned and stared up into his eyes, probing for more information. Something about the way he'd said "all over" made her gut cramp.

He's hiding something, Celeste said.

The Queen had learned, since Knight was so slick, that questioning him about something was pointless. He was master of the art of deception and evasion. She would have to investigate in more cunning ways. She kissed his cheek. "I want a tropical island honeymoon. So I can lay on the beach with my bare ass pointing up at the sun."

Knight ran a giant hand over her hair, smoothing it down from the crown of her head to her shoulders and back. "I'll find us a remote house on an obscure island. After the wedding, we can sail down Lake Erie to the Erie Canal to the Atlantic and down to the island of your choice."

The Queen caressed the beautiful black skin on his bald head. "Someday I'm gonna climb up into your brilliant mind so I can sit down and look around. I need to see what a bionic brain looks like on the inside."

Suddenly Shane hardened and poked into her hip.

She wrapped her fingers around all that lead pipe, watching her ring glisten brightly against the huge black dick snaking over her thigh. "I'll take a bionic blast from that, too."

"Baby Girl, be honest," he whispered. "Two things—Do you have any desire, even an ounce, to fuck another man? And do you have any yearning to return to the white world you left behind?"

"Hell no to both."

Knight stared hard into her eyes, as if invisible hooks were shooting into her brain to pry out the truth. "You've made love with two men in your life," he said. "Me for a year, and Duke for five days before that, is that it?"

The Queen stiffened. "Why would I want to sample chicken nuggets when I get to savor the juiciest lobster in the sea all day, every day?"

Knight tossed back his head. Deep laughter echoed off the shimmery turquoise and beige Egyptian design that was hand-painted on the leather ceiling. "That, Baby Girl, is exactly how I feel about you; this man don't ever need any other pussy than the sweet, creamy meat right here." His brows drew together. "I haven't heard you say yes."

The Queen's pussy throbbed. She said with a sassy-sexy tone, "Celeste wants to whisper it to you."

In one graceful movement, Knight grasped The Queen at the sides of her waist, tossed her into the air as he stood up, and caught her by cupping his open palms under her thighs. Rested the backs of her knees over his shoulders, and pressed his open mouth, his extended tongue, between her legs.

"Whew!" The Queen shrieked playfully. "I'm in heaven up in here!"

His tongue fucked her with lightning speed, while his upper lip pressed into her clit with expert precision.

"Oh my God!" The Queen moaned. Her pussy felt like a pulsating light that flashed purple and lavender and blue and yellow up through her body, down her legs, into her fingertips and brain, where a colorful swirl numbed her to all sensation except euphoria. Her fingertips gripped the back of Knight's smooth, bald head.

He moved his palms to cup right under her butt, which he kneaded.

"Yeah, squeeze my ass like that," she said, grinding her hips to intensify the pressure of his lip on her clit. "Can you hear Celeste screaming the answer?"

Knight groaned so deeply.

The Queen's whole body trembled. Because she was about to cum. She tossed back her head, letting her long black hair tickle down her back.

Knight gripped her harder, digging his fingers into the flesh of her ass.

Wave after wave of shivery love washed up from the depths of her soul to the surface of her hot skin. Knowing that this was just the appetizer—that hours of his big black dick would come right after this—intensified the orgasm to mind-blowing intensity.

"I'm yours!" The Queen moaned as her heels dug into his back, her fingertips gripped his head, and her pussy pulsated around his tongue.

In a flash, she was falling. Down, down, down . . .

Was he dropping her?

Had he been pale earlier because he's sick?

Was he fainting and losing his grip?

Was her pussy suffocating him?

Or sucking the life out of him?

No, God please don't let my mixed-race woman sex powers kill Knight like they killed Mommy. No! Knight is so strong . . .

Or was he sick?

Her eyes flew open. She stared into Knight's lust-widened gaze.

That mischievous smile curling up the corners of his beautiful lips let her know, everything was okay—

Slam! Like a cube of meat dropping down on a metal shish kebob skewer, The Queen's pussy landed on Knight's huge, hard dick.

He tossed back his head, busting out a laugh. "I scared you!" he teased.

She wrapped her legs around his waist, gripped his shoulders. Oh, his shoulders. The Queen loved the ripple of muscle fibers under his dark chocolate skin. When he moved his arm a certain way, and that one indention, between his front and side deltoids, it made her pussy drip. It was so masculine and virile-looking.

The Queen gripped her knees around him in a way that she could *giddy-up!* Fueled by a playful get-you-back attitude for his little dropping trick, she rode with fury, bouncing, slamming her thighs into sides of his hips, and fucking the shit out of that big dick.

"Damn, Baby Girl," he moaned. "Fuck that shit." He cupped the round curves of her ass, from the sides, and helped her slam that pussy down on it.

Her pussy was extra wet right now, halfway between her last period and the next one.

A few months ago, she'd stopped taking the pill, because Knight had said that a love as powerful as theirs should create new lives to carry on their legacy and their DNA, which was predestined to help people and make a positive impact on the world. And they were certainly doing that by providing great sex to anyone who could afford it.

Panting, sweating, trembling, screaming, The Queen slipped into The Erotic Zone. That's where all thoughts tuned out except for the raw pleasure of making love. Her cheeks burned. Eyes only opened halfway. Pussy pumped as much juice as necessary to keep it slippery. And the energy of an Olympic athlete overtook her so that her muscles never ached. So she could fuck endlessly.

"Make love to me, Tinkerbell. Make love to me!" Knight's deep voice boomed so loud, the boat rocked.

"Now," The Queen whispered, "cum with me."

She pumped harder. Shivers wracked her every cell.

"This pussy mine for life," Knight panted. "This Baby Girl mine for life." He stared into her eyes and whispered, "My wife." Then his white teeth flashed. His eyes glowed with the tenderest expression she'd ever seen. And he pulled her ass back and forth with ferocious fury. The friction of his steaming pipe against the walls of her pussy melted their souls as one. Their mouths smashed together. They sucked for dear life. And liquid Knight squirted up into the core of his Queen, to baptize their union forever.

Chapter 5

Knight had to make his heart stop pounding, and his chest stop squeezing, as he obsessed over that "kill-or-be-killed" moment five hours ago. Even though he'd chosen the first option, the thought of killing his baby brother made his heart ache. Here in bed, he hadn't slept a wink.

Li'l Tut might be dead right now. And I pulled the trigger. Twice. But if he's alive, and he survives that fall into the river, and recuperates, he'll be back with a vengeance.

But if Knight had hesitated, he wouldn't have been laying here watching his Queen sleep more peacefully than an angel. He cherished the sensations of the plush sheets, the warmth of her body, and the gentle rocking of the yacht. It was silent except for the lapping water and his heartbeat.

She could see that I didn't feel well. It scared the shit out of her. Especially when I almost dropped her! Won't let that happen again. Ever.

No, his job was to make sure the future Mrs. Johnson never worried another day in life. He didn't have to tell her that after their wedding they'd be leaving Babylon, Detroit, and the United States forever. Stuff was just too crazy around here. For both, it was in their best interests to start a new life together in an exotic place, with a fortune in the bank.

Knight's fingertip traced the dark arc of her eyebrow. Her suntanned skin was so clear and smooth, as fresh as a baby's. What if he'd planted a seed in her tonight?

Intuition said, *Your child is growing inside her right now. A human being created from the kind of soul-deep love that you never saw between your parents or anybody else.*

Knight's chest ached. If he felt this strongly about protecting his beautiful angel Queen from the evils of the world, how would he feel about a defenseless little baby? That only emphasized the importance and brilliance of starting over, far away. It wasn't even a choice.

Knight was twenty-five and had no children yet. Because he'd always been responsible, and when he wasn't, he'd been lucky. Now he imagined his sperm shooting up inside like

57

God's fingers of fire striking Moses' stone tablets to write The Ten Commandments. A cataclysmic fusion of spiritual power was ushering in a new era for their lives.

And what about Mama? They could take her with them. She couldn't live without any of her baby boys. First, Prince got shot to death. Then Knight went to jail. Knight came back, but Li'l Tut disappeared. No more disappearing acts for Mama. After all that struggling by herself to raise her kids in the hood, it was time for her to relax and enjoy life too. Plus, when everything went down, the Feds would come to her too. But not if she were playing nanny on a sun-splashed island with Knight's first baby.

Knight's chest squeezed. He struggled to suck down air. And that made his heart pound harder.

All of them had to get away. Too many question marks kept popping up here. Top among them: *Is Li'l Tut alive?*

Knight's ears rang with his brother's angry outburst. *Kapow! Pow! Pow!*

Three bullets—one from Li'l Tut, which missed, and two from Knight. At least one struck his little brother, because red stained his white T-shirt before he fell backwards into the black waters of the Detroit River.

The Barriors had searched the marina and surrounding areas of the river but found nothing. But the current could have carried his body downriver toward Toledo, or into Lake St. Clair. A freighter or fishing boat could drag it somewhere. Or it could wash up on the island park of Belle Isle, or across the river in Canada.

But what if Li'l Tut were alive? What if he fell into the water with only a graze wound, crawled up on land somewhere nearby, and made his way to someplace where he could recover?

Be for real, Intuition said. *You know damn well that boy was as whacked out on crack as he could be.*

The dark circles under his eyes. Sunken-in cheeks. Dark splotches on his skin. Shirt and pants hanging off his skinny body like he was a fucking clothes hanger. And talking crazy as a mug.

Knight massaged his chest over his heart. It had raced uncontrollably while they made love, especially when he tossed her up to eat her pussy. He had only half-planned the drop; he had actually gone weak and lost his grip. Panic shot through him now, as it had then.

What if I fall out and can't protect her? What if I drop dead? Or what if she thinks that crazy curse shit is comin' true and she rations out the pussy to me but gets some dick from another muthafucka?—

"Stop!" he said out loud. He tried to remember all the visualization techniques that had helped him meditate on positive outcomes for all his problems, including his early release from jail—that's how he'd built Babylon for the past year.

But lately, closing his eyes to meditate only wrenched up a barrage of horrific visions: Prince's dead face; a disgruntled employee spraying bullets inside Babylon; Federal agents snatching The Queen from his side; and piles of money burning.

"Stop," he whispered. He closed his eyes to visualize himself free of any discomfort. But all he saw was Li'l Tut's drug-ravaged face. His heart raced even more intensely.

Perhaps what disturbed Knight most about that was the eerie resemblance they shared. Seeing his mirror image whacked out on crack made him shudder because that's what he would have become if he had taken that hit some fellas in the neighborhood offered when he caught that rape case. Wrongly accused; yes. Wrongly convicted; yes. But vilified in the media nonetheless.

And aching for an escape from the pain, chemical or otherwise.

But Knight was strong. He remembered one of the few words of wisdom their father had offered during his brief appearances during his early childhood: "A man's character is defined by how he handles the bad times."

That muthafucka's character must've been defined as a certified loser, because he disappeared and left Mama to do a man's job. Now Li'l Tut was following in his footsteps.

Knight pressed his lips to The Queen's forehead. Never would he hand this goddess back to the young punk who couldn't appreciate her or treat her the way she deserved.

The same went for Babylon. Li'l Tut had been running the family empire into the ground when Knight came back: Housing a fugitive; allowing a Federal agent to almost sneak into his birthday party and creating inner chaos with his children's mother, Milan, and that knucklehead, Beamer.

Ever since Knight had taken over, it had been nothing but prosperity and expansion.

A sudden squeeze.

Knight gripped his chest.

He had to check his accounts online, to make sure that everything was in order for Manifest Destiny to happen on schedule. He slowly rose from the bed, trying to breathe away the pain, but every time he inhaled, the chest cramp squeezed more tightly.

Bending over as he walked, he slowly made it across the room to the dresser, turned on the laptop, and brought it back to bed. The clock on the upper right corner of the screen said 4:42 a.m.

His fingers clicked across the silver keyboard as the screen danced with numbers for his various overseas accounts. Accounts that in one month would have a balance of $50 million, which would secure his family's future forever, far away from life in the big city.

He clicked onto the high-security website for his world-class financial institution, which handled accounts for Greek shipping moguls, inner-city thugs in hiding, and English royalty alike.

For the password, he typed in CAESAR-RULES.

Knight's Manifest Destiny accounts had been opened in the Bahamas under the name of Julius Mark Anthony. With several more secret passwords and a fictitious profile of a California real estate baron, Knight had set up the accounts with the help of a kinky Caucasian couple, Mr. and Mrs. Marx. The West Coast couple whom he had met years ago, had helped him expand Babylon to the Pacific and were his mentors. Because he had a felony conviction on top of a rap sheet that showed his teenaged run-ins with the law, Knight needed their help to bypass all the rules, regulations and red flags that an urban entrepreneur like himself would raise for the conservative officials who monitored international banking.

I couldn't have done it without them. Now I need them more than ever.

But their high-profile multimedia company, which made adult films and ran a soft-porn cable TV channel, was being investigated for tax evasion. And if the Feds actually indicted the Marxes, Knight worried that his accounts would be traced back to them and seized.

A lightning bolt of pain shot through his chest.

Somehow he would have to get these elaborate accounts switched once again to avoid all risks. He had worked so hard, sleeping only a few hours every night for the past year, to build Babylon to what it was now. So it wasn't an option to leave it all behind without taking the financial fruit of his labor with him.

His brain spun over all the scenarios that could break wide open on his wedding night: The Feds, still searching for Victoria Winston; a raid; Moreno; Li'l Tut plotting a coup with board members and others.

Knight did a mental checklist of his offense and defense: the moat of fire that would create a wall of flames around The Playhouse while he and The Queen disappeared; rooftop snipers; the tunnel to the river; a motorcycle escape, if necessary, down to Yacht #2.

He remembered a rule from The Prince Code: *Think from the end.* He had to envision every detail of those final minutes then plan accordingly, right now. But time was whizzing at the speed of light.

"Fuck," he whispered. The clock on the upper right-hand corner of his laptop screen said 5:55 a.m. He'd already spent more than an hour online and still hadn't figured out a solution for protecting these accounts.

So much to do for Manifest Destiny . . . Time is going too fast . . . I'll never get it all done.

The pain radiated from the sharp clutch around his heart, up his neck, down his arm.

Classic signs of a heart attack.

A panic attack, too.

He set the computer on the blankets, then laid back, holding The Queen's hand. The heat of her fingers comforted him. But when he shifted, the needles pierced his heart.

No, she couldn't wake up to find him dead.

I can control this with my mind. Mind over matter.

Intuition echoed those same words.

But the pain intensified.

He took long, deep breaths to calm himself.

But his heart was racing. And it hurt.

So Knight laid staring wide-eyed at the ceiling.

Am I dying?

Chapter 6

The Queen sat behind her glass desk at Babylon HQ, punching numbers into her sleek, silver laptop computer. She had just finished a conference call with L.A., Chicago, New York and Dallas. Now, finally, it was quiet enough for them to concentrate. Seemed like the phones had been ringing nonstop and employees had been coming in all morning, interrupting their work. She pulled off her gold-framed glasses.

"Knight," she said, focusing on him as he hung up the phone. He'd been hammering out the details of the meeting with Moreno tomorrow afternoon and the board meeting after that. Their every move right now was putting Babylon closer to domination over their competitors.

They had so much work to do between now and the wedding, so they could take off and not give Babylon a single worry. But The Queen was worried that all this work was taking a toll on Knight. He just didn't look right this morning.

Plus they were going to Jamal's studio this afternoon to record their wedding song, which she'd written last night. Seemed like there weren't enough hours in the day. The Queen's muscles tensed. And that triggered her body's automatic urge to relieve stress—have an orgasm.

Yeah, some people smoked when they got tense. Others chugged beer. Lotsa folks around here, and back at her private school for that matter, sucked on a fat blunt to mellow them out. Her sister Melanie ate chocolate chip cookies with warm milk to sweeten a sour mood.

But orgasm is my drug of choice.

She glanced at Knight. Maybe she could slide down on it for a minute and let Shane take care of this.

Damn, he looks pale. Somethin' ain't right.

She froze. Were her mixed-race sex powers taking a toll on Knight? If Duke were dead, the curse had already proven true on him.

But after that supersonic love last night with Knight, and her sense that he wasn't feeling well, she didn't want to wear him out. Her clit throbbed. She could take care of it herself. A quick flick of the fingers and boom—she'd cum and be good to

63

go. However, she'd rather enjoy the sensations of somebody wrapping their lips around it and sucking for a while. Then her muscles would loosen up. Where was Honey when she needed her?

The Queen's mind spun back to when she had first met the assistant whom Duke had assigned to her. It had been only a matter of time before Honey was sitting spread-eagled on the desk, with the molasses-brown curves of her ass forming a sort of platter for Honey's sweet meat. All those luscious folds of shiny, pink-brown flesh, like those party trays with ham and roast beef sliced so thin it looked like a crumpled piece of satin. The memory of tasting all that made The Queen's pussy throb even harder. *Focus!* The Queen studied the green numbers on the computer screen.

"These numbers don't make sense," she said, shifting to make her thong rub against her pussy. "Look at the net and the gross for the past three Bang Squad gigs in The Garage. Somethin's outta whack."

She stood up to let Knight sit down and let his math whiz mind do some calculations. He looked pale, like he had last night.

Maybe he's stressin' about the meetings. But Knight never lets it show. She massaged the back of his shoulders through his crisp white shirt. "Knight, baby, you okay?"

His brows drew together as he focused on the numbers.

"Maybe it's time to add more meat and dairy back into your diet," she said. "Maybe all those vegetables just aren't enough for my African god warrior."

He smiled, turning toward her to let his beautiful genie eyes peer at her squeezed up titties. "I get all the meat and cream I need."

"But maybe you're anemic, not enough iron," she said, pressing her cheek to his and looking at the columns of dollar amounts. "Your cheeks feel hot."

"My whole body's been hotter since I first saw you," he said. "I see the problem here. Somebody neglected to add in the tips and fees. That skewed the numbers."

The Queen could almost hear Knight's mind ticking down a list of suspects. Because if they had done this deliberately, they were stealing money from Babylon. And the last person who had done that had joined Milan and Beamer for a life of sexual servitude down in Mexico.

"CoCo," Knight said without looking up from the screen, "call the accountants to do a computer history on who entered these figures. Not just whose names were on the report, but who logged in and jacked up my dollars."

"Yessir," CoCo said, flipping open her phone. She walked through the double doors to the back offices.

The Queen kissed the top of his bald head. "Brilliant man!" She pressed her lips to his ear. "I love you to the infinity. To the infinity. To the infinity."

He turned to kiss her mouth. Anytime their lips touched, it felt like time stopped.

"A month can't come soon enough," The Queen whispered. "I bet all you need is some rest before your beautiful face is glowin' like rich, dark chocolate again. We'll get that pink blush back on your cheeks, like when we make love—"

He grasped her hands then raised her ring to his mouth to kiss it. "Mrs. Johnson, you got a brotha feelin' so unbelievable."

"Believe it. I'm yours for life."

Big Moe walked in through the front office doors. His linebacker bulk moved like a military tank through the elegant room. Wearing baggy jeans, black boots, and a white turtleneck, his small eyes sparkled over his pear-shaped nose and gap-toothed smile.

"Must be nice bein' in love, mon," he said, setting an envelope on the desk. "Phone records. I won't interrupt nothin'."

"I appreciate cha, man," Knight said.

As soon as he left, someone else knocked on the side door leading to the secretarial cubicles.

"Damn! All these interruptions," The Queen said.

The door opened. In walked Honey in her short white Cleopatra-style dress, gold sandals with straps laced up her juicy calves, and gold bands snaking around her upper arms. Her juicy titties bounced under the sheer fabric as she approached the desk. She curtsied Knight, who nodded back without looking away from the computer.

"Queen," Honey said through full, peach-glossed lips, "here's today's mail and that credit card report you asked for."

"Thank you," The Queen said, inhaling Honey's brown sugar-vanilla scent. She was one of the prettiest women The Queen had ever seen. Her honey-brown eyes sparkled out from under thick black eyelashes, which she batted over her apple-round cheeks. She had a mini-mushroom nose and perfect white squares for teeth. And her molasses skin was so dewy and plump, but not fat, something about it screamed, "Eat me." And The Queen had, many times.

"And there's a woman who wants to see you," Honey said. "She's in the lobby. Says she met you at the sorority party at The Playhouse."

The Queen stiffened. "How'd she find her way over here?"

"CoCo invited her."

"That doesn't sound right," The Queen said. "What's her name?"

"Trina Michaels."

Knight glanced up. "Hell no," he bellowed. "Client or not, no journalist is welcome in Babylon HQ. I don't care if she hires every Stud and Slut for a month-long party. This building is off limits to outsiders. Bring CoCo's little ass back in here."

"Yes, sir," Honey said.

"Baby Girl, turn on the insurance."

The Queen stepped toward the eight-foot, black-and-gold striped mummy cases flanking the glass shelves behind the desk. After opening each one, she pressed a red button and saw a crimson light flash. She did the same with two mummy cases flanking the double doors facing the desk.

CoCo strode in wearing a black pantsuit and spike heeled, pointed-toe black boots. Her fluffy black hair bounced as she walked. Her maroon-glossed lips sparkled as she spoke before spoken to. "I made an exception," CoCo said, "because Ms. Michaels wanted to meet the man behind this enterprise."

"We coulda done that over lunch downtown," Knight said, standing. He stepped down from the marble platform that held the desk. Down three steps, and he towered over CoCo. "What up, CoCo?"

She stared up at him with her usual business toughness. "Well, Ms. Michaels wants to hook up a deal for her annual Christmas party in Washington, D.C."

"Coulda done that elsewhere too. Next."

"She kinda got the hots for The Queen."

Knight shook his head. "Like I said—"

The Queen stepped between them. "What is the deal, CoCo? What, did she lick your pussy so good you agreed to violate Babylon protocol?"

CoCo smiled. "Actually—"

The double doors opened and in walked Honey with Trina Michaels. She wore dark jeans, high-heeled sandals and had a pink pedicure that made her toes look like little pieces of candy. Her nipples poked through the thin fabric of her green blouse, and her long brown hair bounced as she strode in.

"Queen," she exclaimed, smiling. Her big brown eyes glowed with lust and excitement as she shook The Queen's hand.

"Nice to see you again." The Queen's gut cramped at the idea of this nationally known TV reporter stepping into the nerve center of Babylon.

Knight stepped behind the desk and turned off the computer. "How can we help you, Ms. Michaels?" Knight asked. He looked so gorgeous in that starched white dress shirt, black slacks and his diamond KNIGHT belt buckle, and black, pointed-toe boots.

Trina looked up at him like she wanted to slurp him down whole, the same way she'd checked out the Studs at the party.

But Knight stared down at her like he didn't even notice. "I understand you enjoyed the party," he said with a complete business tone.

"Had the time of my life!" she exclaimed, taking The Queen's hand. "This woman has a magnificent mind!"

Honey and CoCo stared with confused expressions.

"What can we do for you?" Knight asked with a more stern tone. "We don't normally hold meetings here. If you'd like to arrange a party, we can do that in our downtown offices."

"Actually, I have an unusual proposal for you," the TV chick said. "I want to do a special on the sex industry, and I—"

Knight nodded so subtly to The Queen, no one could have noticed.

Honey closed and locked the double doors. And CoCo sat down on one of the black and gold striped satin couches against the side wall.

The Queen raised Trina's hand to her mouth, then trailed the woman's knuckles over her hot, parted lips.

Trina gasped.

At the same time, Honey went to the sound system on the glass shelves behind the desk. One of Bang Squad's sexiest slow songs began to play. With a soft bass beat and a woman moaning lyrics about making love every minute of every day, the music electrified the air.

Knight sat in the chair behind the desk.

The Queen stepped closer to Trina. She leaned into her soft brown hair, by her ear, and whispered, "You got the prettiest pussy. Made me think of a pink and brown flower, blooming like there's no tomorrow."

Trina's eyes widened. Her nipples poked even harder through her shirt as The Queen stepped closer. Her arm brushed against one titty, making the woman close her eyes.

She glanced around nervously. "All these people . . ."

"This is what you wanted, isn't it?" The Queen teased. Then her voice hardened. "This is why you schemed your way up where nobody is allowed to enter—ever—isn't it, Trina?"

The woman stepped back, her eyes wide with worry.

The Queen felt the rhythm of the sexy music. Her pussy throbbed at the thought of what was about to go down—fresh meat; with a room full of willing participants. Even Miss "thang" and her conniving self who wasn't neva gonna put Babylon on TV.

The Queen stepped closer to Trina. Standing nose-to-nose with her, she pouted her lips and stared seductively into her eyes. "Trina, you ever ate some pussy?"

"No," she whispered, glancing at Knight and CoCo.

Honey sat on one of the marble steps leading up to the desk. She leaned back on the heels of her hands, offering her beautiful titties up into the air, legs wide so that her bare knees offered a delightful view, down to her thighs, where her white dress fluffed in her lap. Honey swayed gently to the music as she held a gold lighter to a long blunt. Squinting, she sucked down the sweet smoke, then offered it to Trina.

The reporter shook her head. "This isn't what—" Then she shrugged and took the blunt. Sucked down some smoke like a pro. She moaned as smoke poured out of her mouth and her whole body visibly relaxed. She gazed longingly at The Queen and said, "I didn't expect to—"

"I know how you feel," The Queen said, her lip slightly brushing Trina's mouth as she spoke. "Wasn't quite what I expected when we saw you either."

Trina kissed her. She pressed those pretty brown lips straight onto The Queen's mouth. Like she'd been hungering for a girl all her life but was too scared to make it happen.

"Yeah," Knight groaned. "CoCo, call Twister."

"Yes, sir."

Before The Queen closed her eyes, to love the sensation of this new, beautiful woman kissing her, she glimpsed in the corner of her eye, Knight's giant hand stroking the crotch of his pants.

My pipe is steamin' now.

The Queen raised Trina's palms up to the *V* of her blouse. Slid them inside, let Trina feel the hard points of her nipples under her lace bra. "Take your clothes off," The Queen whispered.

CoCo and Honey carried the couch—the Egyptian style with no back, just curly arms at each end—to the foot of the marble steps. Both women undressed.

Damn, her pussy looks good.

WHITE CHOCOLATE

The Queen straddled one end of the couch. "Come taste," she whispered, sliding down to offer her swollen, waxed-bare pussy up to this hungry bitch.

Trina straddled the couch, too, facing The Queen. She leaned down, mouth open, diving toward—

"Oooh, seems like you've done this before," The Queen whispered. "Or does eating pussy just come naturally to you?"

A soft moan was all the response she got.

But she was doing a good job. Lapping like it was momma's milk and she hadn't eaten in days. Good as it was, The Queen wanted to cum. But she wanted Celeste to meet her new playmate.

"Sit up," The Queen said, gently taking the sides of Trina's head and raising her up. The Queen scooted closer and instructed Trina to do the same. "Look at that," she whispered. "Two beautiful pussies saying hello. Two big, fat, swollen clits ready to deliver us to kingdom cum."

Trina's lips parted. Her eyes were at half-mast, as she stared at The Queen's glistening cunt. The two women eased closer, their asses pressing into the satin fabric.

"Ooh, wait, just look at that pretty sight," The Queen said, loving the image of another juicy pussy about to press into hers, to grind them both into erotic oblivion. "Knight, baby, you see this?"

Suddenly Trina looked embarrassed. She must have forgotten that Knight was there, and CoCo.

Honey offered Trina another hit on the blunt.

The Queen delighted in watching this prim and proper professional woman suck down smoke and relax.

Yeah, now she's ready to get turned out in a new way.

Victoria slid even closer and—

"Good gracious!" Trina cried.

The Queen closed her eyes, grinding a slow circle, her whole body trembling with the extreme pleasure of her clit rubbing against another one. The sensation of fat flesh touching more flat flesh was amazing. But the way the swollen skin pressed into the hard ball of clit beneath it, where all the nerve endings formed a luscious starburst, was one of the most delicious sensations The Queen could imagine.

And what made it so good was the way they both ground their hips in slow circles, so the clit balls could circle 'round and 'round each other, sliding on all that pussy juice. The motion caused a friction that activated the fire spot on The Queen's clit, which created the hottest, most intense pleasure and culminated in the most violent of orgasms.

"Yeah, work that pussy," The Queen whispered, staring into Trina's eyes. This Babylon invader was clean, The Queen was sure, because Trina had gotten checked like every other woman before the party.

"Good gracious, I had no idea," Trina whispered, "no idea it could be so divine."

The Queen laid back, so that her back arched and her titties poked up. Honey came to the rescue. She knelt at her side, sucking one hard point into her hot mouth.

CoCo did the same with Trina.

In just a few minutes, Trina convulsed all over the place. Her pulsating pussy made The Queen's throb even harder; she shuddered with orgasm too.

That's when Knight stepped in.

Trina laid back on the couch, legs spread.

"OOOhhh," The Queen groaned, loving the sight of all that female meat, succulent pink-brown folds like a dew-covered flower. Creamy cum making it glisten. And that dark hole wide open, wishing for—

The Queen shoved her fingers up in it.

Trina screamed.

The Queen knelt on the carpet, then lowered her face into the pussy.

Behind her, Knight knelt, too.

Just as The Queen's lips wrapped around Trina's cherry-sized clit, Knight's big dick rammed up into The Queen's pussy from the back.

The Queen sucked like her life depended on it. She licked and finger-fucked, and moaned and shivered with the pleasure of Knight's pipe, pounding into her sweet canal.

On the carpet, nearby, Honey spread her sweet stuff for CoCo to lick as CoCo's finger-fucked herself from behind, her beautiful dark ass poked up in the air, her titties dancing over the carpet as she sucked.

"I'm 'bout to blow," Knight groaned. He pounded harder and harder.

The Queen licked ferociously.

CoCo and Honey spasmed all over the floor.

"Da-yum!" Knight exclaimed as he soaked The Queen inside out.

Trina panted, then collapsed.

And they all laid quiet for a few minutes.

Then, when they were dressed, Trina revisited the TV interview question.

Knight walked to the mummy case. He pulled out a videotape and said, "The answer is no. Hell no. And neva in a million years, unless you'd like to see this on national TV to preview your legal analysis of the day."

Chapter 7

Jamal was diggin' the way CoCo was sucking his dick while he worked the board in his music studio. Life for a 22-year-old brotha from the hood didn't get much better than this fantasy hook-up as a hip-hop music mogul. He was sitting in his big chair, getting blown by his lady, and watching Knight and The Queen through the glass in the sound booth, where they were jammin' on their wedding song, and each other.

The world gon' cum jus' by watchin' the sexiest couple groove in my studio. Knight a bad dude, plannin' his disappearing act like this.

The soft light of white candles all around the sound booth cast the most seductive glow over their nude bodies. They looked like a huge licorice twist around a long caramel sucker, and their love was so hot that they both glistened as if they were melting into one. Both their bodies were so buff; their biceps and abs and asses looked rock-hard, yet tender, curvaceous, yet toned.

As Knight planted his lips on The Queen's shoulder and sucked her skin, making her pretty cinnamon nipples point straight at Jamal, he moaned.

"The world ain't neva seen that kinda love," Jamal whispered. "But I'm 'bout to show 'em." He glanced at the panel of knobs and red lights to his right. Yeah, the cameras were rolling on four angles, including the ceiling, to capture that from every angle. They'd have to edit to make it clean enough for TV, but the Bang Squad knew all kinds of ways to show a lot of bumpin' and grindin' without showing the whole body part.

Jamal swayed his body to the sexy beat he had laid to The Queen's song. It started with The Queen whispering, "Promise you'll always kiss me like this."

Then Knight whispered back, "Promise you'll always look at me the way you're lookin' at me now. Promise me."

After that, The Queen sang in a super-sultry deep voice: "I promise. Promise me you'll always see that we can be, you and me, into eternity, for all to see. Never flee but always free to be

73

in unity. Fly high with me; cry, sigh, lie with me; die with me as our souls float into infinity."

The hook jammed on their hit theme song, "Love You to the Infinity," which had been rocking the charts since its debut.

The fact that Knight and The Queen had refused all media interviews from the hottest hip-hop magazines and TV shows out there only made fans want more. All kinds of rumors were burnin' up cell phones, e-mails and Internet websites about the real identities of The Queen and her Knight.

Some said it was Tupac and Aaliyah reincarnated. Or that they had faked their deaths and were recording from some remote hideaway under aliases. Others said it was some supernatural rising of Marvin Gaye and Phyllis Hyman, that the two superstars had hooked up in heaven then came back to make supernaturally sweet music together.

But nobody except folks at Babylon knew the truth. And they also knew that if they snitched that'd be their ass. So the secret was kept. And sales and rumors would shoot through the roof as soon as Manifest Destiny went into effect.

"Billions," Jamal whispered.

Jamal's dick, well-known in the rap and hip-hop music industry as Beat, threatened to go soft for a minute, even though CoCo was working it like the best of the Sluts did Saturday night at The Garage party.

Do I really wanna buy Babylon? Yeah it would be crazy dough. But Bang Squad, Inc. makin' mad money too. Dang, I can't let my boy Knight down; I gave my word.

Just like Knight, Prince, and Duke had given Jamal their word three years ago that they would bankroll his music until he became the next P. Diddy or Jay-Z. And the Johnson brothers had stuck by their word. They'd done everything, from financing his studio time, to sponsoring his national concert tour, to using their underground network and power plays to get him on the hottest radio stations across America.

So by the time Knight had gotten out of lock-up, Jamal and Bang Squad were so rich and famous that their nasty beats were rockin' cars, flowin' off lips from the cities to the suburbs, and even playing on the soundtrack to a couple in-the-hood-style Hollywood movies.

Jamal's dick threatened to turn to mush. Because if he turned on Knight, he'd be through just as quickly.

I'd be a dead, out-of-bidness muthafucka.

But the idea of taking on an illegitimate business, now that Jamal had huge, legitimate record deals, made something sharp and wicked slice through his gut. Then again, the idea of raking in all those millions that Babylon was making across the good old U.S. of A. suddenly made Jamal's dick stand to attention and pledge allegiance to his boy and their deal.

His dick got even harder as The Queen moaned with real-sex sensuality: "Yeah, baby, promise me we can be wild and free and love to the infinity."

And the video of them, right now, making love like a man and a woman should was so hot, a magical glow lit up the studio like The Queen really was Tinkerbell sprinkling her pixie dust all over the two of them.

"Billions," Jamal whispered, shifting his hips to shove his dick deeper into CoCo Boo's sexy little mouth.

Yeah, this video would show the hip-hop generation what real love was all about. So what if the Bang Squad sang about getting as much pussy and dick as any nigga or bitch could? Jamal needed to let everybody know that, at the same time, they should all be looking for a partner, a soul mate, who could get them through life with hot sex, friendship, and inspiration.

Like me an' CoCo. And Knight an' The Queen.

Knight had agreed as part of the buyout that Jamal could videotape this scene and put it in the video for *A Love Story*.

"CoCo Boo, you doin' it jus' like Daddy love it," Jamal groaned. His phone vibrated on his hip. *Dickman* flashed on the red screen. Raynard would have to wait.

I'll holla back in a minute.

Right now Jamal only had two things on his mind: music and making love. 'Cause Coco had a way of letting lots of spit cover her lips and the inside of her mouth while she slurped up and down on Beat. Plus with his girl, he didn't have to use a condom; they'd both been checked by the Babylon doctors to make sure their blood didn't have any viruses or illnesses, and their sex parts didn't have any nasty bumps or blisters or pus.

On the road with groupies, Jamal jimmied up every time, even just for head. 'Cause the shit he'd seen out there was enough to make a nigga want to whack his own dick forever.

But his Coco Boo was clean. And he trusted her.

I love the way Coco give head 'cause she ain't scary.

Unlike some girls who act like a dick's gonna lurch up and bite them, or get stuck in their throat, or make them sweat out their hair, CoCo always got down and dirty, and acted like she loved that shit. The way she worked her mouth, it was so slippery and hot and form-fitting; better than her sweet, little pussy, because he didn't have to do any work. Except close his eyes and shoot a wad of Beat juice all over her glossy lips and flickering tongue.

A sexy shiver rippled through his six-foot frame as he watched Knight and The Queen through the glass in the sound booth. The Queen's earphones held her hair back over her shoulders as she moaned into the mike that descended from the ceiling. Her hair swayed back and forth, back and forth, over her bare shoulders as Knight drilled her fine ass from the back. So the sexy sounds everybody would hear at the wedding reception would be real. Because they were really fuckin' in the sound booth.

As CoCo squeezed her slippery lips over his dick, up and down, he shifted his hips in the red suede chair.

The Queen let out the sexiest-sounding "Aaaahhhhh." And Knight's face radiated all the macho power and confidence that every nigga in America wished he could feel and flex for a day.

Jamal slid up the bass to capture the full range of The Queen's sexual sounds.

Ain't no betta life than this shit. He couldn't even see CoCo under the board. She had a pillow down there in the darkness, to cushion her knees as she sucked his dick. She didn't need to know how many other chicks craved the privilege of kneeling before this hip-hop throne to pay homage to this musical king.

SEX IN THE HOOD 2

She also didn't know that this king would soon rule Babylon from coast to coast. His Grammy-award-winning musical empire was quickly expanding with hit-making new artists, a clothing line, a custom Bang Squad SUV, cell phones, male and female fragrance, and even restaurants in New York and L.A.

Adding sex to the enterprise would help him build his billions even faster. And it would be easy to hide under all his legitimate and highly respected business endeavors.

Jamal nodded to the sexy beat that he had laid for their wedding song, "Promise Me." He had promised Knight that their deal would be top secret and not revealed until well after he had disappeared into tropical oblivion. All that secrecy, from The Queen and CoCo, from the board of directors at Babylon, from the Studs and Sluts, Barriors and B'Amazons, from everyone, it made Jamal's dick surge with power. He was about to become the most revered and feared gangsta anywhere, ever.

"Damn, look at that muthafucka," Jamal exclaimed, watching Knight jackhammer The Queen nonstop. Her erotic moans into the mike made Jamal shiver. "Yeah, suck that," he said down to CoCo.

She sucked faster.

"Come up here," he said.

She climbed out of the darkness with eager eyes and wet lips. Her black denim mini-dress was already hoisted up over her thighs.

"Sit on my lap."

She was so tiny, she could sit back on Beat and not block his view of the sexiest couple he'd ever seen gettin' it on his studio.

"Oh, fuck," he groaned as her pussy squeezed around Beat.

She ground, round and round, knowing just how to move so that he could still have his hands and forearms on the console.

"Work that shit."

She licked her fingers and pressed them down to her clit. That made her pussy squeeze harder as she rubbed herself.

"Yeah, cum wit' me," Jamal groaned. "Cum wit' me, sweet CoCo."

They faced forward, getting their freak on, watching their best friends do the same, and making beautiful music all at the same time.

And every sexy second of it would debut on world TV, right after Knight signed away the rights of Babylon and made his exit with the same mystery and power that made him a legend in life, and would do it even more in death.

Chapter 8

The Queen felt so wild and rebellious as her ass poked out and back toward the traffic. Riding through downtown Detroit on the back of Knight's super-sleek Suzuki motorcycle, it was as if she were telling the wicked world to kiss her "*juicy*licious," black booty.

"Can we fuck right now?" she said into the microphone wired inside her black helmet. She ground her pussy into the broad leather seat just behind his ass, and gripped her arms around his tapered waist, under his jacket. "Please? Right here at the stoplight?"

Just out of the studio, with music on her mind, she mused on a new rhyme that she'd call "Motorcycle Man." Before Knight could respond to her lusty, lawless request, she spit her rhyme with sexy spoken-word rhythm: "The vibration causes stimulation and gyration, better than masturbation, I'll give a demonstration with a libation of *cream*ation while we're racin' . . ."

Knight revved the engine. The deafening rumble made her bust into laughter. She knew he was smiling as they both turned to admire their reflection in the mirrored windows of an office building.

"That right there, us, is the definition of sexy." Knight's voice boomed into the speakers inside her helmet as the motor quieted.

Their reflection was so sexy, The Queen moaned and shivered. She ground her pussy into the seat and into the back of his muscle-hard ass. "I'ma cum right now," she said, pouting through parted lips that felt as hot as the shiny chrome pipes beneath them.

She mashed her clit into the seam of her black leather pants, making that little starburst shoot flames all up through her. The sensations in her body were like the red racing stripes on the black custom-built bike.

"How you get so fuckin' sexy?" she moaned, staring at Knight's image, which intensified the about-to-cum throb between her legs.

"I wasn't sexy till I found my Queen." He wore a black helmet, a black leather jacket with fringe under the arms and across the back, along with snug leather pants and pointed cowboy boots. His 6 foot, 7 inches of man looked so sexy that The Queen felt dizzy.

"This all fo' you, Baby Girl." Knight let out a low, sexy laugh as he looked around at the vehicles around them at the stoplight. A dude on a lime-green motorcycle two lanes over nodded and revved his engine.

"Don't even think about it, muthafucka," Knight said.

Oooh, that macho power in his deep voice . . . their reflection . . . the rubbing . . .

She closed her eyes, letting the "bike-gasm" roar through her. "I love you," she moaned through trembling lips as she rested the side of her helmet on Knight's broad back.

"Yeah, that's my Baby Girl."

"Pull in someplace secret so we can fuck," she whispered.

"Baby Girl, this ain't the time to get reckless. Plus, with you pregnant, we shouldn't even be on this bike. Gotta get back and get ready to rock Moreno and the board meeting tonight."

"Nothin' can happen to me when I'm with you."

The engine roared.

The bike lurched forward. The Queen held on tight. And Knight took off, screeching through the intersection as the traffic light glowed green on Jefferson Avenue. The Queen closed her eyes as the power rumbled through her so strongly, rousing shivers.

"Yeah, revv me like that, baby," she purred. She needed to write a song called "Life-gasm," about the spasms of love after the chasms of race made her razz 'em by disappearing without a trace.

Knight was driving so fast, the momentum and speed gave her a buzz. Maybe he was zipping through downtown to find a spot where they could park the bike and she could straddle him right here on the seat.

She kept her eyes closed to let that fantasy play out in her mind. The vibrating seat was getting her ready to cum again. Plus, Celeste was still throbbing from the sensuous, candle-lit lovemaking and singing in Jamal's studio. It seemed like the more they made love, the more she wanted. Needed.

She gripped the insides of her thighs along the outsides of his legs. They were touching all the way down to her black boots, which were just behind his.

All her hair was tucked into her helmet because Knight had said they stood out enough and didn't need any more attention. The last time they had taken the bike out, and she'd let her long black hair fly in the wind behind them, somebody in a van had followed them and asked if he could take their picture for the newspaper.

"*Je regrette que je ne parle pas anglais*," The Queen had cooed, later laughing that she'd told the photojournalist in French, "I'm sorry that I don't speak English."

Knight didn't laugh though, because he said it could have been a spy for the FBI, still searching for Victoria Winston, or watching Babylon, or even confusing Knight with some other Most Wanted black man. That's why today, when Knight had at first refused to take the bike out, The Queen told him he was paranoid. She pleaded, saying the fresh air would make him feel great. And it did, because he'd seemed much more relaxed that day in the studio than he had in a long time. Plus, it had helped her sing and perform better.

The Queen opened her eyes. They were speeding west on Jefferson. On their left, the five cylindrical towers of the Renaissance Center, which housed hotels, restaurants, and General Motors' world headquarters, gleamed in the sunshine.

Straight ahead was the Joe Louis monument. The giant black forearm and balled fist—suspended in a triangular frame in the middle of Detroit's busiest street—was a controversial tribute to the legendary boxer. Opponents believed it symbolized a militant black power fist salute. But former Mayor Coleman Young, who had backed the project, insisted that the fist was the perfect way to celebrate that Motor City legend.

The fist always reminded The Queen of her first night in Babylon when Duke had taken her in his cream-colored convertible Porsche and they went out to dinner downtown. She was marveling at it while Duke expressed shock that she'd been so sheltered out in the white suburbs that she'd never been downtown to see even the nicest parts of the mostly black city.

The Queen smiled behind the tinted glass of her helmet. The fist reminded her of something else. "That's how your dick felt the first time we made love," The Queen said, "and I didn't even know it was you."

Knight let out a low laugh. "You don't know the symbolism of that statement, Baby Girl. The black power fist up inside 'Lillywhite.' "

"Yeah, I do. I was like Darth Vader. Stepping onto the Dark Side. And lovin' it."

Knight stopped the bike at a red light at Woodward Avenue so they could admire the fist up close.

"I was like lillywhite but didn't fight the sight or the might of that dynamite stick, your dick that I lick and I light like a wick and trick—"

"Rhyme that, Baby Girl."

"A big black fist that I kissed, never missed I insist the power to devour—"

A deep rumble all around them made her stop.

"Don't turn around," Knight said. "It's gang." Beside them, that lime green bike pulled up on their left, along with an orange one. Two black ones stopped to their right.

"Moreno's muthafuckas."

The Queen froze.

I'm pregnant.

But she knew Knight would handle it like a Hollywood stunt man. The light was still red. They were in the middle of five lanes, surrounded by bikes. City Hall was on their right. TV trucks and police cars usually lined the curb, but today there was only a meter maid, a cab, and a bunch of hoopties.

"Hold on, Baby Girl." Knight proved that his bike really could go from zero to eighty in the blink of an eye. Because he screeched at the speed of light, making a bold right turn onto Woodward from the middle lane. The revving engine beneath them was all the noise they heard for long moments.

SEX IN THE HOOD 2

The Queen's heart pounded as she gripped Knight with her arms around his waist. *We are safe . . . we are safe . . . we are safe . . .* She knew Knight was thinking that he should not have let her talk him into taking the bike to the studio.

She could hear him thinking, *The days of reckless abandon for the sake of fun are over. Until we get to paradise forever. And we will.*

But what did "paradise forever" mean? Marriage? Or something else? This telepathic love connection was kind of a bitch. Because she got these hunches that raised questions that maybe she didn't want to know the answer to.

"Biker One to Cairo," Knight said as he sped toward the city's center, where a park, an outdoor café and a skating rink during the winter converted into a lunchtime concert spot during the summer. Campus Martius was bustling with business people and families as Knight sped over the patterned red brick of the circular boulevard.

The deep roar of bikes behind them made her heart hammer.

"Ramses, over," Gerard answered from the security post back at The Playhouse.

"*HO* delivery. Copak." The Queen knew that meant "Hummer One pick-up at Comerica Park," the downtown baseball stadium where the Detroit Tigers played.

"Ramses, over."

The Queen also knew that Babylon's security system had a lojack installed in every vehicle, including the catering trucks. So that right now, Paul or Gerard, could be watching exactly where their motorcycle was, along with the fleet of Hummers and cars. That way, he could direct Hummer One to the exact spot where they'd meet.

But how could Knight evade this army of evil bikers to get all the way past downtown to the stadium? The Queen half-smiled because she knew Knight could figure his way out of any situation. Plus, both she and Knight were packing, but how could they draw and shoot while speeding through bustling downtown on a motorcycle?

We can't.

"Hold on, Baby Girl." Knight whipped the bike around the circular park. He zipped between a Mercedes and a UPS truck. Then he shot into an alley between two office buildings. He cut a sharp right into another alley, then a left into another.

A few bikes followed; several others rumbled on the streets at the ends of the alleys.

The Queen could hear him thinking, *Here we go. Grip me good.* His mind was ticking down options at the speed of light as he turned down another alley between tall office buildings. Pedestrians jammed the sidewalk at one end. It was an art fair. Vendor booths and food stations packed the streets. That was virtually a dead-end. With brick walls at their sides and bikers behind them, it appeared they were stuck.

Suddenly The Queen realized that her fingers, gripping tightly around Knight's waist, were trembling. And her senses were overwhelmed by that same feeling as when Flame had tried to rape her in the Champagne Room during the party.

This is some dangerous shit!

For all the exhilarating highs, they were pockmarked by these sudden flashes of terror: the threat of rape; the fear of Duke popping back up at anytime seeking revenge; the horrific idea of something bad happening to Knight, whether it was a health crisis or someone trying to take him down and out— leaving her alone and defenseless; the reality that the Feds were after her and might put her in prison or worse if they caught her on the trumped-up charges to punish the little black girl who fled when her daddy died. And now this, out of the blue—a sinister mob of bikers sent by a dude they were supposed to meet with later that day so they could dominate Moreno into submission.

And we will. With a vengeance, if we live through this . . .

But were all the super-high moments of exhilaration worth these life-threatening lows? Was this the type of lifestyle in which she and Knight wanted to raise a child? But if they were to pick up and leave Babylon, where would they go? What would they do? How could they possibly finance this glamorous life that they loved . . . in a way that was safer, legal, and lower-profile?

The questions whizzed through her head as fast as the people, buildings and vehicles around them. They veered past a delivery truck with its back ramp open. A private valet parking lot nestled behind the buildings offered a wide-open space.

In one dizzying flash, Knight spun the bike 180 degrees. Two dozen bikers were heading toward them, straight on. He stopped. His black boots touched the brick alley in a way that said, "Bring it on, muthafuckas!"

They zoomed close. And Knight revved the engine.

The bike sped straight between the gang.

The Queen imagined she and Knight on the bike were like a black bullet shooting past those losers.

She pressed her cheek into Knight's back as he wove between dumpsters and delivery trucks and people. On the street, he zipped between cars. Not a single biker appeared in the rearview mirrors or at the front or sides.

Knight ripped back up Woodward Avenue. He sped past restaurants, a drug store and chic nightclubs and lofts. Then he turned right at Grand Circus Park, just south of the fabulous Fox Theatre where Motown greats once played. He whipped toward the giant stone tigers that greeted fans to Comerica Park.

And he followed the shiny black stealthiness that was Hummer One, just down the street, as it turned onto a back street for their rendezvous.

Chapter 9

Reba and another Slut, Baby Blue, sashayed amongst the mostly black clientele of Northland Mall.

"Girl, admit it," Baby Blue said as a half-dozen teens stopped in their tracks and watched the women switch on high heels—"you a hater."

In a skintight, denim bodysuit, Reba led her best friend into their favorite leather shop that sold the most blingin' styles in D-town. She was treating her girl to an impromptu shopping spree, thanks to the thick stack of "benjamins" that Gerard gave up after their sexy splash in the Jacuzzi last night.

Reba's whole body felt tingly, because by the end of the day, Baby Blue would be her partner to move up and out of ho'in' and into positions of power.

"I don't hate, I plan." Reba stopped at a rack and fingered an orange opalescent leather mini-skirt with cubic zirconia studs. She snatched it and its matching cropped jacket. "I know what I want. I'm gon' get it. An' ain't nobody gon' stop me."

She pointed a long, acrylic nail toward the chick who wore a store name badge but looked as uninterested as a gay dude in Victoria's Secret.

Reba ordered, without making eye contact. "Sweetheart, get me the matching boots in size seven. In orange and black." As her expert shopping vision zoomed in on the sexiest shirts, pants and dresses, Reba thought about all the steps she'd have to make her plan become reality. She was already working every angle.

Reba held up some low-cut Baby Phat jeans with a sparkly pattern on the butt. "Ooohh, girl, these would hug your cute little ass just right." She handed them to Baby Blue, who smiled. "And take that bustier top too."

Baby Blue's eyes got big, making her blue contacts look extra bright against the whites of her eyes. Her long, sandy-blond weave hung straight over the fronts of her shoulders in two ponytails. Her lips—as full and red as Betty Boop's lips on her tight black T-shirt—pulled back as she smiled. "Reba, since when does Christmas come in September? You act like you hit the Lottery."

"I'm 'bout to," Reba said, tapping the Louis Vuitton bag over her shoulder. She glimpsed her phone in a side pouch; in a minute her partner would be calling to check the progress of her recruitment for Plan B. "Yeah, we can both hit the lottery. If you help me."

"How?"

"Aw, shit!" Reba exclaimed, striding quickly on her high-heeled sandals to pick up a royal blue crochet dress. "Ain't you got a bikini like this? Girl, wear that under this dress. You'd have niggas lickin' yo' toes."

"Already got that"—Baby Blue giggled—"and my pussy."

"That ain't all who's lickin' yo' shit," Reba said. "I heard The Queen turnt you out the otha night. Why you didn't tell me? Ain't I still yo' girl?"

Baby Blue turned away like she was looking at the baby T-shirts against the wall. "It ain't somethin' I like to talk about."

"How you gon' go from bein' the freak of the week, puttin' all kin' o' stuff up in yo' pussy while you on stage at The Garage, and now you shy wit' yo' girl?"

Baby Blue's cheeks turned red. She stepped to a nearby table displaying a rainbow of lace thongs. She chose three, each a different shade of blue. "I hit the jackpot. These are my favorite brand. This stretch material don't cut into my crack like the regular ones."

"You ain't hearin' me," Reba said playfully to hide her pissed off feelings inside. Maybe Baby Blue wouldn't be as easy to convince as she thought. "Knight and his snowball got you on some kinda gag order?"

Baby Blue snapped. "Don't ask me what I do wit' them. Just 'cause you saw her eat my pussy last year at Duke's birthday party don't mean somethin's goin' on now."

"Yeeeeaaah . . . right!" Reba flitted toward a fur bikini in the corner. "Girl, the yacht party comin' up. Check this out!"

"I like the blue leather one better," Baby Blue said, picking up a thong bikini with turquoise beads sewn in star patterns over the nipples. "I can wear this in the Sexiest Slut contest during The Games. Girl, if I win all that money, I can seriously think about retiring."

"That ain't no money compared to what you can make wit' me," Reba said.

Baby Blue laughed. "I wouldn't call a hundred grand 'no money.' Plus, last year's winner impressed one of the celebrity judges so tough, he married her. Now she lives in some mansion in New Jersey."

Reba fingered the blue leather bikini and said, "Dream on, girlfriend."

"So what else you wanna ask me?"

"Be my partner," Reba said. "I cain't tell you the details just yet, but know that you'll get paid when it all go down in a couple weeks."

"Sounds too vague," Baby Blue said. "And if you tryin' to buy me in"—She put the bikini back—"then I can buy my own shit."

"Naw, girl!" Reba grabbed the bikini and put it back in Baby Blue's hands.

I'm gon' make this bitch cooperate wit' my plan if I have to. She the only one I trust enough to make it happen, now, 'cause Duke only gave me three days to recruit my team. Smiling, Reba said sweetly, "This just a treat 'cause you my girl. C'mon, let's go try this on."

As Reba marched toward the dressing rooms with an armful of clothes, the Bang Squad's hit song, "Freakalicious," blasted from her phone. "Girl, just a minute. It's Gerard. This pussy gave him a lobotomy last night. Bet he callin' to ask for help rememberin' his own damn name."

Reba held the phone so Baby Blue couldn't see ANTOINE flash on the display. "Hey, big daddy. We shoppin' thanks to you." Reba smiled at Baby Blue, who looked tense.

"Yeah, I do. Ain't nothin' like help from a fine-ass man to save the day for D-town's workin' girls."

 Baby Blue drew her brows together and mouthed, "Fine?" She rolled her eyes, knowing damn well Gerard was not fine.

"Yeah, big daddy, I'll keep it hot."

She hung up.

"Girl, you dangerous," Baby Blue said. "The chief of security ain't a smart choice to be fuckin' around with. He can watch your every move—"

"Why you so scary about every damn thing?" Reba snapped as the Arabic-speaking store owner led them into the dressing room. "An' why you all of a sudden followin' the rules when you shit on Slut Rule #5—Never date your clients."

"I haven't seen Brian in six months," Baby Blue said, staring at the floor. "That crazy white boy loved black booty an' rap music an' dressin' like a thug. But he was racist as hell."

"But he was a Babylon client—till you started givin' it away free."

"He wanted to marry me," Baby Blue said as they stepped into the spacious dressing room with red velvet chairs and mirrored walls, "but his parents said if he married a black chick, he wouldn't get his trust fund money when he turn twenty-five."

Reba admired herself in the mirror. "Sheee-it. He must have money. I'd wait. Keep the love tip on the down low from his parents. Get the money then say, 'Guess who's comin' to dinner?' " Her ponytail bounced as she laughed.

"I don't want no part of that," Baby Blue said. "Besides, I'll do dick for work, but personally, I'd rather get wit' a girl."

Reba rolled her eyes. "You know damn well you'd be all ova some dude who wanted to get married, have babies and live large in the suburbs. You'd be done trickin', girl. I think every Slut dream about—"

Baby Blue shook her head. "I see it like this. I can find a rich woman to take care of me. Make me her sex kitten, you know. Like Shar Miller . . . remember her? She old now, but she got fat money 'cause she runnin' Babylon in Vegas."

"She a freak," Reba said. "Got a whole harem of dudes an' pussy. Go 'head, girl. You qualified."

Baby Blue rubbed her fingertips over her nipples, dropped and rolled her ass. "When she see me dance at The Games an' win the Sexiest Slut contest, I'll be her playmate numba one."

"Yeeaah, right!" Reba held the orange leather ensemble up to her body, admired herself in the mirror, then popped her hips. "You betta get in line for that Sugar Momma!"

Baby Blue smiled. "I'll keep her cummin'."

"Dream on," Reba said. "These clothes gon' be my costume for a serious man-gettin' mission. And it will be accomplished."

"Who's the man?" Baby Blue asked, hanging clothes on hooks.

"Knight."

"*You* dream on, girl! You sound like Milan when she was goin' after Duke. You can only lose; look what happened to that stuck-up snob."

"Got her due for lookin' down her nose at us for so many years," Reba said as she pulled off her jumpsuit.

"You playin' wit' fire. I don't care how prissy you think Miss White Chocolate be. She don't mess around when it come to her man."

"I ain't scared o' that bitch," Reba said, admiring her big, brown titties in the mirror. They pointed out just enough to make her waist look extra tapered, her hips extra juicy. Especially when she wore this red satin G-string that curved up over her hip bones down to barely cover the tiny pouf of pussy hair that she got waved into a heart shape.

"Neither was Janet." Baby Blue peeled off her T-shirt and low-cut jeans.

"Damn, girl! You nasty—no panties."

"I like the way my jeans rub up on my clit." Baby Blue tapped her fingertips to the top of her fat pussy. It looked like two extra-large hamburger buns holding a thin slice of meat in the middle.

"Hey now, how I'm gon' resist all that shit in my face?" Reba moaned. She dropped to her knees. "Tell me you ain't givin' me leftovers after snow white took a bite of this juicy apple," Reba said.

"Eat!" Baby Blue ordered, falling back on a chair, spreading her legs.

Kneeling on the zebra-striped carpet, Reba rubbed her fingertips on top of that slippery brown berry. She pulled her index finger back, watching clear pussy juice stretch an inch upward. "Damn! Yo' pussy get wet."

"I'm ovulating," Baby Blue said, loving the explosion brewing in her cunt. "Right between your periods, makes your pussy juice stretchy and sticky to catch cum and get you pregnant."

"I ain't got no sperm."

"Naw, but yo' clit so long, might as well be a dick."

Baby Blue moaned. "Ooh, I see your ass in the mirror. Your pussy tryin' to expand out between your thighs."

Reba's ass pooted up in the air. The round mounds curved down just right to her just-thick-enough thighs. And her red G-string rested between her pussy lips, like when a man holds a rose between his teeth. As she moved her hand, the lips closed, then opened, around the red strip. "I got yo' ass now," she said. "Say you gon' help me."

A knock on the door.

"Ladies, a man is coming here to see you," the store owner said with a heavy accent.

Reba faked a confused expression.

"Can't they wait till I get my nut first?" Baby Blue moaned.

"You will." Reba didn't bother to cover up as she opened the door.

Antoine stood there with a big bulge in his jeans. His brown sandals matched the mesh style of his long-sleeved shirt, which showed off his flat stomach and upper body muscles.

Reba said, "You like Superman—you know when it's some bitches in need an' you show up wit' just the right tools."

"At your service," Antoine said, stepping in.

The manager rolled his eyes and walked away.

Reba closed the door. "Shoot! As much money as I spend in this joint, he bet' not say nothin'."

Baby Blue sat up, closing her legs. "Is this just a coincidence or a set-up?"

"I was shopping next door and I saw you two fine ladies stoppin' traffic out in the mall," Antoine bullshitted. "I knew you'd get freaky up in here, so I came to offer my services."

"I don't fuck Studs," Baby Blue said.

"A Slut standing on high moral ground," Antoine said. "Betta watch out. A flash-flood can come along, cause a mudslide, and you'll be slippin' into the cesspool with the rest of us unscrupulous muthafuckas."

Baby Blue glared at Reba. "Girl, you know I can't stand his pretty ass. I'm outta here." She stood and reached for her clothes.

"Sit the fuck down," Reba said with a hard tone. "I was tryin' to be nice, but now I see I gotta go ghetto on your 'sew-ditty' ass."

Antoine sat on the arm of the chair beside Baby Blue and cast a fake smile down at her.

"Why you look all jumpy an' nervous?" Reba teased. "I'm 'bout to make you rich."

"I have enough money," Baby Blue said; "my life is just fine the way it is."

"Don't think small," Reba said. "You an' me, as little girls in that rat-hole apartment our trick-ass mommas shared, they taught us to think small. Like yo' little hook-up at Babylon all you need."

Antoine laughed. "Time to get your juicy slice of Babylon's pie. You'll never have to work again."

"Yeah," Reba said. "Think big. Be big."

Baby Blue crossed her arms over her bare titties. Then she crossed her legs. "You both crazy. If you think bum-rushin' me with a hot pussy in a dressing room will intimidate me into doing your death wish, forget about it."

Reba snatched her phone out of her purse. "I'll call Knight right now and tell him about you dating a Babylon client for six months, giving away thousands of dollars' worth of pussy."

Baby Blue shrugged. "Call him. I'll pay it back. I learned my lesson. And Knight would understand."

"You ain't hearin' me, bitch!" Reba raked her fingernails into the back of Baby Blue's head, grabbed a fistful of hair, and pulled back hard.

Baby Blue's eyes got huge.

"You gon' help us," Reba said, "an' you gon' get paid, so listen."

Chapter 10

In the small apartment over his mother's garage, Duke searched the doctor's eyes for more answers than the vague-ass words that were coming out of her mouth. He needed to recover from this bullshit ASAP so he could get back to the work of taking what was his.

"It looks nasty as hell," he said, laying on the bed and staring at the shredded skin near his right ribcage. "Tell me it ain't as bad as that shit looks."

Doc Reynolds dabbed a cotton ball with white cream on the wound where Knight's bullet had grazed him. "I'm afraid you need stitches," she said, examining him through her purple-framed glasses. "And all that time in the water, you were exposed to bacteria and possibly toxins that are causing a bad infection." She leaned down to his leg. She shook her head. "And this wound . . . I'm afraid you shouldn't walk on this."

"It's just a cut," Duke said, remembering the ripping sound as he went overboard and the sharp tip of the rope notches sliced open his thigh. "Good thing ain't no sharks in the Detroit River. I woulda been chum like a mug."

Doc Reynolds shook her head. "I'm afraid you need stitches there too. But the infection—"

Duke tried to get up. "I ain't got time to lay up in bed. I got—"

Her gentle hand on his chest pushed him back down. "Duke, if you were as healthy as you were a year ago, you'd recover quickly and easily. But the drugs have severely compromised your body's ability to heal. And the blood test, I'm afraid—"

"Quit sayin' you afraid; just tell me, goddammit!"

"Sometime over the past year, you contracted HIV," the doctor said. "Whether it was from unprotected sex or sharing a needle—"

"Muthafuck me!" Duke shouted. "How long I got to live?"

"If you get on medication now, it can prolong the onset of AIDS. But those drugs are costly."

SEX IN THE HOOD 2

Doc Reynolds was once the top physician for the Sex Squad, giving them their weekly check-ups at the clinic in Babylon HQ, but Knight had ousted her and replaced her with fancier doctors. Now Duke was recruiting her to work for him again, once he got things back up and running. After he got his body back up and running.

"Give me all the drugs I need," Duke said. "Pump me up; make me into a fuckin' bionic man. Like Lee Majors on that TV show, *The Six Million Dollar Man.*"

Doc Reynolds shook her head, making her smooth black French roll move from side to side. She crossed her arms over her all-white uniform. "I can start you off with the small supply, maybe a month's worth, that I have at the clinic, but since I left Babylon, I don't have unlimited access to free meds—"

Duke ground his teeth. "I'll get the money." And he'd get it from the folks running Babylon in two of America's sexiest cities—Miami and Las Vegas. Shar Miller and Leroy Lewis were sick of Knight's totalitarian regime and all his tight-ass rules. They were ready to bust out on their own, or bolster their bank as part of Duke's new empire—Oz.

And I'm the new muthafuckin' wizard.

Duke had just spoken with Shar and Leroy, who had both promised to put out feelers to recruit more Babylon-controlled cities into Oz. Next, Duke was going to talk with sleazy-ass Moreno. Not for the meeting he'd planned a year ago in which Duke would seize all power from their family's empire. This time, Duke would be teaming up with them, to bring down their common enemy: Knight. But first Duke had to get his body back in top shape to run an empire and win back his Timbo-lovin' Duchess.

"Now I'm going to prep you so I can stitch up those wounds," Doc Reynolds said. "I have to go to my car for supplies." As she opened the door, Mama stood there crying. The dinner plate in her hand trembled so badly, the doctor grabbed it.

"Mrs. Johnson, I'm so sorry," Doc Reynolds said, leading her inside.

"Boy, look at the mess you done made!" Mama shrieked. "No wonder Knight took control of e'rythang. You cain't no more run a business than stay alive. Now done gone and caught the AIDS?" She grabbed a pillow and whacked him in the head. "Boy, you ain't nothin' but a dead junkie now. Ain't no point sewin' you up."

"Mama, admit it now—I cain't neva be as good as Knight in yo' eyes. You, him, an' Prince never did look at me as nothin' but a knuckle-headed punk!"

Duke wanted to stand but his body hurt too much. All the rage from twenty-two years of feeling lesser than his brothers in their mother's eyes suddenly surged up and shot out of his mouth like bullets at the woman who had both birthed him, and killed him inside. "You think I'm such an 'ain't-shit muthafucka', Mama; I'll be better off dead anyways. So go on back to church; tell God thank you for knockin' off your no-good baby boy. You and Knight can live happily ever after."

Duchess' face flashed in his mind.

"You even like his lady now, but you hated her when she was wit' me!" He snatched the pillow and threw it at his mother. "Get the fuck out, Mama! You ain't neva gotta look at this triflin'-ass muthafucka again."

Mama burst into tears. "Baby, I'm sorry. I'm just so mad you don' throwed yo' life away. Now it ain't hardly nothin' to save." She spread her arms and leaned down to hug him. "I'm sorry, baby."

Duke pushed her away. "Doc, take me outta here."

"Baby!" Mama shrieked. "Baby, stay! You need rest! I'll take care of you."

Duke grimaced and gripped his leg and side as he angled his body to the edge of the bed. He pressed on the nightstand and forced himself to stand up, despite the blinding pain.

"Baby, stay!"

"I'm sorry, Mrs. Johnson," the doctor said as she put Duke's arm over her shoulder and led him toward the door.

Duke turned back, focusing on the floor. "I ain't stayin' where don't nobody love me. Bye, Mama."

She screamed.

SEX IN THE HOOD 2

He slammed the door.

Chapter 11

The Queen had never met the Moreno Triplets, but she strutted toward them like she owned the whole damn universe. Because after she got through with them, she would. At least the universe of organized sex-for-sale anywhere near D-town and a dozen big cities across America.

And that little bike chase this afternoon had shifted her all the way into bitch overdrive. If ever she wanted to use her mixed-race sex powers, she was about to whip some *femme fatale* on these muthafuckas to make them bow down and kiss her baby toes.

When I get done, they won't know their dicks from a do-rag. They'll be beggin' for scraps. And I won't even toss 'em a muthafuckin' bone . . .

The Queen's pussy contracted as if she were holding a dick up inside its hot, creamy walls. Duke used to marvel that she had balls as big as his. Now her pussy meat felt so swollen, she actually felt full. As if she were carrying around inside her a phantom dick to overpower these high-class hoodlums with super-sexy style.

Knight's contacts had done extensive research on just what the Morenos controlled and wanted to acquire. They had massage parlors, escort services, and strip clubs. Now they were trying to muscle in on the traditional pussy-party circuit—the kind that entertained men. But it turned out, Babylon had them beat in a big way, thanks to The Queen's aggressive thrust into the female market.

Only problem was, Moreno wanted what Babylon had. And this was the day to fuck them out of business entirely.

"Now it's time for us to execute Prince's Rule #4: *Crush Your Enemies Entirely*," Knight had said as they were chauffeured here by Ping and Pong in Hummer One. "But at the same time, they'll never know they're being smashed. The trick is to make them feel like they're being praised as the kings."

The Queen kept that in mind as she led Knight, Ping, and Pong into the private room of a five-star restaurant on the 72nd floor of the Renaissance Center. The all-glass walls offered a breathtaking view of downtown Detroit, Windsor, and far beyond.

I love this shit. We're on top of the world. And we're stayin'.

The Queen loved the way her super-spiky, high gold heels cut into the carpet with her every step.

A hostess led them to the sleek meeting room with walls made of beige suede and glass blocks. Inside, at a large, square glass table sat the notorious Moreno Triplets, along with a heavyset, light-skinned guy with thick facial features and a bald head. Beside him, a freakishly skinny blond chick in a tight white pantsuit perched on one of the brown suede chairs. Behind them stood one bodyguard; he was a handsome, African-black giant wearing a brown suit. A glass-block wall that shielded them from the sophisticated crowd in the bustling restaurant set a chic backdrop for this gang of six.

Now, The Queen loved how all of their eyes became enchanted and danced all over her as she entered. A rhyme popped into her head; she'd have to write it down later and put it into a song she'd call "A Bad Bitch."

As I switch without a glitch they call me A Bad Bitch
'Cause I mesmerize as I glamorize the eyes of guys
Whose sighs and size sensualize
With cries of sex as I vex their minds
I wind with my walk and my talk don't balk
Just chalk it up to my desire to make you on fire
Hotwire you liars . . . you booty buyers
I'm 'bout to steamroll you like monsta truck tires
So slick with my trick that you'll love me
Your dick, your prick will ache for my sweet meat
But I beat you and now it's time to meet,
Treat you, defeat you ...

The Queen loved the way everyone, including that chick who needed a few good meals, focused first down on her red-jeweled Manolo Blahnik sandals that framed her tiny red toenails, ran up the centers of the tops of her feet, and circled around her ankles with faux red rubies and topaz stones.

WHITE CHOCOLATE

All their eyes trailed up her long, tanned and bare legs, and over her snug red mini-skirt. A painfully horny expression radiated from their eyes as their stares paused to assess the gap between her thighs, where only she knew that the soft curves of her legs guarded the red satin thong that was rubbing against her swollen clit with tantalizing friction and heat.

After a moment, their stares rose up to the tiny waist of her tailored jacket, which fastened with a large topaz button to cinch her small waist before the soft red leather flounced in an oh-so-sassy way over her hips. The sleeveless jacket revealed her toned, bronzed arms and the golden Cleopatra-style bracelets that accentuated the buff curves between her biceps and her deltoid muscles on each arm. The cuffs were made of half-inch-wide gold that circled at the fronts of her arms into two coils ending with asps, whose eyes were real diamonds.

They neva seen nothin' like me.

The Queen held back a smile as these new onlookers downright ogled the explosion of titties in the scandalously low-cut lapels that pressed two humps of hot bronze decadence up and into their faces. She had spread some iridescent lotion over her titties to make them shimmer as they bounced with her strut-walk. Plus her newest tattoo announced in cobalt blue scroll across the tops of her titties: *Cleopatra of the Knight.*

Wearing ski-goggle-style sunglasses that were gold-tinted and sexy as hell, The Queen let her long hair sway down her back as she approached the men and the one chick. All of them looked at her like she was the lunch that would be served on the table full of cream-colored china, silverware, and crystal glasses.

Yet their lust mixed with evil was so strong in the air, she could taste it. In fact, a chill hung inside this small glass-blocked room, even though the rest of the restaurant felt warm and cosy as they'd entered from the elevator. While she had savored the scents of garlic, steak, and seafood cooking as they approached, this room had the choking odor of cigar smoke and too much expensive cologne.

100

SEX IN THE HOOD 2

"Queen," the men said in unison, rising to bow slightly. Each wore a white suit, shirt, and silk tie. Their skin was beige, which could have made them Bolivian, Italian, Arabic, Yugoslavian, or even Spanish.

Knight had said they were from a small island in the Mediterranean Sea, but they had lived in Colombia and South Africa before joining an elderly uncle here in Detroit to stake their claim on his underworld empire before he died.

The Queen forced herself not to shiver as she checked out the diabolical vibe in their identical hazel eyes set in fleshy, clean-shaven faces with hook noses and thick black brows that were professionally sculpted into upside-down Nike swooshes. Their lips were unnaturally red, and their skin looked so pampered, it shone as if it were made of wax.

The one in the middle wore his long, auburn curls pulled back in a white satin ribbon. The other two, flanking the redhead, had close-cropped, kinky black hair with long sideburns.

Were they somehow familiar? Had she seen them before, or had Duke and Knight mentioned them so many times that she felt she already knew them? Or had she seen their faces and heard their names even before she'd come to Babylon? Had Moreno been among the names on those files that Daddy had asked her to feed into the shredder on that frantic Wednesday night before he blew his brains out?

The Queen's mind spun, but her face was as cool and seductive as a Cleopatra mask. She stared hard into the redhead's eyes as she purred, "You're as gorgeous as legend has it."

He stood and extended his waxy-looking, hairless hand. His manicured, polished fingernails shined under the light of the modern chandelier. And his white jacket fell open to reveal a huge bulge in his pants. The white fabric was thin enough to reveal that he wore no boxers or briefs; the rim of the head of his big dick pressed like a face against glass inside the pleated polyester of his pants beside his front zipper.

"*Enchanté*," he said, his eyes blazing with lust. "I meet beautiful women of every race around the world, but you are by far the most exquisite specimen of the black female I have ever had the delight of meeting."

I ain't a muthafuckin' specimen in a science lab, but I'm glad you're taking the bait. The Queen's lips felt hot as she smiled and made her eyes glow with seduction. She did a slow body scan over him, holding her gaze at his bulge, before she looked back into his eyes.

This dude was gorgeous. But he was fine in that slick, mafia-type way that flashed DANGER in her mind. He reminded her—Wait, maybe he was the man she had always seen at those super rich, prestigious parties at her ex-boyfriend Brian's mansion and at gatherings hosted by the parents of her ex-best friend, Tiffany. Daddy had even greeted that man, who always had dark, slicked-back hair, expensive-looking suits, and that sexy-as-hell Asian chick on his arm: the one who was always wearing leopard print catsuits or patent leather white pants with a matching bra or see-through bodysuits, with patches of fur in a few strategic places.

The Queen remembered staring at that woman, wondering what her life was like as the sex kitten arm ornament for a gangster who was hooked into that very legitimate circle of CEOs, lawyers, doctors, and moguls.

Now I'm just like her. Only I got the power too.

That world, The Queen remembered, would accept a quiet, passive Asian ornament. But they rejected the bone-colored China that they thought was porcelain but was actually tarnished with black on the inside.

Right now, somehow, the Morenos were guilty of racism by association. Whether they were as wicked as Brian and Tiffany and their parents—or whether they were down with African Americans—it didn't matter.

Looking at them right now, and feeling their very bad vibe, roused up all the horrible feelings that The Queen had kept buried for more than a year. Since that day Brian had tried to rape her when he found out she was black. And his parents refused to let her live in their mansion when she faced going to live with her black grandmother in Detroit's worst ghetto. Pain rose up that The Queen had also repressed since Tiffany and

102

her parents had turned on her after the local newspapers "outed" her for being black.

Suddenly, a red mist of rage in The Queen's mind cast a sinister haze over this creepy cast of characters. All the anger and disappointment and sadness that she had felt when Brian, and Tiffany and their parents kicked her out of their lives came surging up in a tongue-load of cuss words that she now knew how to launch with hood-style precision and power.

Naw, hold that. These muthafuckas ain't Brian or Tiffany. They just punks cut from the same sleazy, backstabbin' cloth.

Behind her, Knight must have sensed her angst. Because she heard him speak in her mind: *Keep complete and constant control of your emotions.* He had said that earlier, one of The Prince Codes, and he was no doubt projecting that thought on her right now.

"Thank you," The Queen said to the auburn-haired Moreno.

"I'm Red," he said, his long, hot fingers still gripping hers. "These are my brothers, Marco and Liam. We've been greatly anticipating this encounter with the singular woman who could meet Knight's superhuman standards of excellence." Red nodded at Knight, who was still behind her. The man gripped The Queen's hand harder and bowed toward her. His ponytail flipped over his shoulder so that its curly-cue end slithered like a red snake down the padded white fabric on his chest.

The Queen allowed him to continue holding her hand as she stared into his eyes. They were like a marquis flashing DEVIL. The attractive shade of hazel coloring his irises did nothing to hide the violence and betrayal and greed that roiled in his soul. In fact, an aura of malice radiated around the three brothers so intensely, The Queen could almost see pale green vapors rising up around them, like she'd seen in a picture book around an evil dragon that Mommy would read to her as a little girl.

In that story, the beautiful princess always defeated the dragon with her charms, so she could free the handsome prince inside the dragon's scary cave. In the end, the prince and princess tamed the dragon as their pet; he even sang sweet songs instead of breathing fire.

That was their plan with Moreno. But he didn't breathe fire. No, he spoke with an accent that to anybody else would be a dramatic "smoke-and-mirrors-type" distraction to trick them into thinking he was an international aristocrat.

It didn't work on The Queen, though. Working with Daddy at his business, she had met authentic rich people and royalty who spoke with beautiful accents from Great Britain, Australia, Italy, Japan, France, and even Zimbabwe.

But this dude was perpetrating like a mug. His fake accent was a cross between a Transylvanian vampire and a British wannabe. She bit her lip to stop a sudden burst of laughter. In her eyes, despite his expensive suit and impeccable grooming, he was a Eurotrash perpetrator who deserved nothing more than to get double-crossed so Babylon could keep all that it had and get whatever else it wanted.

"These are my partners in charge of operations here in southeast Michigan," Moreno said. He nodded toward the heavyset brunette guy and the skinny blond chick. "We met on holiday in Monaco, when they were celebrating their honeymoon at my favorite casino. They both possess brilliant business minds, thanks to their pedigreed family back-grounds."

The Queen froze.

Why did they look so familiar?

The guy and the chick stared back with equal intrigue.

Brian. And Tiffany. Those snobby, racist punks were work-ing for a gangster now? Was this man the same dude she'd seen at the fancy parties with her friends from her white life? And was there a connection to Daddy's death?

The Queen's insides reeled with shock. If any of them identified her, they would be able to trump her power play by threatening to tell the Feds exactly where she was. Plus that would crush Knight's leverage because they would hold all the juice in the deal.

That would kill us. And Knight has no idea that this little sub-drama could be going on.

SEX IN THE HOOD 2

The Queen smiled.

*Ain't no way in hell they can recognize me right now. None of
'em.*

She looked different—behind sunglasses, super-sexy
clothes, ten extra pounds and a dark tan. All that had
transformed her from the color of the inside of an almond to
deep, bronze-brown. She talked different—ghetto as she
wanted to be. Tough, assertive, nasty, and she acted different—radiating sex power that could singe the senses of
anyone, male or female, with one glance.

*I am someone else. I am The Queen. And I'll crush all their
racist asses too.*

"How y'aw doin'?" She nodded toward them.

Knight stepped forward to shake Red's hand. His tall, dark
height beside her underscored her sense of power. Her former
boyfriend and best friend had never seen Victoria around any
black people except for the maids in their houses, the janitors
and cafeteria staff in their school and CoCo in Daddy's office.
And even CoCo had been someone else when she worked as
his assistant—a navy blue suited, studious nerd named
Marlene.

And if anything did go down up in here, The Queen knew
that Ping and Pong, who were flanking the closed wooden door
leading out to the restaurant, would handle it.

Brian and Tiffany were staring. Had her departure from
their lives somehow inspired them to step onto the dark side
too? They hadn't turned black like The Queen, but they had
crossed over from a super-white, rich world into the sexy
domain of illegitimate enterprises.

Like a reflex, her right hand balled into a fist, the way Lee
Lee had taught her in self-defense kick-boxing class back at
the Babylon gym. She could actually see in her mind's eye her
squared-off knuckles extending straight out from her
shoulder, popping Brian in his nose, then calmly drawing back
to her shoulder and back. She glanced at Tiffany and imagined
doing the same thing, smashing her tiny little beak of a nose
to bits.

WHITE CHOCOLATE

Those two backstabbing hypocrites deserve each other. I'll christen their marriage in Hell—now and forever.

A year ago, she had considered them dead and gone from her mind, her life, the planet. They still were. And what an idiot this Moreno dude must have been to pluck those two from suburbia and expect them to do his dirty work. Unless they'd had immersion training in the hood like The Queen had under Duke and Knight at Babylon, they couldn't possibly have been adequately trained for the rigors of this business. As far as she was concerned right now, they were invisible. Irrelevant. Tiny ants trying to flex like the mighty black butterfly that she had become.

Knight, looking gorgeous in a custom-made, three-button black suit, cream silk tie, and starched shirt, pulled out a chair for The Queen so that she could sit close to Red.

She sat down, feeling his eyes on her crotch to no doubt catch a *Basic Instinct* glimpse of whatever might flash as her miniskirt rose up higher over her thighs.

"We've got a proposal that creates a triple win-win for all of us," Knight said as he sat beside The Queen. "We keep an open mind and work together. Then the billions are ours for the taking."

Damn, I love that man. The thrill of the fight must have given him strength today because ever since the motorcycle chase—and the good love in the music studio—his cheeks had been glowing with that pinkish hue on ripe, dark cherries that came from Northern Michigan.

The Queen peered through the mirrored shimmer of her sunglasses into Red's piercing eyes. "We propose that immediately following The Games we create a collaboration."

Red's gaze lowered to her QUEEN diamond necklace, then her CLEOPATRA OF THE KNIGHT tattoo for a moment. He nodded then looked back into her eyes. "Tell me more."

"It's essentially a situation where you keep yours, we keep ours, but together we create something much more powerful."

Brian and Tiffany were staring so hard at her left cheek that it felt hot.

They can't possibly know who I am . . .

106

At first glance, when she walked in, she had thought that Brian was a brotha. When she knew him, he was a *wigger*, a wannabe, always listening to rap music and talking shit, but he'd quake in his boots if a black guy even approached them on the street to ask for directions. *Punk.*

Now, he looked terrible. All the weight Tiffany had lost, Brian had found, times ten. It distorted his face, thickening his nose, his lips, and the skin around his blue eyes, which still glinted with the same malice.

"Why should we trust you?" Brian asked, twirling his gold ring imprinted with the Martin's family coat of arms. His voice raked over the scabs he had left on her soul.

She imagined herself getting up from the table, walking around the Moreno Triplets, and raising her stiletto heel with the lightning speed and lethal force that Lee Lee had taught her. Her heel would bash straight into his nose and he'd shut the fuck up.

Yeah, I will find the chance to whip some black "Charlie's Angels" action on that muthafucka. And he won't even know what hit him.

"Trust," The Queen said playfully. "What do you feel in your gut right now?"

Brian let out a sexy laugh. "I don't want to get crass while we're doing business. Because what I feel in my gut has nothing to do with—"

"I believe it does," she says. "You feel sex." The word sex came out of her mouth in such a seductive and powerful way that everyone at the table visibly winced.

"And sex is the name of this game," The Queen said. "Trust *that.*"

Knight watched her speak. His poker face hid his expression from the others, but The Queen saw a sparkle of pride that she was doing her thing. Little bits of jade and topaz flickered in the onyx irises of his beautiful eyes. And it made her pussy throb.

This is love. Teamwork making the dream work.

As her seductive words hung in the silent, still air like the salty-sweet aroma of sex at a Babylon pussy party, Brian grinned. Tiffany's nipples poked against the chest of her tight suit jacket. It appeared as though she had starved off her titties, so those two little points made her look like a pre-teen who was just developing.

"Trust is not a question," Red said to Brian. "If it were, we would not be sitting here right now. The question is"—He turned to The Queen—"how will this collaboration work?"

"We structure events based on the already established territorial lines," she said. "Anything you host within the city limits, we split fifty-fifty. Anything we host in the suburbs, you share half-and-half with us." The Queen radiated a smile from her eyes. "And to make it fun, we add a high-stakes gamble to the mix to show our good will."

Liam shifted in his chair, casting a nervous glance at Red, who remained perfectly still.

"I like gambles." Red cast a hungry ogle down on the tops of her titties. His eyes seemed to trace every letter to her tattoo, as if he were writing the words with flames of lust shooting from his eyes. "Tell me more."

The Queen said, "In the past, Babylon has banned Moreno Enterprises from participating in The Games."

Red's lips tightened as he raised a hand up to his ponytail. His index finger parted its curlicue end, dividing it in two. He dropped it back to the front of his shoulder, where it rolled slightly, as if it were flickering like the forked tongue of a snake.

"This year," The Queen said, "to celebrate this historical collaboration, we invite you to participate in The Games. As you know, there's a million-dollar prize for each team that can perform in each event with the best style, endurance, and technique."

The triplets grinned all at once.

"We bring our own security," Liam said nervously with that same whack accent. "We don't go into that territory—"

Red cut his hand through the air. "Winner gets the convention circuit—Detroit, New York, Miami, L.A., and Chicago. Male and female."

The Queen cast a charming gaze at him.

SEX IN THE HOOD 2

Hell naw! That's mine!

But the Morenos weren't going to win The Games anyway, so it was a moot point to discuss.

"Bet," Knight said. "Then we make the same toss at next year's Games. Upping the ante will make for more exciting competitions. More bets."

"And hotter sex," Marco said, holding a martini glass so that the red liquid swirled over the edge onto his hand. He licked it slowly, staring at The Queen.

"Let's add a little more excitement to the deal," Red said, devouring The Queen with his eyes. "The winner gets an evening alone with this Cleopatra of the Knight." Red raised his waxed-perfect black eyebrows to underscore this scandalous question as he looked at Knight.

The Queen could feel Knight's rage so strong, she heard his thoughts echo inside her mind.

He's through, Knight was thinking. *This muthafucka betta enjoy his last gulps of oxygen.*

Knight didn't move. His face remained cool and calm. And he let out his most charming laugh, the kind that Daddy would always use when he was annoyed as hell at a client. But he never let his emotions interfere with business. "All men should strive for your level of confidence," Knight said with a charming, almost chuckling tone. "However, this territory is not open for negotiation. Right now. I'll have to discuss your proposal with The Queen in private and get back with you on that." Knight glanced at The Queen. "I'm sure you can appreciate that it takes teamwork to make the dream work," he said, turning back to Red. "She may in fact be open to your request."

The Queen let her lips part as she widened her eyes at Red.

His waxy beige cheeks grew pink.

"I like your style," The Queen said, smiling at that disrespectful muthafucka.

"Security," Brian said. "We need to work out protection for us as we watch and our teams as they arrive, compete, and leave with several mill."

Red nodded back to the enormous black man behind him. "Nikolai handles that. Our only duty at this time is to agree to this historical collaboration that will fill the coffers of both Babylon and Moreno Enterprises with even more riches. And perhaps bring with it some extraordinary opportunities for pleasure." Red raised a shotglass full of light brown liquid.

"To the deal of the millennium," he said. Without waiting for anyone else to raise a glass, as The Queen and Knight had not even been served, he chugged back the shot. He did not wince before he said with glistening lips, "The truce is a new beginning for all of us, my brother."

"Bet," Knight said.

For the next twenty minutes, they chatted about The Games, the weather, and the upcoming wedding.

*

"Excuse me," The Queen said. "I'm going to the ladies room."

Tiffany stood. "Me too." She was so skinny that when she turned sideways in that white pantsuit, she almost disappeared against the lighted glass-block wall. She had no ass; the dark red pinstripes on her pants made her backside look like a wishbone.

Pong followed as The Queen left the room,. She took long strides through the restaurant, loving the way men and women froze to stare at her. It reminded her of the night she and Duke had met and had gone to a restaurant where former colleagues of her father had screamed obscenities at her and glared because she was with a tall, god-like Mandingo warrior.

Now, nobody would dare. She looked like the black diva that she had become, and she radiated sex power that made a middle-aged woman hold a forkful of lobster mid-air. And that young guy stopped mid-bite with a buttered dinner roll between his lips. And a thirty-something businessman locked his blue eyes on her and dropped his sandwich to his plate.

All so they could hail The Queen. Yeah, her ego was out there. *Ova the top.* But she was lovin' it. And better this than that panicky, depressed, and hopeless place where her mind had gone when she had first come to live in the ghetto.

110

SEX IN THE HOOD 2

"I've never met anyone like you," Tiffany said, taking quick, tiny steps to catch up and keep The Queen's pace. "Ever."

Yes you have. We used to be best friends, bitch.

"What was your name again?" The Queen asked. "Red never mentioned you and your husband's names."

"I'm Birdie; he's *B*-boy. And we're not really married."

As The Queen pushed open the bathroom door, she saw in her periphery that Brian was going into the men's bathroom. She didn't have to look to know that Pong would wait outside the women's lounge to listen for any problems and escort her back to Knight.

When she entered, another woman came in from a door at the opposite side of the restaurant.

Be careful, Celeste said. *This bathroom isn't as secure as you thought.* She thought about letting Pong know that, but she had Smith & Wesson strapped to her waist, so she'd be fine. Even with tiny Tiffany in tow.

The Queen dashed into a stall. Lately it seemed she had to pee a lot. So she pulled down her thong, squatted, and let it rain. She loved that sensation of relieving the pressure of pent-up pee, especially when she'd been holding it. It created a shiver over her whole body.

And suddenly the tension that had gripped her body in that meeting was craving the sedative opium of orgasm. Again. Tonight, after the board meeting, she and Knight could give each other some sexual healing.

"Does everybody call you The Queen?" Tiffany asked from another stall. Her voice was higher-pitched, as if it had lost weight too; her chirpiness echoed off the dark-blue-tiled floor and walls. "I mean, like I don't know, I guess something about you seems so familiar."

All the negative emotions that Tiffany's speech cadence was rousing inside The Queen made her pussy ache. She needed sex to pound down these thoughts and feelings. But the girl with whom Victoria Winston had shared so many secrets and pledged to be best friends for life, kept clanging against her senses.

111

"When my best friend died last year," Tiffany said, "it was so tragic. You remind me of her."

"How'd she die?" The Queen forced the words up and out like sour, slimy chunks of vomit.

"Oh my gosh! It was so, like, tragic," Tiffany said as her pee struck the toilet water. "Her dad, he died, and she, like, got sent to live in the worst part of Detroit. And she, like, couldn't handle it. And her dad had been like, really into some shady deals that she helped him hide from the IRS. Red says Dan Winston was really a shady dude who did him wrong."

The Queen wanted to puke. Daddy did business with Moreno? Had that gangster threatened her father when the Feds closed in with their audit? Had they threatened to hurt him or his three kids? The Queen choked out the words. She had to relieve these feelings, quickly. "Did him wrong, how?"

Tiffany let out a disgusted sigh. "Oh I'm not supposed to talk about this, but they're all dead, so it doesn't matter. I guess, like, Red had hired Mr. Winston to handle some of his deals. But the money got mixed up and, like, the IRS clamped down—"

The Queen coughed. Just like other people craved a cigarette when they were stressed, and some folks smoked a joint, while others gambled, The Queen needed to calm herself by cumming. She pressed her middle finger to her clit. Yeah, the ultimate mind mellower. "MMmmmmm," she moaned softly.

"You okay?" Tiffany chirped while hitting the toilet paper dispenser and unrolling it.

"Mmmmm-hhmmmm."

"Well," Tiffany said, "it all worked out because I remember my friend said her dad had her shred some papers. The Feds never found anything on Moreno, but he was highly pissed."

The Queen's fingers danced over her clit with lightning speed. Her mind swirled with thoughts of Knight's giant dick slamming up into her slippery hole and banging, banging, banging until The Queen couldn't think straight or walk across the room or even say her name. Yeah, right now she needed love to smash away this pain. And shut Tiffany the fuck up.

"So my friend, she was so sweet, but she killed herself. They found the body of a girl who fit her description inside her dad's mansion, like, a few weeks after the funeral."

The Queen gasped. She shoved the fingers on her other hand up into her pussy, fucking herself so that she wouldn't have to let those words register.

They think I killed myself? And they found a body in my childhood home?

This was the first she'd heard of that. A year ago, she had followed news reports about herself, watching TV and reading the newspapers to track the Feds' movement on her case. But after a while, as she immersed deeper into the *incomunicado* underground world of Babylon and blackness—and decided that she wanted to stay there for life—she had stopped paying attention to media lies about Victoria Winston.

That girl was, in fact, dead. And reincarnated as The Queen. Now the body was trembling, about to cum in this marble bathroom 72 floors above D-town. So what body had they found in the Winston's abandoned mansion? Could it have been her sister Melanie? After all, The Queen had not seen her since the funeral, when Melanie had vowed to enter a convent.

"It was weird," Tiffany said over the rustle of clothes that must have been her pulling those tiny pants over her even tinier skeleton. "They showed the girl's picture on the news and said it was Vikki. But I woulda bet money that it was, like, her sister Melanie, 'cause Vikki had eyes like yours but Melanie had brown eyes, and the girl on the news had dark eyes."

The Queen stabbed her fingers inside the creamy heat between her legs to numb her pain. She wished she had four hands so that she could work her pussy and cover her ears all at once. So she wouldn't have to hear Tiffany's mile-a-minute chatter that was jackin' her cool.

"Plus the news said she hung herself from the banister, but I heard it was blunt force trauma to the head." Tiffany let out a nervous laugh. "I don't know why I'm telling you this. I guess 'cause, like, I don't have anybody else to talk to about it."

Who would kill Melanie to trick the world into thinking Victoria were dead?

Duke. No one else cared.

The Queen let her fingertips circle her clit, 'round and 'round, to still the horrific hurricane in her mind.

But Celeste spoke loud and clear: *Duke had them find a female body in the mansion so they'd stop tracking her. A body that looked just like Victoria. Dead girl, case closed. No more worries about the Feds sniffin' around Babylon for Victoria Winston.* That was how Duke thought. And he must have done it before Knight had rolled back into town.

The outrage of Duke killing her sister, and anguish of knowing that her sister was dead, made her ache from head to toe.

So The Queen tickled her swollen pussy with expert precision on that fire spot at the tip of her clit. That was the most sensitive place of all. And it protected her from having either, the energy, the ability, or the desire to think about the fact that Duke had committed murder to protect her new position in Babylon.

"I don't know why they keep saying on the news that they're still looking for Victoria when we know she's dead." Tiffany flushed. She unclinked the stall lock. Her heels tapped across the tiles, then the water hissed in the sink.

"What makes it, like, even more sad, is that Vikki had tricked so many people. We thought she was white, but she was tricking us. She was actually black, and her mom had died in this sex scandal. So me and my family, well it wasn't, like, the black part bothered us. I mean I have a lot of black friends, but the fact that she lied—"

A low moan escaped The Queen's trembling lips.

"Victoria pissed us all off by not fessin' up to the fact that she was black," Tiffany said. "I mean, you're beautiful and you're black. But you're not trying to hide it."

The Queen moaned again.

"You okay in there?"

SEX IN THE HOOD 2

The Queen wanted to scream because she was about to cum. The more tense she felt, the easier it was to orgasm. So Tiffany's fucked-up recollection of how their friendship ended along with the life of a rich, white girl named Victoria Winston, was making it easy.

In fact, her whack chatter was an aphrodisiac of sorts.

Because all of The Queen's senses jammed into one emotional mash—good or bad, stressed or sexy. And she had one sure-fire, erotic remedy.

Damn, I wish Knight were in here to slam it real quick.

The Queen raised one foot onto the closed toilet seat so she could open her legs wider. With the thong pulled to one side, and her gun perfectly poised, the waistband of her red leather skirt, she leaned against the stall wall and stuck her left fingers even deeper up her pussy. All the while, her right fingertips danced over Celeste with expert precision and speed.

"Hello?" Tiffany called again.

"I'm fine, sweetheart," she said as the little fireball between her legs radiated up her abdomen, down her trembling legs and arms.

"See ya back there," Tiffany said, walking toward the door, which *swooshed* open and closed.

The Queen's pussy walls pulsated around her wet fingers. Her clit convulsed under her fingertips. And the starburst exploded. She lay back her head, panted quietly, and let her body's opium mellow her mind. The silent stillness of the bathroom was just what she needed before heading back into the bad vibes of those three gangsters.

Damn, I feel better.

All the junk that Tiffany had just spewed had vaporized under the sizzlin' sex power of The Queen's mind and body. So, after wiping the hot cream from between her legs and putting her thong back in place, she stepped out of the stall.

Oh, fuck.

Brian was standing against the shimmery blue wall facing her. "Vee, I thought you were dead," he groaned, rubbing his open palm over the crotch of his pants. "I'm still yours forever. You've never looked better."

WHITE CHOCOLATE

The Queen raised her chin and strutted to the sink. "It's The Queen," she said calmly, watching him in the mirror. "And unless you're trying to get kronked beyond recognition, you betta show some respect and get the fuck out."

She could hear Knight reciting one of the rules of The Prince Code: *Kill or be killed.*

Brian stepped close behind her. In the mirror, his eyes glowed with lust from his puffy face. "Congratulations on your music," he said. "Who knew my little lillywhite, prep school prude with the coffee-house rhymes would rock her way up the charts with some freakin' black girl beats?"

The recessed lights over the vanity glowed down on his head, casting eerie dark shadows around his eyes while his nose became extra bright.

How had this high-school football star gained so much weight?

"You got me sadly and dangerously confused wit' anotha bitch," The Queen said. "So unless you gon' change into a dress up in this *ladies* bathroom, punk, you betta step the fuck on."

He said with a low, sinister tone, "Vee, your acting skills are superb. All that practice in the school plays really paid off. You could win an Oscar for best actress playing a blackface minstrel. Let's call your movie, *Ho in the Hood* or *New Black Titty.*" He laughed by himself.

The Queen rolled her eyes.

"Or you could put your Hollywood skills to work for me and Red. Travel the world with us. You saw the way he looked at you. The globe is yours on a silver platter—"

The Queen squeezed her still throbbing pussy to calm her emotions. Especially the rage at his bold disrespect of her and Knight. "Sorry," she said, coolly washing her hands and meeting his stare in the mirror. "You're making me an offer I'm afraid I'll have to refuse."

Brian's eyes sparkled. "You can make the world be your playground. I've been all over with Red—Rio, Rome, Sydney, Nairobi, Osaka, Beijing. Any woman who looks like you is usually seen but not heard. But you could rule. Not some ghetto underworld. But the real world. Vee, think of it, the whole world at your fingertips with—"

The Queen spun on her sharp heel to stare into his ridiculous eyes. She rapped with a slight neck jerk: "This Vee, you see, she ain't me, and I don't be makin' bathroom deals wit' a dude who steals my time. You got me confused wit' a chick who might think you slick, but I say you a prick, so stick yo' shit in a place out my face." The Queen raised her chin and strutted past him.

His chubby hand gripped her elbow, just below her Cleopatra bracelet on her upper arm.

Oh no he didn't.

He pulled her close, breathing sour alcohol breath on her. "Vee, you promised we'd be together forever. You're mine. And I know you're givin' it up to that ghetto thug."

She spat in his eye. Saliva dripped down his pudgy cheek.

He leaned close to kiss her.

Right now she could scream, and Pong would come in here and squash this punk muthafucka like a bug. She could pull the gun out of her waistband and blow him away, but that would draw too much attention. "You got one last chance to get ya hands the fuck off me," The Queen said coolly. Her insides tingled with excitement because she'd been hoping for this moment ever since he'd tried to rape her while his parents sat downstairs in their mansion devouring every word of those racist newspaper articles.

"My dick is so hard," Brian said, yanking out his dark-pink dick. "Sweet little Victoria is such a tough girl."

"Put that shit away. If Knight comes in here, he'll cut it off."

Brian laughed with a sinister glow in his eyes. "Oh, I'm real scared of that illiterate gorilla. I bet he shoves his big black cock up the sweet pussy you refused to give me."

The Queen smiled. "And I *looooooove* it."

Brian's cheeks turned red as if her words had slapped him. "Think of it, Vee—you and me together, our dream, college together, our company. Promise you'll come back to me. We can travel the world with Moreno till I'm 25. Then I get my trust fund and we can get married. Set for life with millions. You and me, Vee."

The Queen pressed her hands to his shoulders. "You sick. Firs', you don't know who the fuck you fuckin' wit'; secon', you obviously didn't see my fiancé; an' third, what lyin' bitch said you got it like that, where I'd want to leave my African god to get wit' yo' fat ass?"

His hand grabbed her left tit. He smashed his slimy mouth into hers.

She pushed his shoulders back.

He fell backwards, but lurched back at her.

As she had been trained by Lee Lee and the soldiers, she extended a lightning quick and brutally hard heel of the hand. *Smash!*—into his nose. At the same time, her knee slammed his groin.

He doubled over, groaning.

The Queen stepped back. Her whole body tingled with excitement. She felt superhuman strength as rage and disappointment and sadness pumped through her red-hot veins. She blasted her pointed heel into the side of his fleshy gut.

He let out a grotesque groan and stood, glaring at her with glassy eyes. His left hand cupped his nose. Blood dripped down his chin. "Vee, you'll come to your senses," he said with a calm mouth but eyes glowing like a rabid dog.

"So will you," she said, balling her fist. She extended her arm. *Wham!*—She crashed her knuckles into his lips then straight-kicked his gut with the sharp point of her heel. And she whacked his left jaw with a punch, followed by an uppercut to his chin. And a final punch to the center of his chest with her right hand.

Blood dripped from his vile mouth that had spewed racist insults at her. He slumped on the floor like the pile of trash that he was.

"Stupid racist punk," The Queen whispered. "You just fucked with the wrong nigga bitch. Hope you ain't mixed up no more about who I am. I'm The Queen, bitch. The one and only. The Queen."

SEX IN THE HOOD 2

The sweet taste of revenge delighted her mouth as if she'd sucked on a Jolly Rancher. She strutted to the sink, ran cold water over her throbbing knuckles, smoothed down her hair, and strode out of the bathroom humming her song, "A Bad Bitch."

Chapter 12

Later that evening, Knight stood at the head of the sleek black conference table, looking each of the fifteen Board members in the eye. One at a time, he had to filter their vibes through Intuition before he proceeded with the meeting here at Babylon's headquarters.

"I'm always glad to see our top brass gathered in one room," Knight said, looking each one in the eyes. These pimps and madames from across America, most in their mid-twenties and dressed in suits with Rolex watches and diamond earrings, were so high-class and business savvy, they made the meeting feel like a Fortune 500 conference.

Tonight I'll bedazzle them with bullshit. The less they know about anything right now, the better.

"On the agenda tonight, we're focusing on The Games and the rapid growth of Babylon over the past year," Knight said.

The Board members knew Babylon was extremely vulnerable to inside and outside forces, because rapid expansion always had the potential to cause serious growing pains. Most of these cats loathed the idea of playing anything but war with Moreno. So the positive outcome of today's meeting was not on the agenda with the Board.

And no one, even The Queen, now seated beside Knight, knew about the mega deal to sell Babylon in one month's time. Nor did anyone even know about their meeting with Moreno today.

Knight wore his best mask of mystery and power while his insides bubbled with love and pride as he gazed at The Queen. Paul had been monitoring every second of her little foray into danger in the bathroom of that restaurant today with Moreno's cat named B-Boy, Brian, punk of the century. Pong had been poised to bust in and take care of it, if necessary.

But like always, The Queen had passed that test with flying colors. This was not a test that Knight had set up in advance. This was the kind of test that he allowed to unfold, to see how his Baby Girl would handle it. And she had finessed it with the style and sass of a certified sista.

Left no fingerprints. Nobody in the private room had a clue about what had gone down by the way she strutted back in and titillated them with details about The Games. And nobody had questioned their bodyguard's announcement that B-Boy had called to say he had to go make a run so he wouldn't be back.

Knight smiled inwardly. *Yeah, a run to the dentist to get his front teeth back.* Arrangements were being made to secretly alert his parents of their beloved son's underworld lifestyle, so that he could stop counting on his trust fund at age 25. And Brian was also being informed in the most convincing way that any more attempts to contact The Queen or even speak her name to anyone would result in swift and permanent consequences for him.

The theme song for Babylon played on the hidden Bose speakers throughout the conference room: "Babylon rule, wit' D-town cool, urban jewel, win any duel, jack a fool, sexy seductive, serve an' protect, in Babylon, Knight an' his Queen get respect."

Of course Knight had had the song changed from the one that had praised Li'l Tut and his Duchess.

His favorite part was when the male chorus faded as the girls rapped over a belly dancer beat. "Babylon men, I'll take ten, rock this ass, oh so fast, they last an' last like a rocket blast. Knight an' Queen, they rule, wit' D-town cool."

Several people rocked in their seats as they tapped expensive Mont Blanc pens to the agendas and jotted down notes in their monogrammed leather organizers. Some of these folks knew and loved Jamal; others didn't. With him as the proud new owner of Babylon, they would all be well taken care of, and still earn their fortunes in their respective cities.

But with all those millions on the line, Knight had no time for mutiny in the ranks.

So secrecy was the name of his game for the next four weeks. Then he'd do the deals, get married, and disappear before the announcement was made that Babylon was under new management.

Plus, Mama's tearful visit just minutes ago to the Penthouse had him rattled. Li'l Tut was alive. HIV positive. Crazed. And on the run. Now the Barriors were on a mission to finish what Knight had started on the boat.

Li'l Tut is capable of anything now. He has nothing to live for except a nasty date with death.

And The Queen had heard it all as Mama had sobbed into Knight's shoulder. Knight had immediately called Paul to put all of Babylon on Red Alert—the highest security level. It also meant that The Queen would be packing at all times. In fact, after this meeting, Knight would take her to the firing range downstairs, to make sure her shot could blow a muthafucka's block off, if necessary; because if Duke somehow got to her, and took what he wanted, his poisonous dick was as good as a gun to her head.

Gotta take him out. Now! But where the fuck was he?

Suddenly Knight's chest squeezed. He froze. Didn't even want to inhale. Because any movement, he feared, might make those tiny needles stab harder into his heart.

The Queen's eyes locked on him. Her lips were tense and tight; her eyes flashing fear. In his mind, he heard her voice say, *I can feel your pain.*

The silver dollar blue moons that were her eyes had never looked like that. The deep love radiating from them numbed his pain for a minute. It even roused burning tears; that was the kind of look that every man wished a beautiful, caring woman would cast on him in sickness and in health.

I have it. I'm only 25, and I'm blessed with this once-in-a-lifetime love. Now I have to make sure I live long enough for a lifetime.

Knight inhaled deeply. He had the power over his mind to control his body. And he would do that. To live the bliss of a monogamous relationship that niggas from the hood weren't supposed to enjoy. They'd never seen it, never felt it and, as a result, didn't want it.

But it was Knight's responsibility as a socially conscious, self-educated black man to show as the example that black love could survive and thrive in the inner city. In prison, he had read W.E.B. DuBois' *The Souls of Black Folk*, which the legendary black author had written during the Harlem Renaissance of the 1920s. Knight viewed himself as part of what DuBois called The Talented Tenth, which was the percentage of African-Americans whose accomplishments, talent, and intelligence elevated them to positions of leadership to uplift the rest of the race.

And it all started with love. So for the love of himself, and his woman, and his people, Knight had to cure his body. He had to leave a legacy on the world that all the statistics that were stacked against him at birth could be defied.

It was also on him to prove that greatness could rise from this black giant from the ghetto. He inhaled deeply. *My body is a precision-tuned, superhuman machine. I am well. I am well. It's just stress. It'll all be over in 29 days. I can make it to paradise.*

He inhaled again, very slowly. And the pain dissolved to a dull ache. But this health crisis, he feared, was eroding the cool, calm confidence that was his trademark as the CEO of Babylon.

Now, in the board meeting, he had to walk a tightrope to keep the members happy without revealing the secret deal. Or that Li'l Tut was back with a vengeance, armed and dangerous. Telling that would give the schemers in the room ammunition to make a power play. They also didn't need to know that one of his Fed sources had tipped him off to a possible raid during The Games.

A Babylon party had never been raided, because Prince and Knight always knew how to muzzle the right mouths. Bricks of benjamins always had the power to do that. But Li'l Tut had been fucking things up last year to the point that undercover snitches were sneaking into his birthday party, standing in the offices talking about a warrant.

Hell, naw.

Knight had to do an expensive clean-up after that, to make sure what they'd seen and heard was long forgotten.

That was even more information that the Board didn't need to hear about. Knight had to finesse this meeting so that no wild cards got tossed into the mix.

"Excuse me." Reba came through the door with a silver tray holding glass bottles of water and crystal tumblers. Her white jumpsuit did little to conceal the dark circles and points of her nipples. And the tight crotch separated the two fat folds of her pussy lips and gripped her ass like second skin. "How's everybody doin'?" She placed a bottle and glass before Knight's seat. She wedged between him and The Queen, brushing her ass against Knight's leg.

He immediately stepped back.

"Hey, boss lady," Reba said, smiling down and sticking her pushed-up titties inches from The Queen's face as she served the water. "That pantsuit is sharp."

The Queen cast her steel-gray eyes up at what she knew was a ho scheming to steal her man.

Knight focused on his typed agenda.

Reba is through. Can't have her agitating like this.

All eyes in the room were on Reba's highly glossed lips, her titties, and her ass. These bosses from Babylon offices across the country saw pussy like that all day long, but they were looking at Reba like she was the first jaw-droppingly gorgeous vixen they'd ever seen.

"Quickly, Reba," Knight snapped. "We're about to get started. You can greet everybody at the party down in the garage, after our meeting."

Reba continued serving around the table.

Knight got on with the task of feeling out everybody's state of mind. As he stared into Marcus Reed's eyes, the cool cat from L.A. looked as honest as Abe Lincoln.

But Shar Miller, a former D-town Slut who moved to Las Vegas to head up Babylon operations there, was avoiding eye contact and crossing her legs repeatedly.

She's hiding something, Intuition said. *Possibly a link to her past with Duke.*

Just like Leroy Lewis from Miami. He kept shifting on the high-backed, black leather chair and blinking.

He's mad, Intuition said. *Wants more power. Fears he'll never get it unless he takes it under the table.*

And Knight didn't like the way Raynard "Dickman" Ingalls from Chicago was glancing around the all-black, windowless room. Wearing a red, black, and white padded leather jacket with the Bulls logo on the back, and a matching baseball cap cocked to the side, the young brotha stared into the bright white light radiating from the huge clear glass blocks, high over the table, spelling BABYLON.

He's looking for a way out, to elevate himself to higher ground, Intuition said.

As Reba left the room, Knight ignored the tightness in his chest. He had to fake it till he made it.

"I'm grateful that all of you were able to make it today," Knight said, "because our plan for the next month is extremely ambitious. But I believe it's attainable, given the rapid growth of the past year."

Knight loved the crisp, concise, and clear way that words poured out from his mouth. In prison, he'd listened to audio tapes and practiced how to speak so-called proper English, after years of expressing himself in Ebonics. Because that was all that he'd ever heard.

Watching TV, especially westerns, had trained him somewhat. But the special study kit that he'd ordered off the Internet taught him like an ESL course or English as a Second Language, on how to say *ask* instead of *ax* and *she is going to the store* as opposed to *she be goin' to the store.*

As a kid, the boys in his hood had teased anyone who "talked white." But as an adult, especially when he had met the rich white couple, Mr. and Mrs. Marx, who had schooled him on how to transform Babylon into a national phenomenon, Knight had felt an urgent need to speak their language the way they spoke it.

So he read voraciously. And studied the way articulate people spoke. He was still keeping pace with his speech training to learn one new vocabulary word every day. Today's word was "exquisite," meaning unusually delightful or beautiful. He'd have to find a way to work it into the meeting.

Plus, The Queen's ability to speak the King's English, without even thinking about it, made Knight's dick hard. He believed that being around her would, by osmosis, improve his own vocabulary and ability to roll big words off his tongue effortlessly. And now, tonight, was another chance to showcase his hard work.

He held up the schedule; papers rattled throughout the room as everyone else followed suit. "These are the major deals and events on the horizon," Knight said. "Skip down to the bottom. If you haven't heard, you'll see that The Queen and I are getting married the day after The Games, on October first. The Games will be our bachelor/bachelorette party."

Leroy Lewis's angry tone cut through the chorus of congratulations. "Your planning is fucked-up." His diamond pinkie ring sparkled as he twisted the edge of his pencil-thin mustache. "A huge distraction. Babylon can't afford to derail our focus on the frivolity of a wedding."

Several people let out annoyed groans.

"I agree," Shar Miller said, shaking her spiky black hair. "Makes us vulnerable to outside forces. The Feds, the competition, and Moreno's wicked tricks. Too many wild cards out there could deal us a fatal blow. And everybody knows if Duke is still alive, he could come back with a vengeance."

Marcus Reed shot up to his feet and threw his silver pen down on the table. "Why y'awl gotta hate on a brotha wit' good news? Damn! Cain't stand a hater!" He slapped the back of Leroy's chair. "If you got a legit beef wit' the brotha, speak on it. But if you just gripin' to flex, then shut the fuck up."

Most people around the table applauded.

"What Knight done wit' Babylon over the past year ain't nothin' but a miracle." Marcus strode toward The Queen and stood behind her chair. "An' this young, talented lady done made millions for all o' y'awl in the women's market. So e'rybody, let the brilliant brotha speak."

Knight nodded. "I couldn't have said it better myself. That was exquisite, my brotha."

Several people laughed.

But Leroy and Shar were like two smokestacks. Fuming toxic vapors. Just like Flame, they'd both get cooled down in a heartbeat.

Knight didn't even look at them. "Between the wedding and The Games, we have the Moreno meeting tomorrow. And the last yacht party of the season, to recruit clients and associates, will be next week at The Playhouse."

Leroy raised his hand and spoke at the same time: "I heard a rumor around here today that Duke is back. Is that true?"

Knight's chest squeezed. He swallowed a cough. Shooting pains radiated like poison darts from his heart, up his neck, down his arm.

I'm having a heart attack. Can't breathe.

His face remained as stiff as a mask, but he could hear The Queen's panicky thoughts.

I cannot, will not, fall out in this meeting. My power depends on my strength.

Knight took three long strides to the door. He felt like he was holding his breath; just had to swim faster up to the surface, so he could gulp down air. Opened the door. Stepped out. Closed the door. Inhaled.

The pain eased.

The four Barriors and B'Amazons who had been guarding the meeting watched attentively but gave him space.

Then a gush of alarmed voices shot out from the room as the door opened again.

Out came The Queen, eyes wide and roiling with questions. In them he saw that she felt his pain and fear as intensely as he did.

"Knight, baby," she cried, stroking his back as he coughed to hide that he was gasping for breath. She held up her cell phone. "I'm calling an ambu—"

"No, I'm fine. Handle the meeting," he wheezed, holding his chest. "Say I got stomach flu. I'll be upstairs."

A sound he'd never heard shot out from between her lips. It was like a cry of pain, a shriek of horror, but muted so only he could hear it.

And it made his heart ache more.

Chapter 13

I'm killin' him with my pussy.

The Queen studied her terrified eyes in the mirror. She had locked herself in the huge, marble bathroom of their Penthouse.

We make love so much, it's sucking the life out of him. I have to stay away from him. No more pussy for Knight until he's better . . . if he gets better, because if he dies, I'll die too.

She had warned him, but he, like Duke, had laughed when she told them about the killing powers of her pussy. Powers she had inherited from her Native American grandmother and her black grandfather and her mother whose sex appeal was so strong that she inspired her father to make love to her so much that it killed her.

In the mirror, Celeste appeared bald and plump, cradling her clit. Right now, in this depressed mindset, her clit reflected her bad mood by shrinking into what looked like the tip of a dark-pink carnation. When she was hot and horny, though, her clit bloomed into a big, juicy red cherry, ripe for the picking.

Poison fruit. Like Eve's poison apple. Taste it in heaven, end up in hell.

The Queen imagined covering her crotch with a yellow and black striped sign that said DANGER, like those stickers on X-ray machines and those red boxes labeled "biohazardous." There was one down in the clinic, where Doc Roberts disposed of used needles after blood tests.

She crossed her legs. If she and Knight never made love again, that would kill her too. Because she was him, and he was her, and without their daily charge, plugging into each other's bodies, they would both fizzle out on every level.

"Baby Girl!" He pounded on the locked door. "Let me in."

"Will you go to the doctor?"

"We need to talk."

That meant no, but she had to convince Knight to get medical help. A doctor or specialist could figure out what was going on. Maybe it was something as simple and controllable as asthma. He could just get an inhaler and some breathing treatments, and he'd be fine. Or perhaps he had some type of virus that could be cured with rest. As much as he was working lately, he hardly slept. Maybe he was just fatigued.

But Knight was so suspicious of doctors, except the ones here at Babylon who made sure everyone was free of STD's and other contagious illnesses.

The Queen crossed her legs more tightly, as if she had to pee and was holding it in.

My biggest fear is coming true.

*

She had known, the minute she felt tempted to fuck Duke a year ago, that she would unleash powers that were proven to kill. She had inherited the same mixed-race sex powers that had killed her mother. She had told Duke that her father had been so addicted to making love with her mother that she had died from a sex overdose.

And the day of her funeral, little Victoria decided that she would never do whatever it was Mommy and Daddy were doing so much of that proved fatal. Because she didn't know if it had the power to kill her, or to kill someone else.

All she knew was that Mommy had told her that she did have special powers. And even though, the first time she made love with Duke, she had heard her mother's voice telling her that this pleasure was the power, and that she could use it to get anything in life that she wanted, The Queen still believed that it was deadly.

And life was proving her belief true. Her first victim, Duke, was dying because he lost her and Babylon to his big brother—on his twenty-first birthday, no less. That sent him on a kamikaze flight into the hard streets of wherever the hell he'd been. The pain and disappointment of that cruel blow shattered his religious devotion to safe sex, and he'd caught a wicked virus.

He's gonna die. And it's partly my fault.

The Queen raked her fingers through her loose hair. In the mirror, her new diamond ring sparkled so brightly, she gasped.

I'm about to have it all, but the curse is sucking the life out of it. No!

But Knight looked like he was dying. Pale, weak and hurting, he was The Queen's victim number two. And both brothers blew her off when she divulged the curse.

*

"Baby Girl," Knight called through the locked door. "Baby Girl, you okay?"

"No, I'm not okay—neither is your ass."

"Come out, or I'll come in."

She rolled her eyes. "You can't. It's locked."

He was silent. But in her mind, she could hear him say, *You know a lock never stopped me. I snuck into Babylon, and into my brother's bed, to get you.*

The Queen shook her head. Why was she hearing his thoughts?

Because the two of you are one, Celeste answered. *You're on a different wavelength that's so high, so divine, it defies logic. It's supernatural.*

A click echoed over the marble bathroom, and the door opened.

Knight walked in.

She didn't bother to ask how he had entered. Knight was all-powerful. Except, suddenly, over his health.

"It's my curse," she said, facing the mirror, looking into his tired eyes. They were bloodshot and dull, as if dusty rocks had replaced the sparkling gems in his irises. Plum arcs of fatigue framed his lower lashes, and a grayish pallor covered his normally radiant and dark skin.

"Knight, admit it—my curse is suckin' the life outta you."

Wearing a plush white robe with KNIGHT embroidered in gold on the left breast, he stood behind her, resting his chin on the top of her head. His huge, black hands rested on her waist, tickling her bare skin.

She was nude, her long black hair falling over her shoulders and breasts and over Knight's hands. A diamond sparkled in her pierced belly button.

"Look in my eyes," he said. Even his delicious sucka lips looked thinner and tense. "What do you see?"

"Sadness, fear . . . all the things I've never seen there before—because my pussy power is killing you."

Knight shook his head. "Baby Girl, that's ridiculous. How can you think that?"

She cocked her neck. "Because I've been thinking about it ever since I was six years old and I went to my young, healthy momma's funeral and my cousin said she got fucked to death."

Knight took her hands into his. "Baby Girl, there's no medical ailment showing you can die from making love. It creates life, literally and figuratively. It heals. Since I've been with you, I've felt more alive than—"

"Yeah, I could tell when you almost fell out in the meeting tonight," The Queen snapped sarcastically. "I've never seen you look so alive, so vibrant, so radiant with health."

"It's just the pressure of everything piling up—"

"Right on your chest. You hardly sleep, you're constantly working, you're running yourself ragged, and you won't even go to the doctor."

"I'll go tomorrow."

"You need to go right now." The Queen spun around. His face blurred through her tears. "Knight, if anything happens to you, I'll just die."

"Tinkerbell, watch your magic words; they have power. Anything you say can and will come true, Baby Girl, if you put it out there."

"Then read my lips, Knight—If anything ever happens to you, I'll just die. You hear me? I'll scream it while we're making love, to give it that extra power."

Knight scooped her into his arms. "I'm going to make love to you right now to prove that I'm fine. We'll concentrate on the good things we want. Don't speak those words again."

As he walked, she cupped her hands over his jaw and stared into his beautiful eyes. She had to make him well again.

But I'm making him lovesick. Literally.

She imagined he were a picture that she could airbrush back to perfection. "Look at my Knight," she whispered. "I gotta get the color back in your cheeks. And erase those dark circles."

"Give me some love therapy."

"No," she said softly. Just the idea of him not feeling his best because of her made her stomach ache. "I don't want to make love until you feel better. And look better."

Their sensuous theme song, "Love You to the Infinity," which she'd recorded with the Bang Squad, played softly in the huge bedroom. Dozens of white, gardenia-scented candles cast a soft glow on the gold sheers around the giant, Egyptian-style canopy bed with mahogany pillars.

He swung her onto the shimmery gold silk bedspread so that he could sit down with his legs outstretched and she could straddle his lap, facing him.

"I'm gonna heal you of whatever is wrong, but not with sex," The Queen whispered, pressing her lips to each of his cheeks for long moments. Her bare behind rested on his thighs. Her hair was long and loose down her back, tickling the tops of his hands around her waist. "If you hurt," she said, "I hurt. If you cry, I cry. If you die, I die."

He groaned. "Baby Girl, don't say that."

"If you die, I die," she said more forcefully. "It's the honest 'Romeo-and-Juliet' truth, so hear it."

"No, no, Baby Girl."

"Yes, yes, beautiful Knight. You're all I got in this whole world—one million lifetimes of love all rolled into one."

A tear rolled down his cheek.

"I've never seen you cry," she whispered, licking the tear with the tip of her tongue.

"I don't," he said. "But where I come from, you don't see this—love that's pure, untainted by insecurity and jealousy."

The Queen laughed softly. "I was ready to knock that Reba bitch's block off when she rubbed her fat ass up against you in the meeting."

Knight smiled. "But you didn't 'cause you're secure. You know even the sexiest woman can't steal a man unless he's already put himself at risk for theft."

"My parents had this kind of love. Love so good it kills."

"We'll use our lovemaking power together to make me feel invincible again," Knight said. "And we'll exorcise your mind of that ridiculous curse."

"It's not ridiculous," she snapped.

"Kiss me, Baby Girl."

"Not until you—"

The heat of his mouth lobotomized her. She felt, thought, feared nothing as his hot satin lips pressed into hers. She breathed in the air that he exhaled through his nose; it smelled clean and masculine and luscious. It had circulated through his body, keeping him alive, and was now entering her bloodstream through her lungs.

As they had so many times before, The Queen and Knight synchronized their breath. Both breathed in deeply, slowly, with the same pace and rhythm, then they breathed out just the same, all the while never separating their mouths from each other. They held their hands up, pressing their fingertips and palms together.

After a good few minutes, Knight raised himself by sliding his legs back and sliding The Queen's ass onto the bed. In one graceful movement, he laid her back and position himself over her.

She stared into his beautiful black eyes and concentrated on the words *perfect health*. And if he needed to make love to her to get perfect health, then she would give every drop of her blood to keep his heart beating. Curse or no curse, they would live and love together. Or share their final breath.

Her body beneath him was soft and limp. Totally surrendering to the need in his eyes. With her feet on the bed and her knees raised, her legs were open for him. As his body came forward, the insides of her knees pressed the outer curves of his waist.

And then the magic.

A soft cry of pleasure surged up from her soul.

As he penetrated her most intimate space, Knight was so long, so big, that she could almost feel him reach up and stroke her heart.

She closed her eyes. Blue and purple sparks glittered like tiny stars behind the blackness of her closed eyelids. Her mind went numb, and her body tingled; she felt her spirit rise up and dance with Knight's, around their bodies.

Opening her eyes, she loved every detail of this man—the ebony lashes around his genie eyes that sparkled down on her. His perfect Indian-chief nose. His sculpted cheeks, dark-pink with the heat of passion, and his so soft and smooth bald head.

And those rippling muscles on his broad shoulders. That, plus his masculine natural scent mixed with Black Cashmere cologne, and the heat of his smooth satiny skin against hers, and the way his eyes radiated so tenderly.

I love you to the infinity, The Queen thought.

Knight's eyes sparkled.

I love you to the infinity, Baby Girl.

Though their lips were still connected in a kiss, The Queen couldn't stop herself from gasping.

Knight's lips felt like they were twisting into a smile too. He pulled back. "You heard me think," he whispered.

"You heard me first." She giggled.

"We are one mind," he said. "One heart. One soul." Knight smiled as he thrust harder.

"So divine," she sang softly along with the music, "you're mine, no line between our mind, we find that behind the soul lies heaven in you, so true, I do . . . love you to the infinity . . . love you to the infinity."

As her body shuddered, her mind danced and her soul spun, The Queen stared into his eyes. The energy between their faces right now, she was sure, was so strong, it could melt gold. Or split a diamond. Or create thunder and lightning.

Then surely it could heal whatever ailed him.

The Queen envisioned a giant balloon being filled with their sex power energy then sucking Knight's entire body inside, where he could float on the fumes of this miracle cure called love. In her vision she saw him smiling, his face glowing with health and happiness. His voice booming with power.

There, his body was long, lean, and strong.

And cradling a baby. Their baby. A plump, little, caramel butterball boy with a 'fro-sized shock of black curls.

The Queen's eyes opened quickly. And Knight's beautiful face, looking down on her, blurred as hot tears filled her eyes.

Splat.

Something hot and wet fell on her cheek. Then another into her eye. Knight's tears.

"I see him too," Knight whispered. "Our son." His eyes sparkled with joy.

Until terror flashed in them. And all the expressions she had seen on his face in the conference room. He coughed.

"Knight!"

He kissed her, as if trying to suck fresh life from her to resuscitate something deep inside himself.

She kissed him back passionately, feverishly, hoping her heart, lungs, and brain would become his life support until his own body jolted back to normal. They had to. Or she'd have cardiac arrest right along with him.

Chapter 14

As he left the dentist's office, all Brian wanted to do was punish the black bitch that his sweet Victoria had become. He ran his tongue over the new caps and veneers to replace the jagged front teeth that had remained after his run-in with the so-called Queen.

"Kill the bitch!" his favorite gangsta rappers shouted from his stereo as he climbed into his new Range Rover and turned the key in the ignition. "Killa, killa, killa!"

The pounding beat made him clench his fists with the need to blast her back in the mouth, and other places, as she had done to him. She'd become the dirty whore of that inner-city kingpin whose cock was probably like a black python, poisoning the pussy that Brian had once wanted so much.

But she never gave it to me, the fat-ass bitch.

And now he didn't even want the tainted shit. He just wanted to destroy it.

All that time, after he'd seen her look-alike sister Melanie's picture on TV, he'd thought Victoria was dead.

She tricked me.

His stomach gurgled. He hadn't been eating because his teeth were hurting so bad. And now he hungered for vengeance.

Nobody treated Brian Martin like that. Not only was he working for one of the most powerful men in the world, but his pedigreed, white blood entitled him to respect.

Every inch of him, from his chubby fingers down to his swollen dick, throbbed with rage. It blinded him to the fact that he'd be double-crossing his boss, Red Moreno, who wanted "Cleopatra" for himself.

Not gonna happen, Red. She'd probably love the life you'd give her, even if you were sellin' her pussy to your international gang of thieves. Nope, I got my own plans for this one.

Brian flipped open his cell phone, punched in the code that would make his call untraceable, and dialed the FBI. They finally connected him with a dude named Rick Reed.

136

Brian imitated the way his father spoke when handling the details of multi-million-dollar business deals. He deepened his voice and said, "Good afternoon, Mr. Reed. I'm calling to alert you of the whereabouts of Victoria Winston, who's been wanted for more than a year after—"

"I know who she is." The dude spoke proper; Brian couldn't tell if he were black or white. "Where can I find her?"

"Mr. Reed, I'm about to make you a hero. Because she's your dreamcatcher. Find her; you'll solve the murder of Melanie Winston. You'll step into an inner-city prostitution ring that's bigger and more organized than you'll believe. And I can tell you exactly how and when to do it."

"Let's deal."

Chapter 15

The "gold-digger glint" in Reba's eyes let Duke know she was his for the taking. And she'd do anything to get what she thought he could give her. Even though he was a shot-up, cracked-down, HIV-blowed out muthafucka right now, who was letting her foot the bill for this hotel room while he recovered from Knight's gunshots.

She stood over the bed, pulling down the sheets to inspect his wounds.

Duke was laying on his good side, resting his cheek on the pillow. "Reba," he called playfully. He sang, "Suga, suga, how ya get so fine?"

His gaze raked over her skintight jeans that were so low-cut, they revealed the top of that little heart-shaped pouf of hair over her pussy. Her nipples poked two points in her orange-cropped top that matched her baseball cap. He reached out to touch the orange rhinestone star in her belly button.

"Quit, boy!" she played with her high-pitched, little-girl voice. "You need to rest. Get yo' strength. So you can be king again."

Duke stared up into the dollar signs flashing in her eyes.

She wanted nothing more than to be at his side as he "bogarted" his way back to the top of Babylon. So she could live her ghetto fabulous fantasy as his wife.

She fine, but she ain't Duchess.

And his dream wouldn't be complete without the woman he chose right off the TV screen to be his partner for life. Duke remembered the heart-stopping moment when he had first seen The Duchess on the news. It was a report about her Daddy sucking down some bullets in his office as the Feds closed in on him.

Then the news had shown Victoria Winston and said the 18-year-old would be sent to live with her African American grandmother in one of Detroit's most notorious ghettos.

Duke to the rescue. And he was fuckin' her that same night. All it took was one look at the sexercise class and that horny-ass virgin was drippin' for Timbo.

138

And damn, was it good.

That was the best pussy I eva had in life. Eva.

But for now, Reba would do. She was devious enough to carry out any command he ordered in his war against Knight. And she was mad enough at Knight, for rejecting her, to enjoy his execution.

She's using me, I'm using her; we even. An' we gon' get rich together, or die tryin'.

He watched her ass pop like two round balloons covered in denim. Every step toward the bathroom made one rise up, and then the other go down.

Timbo swelled like a tree trunk—thick, hard, and long. But now his dick was a killing machine. Nobody would fuck him if they knew, so he wouldn't tell.

Duke's insides felt like a whirlpool of dirty water spinning down into a drain in the gutter. Because he was filthy. How had he gone from being meticulous about his personal health—using condoms, getting regular check-ups and HIV tests like all the folks at Babylon—to this nasty-ass leper status?

A hot melting sensation made his throat hurt. His eyes stung. But hell no, he would not cry; he would just get revenge.

"Reba," he said playfully. "Reba Sheba be my girl."

Her little girl laughter echoed from the bathroom. "Why you sayin' my name like you wanna fuck?" she cooed over the sound of water wringing out of a washcloth into the sink. She giggled, peering from the doorway. "Boy, you could kill yo'self tryin' to fuck right now. Bleed to death. Pass out from no strength. You betta quit!"

She strutted back toward him with the washcloth and bandages. The warm cotton on his face, and her gentle touch, made him close his eyes and wish he were a little boy getting some "Mama love," but Mama had kicked him out, and this was a ho polishing up her ticket to the jackpot.

"Dang, Duke!" She flitted her long ponytail over her shoulder. A whiff of expensive perfume overwhelmed him. "Every time I look at you, I have to remember. You don't hardly look like—naw, let me stop." She folded her big, juicy lips inward, then nodded. "Knight always says, 'Make it positive.' So, we gon' fix you back up so you even more healthy and fine than you was a year ago."

"You gon' be my nurse?" he asked, rubbing his knuckles against her right nipple. "You gon' help me?"

"Read my lips," she whispered, her face just inches from his. "Reba at your service. Ain't nothin' too much to ask. I'ma do any- an' everything to get us where we need to be."

Duke grinned.

"That's my suga-pie." She smiled and pressed those juicy lips to his forehead. "We the new Bonnie an' Clyde. Takin' D-town by storm, baby!"

Duke roared—"Oh, shit!" he grimaced. "I forgot . . . I cain't laugh like that no more. That muthafucka fucked me up!"

Reba shot up, stepping toward the dresser. "Let me get you another pill." She pulled open the drawer where the doctor had stashed all of his medicine—painkillers, antibiotics, and his HIV cocktail—in the top drawer under his shirts. "Damn! You got a whole drug store in here."

"No!" Duke shouted. "Don't nobody but the doctor need to give me my drugs. She gon' be here at four."

"That's in three more hours." Reba's tone was sassy: "But you need some now. How we gon' make plans an' you cain't barely see straight 'cause it hurt so much?"

Time stood still as she pulled back the sweaters and stared down. If she knew the name of an HIV drug when she saw one, he'd be busted. An' his plan wouldn't work 'cause her motivation was the rock she thought he'd put on her finger just before saying, "I do," a short time later.

Locked into all that money for life as his wife. A short life, if she got infected. But life was short anyway. And she'd get to live large until the end.

"Bitch, shut the drawer. Come back ova here."

Reba sucked her teeth and slammed the drawer.

A hard knock on the door made Duke reach under the blankets and grip a gun.

"Who the fuck?" Duke whispered.

SEX IN THE HOOD 2

*

Reba had made arrangements to cancel maid service at this upscale, downtown Detroit hotel. And it wasn't room service; she had brought in a lunch of pizza and salad.

And all the other folks he was scheming with to topple his big brother—Shar and Leroy and now Raynard Ingalls of Chicago—they knew better than to show up at his hotel room. All those deals were handled over the phone for now, but their meetings before Knight shot him had established exactly how the coup would go down.

And so it is written, and so it is done, Duke thought, focusing on his favorite line that King Ramses always said in the movie *The Ten Commandments*. Ever since Duke and his brothers had watched that movie as kids, Duke had modeled himself after bad-ass Yule Brynner's portrayal of the powerful Egyptian king. That's why Knight called him Li'l Tut, after the boy king Tutankhamen. And that's why they'd decorated Babylon HQ like an Egyptian palace. And his Duchess had slipped right into the most ghetto-fabulous Cleopatra style.

Duke had used his favorite line to make the Universe know that Victoria would become his Duchess. It had been done for a Motor City minute, until Knight had taken her and she became The Queen. Now, as soon as Duke seized Babylon back under his control, The Queen would become Duchess once more. Married to The Duke forever.

*

An' no punk knockin' uninvited at my door gon' block my jock. Duke gripped his gun. Ready to blast like *Butch Cassidy and the Sundance Kid* if he had to, even while he was fucked up in this bed.

"It's probably Antoine," Reba whispered as she tiptoed to the peephole. "Yup."

"I don't want that muthafucka to see me."

"We cain't make a plan without him." Reba unhooked the chain lock and turned the bolt. "Sorry, Duke, but two ain't enough to bring down a kingdom."

Duke had already suffered the shame of his brother, his mother, his doctor, and Reba staring into his face with pity and shock. Now he didn't want one of the finest Studs in Babylon to do the same. "Reba don't open that muthafuckin' door."

She opened it quickly.

Antoine glanced both ways down the hall and slipped in. Yo," he said with a quick wave, "Duke, good to see you, man."

Duke glared at that caramel-colored pretty boy with a healthy dick. No bullet wounds. No crack-ravaged blood, bones and body.

A healthy Stud muthafucka like I used to be. The kinda stud that The Duchess couldn't wait to fuck.

Duke closed his eyes to escape this nightmare, but Reba's girlie voice, talking about the time schedule, snagged him back to reality.

Duke stared hard into Antoine's eyes. "How we know you ain't got an allegiance wit' Knight?"

"You don't." Antoine shrugged. "All I got is my word. An' you remember from back in the day, we was tight like that." Antoine stared back hard in a way that said, "Follow me if you need to."

Reba play-slapped his hand. "Duke, I ain't gon' bring somebody up in here who ain't on the team. An' you ain't in no position to go out recruitin'. Antoine all right."

"Bet." Duke shot him a hard look. "You play right an' you gon' get ova real good."

"I'm in," Antoine said, pulling up a chair for himself and another for Reba.

"Now, this the way it—" Duke grimaced in pain. "It gon' go down the night o' The Games. An' anybody who stand in my way gon' get steamrolled."

Chapter 16

Knight stood beside The Queen, studying how the clear safety glasses made her eyes look extra big and beautiful. With her hair pulled back in a ponytail, and the orange plugs in her ears, she focused straight ahead, over the tiny viewfinder above the barrel.

All his chest-crushing anxiety about Manifest Destiny had dissolved the moment they had stepped down into this gun range in the basement of Babylon HQ; they had an arsenal that could arm a small country. But right now he had to make sure that The Queen's target practice, twice a month, was preparing her to fight to the death if necessary. Her self-defense classes with Lee Lee were doing the same, as she'd proven with that punk, Brian, after their Moreno meeting.

Knight was making plans to take care of Brian and Moreno, too. They'd be out of the way for Babylon to thrive under Jamal's reign, as Knight and The Queen could flee their urban underworld and live in the sunshine in peace forever.

Even if all hell broke loose on their wedding night—a power coup, a robbery, a siege—he had to make sure The Queen could handle herself and get out alive.

Knight's thoughts popped as quickly and as intensely as the gunfire of two dozen B'Amazons and Barriors who were doing target practice in adjacent lanes.

"No emotion," Knight said close to her ear. "Kill or be killed."

The Queen's diamond engagement ring glistened as she gripped the pistol with both hands. She aimed at the man-sized target. *Pow!*

The bullet blasted into the red bull's-eye on the man's chest.

The Barriors and B'Amazons around them stopped to admire The Queen's sharpshooter skills.

"You doin' it, Baby Girl!" Knight exclaimed.

She stared forward, hard, not reacting. "Duke's dick is like a loaded gun right now. If that muthafucka comes near me, I got a lead cure for his ailment—"

143

"Brother or no brother," Knight said with a sad but serious tone, "This is a prime example of The Prince's Code #3: *Kill or be killed.*"

Pow! Another bullet pierced the heart zone on the target.

"Baby Girl!" Knight said with awe. "You shoot better than some of the B'Amazons."

"'Cause I'm The Queen," she said without taking her eyes off the target or lowering the gun. "I dare a muthafucka—" She turned to look into Knight's eyes.

The potency in her stare was so powerful, Knight shivered. It was like looking in the mirror, on his best days, when he felt like the African god that he was, ruling over his kingdom and making his minions quake in their boots with a glance.

The Queen smiled.

She knows what you're thinking, Intuition said. *You're the perfect power couple. Gotta be careful, though.*

There was a glint in The Queen's eyes.

"Your cry for help is '*Isis! Osiris!*' You yell that out if anything happens while you're in The Penthouse, the wedding suite, or anywhere else. Shout it over and over until the Barriors and B'Amazons get there."

The Queen stared back with a suspicious glint.

"We're monitoring every sound and every movement in The Playhouse and HQ. So know that somebody will be there. Until they arrive, though, you can handle it. Stay armed at all times. Does your holster fit okay?"

"It's fine."

He glanced down the form-fitting curves of her baby tee. The lace edges framed her *Cleopatra of the Knight* tattoo scrolled in cobalt blue ink over the beautiful bronze mounds of her pushed-up breasts. The baby tee also showcased the sculpted curves of her deltoids and her slim waist. The diamond flower in her pierced belly button shimmered. And the brown leather holster hung just below the belt loops on her low-cut jeans.

"Good. Stay armed at all times, even if you're with security. Even if you think you're in a place that's completely safe."

"Even with you?" she said with a flat tone, staring hard. She put the gun on safety and slipped it into the brown leather holster belt around the waist of her low-cut jeans. "You won't go to the fuckin' doctor, you could fall out any minute. An' I'm just standin' there like a sorry bitch outta muthafuckin' luck."

The anger in her voice made Knight's cheeks burn as if he'd been slapped. He took a deep breath.

"Baby Girl—"

"Naw, I ain't a baby right now." She jerked her neck. "I'm a grown-ass woman who's worried about her man who supposed to keep my ass safe, but the way you—"

Knight grasped her arm. Nobody needed to see anything other than complete harmony among them. He pulled her into the small office where men and women had to scan their ID cards to gain entry and check out extra weapons if necessary. Then he guided her with a tight grip on her arm, through a small door to the gun room. Knight closed the door behind them, staring hard at The Queen as she stood framed by a row of rifles. "Never show a public display of anger like that again. This a dangerous time at Babylon. We can trust no one. Because they will divide and conquer if we show even the slightest crack in the veneer."

The Queen rolled her eyes. "You actin' way too paranoid lately . . . like you ain't bein' straight wit' me about what's really 'bout to go down when we get married."

Knight took another deep breath to force down any conscious thoughts about his plan.

She had heard something broadcast over their telepathic love connection. And it had tipped her off. Now she was going purely on a hunch.

No information. She has no information. There is no information. He let the words *no information* play over and over in the back of his mind.

"I see some scheme, Knight. An' I ain't diggin' it—"

Knight squinted slightly as he looked down at her. "Baby Girl, you're acting and talking a little too black—"

She crossed her arms. "How the king of black pride gon' tell me I'm actin' too black? An' how can my half-white ass possibly act too black?"

"You had a happy medium for a minute, but you've gone a little overboard. You won't have to put up such a front when we—" Knight stopped himself. He wanted to say, "When we disappear . . .," but he forced the words no *information* to play again and again so she wouldn't hear that.

Her eyes grew enormous, like two blue-gray saucers. She spun around, making her ponytail slap his arm as she turned her back to him. The holster gripped her hips so that the brown leather hung just below her QUEEN OF THE KNIGHT tattoo, as if the gun belt were underlining her title, her position in this urban underworld into which her family's tragedy had thrust her. She tapped her foot, making the bottom of her straight black ponytail sway a few inches above her tattoo along the bottom edge of her tight, white lace-trimmed baby tee.

She's biting her lip so she won't say anything else, Intuition said. *Calm her down.*

A twinge of sympathy halted the words that were about to jump off the tip of Knight's tongue. He should not have been so harsh. The Queen was fitting into this foreign world so well that she was ruling and profiting far beyond his expectations. Now in this climate of fear and distrust, and Li'l Tut on the loose with poisonous and power-hungry intentions, who could blame her for putting up a tough-girl defense?

"Baby Girl, I apologize," Knight said softly, noticing how much darker her skin was today compared to when he'd met her just over a year ago. Then, she'd been sun-kissed beige. Now, her nude visits to the tanning booth in The Penthouse had deepened her whole body's color to a deep bronze-brown.

"Baby Girl," Knight said with a tone that demanded a response, "turn around, please."

She made an annoyed sucking noise.

"Baby Girl—"

SEX IN THE HOOD 2

She spun on her silver stiletto heel so hard, she could have drilled a hole in the floor. She sharpened her eyes on Knight in a way that made him freeze.

"I didn't have no place else to go," she said through tight lips. "Duke was always talkin' about survival of the fittest in the urban jungle. An' I wasn't about to get eaten up an' spit out by nobody!"

Knight wanted to smile. The power radiating from this goddess made Shane hard as hell in a single heartbeat.

"No time to grieve!" she exclaimed. "Snatched out of my white mansion and thrown into the ghetto. Horny as hell, an' turnt out in a matter of hours."

Knight looked back without feeling a single pang of possessiveness or anger that Li'l Tut had plucked her cherry. All his little brother had been doing was preparing her for Master Knight to lay his giant steam pipe in that fertile feminine ground. Baby bro' had handled the painful part and gotten her warmed up for the real deal, and for that, Knight was thankful.

Together, he and Li'l Tut had created this magnificent, sexy monster named The Queen.

"I couldn't wait to get the fuck outta here," The Queen said. "The blackest thing I came across in prep school was the coffee I drank in the morning. Sex?" She held up her right hand. "This was all the dick Celeste was gettin'."

The corner of Knight's mouth curled up slightly.

"I cain't hardly believe it myself," she said, "but I love this shit. I love this life—the sex, the power, the money and, most of all, your ass." Her eyes became shiny and silvery as they filled with tears. "I love you, Knight. I love the idea of spending the rest of my life here in Babylon beside you, runnin' things an' raising our family."

Knight's throat burned. He wanted to pull her into his arms, cover her with kisses and whisper that he would always protect her and make her smile and make her cum and be the perfect mate. But he was frozen by guilt. It sliced through his gut like a giant knife.

I'm deceiving her. She trusts me with her life, and I'm tricking her. If she fooled me, it would forever destroy my trust. So how will she forgive me once everything shakes down and we wake up in another life?

Something flickered in her eyes. "I got this feeling with Duke too," she said with a weak tone, as if she were about to vomit. "You betta tune your thoughts back to a better frequency where you ain't givin' off that vibe I just felt. I don't like it. An' I'll slip off your radar before I let you or anybody else play me—The Queen don't get played."

Knight stepped close to her and rested his hands on her shoulders. "Everything I do is for us." He lowered an open palm to the soft, warm swath of belly exposed by her low-cut jeans. The diamond in her belly button seemed to wink up at him. "For us and for Baby Prince." Knight kissed her.

Their lips did not move. But the heat and the energy passing between them caused The Queen's tense shoulder to relax under his hand, and her belly quaked slightly. She gripped the crotch of his black jeans.

Shane surged to attention.

"Make love to me," she whispered, grabbing the big silver belt buckle that said KNIGHT. She dropped to her knees, unfastened his belt, unzipped his pants, and pulled hard-as-lead Shane in front of her face.

He surged out like a black python.

The Queen had the power and concentration of a snake charmer in her eyes as she stared at his dick as if it held all the secrets to the meaning of life and love.

Knight almost smiled. He couldn't think of any situation in a relationship that didn't get resolved with some good dick therapy. Because sheer bliss glowed in The Queen's eyes as she parted her lips and stuck out her tongue to slide it under the giant black head and lure him into the hot chamber of her mouth.

This is the answer.

Having her mouth on Shane twenty-four/seven was the remedy for his health crisis, because as soon as her steaming hot mouth closed around his cock, it sparked a chemical reaction in his body. The stress and worries that caused tight sensations in his muscles and made his mind reel, suddenly transformed into a warm swirl of liquid opium.

"Aw, Baby Girl," he groaned as she rimmed her tongue around Shane's head and worked her hands up and down the shaft with a twisting motion.

She spat into her palms to make her hands slippery, and the friction heated them as she massaged up and down.

I know her pussy's drippin'.

It is, her voice answered with a seductive tone, in his mind.

She put her whole body into it, moving her shoulders and grinding her ass into the air behind her as she worked his dick. With a slurping sound, she pulled her mouth off and stood up. She yanked back the top of her baby tee where the white lace framed the creamy mounds of her full titties. They were as golden brown as the buttered tops of corn muffins.

Knight bent down to take a suck.

Her nipple popped out just as his mouth reached the tip of her beautiful breast. That hard, hot sensation in his mouth, and her fingertips gently pressing his bald head as she pulled him close, made Shane triple hard.

She let out her other tittie, which he sucked into his mouth at the same time.

His tongue made a figure eight over both nipples as he pressed her breasts together from the sides. With two handfuls of soft, curving flesh, he buried his face between them, inhaling her sweet skin.

"Make love to me," she whispered with a desperate tone. "Make love to *me!*"

They quickly undressed, carefully placing her holster on the countertop.

Then Knight raised her onto the desk, onto her hands and knees, with her ass aiming straight up at him. "Spread your legs wider," he said, staring at the brown mounds of her plump ass.

Her knees split wide, causing her booty cheeks to part.

He loved how her tattoo reminded him and everyone that this ass was like prime USDA meat marked QUEEN OF THE

KNIGHT. He pulled her hair out of that ponytail so that long black locks spilled down her back and over the sides of her small waist. Her hair let off a flowery aroma from her shampoo, which Knight inhaled because he loved her clean scent. Clean mouth, clean hair, clean fingernails, clean ears, clean pussy, clean toes.

Yeah, The Queen was clean enough to eat off of any surface or hole on her body. Even her ass.

Knight stroked his dick as he stared at the prettiest asshole he'd ever seen. It was all smooth skin with tiny lines that aimed down into a little brown dot of a hole that was closed. It reminded him of the end of a sausage, where the skin was drawn together and made little lines and folds as it curved to the point.

The hole glistened with pussy juice that smeared thick and shiny over that small stretch of skin between the asshole and her pussy. The lips were wet and swollen and red. Since she was on her hands and knees, her pussy looked upside down—the vagina hole at the top, the big, meaty clit at the bottom.

He shoved his face between her ass cheeks. He inhaled. Her ass had no odor and was always clean. So he stuck out his tongue and ran it 'round and 'round that tight, pretty hole. He sucked on the curving parts of her juicy ass and let his tongue slide down to dip into her pussy for some of that sticky-sweet cream.

He pulled back, licking his lips and jacking his dick, just staring at what he was about to drill with perfect precision. "Yeah, dance it for me, Baby Girl," he groaned. He leaned close again to inhale that sweet-salty scent. Her pheromones made Knight shiver. He stared in awe at The Queen's body. She was super-toned and strong from working out in the gym.

But she also exercised her sex muscles. So she knew how to make her clit dance like a freaky red animal, rippling and rolling as if it would jump up and attack some dick. And she was making her pussy lips move as if they were a mouth talking—open, close, open, close—exposing the luscious pink satin chambers of her regal temple, then shutting the golden doors like a sudden burst of modesty. But she kept teasing, flashing the glistening jewel just enough to make him crazy.

With her left hand, she reached between her legs and slid her middle finger into her pussy. Her diamond wedding ring sparkled as she pulled her finger out, covered with juice, which she spread around the already-wet lips. She finger fucked herself a little more, then made tiny circles with her fingertip over that delicious meatball that was her clit.

Shane was hard enough to cut diamonds.

And she was wet enough to take him all in with a single stroke.

Knight stepped forward. He aimed Shane's giant head at her pussy hole, and with one smooth thrust, his black python slithered up into its luxurious velvet nest.

"Ooooooh, Knight, baby, do me so good." She let out the sexiest sound that was a combination of a moan and a shriek.

He pulled back and thrust again. His reward was that little sound again.

And she squeezed her pussy from the inside. Starting at the top, around Shane's head, she made little rings of muscle contractions that rippled down the shaft. It felt like she was milking his dick, working the muscles from the top all the way down his dick to her pussy lips.

This pussy looks pretty, smells clean, and does acrobatic tricks!

Knight groaned at this "sextravaganza" with the perfect woman who would be his wife for life. In mind, body and spirit, they were one. His plan was best for them. It would save their lives.

But he was not being honest. Guilt rippled through him like a splash of cold water. He was tricking her and would have to continue doing so for several more weeks.

More guilt surged through his veins like crushed ice. And Shane went soft.

The Queen's head spun back. She turned and stared over her shoulder with eyes that glowed like a hungry wolf in the wilderness.

Knight don't choke. I am an African god. A Mandingo warrior.

Blood surged back into Shane.

Knight's giant fingertips grasped the soft flesh of The Queen's pretty hips. And he jack hammered her until she screamed his name.

Chapter 17

Trina Michaels hurried into her office at the Global News TV Network in Washington, D.C. She was trembling with a nasty mix of emotions, ranging from fear to excitement and anticipation, to disappointment and rage.

I'm never gonna fuck again. Sex never led to anything but trouble.

That was the whole reason she had married her first husband. And her second husband. And that jerk she left at the altar last year, when she realized that sex was her only motive for wanting to tie the knot with him too.

Otherwise, she didn't give half a shit about those cavemen. Cavemen who had gone to the best schools, granted. And cavemen who came from the best, most bourgeoisie families on the East Coast, but cavemen, nonetheless. They all were. Just big apes playing with the bananas between their legs, hoping to hump it into any and every female they encountered while swinging from tree to tree.

"So why does sex make me so stupid too?" she asked aloud as she set down her suitcase and perched on the chair at her desk. "Why do I think that in order to feel clean and respectable, I have to marry the dick of the day?"

And how come, the first time she decides to indulge her curiosity for sex with women, she gets mixed up with some inner-city bandits who try to frame her by videotaping the female sexcapades? When in her 35 years on this planet did Trina Michaels ever have sex that didn't end up a mess?

That abortion just before the senior prom, so she could go to college; Chlamydia after pulling a train at that frat party during her sophomore year at Georgetown University; the rumors and lies that the married anchor spread about her at the first TV station where she worked, in that dusty little hick town in Kentucky; the catfight in the newsroom at her next station, in Atlanta, when she and another female reporter had gone to blows over the hottest guy in TV news at the time.

"Talk about drama," Trina said out loud as she logged onto the blue screen of her computer.

This last situation clearly took the cake over everything else. Even that white network TV headhunter who promised an extra $25,000 in her contract if she fucked him after the interview. When she negotiated it to $35,000, she thought of it as a signing bonus, which helped her get a luxury sports car that projected the appropriately glamorous image for a serious TV reporter in the nation's capitol.

So there was no way that anybody, especially that thug and "thugette" in Detroit, was going to stop her now. Nope, onward and upward. Alone. Without sex.

"Those niggers in Detroit think they got somethin' on me, but I'm gonna do a report that blows them outta the water."

Yes, when The Queen and her caveman, The Knight, first threatened her, Trina felt scared for her safety, her career, her reputation. But as she fumed on the plane ride back to D.C., she realized, in this day and age of technology and computer manipulation of video, nobody could ever prove that was GNN's Trina Michaels on that nasty tape. Plus, she did so many negative reports about vile people, and the court cases they generated, dozens, if not hundreds, of people in America would've loved nothing better than to destroy her.

Now she could add those Detroit sex freaks to the list.

I'll say they forged the video using my face from TV and another woman's body. Another woman who was smoking marijuana. Then they'll be busting on their own asses, after my report blasts their little empire to smithereens.

*

Trina wasn't stupid. She'd grown up with street hoods just like that on the South Side of Chicago, always hustling to make a dollar. No matter what toll it took on someone's body or mind or soul.

A pimp and a ho were a pimp and a ho, no matter how classy, sophisticated, or beautiful their whole spiel appeared to be. They were breaking the law. And they would have to stop. Soon. And she wasn't buying that sob story 'bout growing up in the hood and not having any opportunities. *Stupid idiots. Go to school. Stay there. Don't get pregnant. Get a scholarship and go to college. Become something. Ugh!*

SEX IN THE HOOD 2

And their black English. The way so many of them
butchered perfectly whole words to little itty-bitty bits flying
out of their mouths with no thought beforehand, replacing *th*
with *d*, *this* and *that* with *dis* and *dat*, yes with *yeah*, using
ain't with too many things, and *fuck* as a noun, a verb, and an
adjective.

Her parents were both honest, hard-working people, who
taught her the right values. Mother worked downtown as a
seamstress at a clothing boutique, and Father had a good job
in the U.S. Post Office. Her brother was a lawyer, thanks to
Harvard, and her sister was a stay-at-home mom, married to a
stockbroker.

Yep, the Michaels family was as American as apple pie.
Whereas The Queen and The Knight represented the dark,
rotting core that threatened to bring this great country down
through moral corruption and blatant disregard for the law.

But not if Trina could stop them first.

*

"Now, where is that picture?" Trina said out loud as she
typed the name Victoria Winston into the GNN video archives.

No, Trina had busted her ass to get where she was. And she
wasn't going to allow it to be ruined by that horny mulatto
bitch living some ghetto girl dream. Or nightmare, depending
on who was talking.

And that Knight guy. Whew! What a piece of work!

Trina hated the way he just sat there silently like the king,
as if everybody should read his thoughts and act accordingly,
or else . . .

Men. The male ego knew no bounds as far as being selfish
and self-centered. He should be ashamed of himself, too,
hiding that girl from the authorities. And the price for her
room and board?—Running his illegal underworld.

Trina shivered under her dark brown pantsuit. Her nipples
poked through her lace bra and pushed into her white satin
blouse.

Babylon, schmabylon. Bad ending or not, that was un-
doubtedly the best sex she'd ever had.

WHITE CHOCOLATE

True, she hated that she could indulge in her most animalistic instincts and fuck like a dog without any emotional attachment whatsoever to the dick or the guy it was growing out of. Hell, she didn't even know his name. Or the name of that other guy. Or the one after that.

She did, however, know The Queen's name. Something had seemed so familiar about her unusual gray-blue eyes and her long black hair. Her skin was darker, and her speech was tainted by Ebonics, as opposed to the proper white English that Trina remembered hearing Victoria Winston speak in news reports.

"Now, if I can just get some proof." Trina stared at her screen.

Ching! The computer chimed. And up popped her report about the rich girl who had disappeared after her father's mysterious suicide. There was the girl wanted by the FBI who had serious questions about her father's alleged money laundering schemes through his multi-million-dollar business.

"Yes!" Trina pumped her arm for emphasis. "The investigative journalism gods are smiling down on me now. Thank you!"

Staring back from the screen was The Queen. Also known as Victoria Winston, a federal fugitive who was now part of an illegal sex-for-sale underworld.

"And I know exactly where to find her! Better yet, I'm gonna bring her down before she can bring me down!"

Now, Trina just had to strategize just how to do it. If only she'd taken the hidden cameras into the party. That video would make her a superstar! She would win awards and be celebrated as the toughest investigative reporter in America. That story would be her Emmy, the highest and most prestigious prize in TV journalism.

Nobody had to know that she went to the party at Babylon because she wanted to; it had nothing to do with a story, although she was curious.

But once she saw the huge scale of sex for sale and tasted the rage of betrayal after that bisexual extravaganza, well, it was only natural now to do the exposé of the century.

22

"HHhhhmmmmm," she said, staring at The Queen's picture on her computer screen. Those full lips made her panties get wet instantly.

Those lips that made me cum so, so good. Hey, if I give up sex with men, maybe I can stick to strictly women. After all, The Queen ate me out, but I didn't get to taste hers, or CoCo's, or Honey's.

"Concentrate, Trina Michaels! Now, what angle can I take here?" Trina thought back to the snippets of conversations that she'd overheard during the party, and when she walked around Babylon HQ with CoCo and Honey.

"The Games!" Trina exclaimed, springing up in her seat. "People kept mentioning The Games. I'll send a female reporter to that event, whatever it is, get secret video, and *voilà!*—I am a superstar!"

Chapter 18

Duke wanted to fuck Reba right away, but she was acting all in a hurry to leave and do a party at The Garage.

"Why you gotta leave?" Duke stroked Timbo. He was nude, sitting up on the bed, his back against the headboard, his legs outstretched, and his dick in his hand.

"Ooooh you got a pretty dick." Reba stepped closer.

"I need some sexual healing," Duke said. "Doc said it was okay."

"*I* say it ain't."

"If you gon' marry me," Duke said, "I need a test-drive first. How I know you cain't grind down on it like I like?"

"You *do* know," Reba said, straddling the top of his thighs. Her hot ass in tight jeans against his skin made his dick throb harder. "Or did fuckin' Miss White Chocolate erase all memories of the sistas you used to kick it wit'?"

Duke wrapped his hands around her thighs and stared at her crotch. "My memories live as Memorex—take off yo' top."

Reba pressed her fingertips to her nipples, caressing them through her shirt. They got even harder, poking like juicy grapes through her top. "Why you wanna see my titties?"

Duke stroked his dick. "It's gon' make me heal faster."

She shifted to his kneecap then ground her crotch into him.

"Work that shit," he said. "An' suck on Timbo."

Reba leaped off and stood beside the bed. "Duke, you ain't in no condition to mess around. You cain't even laugh without pain."

"Get on top," he said; "take a ride. Gimme some sexual healing."

"You been checked?" Reba asked. "Lemme see yo' card, 'cause I'm still workin' for Babylon. But if I catch somethin', I'm out on my ass. An' this plan ain't gon' work from the outside. So—"

"You think I'm some kinda infected muthafucka?"

"Duke, you know damn well that half the shit out there ain't got no symptoms. Especially HIV. An' you cain't tell by

158

lookin' at even the finest bitch if she got that rank-ass virus lurkin' up in her pussy."

"You know how careful I was when we was fuckin' before."

"But when you out on the street, doin' what you was doin' . . . no offense, Duke, but y'all gets sloppy."

" 'Y'all'?—What the fuck you mean?"

"It mean Reba don't fuck no dick that ain't been checked. My pussy clean and I'm keepin' it that way." Reba cupped his jaw in her hands. "Duke, this can wait. I don't think—"

He grabbed her jaw and pulled her close. He planted a hot, juicy kiss on her lips.

She resisted, grabbing his wrists to pull.

He didn't let go; her lips were tense and shut. But he pressed harder. Then he grabbed her ass and pulled her closer so that her crotch rubbed up against Timbo.

She moaned. And her lips relaxed.

He slid his tongue into her mouth.

She moaned and ground on his dick.

He pulled her ponytail back, yanked her head. Pulled up her shirt, buried his face in those big, delicious titties. Then his fingers pried at the metal button on the waist of her jeans.

She protested. "Duke . . ."

"I'll wear a condom, then I'll have Doc check me out."

Duke wanted the pussy, but he could get by without it.

Truth was, he was sleepy as hell from the painkiller. But he needed to see just how far Reba would go to prove her loyalty to him and his plan. "Baby, I promise I'm clean," he whispered, pulling her close again for a kiss.

Chapter 19

Something in Reba's gut told her don't play with fire, because as bad as Duke looked right now, somethin' wasn't right. Maybe it was just hard life wherever the hell he had been for a year. Maybe it was the drugs. Maybe HIV was the reason he was so skinny and pale, and his skin was all jacked up with blemishes.

And Reba didn't want any money so bad she'd risk her life for it. What good would that do?—Getting what you want and then dying with it in your hands? Not just dying, though, in the peaceful way that some people go to sleep and never wake up. Or in a split second get hit by a car or have a heart attack and die on the spot.

No, AIDS took its time, like it was a felon of Fate inside your body, gloating at the horrible ways that it vandalized your skin, maliciously destroyed your body functions, and attempted to kill many terrifying times before finally committing a homicide. That's what it seemed like when some muthafucka pulled his trigger inside Lucille and shot up her insides with a spray of HIV-infected sperm.

Reba had watched her sister waste away into a skeleton with chronic diarrhea and throat infections. Hearing her gasp for her last breaths convinced Reba that HIV was nothing to play with. That's why she loved Babylon. If she was gonna trick, then she had the best-case scenario.

That computer card with the chip in her purse, the one that all the Sluts and Studs were required to carry and get updated weekly, was her life insurance. Clients carried the cards too, and had to get checked before every party.

Reba thought of her sister every day, to remind her how precious her health and life were. Yeah, this girl from the hood was doing just fine right now—a nice apartment at Babylon HQ, plenty of money, and tons of men to fuck her, flatter her, and buy her anything she wanted.

I ain't drivin' my yellow Corvette outside an' wearin' designer clothes 'cause I'm strugglin'.

160

SEX IN THE HOOD 2

*

She had to admit something to herself, even though she acted so tough to the world, and she dogged the idea of marriage, deep down it was her lifelong dream. Just like it was for every little girl.

Not that she'd seen examples in real life. No, when you grow up watching your ho-ass momma do her business in your face, the word *trick* takes on a whole new meaning. Trick or treat wasn't about Halloween. It was about the treats that Momma would buy for Reba and Lucille if she let a trick come while the girls were home.

Momma would give each daughter a dollar from the money that she'd earned for suckin' some crusty negro's dick, then she'd send the girls skipping down to the corner liquor store to buy whatever she and her trick wanted.

Baby Blue's mother, who used to stay in their tiny extra bedroom, while all three girls curled up to sleep together every night on the sofabed in the living room, did the same thing—treats for their daughters after their tricks left.

Reba's favorite was a long red popsicle, which she would lick and suck the same way she'd seen Momma do all them dudes dicks. Momma took all those muthafuckas into the bedroom, but Reba and Lucille would still watch through the keyhole in the door.

Lucille's treat, though, was barbecue potato chips. She'd eat so many that her lips would burn, crack, and bleed from the salt and spices, because Lucille had the idea that love should hurt; that a treat from Momma would only cause pain. So she followed in Momma's nasty footsteps, as a street ho. She dropped out of school, got hooked on drugs, and worked for a pimp who put blue marks on her black ass.

But Reba wanted to live a nicer life, like the white people she saw on TV. Somewhere out there was a better way. And all the boys and girls on TV who grew up to be somebody had to finish school first. So Reba kept going to middle school and high school.

But when Baby Blue took her to a party at Babylon, and she saw all those rappers and dancers and fine-ass niggas with rolls of dough in their pockets, Reba felt like she'd just stepped into ghetto paradise. This was the better place she knew had been out there somewhere, waiting for her to find it.

Then Baby Blue, who was already working as a Slut since dropping out of ninth grade, introduced her to Duke. Reba fucked him that night, and it was all over.

He loved her stuff so much she joined the Sex Squad and started working the next day. She even moved into Babylon, sharing an apartment with Baby Blue. It was a nicer place than she'd ever had. Shoot, just the fact that she had heat, hot water, plenty of good food, and no roaches made it an inner-city Taj Mahal when compared to the rat hole Momma had kept her and Lucille in.

At Babylon, to keep living this glamorous life, all Reba had to do was do what she already loved to do—fuck—and everything was taken care of. But now, too many years later, she was tired of humpin' for a living. She didn't want to do this hard work for the rest of her life. No, she was looking for early retirement. And this dude name Duke, sitting here in a hotel room with bullet wounds, a big dream and his dick in his hand, was her 401K plan.

*

"Get some papers or your card from Doc, an' this pussy yours for life," Reba said. "Until then, I can polish yo' knob wit' my hands."

"Naw, baby," Duke said with a deep, almost sinister tone. "If we ain't down all the way like this, it ain't a done deal."

Reba watched his chapped lips as he talked. She remembered how the girls used to say Duke had sucka lips. They were so sexy, that when he talked, all you could think about was wanting to suck on his bottom lip or his top lip or both at once, for a long time—while he drilled some of that good "Energizer Bunny" dick named Timbo, which everybody loved.

Back then, his lips had been so distracting that he had a reputation for getting any pussy he wanted, anytime, because all he had to do was talk, say anything, and the females would cream their panties so fast, they'd be peelin' them off and letting him press those pretty lips of his between their legs in what he always called a Motor City minute.

But right now, the dry skin made little vertical white lines up and down his lips. And while he talked, Reba thought she saw a red sore just inside his mouth. That could be a herpes blister or a syphilis chancre or a burn from a pipe or blunt. And all that made the thought of kissing him about as appetizing as licking a public toilet seat.

"Duke, I got rules for myself. You know how strict it be at Babylon." Reba got a whiff of funk from his underarms. "Don't ask me to toss 'em to the wind jus' so you can blow yo' nut."

"Bye." His word shot through the air like a bullet. "Get yo' ass outta here. Bonnie an' Clyde splittin' up. Clyde gon' get anotha bitch to get paid wit'."

Reba stared into his angry eyes. "You bluffin'."

"Bye."

She stood up, turned her back to him, unzipped her jeans, pulled them down (She wore no panties.) and bent over at the waist.

"Now that's what I'm talkin' 'bout—pussy wet as a mug."

As she faced the floor, she pulled off her shirt, letting her titties dangle. Then, as she stepped out of her jeans and shoes, she pulled a condom from her front right pocket. She ripped it open, then turned around.

"Da-yum!" Duke stroked Timbo.

She stepped onto the bed. With lightning speed, she rolled the condom down on his dick. Then she slid down on it before he could say jack.

"You slick," he said; "da's a'ight."

He grimaced in pleasure and pain as he pounded up into the pussy; she slammed down at the same time.

And they kissed.

Reba gripped his shoulders. But the sensation of rough scabs on his back made her raise her hands up to the back of his head. Normally shaved bald, it was prickly with a week's worth of hair growth. "Oooh, you know how to fuck," Reba moaned.

WHITE CHOCOLATE

"This some good pussy." Duke stared up into her eyes. "Say you love me."

The desperation in his eyes made Reba's gut cramp. "I love you," she said as sensuously as a movie star in a love scene would. "I love you, Duke."

"Say it while I cum," he said, fucking her harder. And harder. And frantically. Breathing hard, like he'd just run down the block.

Damn, he didn't even try to let me cum first. Not wit' his fingers. Or his dick.

But whatever. The sooner this dangerous shit was over with, the better. She could relax and enjoy it when she knew he was healthy.

Good thing she had super-strength, super-sized condoms. But the way he was drilling up, he could split steel with that dick. Plus, she was getting dry because she wasn't that into it. And a dry pussy, hard fucking, and a huge dick created the perfect formula for a broken condom—and infection with whatever the fuck he might have.

"Duke, wait, let me check the condom," she said, looking down past her orange-rhinestone-studded belly button, to her heart-shaped pouf of hair, to her pussy lips spread around his dark-chocolate dick. The white edges of the condom remained intact where it gripped the base of his dick. It was rolled down almost to the hairline.

He pulled out. The whole condom still covered every inch of him.

"Okay." She spat into her hand then rubbed the spit all up and down the outside of the condom. Then she slid Timbo back into her pussy.

Yeah, it felt good, but all this worry wouldn't be worth it, no matter how out-of-this-world the dick was.

"Oh, baby, I'm 'bout to cum," he groaned. Sweat beaded on his forehead. He was breathing so hard, he was wheezing. All that smoking.

Reba glanced at the clock on the nightstand. Her heart was pounding, but it was out of fear. The image of her sister Lucille, laying on her deathbed, trembling, sweating and

164

making unhuman groan noises, flashed through her mind. For a second, Duke's face even transformed into Lucille's, her paper-thin skin stretched so tight over protruding cheekbones, it looked like the bone would slice right through.

"Ah!" Reba cried out. Not in pleasure but in terror. She never took risks like this. Didn't have to, because everything at Babylon was so medically checked and safe. She couldn't wait to get this over with. She'd carefully slide off the condom, go take a long, hot shower, and never put her life on the line again.

"Oh fuck!" Duke shouted. He threw his head back.

She glimpsed his teeth that used to be sparkly white but now were dull yellow, like French vanilla ice-cream. And his breath was kind o' mediciny.

"Say you love me, girl!"

Reba stared at him. Was any money worth this? She did not love this nigga. She loved what this deal represented—paid for life as his wife. He'd be cleaned up, healed, and back to his regular fine-ass self, giving her this big dick under better conditions.

She saw herself in a black Benz convertible, shopping, taking fancy trips, bein' the baddest bitch around and loaded with cash. "I love you," she whispered, staring into his eyes.

"Yeah, love me!" he shouted. "Fuck!" Finally, he trembled with orgasm. "Damn," Duke smiled, still huffing. "That was the best fuck I eva had. 'Cause we was makin' love, not fuckin'."

Reba couldn't wait to get off this lyin' muthafucka. She knew damn well he had said those same words to countless women, including The Queen. Especially The Queen. Reba pinched the top of the condom around the base of his dick. She started to slide upward.

"Wait," Duke said, pressing down her thighs. "I love you, Reba Sheba." He stared tenderly into her eyes.

For a split second, the idea of a man saying he loved her and looking at her like that, made her want to cry. Because it had never happened. Unless it was a fake act like this, when a man wanted to get something from her. And she, of course, was getting something from him—money.

And that was all she wanted from Duke—no viruses, no infections, and no bogus-ass words.

"I cain't tell you," Duke said, "how good it feel for somebody to give me some love. Not just pussy, but some real love. I ain't felt that since fo'eva."

Reba wanted so desperately to feel that, she kissed his forehead. Because his ass was as pathetic as she was. And they were both perpetrating like they were tough. But at the core they were just two sorry-ass fools trying to play each other to get the prize.

After a long moment of pretending this was her husband who adored her for her, she pinched the base of the condom again. Holding tight to keep it in place and not spill sperm around her pussy, she carefully slid up and off—and shredded rubber flopped down the sides of Duke's cum-covered dick.

Chapter 20

Knight's deep voice echoed off the damp, black walls of the tunnel as he spoke to Crew Q. He had hand-picked these fifty Barriors and B'Amazons to execute important tasks during the Wedding and The Games—or so they thought. Knight knew Li'l Tut, and these muthafuckas were scheming to steal his secret maneuvers and plans, report them back to his brother and his team of bandits, and dare to think they could plunder the riches that Babylon would accumulate the night of The Games.

Knight could hear his older brother, Prince, urging him to follow one of his rules of power: "Crush your enemies." Actually Knight was about to let them crush themselves as they attempted to execute their most misguided, knuckle-headed plan that would backfire in the most tragic of ways as Manifest Destiny triumphed.

"Twenty-one days," Knight said in the dim fluorescent light that flickered from a square panel on the ceiling.

In black scuba suits, Ping and Pong stood at his sides, along with his most trusted B'Amazons, Lee Lee and Dayna. All four of them held rifles. And they needed to know the bogus plan for Crew Q for when they carried out the real deal to whisk the money, Knight, and The Queen far and away from Babylon.

"We have zero tolerance for error," Knight said over the sound of dripping water. Though the air was rank with mold and musk, he breathed calmly and deeply.

After years in a prison cell, he felt perfectly at ease in the confines of this hot, humid chamber, its metal walls glistening with greasy grime and patches of green moss. His face and body felt cool, his black ninja suit dry. But sweat glistened on the tense faces and bare, muscular arms of the troops to whom he spoke.

"Hesitation will get you killed." Knight knocked on the wall behind him in the twelve-foot-high, twelve-foot-wide area. "Down here, thirty feet below the water's surface, the Detroit River shows no mercy."

167

He stared into the serious, yet scared eyes of the soldiers, especially Antoine's look-alike brother, Ben. He, like the others, wore fatigues, black boots, and black tank tops.

"So when this door goes up," Knight said, "it's game time. Anybody who misses their play, well, you get a permanent time out—for life." Knight looked over the heads of the men and women, into the thick blackness of a dozen more feet of tunnel behind them.

"Retreat back into that black hole"—Knight slammed his huge hand against the metal door, which clanged eerily, and water sloshed around its edges and dripped down its sludge-smudged surface. "And whatever's going down in The Playhouse will show even less mercy."

Knight took a rifle from Ping. He cocked it quickly. The metallic clanking echoed off the walls. "This is your back-up," he said, nodding toward the metal door behind him, "until the gate goes up. Then—"

Pong handed him a knife in a black sheath.

Knight pulled out the long, silver-bladed knife, the kind scuba divers use in shark-infested waters. It shimmered in the dim light. "—you switch into manual offense and defense. Everybody hear me?"

They answered with military punctuality and speed, "Yes, sir!"

Knight took a large canvas backpack from Pong. He pulled open a zippered slot. "Remember, this holds your flotation device. But don't use it or any heat, or enemies on the water will shoot first, ask questions later—after they snatch the cash." Knight held open the backpack's large inner bag.

"This waterproof pouch will hold the money. Lose it—put on some cement shoes and don't try to float. Your goal is to make it the half-mile down the river to the boat with the underwater hatch."

Knight glared into the shifty eyes of that face that looked too much like Antoine to be trusted. "You got that, Ben?"

"Yes, sir!" he boomed back.

"Good." Knight probed his eyes with a hard gaze. The cat's only crime was nature's cruel trick of modeling him after his brother, whose misdirected lust at The Queen was about to get him jacked. Otherwise, Ben exhibited no physical or visceral signs of scheme.

That didn't make him exempt, though, from Crew Q—Q as in *question*, about their loyalty. Every man and woman down here right now had some mark against them. That mark could have been a rumor that they were Duke sympathizers, or a glance toward Knight that flashed hostility or game. Perhaps they'd shared phone conversations, e-mails or personal contact with Babylon board members who were contemplating a power coup.

So giving directives to Crew Q was the best way to divert all the Barriors and B'Amazons who were vulnerable to conspiring with competitors, especially Duke. Informants had clued Knight in on his baby brother's plan for a heist, followed by the rape and plunder of Babylon's riches. And anybody who helped make it happen would share the wealth, power, and future of Babylon.

At least that's what Duke had promised.

Now, the eagerness in several of the soldiers' eyes confirmed Knight's suspicions. They were looking at him but mentally ticking down all the details they would report back to Duke.

"I'm glad I've got your rapt attention," Knight said. "Now, if at any time during that twenty-four-hour period, you get the star signal, you are to report immediately to this tunnel. Not from the outside port, but from the basement inside The Playhouse. Everybody hear me?"

Knight could call this little exercise a test or a diversion or a trick. But he had to do whatever was necessary to make sure Manifest Destiny unfolded with perfect precision.

"One mistake could be your last." Knight's words reverberated through his chest. A dull ache was all that remained there now, thanks to the sexual healing powers that he and The Queen had conjured up while making love every morning and night since the Board meeting.

Plus, in his mind, he found strength by envisioning that baby boy growing inside the warm, nurturing flesh of The Queen's womb.

I have the power to heal myself and slip away with my wife and unborn child to a better place.

Knight tapped the metal door wall. "Out in the river," Knight said, "that current is ruthless. There's boat traffic too. But here at the edge, you're safe—except watch for floating debris; sometimes it's sharp or toxic."

Someone let out an annoyed groan.

"So wear your goggles," Knight said. "And just like we did in the drill over the summer; grab onto the metal handles in the river wall. Hold tight or that current will suck you down to the Rouge Plant and your bones will end up in the metal frame of somebody's new Ford."

One of the B'Amazons at the back of the group sucked her teeth and whispered, "Sheeit, this ain't worth it."

"Officer Sykes, step forward," Knight commanded. He had not seen her face.

Crew Q parted like water in the Red Sea. The woman slunk between them. Her muscular brown shoulders slumped; her close-cropped head hung shamefully in front of Knight.

He spoke softly, "Get the fuck out."

The rest of the crew was silent as Lee Lee took her arm.

Pong aimed a small silver remote at the blackness at the rear of the tunnel. Squeaking hinges and the clankety-clank of a rising metal gate echoed with spine-chilling screeches.

"Lee Lee, bring me back her discharge papers." Knight stared hard into the eyes of Crew Q.

They stood still and silent as statues. Everybody knew life after Babylon was hell. Even if you left town. It was the ultimate blacklist.

First, the reason most folks came to work at Babylon was because life in the mainstream world had done them wrong— prison convictions, fraud, on the run from somebody or something. So for the already disenfranchised, this was a sanctuary from all the rules and bureaucracy and bullshit of real life for a black man or woman in America. Life at Babylon meant food, clothing, a decent apartment in the Barrior and B'Amazon barracks, and a family-like network. Life away from here meant struggle, more struggle, and usually death.

"Anyone else?" Knight raised his hand toward the bluish light dancing on the thick, humid air now that that the back gate had risen. His laughter echoed in a way that made Crew Q look spooked. "After all, we are standing in a tunnel that led to freedom on the Underground Railroad, through which escaped slaves came North through Detroit, then fled across the river to Canada. Then in the 1920s, bootleggers passed where you stand right now to smuggle booze into D-town."

Ping nodded and said with a chuckle, "Find freedom or get fucked up, or both."

Knight smiled. "Now's your moment. Whether you're looking for a freedom ride or to smuggle your way out of here, speak now or forever hold"—He tapped the black Glock strapped to his hip—"your piece."

He took the remote from Pong's hand. His finger poised over the red button, he said, "Any defectors are welcome to take the waterway out." Knight pointed the silver square at the metal wall leading to the depths of the Detroit River. He pushed the button. With a deafening squeak, the door began to rise. Water crashed in, flooding the floor.

Several Barriors and B'Amazons jumped to avoid the frothy white water that filled the chamber with a strong fish odor. But Knight remained perfectly still. His waterproof boots rested firmly on the metal floor.

Suddenly his mind was illuminated with a thrilling "Aha! moment."

I have no ache in my chest. No sensation in my heart, except for normal, healthy beating. I can do this!

He was in the zone. And for Knight, the zone meant total concentration and focus on a goal. No distractions. No hesitation. No second thoughts.

With this and everything else, he set a goal and accomplished it with laser-beam precision. And that's what he would do the night of his wedding. His life and future—and that of his wife and family—depended on it.

"Ben!" he shouted over the loud splashing sounds. "Ready to swim?"

Ben's huge eyes peered down at the foot-high gush of water under the metal door.

"Yyyyyy-eeeehhhhsssssssiiiirrrr," Ben stammered without stepping forward.

Knight tossed his head back; his laughter echoed off the wet metal walls. The door slammed down. The only sound was the soft fizz of calming waves and bubbles around their feet.

And Knight's deep laughter.

"Crew *Q*!" he shouted. "How can I trust you to execute this plan when you're all standing here quaking like a bunch of pussies?"

Ben squared his shoulders. "Master Knight," he said. "What if it's somebody in the basement? Like they followin' us or somethin'."

"Stop them in their tracks," Knight said. "And follow through." He stared hard into Ben's pretty-boy face, knowing that he would snitch every detail back to his conniving brother. Who would then tell Reba, who would then tell Duke.

Don't they know I'm ten steps ahead of them and everyone else?

There was one glitch—Knight didn't know where Duke was staying. The Barriors had followed Reba to The Suites downtown hotel, and even identified Duke's room. But when they busted in to take care of him and eliminate this need for Plan *Q* altogether, the Barriors found the room abandoned.

All they found were a used, broken condom on the disheveled bed; some bloody bandages in the bathroom; a clump of long, brown-haired weave that was the same color as Reba's ponytail; and a raggedy, extra-large white T-shirt similar to the one that Duke was wearing when Knight shot him. Except this one was not bloody or ripped.

The Barriors had reported back that fresh funk and sex vapors hung heavily in the warm air, so it was clear that Duke and a now-infected female had just fled.

We'll find him. Quickly.

But Plan *Q* would still be in effect. Just in case the likes of Shar Miller and other conspirators had any bad ideas about claiming the millions in cash that would be on the premises the night of The Games.

"Now, assuming that you do not get the star signal, and everything is going smoothly," Knight said, "I'm dividing you into driving teams for the drop."

The men and women nodded.

"When Ping and Pong make the drop in Hummer One," Knight said, "we'll have three decoy vehicles. Three other black armored Hummers will take separate routes: one to the vault at HQ; another to a boat downriver; and the third to the warehouse."

The warehouse owned by Jamal, who by then would be the rightful owner of Babylon.

But these turncoat backstabbers didn't need to know that. Nobody did.

Until I'm gone with my Queen and little Prince.

Knight's insides smiled while his face maintained a serious expression. He and The Queen had decided that they would name their son after Knight's older brother, who had died early in Babylon's creation. But Prince would live a life far away from the violent streets, gunfire, and turf wars that had claimed his uncle. On their island paradise, Prince would study and smile and play and prepare for a life of greatness. The best tutors and discreet, international travel would prepare this boy to become a prophet to help all people unite over lines of race, religion, class, and culture.

Our Prince of Peace.

The night before, Knight and The Queen had thought, then said exactly those words, "Our Prince of Peace," at the same time. Their simultaneous thoughts and spoken words were so sudden and supernatural, they both gasped and stared wide-eyed into each other's ecstatic faces.

Now, suddenly Knight felt warm inside. The Queen was thinking the same thing, feeling the same amazing sensations. This time their soul-deep connection had transcended words.

He'd have to be careful, though, so she didn't get any hunches about his real plans for their wedding night and the rest of their lives.

"This information does not leave the confines of these slimy walls, except in your heads," Knight commanded. "Does everybody hear me?"

A Barrior named Deuce stepped forward with a grim expression. "Master Knight," he said softly, "I cain't swim. I need a reassignment up in The Playhouse, or I'll drown in a Motor City minute."

Knight glared at him, not just because the cat just used one of Li'l Tut's favorite references for time.

"All of you took rigorous swimming tests as part of Boot Camp," Knight said with an accusatory tone. He nodded at Pong, who stepped close to the cat. "If you somehow cheated, give me the name of the Sergeant who helped you commit fraud against Babylon."

The Barrior squealed like a girl. "Sir, I ain't tryin' to get nobody in trouble. I take full responsibi—"

Pong whacked him across the mouth.

"Do you realize that your cowardice could have put your fellow Barriors and B'Amazons at risk?" Knight shouted. "All of you!"

Knight's phone vibrated. *Reba* flashed on the display screen. He pushed the little silver button to put her into voicemail. Didn't that bitch remember he'd told her never to call him again? "Now everybody hit the gym," Knight ordered. "Sixty minutes of cardio kickboxing. Now!"

The phone vibrated again. *Reba*. He flipped it open. "What?" he snapped.

"I ain't tellin' you nothin' you don't already know when I say Duke tryin' to bring you down," she said with a nasal tone, like she'd been crying. "But that nasty ho playin' wit' people lives."

"Reba," Knight said calmly, "have you talked with him?"

"Yeah, 'bout how he gon' take Babylon back. But he sick. He crazy. He done gone renegade—"

"Where is he?"

"I ain't tellin' you nothin' else wit'out cuttin' a deal . . . so I can *G-T-F-O* when I need to."

SEX IN THE HOOD 2

Knight started to propose that she meet him somewhere to talk. But was this a set-up? Was she going to lure him to a remote place so that Duke could pounce on him?

She's for real, Intuition said. *Go.*

But where? He needed someplace where nobody would see them, and if prying eyes did catch a glimpse of their meeting, he'd have a legitimate explanation.

"Reba, meet me by the bar in The Garage. Fifteen minutes."

175

Chapter 21

As they stepped into the elevator and its doors closed, The Queen, CoCo, and Honey talked about plans for the dickfest that was scheduled for tonight in The Garage. Babylon would be hosting the VIP after-party for some of the country's hottest female rappers, who were giving a sold-out concert downtown.

"Make sure the bar is stocked," The Queen said as CoCo used her pink rhinestone pen to check-off tasks on her clipboard. "We need some extra Studs to walk around with bowls of condoms, hot washcloths, and bags for the wrappers."

As her mind reviewed all the tasks they had to complete that day, The Queen stared at the way Honey's tits curved up and out of the top of the Egyptian-style white dress that was the uniform for all women who worked in the Babylon offices.

A hot, swollen sensation delighted her between her legs. But Celeste was feeling something else too. Something about Knight. It was hazy and vague, like he was deliberately blocking their supernatural mind connection right now, which he seemed to be doing a lot lately so she wouldn't know what he was thinking or doing.

The stomach-flipping sensations of the descending elevator intensified this out-of-whack vibe that she didn't like. At all. She had to figure out what the hell was causing this, so she could squash that shit. With all the work they had to do, the last thing she needed was this distraction.

I'll call him . . . Naw . . .

Calling Knight when this happened always proved pointless. If he didn't answer his cell phone, that first click of his recorded message would send her thoughts packing on a paranoid mind trip. If he did answer, he would always give a perfect account of what he was doing, and that would only make her more suspicious.

The way that Reba "ho" had been acting lately, even having the "bitchitude" to rub her ass against Knight in the Board meeting, well who knew how bold that Slut would get if she got him alone?

176

SEX IN THE HOOD 2

It didn't help that some of the girls had been talking in the gym about how every man likes to get some extra pussy before he ties the knot. No matter how pretty his bride was, or how much he was in love. The idea of locking down with one pussy for life was enough to make any man lose his mind in the worst way, the girls had said. And he would usually do it while blowing his nut all over any bitch who indulged him in his last-minute premarital pussy binge.

No, Knight is different. He told me he doesn't want to squander his energy or time or love on anyone except me.

The Queen was sure that, because of their psychic love connection, she would know if he even kissed another chick. She would feel it in her bones, her heart, her pussy.

But deep down, it wasn't that she thought he was fucking around. It was more like, as Duke used to say, he was scheming. Plotting something that would affect her, but without consulting her first. Like she was a little girl. Didn't he know that in the game of chess, The Queen had much more power than the Knight? If they truly were a team, working as partners to make Babylon all that it could be, then she needed to contribute to any and every decision and plan.

"Queen," CoCo said, "come back to Babylon. You lost in outer space."

The Queen shook her head to focus her thoughts back on that night's party. "The last time Emcee Sexarella and her crew were up in here," she said, "they wore the Studs out. These girls some crazy nymphomaniac bitches. So I want extra Barriors and B'Amazons on hand to keep they shit in check."

CoCo nodded. "I have here that she ordered fifty Sluts as well."

The Queen smiled. "Yeah, the freaky bitch."

As the elevator hummed past the VIP balcony, The Queen noticed how the recessed lighting cast a soft glow around her and her inner circle. "Hey, y'aw', look." The Queen smiled and motioned for them to turn and face the mirror next to the row of elevator buttons. "Check us out. Fine, fabulous an' runnin' the shit!"

WHITE CHOCOLATE

The Queen loved the sense of camaraderie she felt with CoCo and Honey. Sometimes the three of them would sit in flannel pajamas up in The Penthouse, pop some corn, and watch corny romantic comedies on the huge, flat-screen TV in her and Knight's home theatre. Other times, they'd hit the upscale Somerset Collection to shop, go to the Nordstrom Spa and have lunch at P.F. Chang's. And they always worked out together in the Babylon gym for sexercise, exotic dance lessons, and cardio and strength training.

"Friends for life," Coco said, taking both their hands.

The Queen smiled. When she had first come to Babylon, it had taken her awhile to feel this kind of girlfriendly vibe with anyone in the wake of grief, shock, and Tiffany's betrayal. She'd gotten right down to business with CoCo. And even though she and Honey had hit it off on the sex tip—in fact Honey was The Queen's first girl—that had been all physical.

"Oh, before I forget," The Queen said with a gushing, chick-chat cadence, "we gotta meet wit' the seamstress after this up in The Penthouse."

CoCo nodded. "I told her to bring your veil and our shoes and purses. This is the final fitting before the big day."

Honey's mocha-hued face beamed as she gave off a waft of brown sugar-vanilla perfume. "Queen, you inspire me so much. You got the fairy-tale hook-up we all dream about."

The Queen kissed their cheeks. "You're both livin' it too. So let's get this work done so we can play!"

The elevator doors opened onto the huge garage. Big enough to hold a football field, its ceiling was three stories high with a silver network of exposed pipes and whirring fans. Brick walls displayed airbrushed murals of ghetto fabulous city scenes in vivid cobalt blue, magenta, and bright yellow. A giant sign made from neon-blue block letters said BABYLYN across the left wall.

"I remember the first time I saw this," The Queen said, leading them onto the silver floor, which was made of metal tire-tread. "Duke had me in his Porsche and we rolled up in here. Felt like I was on a movie set. Unreal."

SEX IN THE HOOD 2

So was this annoying-ass feeling in her gut about Knight. Was he all right?

Knight, baby, talk to me.

All she heard was the tapping of their heels on the floor as they walked quickly past rows and rows of Navigators, Hummers, and Escalades. On raised platforms, a red H2, a gold Lamborghini, and a baby blue Bentley sparkled like new.

In a matter of hours, every inch of this giant space would be "orgified" with hundreds of girl rappers, their groupies, and as many Studs fucking them up, down, and sideways. Sitting on top of cars, bending over the bar, twisting up on the plush cobalt blue couches situated in cozy seating areas, and on the stage.

"Where the hell are the cages?" The Queen demanded as she pointed to the huge, black stage that was framed by towering speakers. "Emcee Sexarella specifically ordered four cages, two on the stage, two on raised platforms, with dancing Studs inside."

CoCo checked her clipboard. "The cages are scheduled for installment within the hour." She pointed to a bed that was the size of a boxing ring, sitting in the center of the stage. "The crew set up the bed first."

The Queen turned toward the far corner, which looked like a nightclub with a long bar and sleek silver stools. Silver poles extended up from the bar, so that strippers could pop their asses in dudes' faces as they sipped Hennessy and Moet.

"Make sure they stock the bar with all the girl drink supplies." The Queen scanned the glass shelves holding hundreds of bottles of booze and glasses. "Emcee Sexarella only drinks shit that's blue, but her crew loves them green-apple cosmopolitans."

"MMMmm," Honey said. "Me too. I personally made sure this morning that we've got extra cases of the mix. And the bartenders know how to mix 'em just right." Her nipples hardened and poked through the front of her dress. "I'll never forget the party she had last year when she had those four Studs fuck her so long, one of them *passed out.*"

CoCo laughed, but The Queen stiffened.

179

Could Knight be passed out somewhere right now?

A low rumble echoed through The Garage; that sound underscored The Queen's worries. Blinding sunshine poured in as the huge metal door rose.

Knight, baby, how come the telepathic shit don't work when I'm stressin'?

Celeste answered, *Relax. He's handling business.*

"Babylon!" The deep chorus of many voices boomed into the huge, hollow space. Their cadence made it sound like a military chant as they exclaimed "Baby*lon!*" with a proud upward swing at the end, like U.S. military leaders bark, "Atten*tion!*"

The Queen, CoCo, and Honey turned to watch part of the Army file in with a gust of strength and sex power that was so strong, every tiny hair on The Queen's body stood on end.

"Damn, that's sexy as hell," The Queen whispered as CoCo and Honey watched with open mouths.

Jogging toward them were four columns of twelve shirtless men in black-white-gray camouflage pants. Their black combat boots hit the floor in unison to create a powerful rhythm. In fact, it sounded so hype, The Queen had Jamal record it and use it in one of the tracks on the *Dick Chicks Party Mix* album, in the song "Bangin' Babylon Boys."

Their bare chests glistened with sweat over their pumped-up muscles. A BABYLON tattoo marked each of their left pecs over their hearts. Their skin formed a breathtaking mosaic of the human spectrum: jet black, cinnamon, nutmeg, oatmeal, redwood, cocoa, and cream as white as The Queen used to be. Their hair showcased every color and texture imaginable: waves and ringlet curls pulled back in ponytails; huge, wild afros; braids of every length; bald domes shining with sweat; and sexy fades.

The Queen shivered. These were Barriors, whose work was strictly security. But Babylon was growing so fast, she was recruiting many of them to work as Studs as well. And every one of them looked qualified to offer "secret service" on the most personal level.

SEX IN THE HOOD 2

A hot sheen of sweat prickled on The Queen's skin, from her long hair that was pulled back in a ponytail, under her wispy, Egyptian-style camisole and under her snug jeans. She wanted to peel them off and rub Celeste right now. But she had work to do.

She checked out the sexy contours of the men's broad backs as they marched up the staircase in the far corner, making their way to the gym. That valley of muscle around a man's spine was so damn sexy, she just gawked at the marvels of the male anatomy.

And no man's back was as beautiful as Knight's. The velvet black skin stretched without a single blemish over his shoulder blades, down the *V*-shape of his back. It sloped from the curving hills of his back muscles down into that valley of his strong spine, which all teased the eye toward his perfect ass. Yeah, his glutes were round, rock-hard, and baby soft, all at once.

I'm gonna call him right now to come fuck me on that giant bed on stage.

The Queen reached for her cell phone clipped to her belt loop.

Do your work first, Celeste ordered.

But something didn't feel right. A bad vibe about Knight was cramping her gut.

"Babylon!" a female chorus chanted over and over as the B'Amazons marched into the garage. Also sporting fatigues and boots, they wore tank tops and bras.

"Poetry in motion," CoCo said with an awe-struck tone. "The first time I saw this I almost came on myself 'cause I kept thinkin' about the male soldiers getting with the female soldiers and—"

"Huuu-uuut!" a deep female voice called.

This cornucopia of women was so beautiful with their sexy-sweaty-shiny skin that ranged from pinky white to black satin. In shades of black, brown, red, and silver, their braids, ponytails, naturals, and perms bounced over their muscle-pumped shoulders.

They radiated an aura of womanpower so strong that The Queen wished she could bottle it and hand it out to every girl on the planet, so that no matter how society or her mother or her abusive boyfriend or sexist husband or boss made her feel she wasn't good enough, she could take a swig of this and feel like Superwoman in an instant.

That was the power of Babylon, which was tattooed on the women's chiseled biceps. They followed the men up the stairs. Not far from them, a circular staircase led up to the VIP Balcony.

"Honey," The Queen said, "make sure they got buckets for jimmy wrappers up there. And ashtrays. The kitchen knows Sexarella ordered the seafood buffet for the balcony, while folks down here'll have to grub on chicken wings and pizza."

The silver rail along the balcony lounge reminded The Queen of the night that Babylon welcomed her during Duke's birthday party. She'd spat a rhyme about her "fade to black," and they had loved it. Then, sitting in their golden thrones, she had enjoyed psychedelic sex with Baby Blue and Duke, until Knight walked in and seized control.

Where the hell was Knight now?

She did a 180 to face the row of doors in the wall leading out from the bar. "CoCo, make sure they locked those doors. We don't need nobody fuckin' in the supply rooms and offices—"

An ear-splitting siren blared.

"Oh my God!" The Queen shouted. She cupped her palms over her ears as the noise echoed horribly off the floor and walls of The Garage.

"It's a test of the alarm system," CoCo shouted.

The Queen read her lips because it was impossible to hear her.

"Gotta check it for The Games."

The siren amped up that vibe that something wasn't right with Knight. How long would that noise last? She, CoCo, and Honey stood covering their ears, looking around.

Knight, where are you?!

SEX IN THE HOOD 2

The Queen wanted to phone Paul and tell him, "Yes, the alarm works in The Garage—now turn that shit off!" But he'd never hear her over the phone, so she looked around helplessly. She noticed that one of the office doors was opening.

And out stepped Knight with Reba.

Chapter 22

The crimson velvet couches inside one of D-town's hottest nightclubs set the perfect tone for Duke to hold this first meeting with the leaders of his coup. Up here in the VIP lounge, with its sexy Moroccan-style décor, Duke took a minute to congratulate himself. Because downstairs in the many private rooms and lounges and dance bar areas of the club, the first pussy party thrown by Oz was in full effect. And the folks who would rake in all that bank were sitting right here before the young wizard of their new Emerald City.

"How e'rybody feel tonight?" Duke asked, raising his crystal flute as butt-naked waitresses poured Cristal for him and his new crew. Timbo was staying hard at the idea that Duke was in another world, one very different from the crack houses where he'd puffed away his troubles.

The Duke back to rule like the king that I am.

The light of low-hanging, fringed red lamps cast a sexy pink glow over the waitresses' asses and titties as they walked on clear spike heels to pour bubbly for everybody: Shar Miller with her Stud and Baby Blue, Leroy Lewis, Raynard "Dickman" Ingalls, Red, Marco and Liam Moreno with that big black bodyguard, their white local operations managers, B-Boy and Birdie, the Stud Antoine, and Duke's lady, Reba Sheba.

She'd been one crazy bitch after that condom broke, until Duke had shown her the HIV negative reading on his doctored-up sex health card. He knew he was putting her life at risk. In fact, he had probably already assigned her a date with death as his HIV virus took up residence up in her fat pussy.

But a gold-digging ho always got what she deserved. He was using her just like she was using him, and they'd both get their due in the end. Plus, her days were numbered anyway, because she'd get tossed out like yesterday's meat scraps once he got his Duchess back.

But I ain't gonna stop fuckin' in the interim.

Since Doc Reynolds had gotten him all that medication and he'd been eating better, his skin was clearing up and he was putting on a little weight. Just like Magic. At twenty-one, Duke was already middle-aged for a brotha from the hood. So if he lived another ten, twenty, or thirty years on the HIV drugs, he'd be doing better than a lot of other muthafuckas he knew.

Plus, whoever he infected—whether Reba Sheba or even his Duchess—their status would keep them together in life and in death.

I won't have to worry about her givin' my fortune to some otha nigga after I go, 'cause she'll go wit' me.

Duke suddenly stood taller and felt stronger than he had in a year. Even the constant ache of his healing bullet wounds subsided. He suddenly felt ridiculously powerful and invincible. This was his destiny—to rule like a king. And if he had to knock off his brother and steal his lady back to do that, then so be it.

And so it is written, and so it is done.

It would be done in just a few weeks.

"Here's a toast to the zillions we gon' make from D-town to aroun' the world," Duke said, raising his glass. "Bigger an' better an' bolder than Babylon."

Glasses clinked as everybody toasted each other.

"Now, we gon' talk bidness for a hot minute to make sure we all on point for the night of The Games when the real shit go down. Then we gon' celebrate."

Something in Moreno's eyes still didn't feel right. Yeah, this was honor among thieves. And yeah, Moreno had the overseas contacts and expertise to handle the bank accounts where they'd deposit the millions from The Games. But Duke had to find some leverage to wield over Moreno's sneaky ass.

Let that muthafucka know The Duke don't play.

The funky electric beat from the party downstairs was loud enough in there to get several folks bobbing their heads. And not just in the dancing way.

Three of the waitresses were already on their knees in front of the Moreno triplets. Their pretty asses aimed back at Duke as they sucked dick.

"I said we'd party after we talk bidness," Duke said loudly.

"We heard you," Red said, smiling and squinting behind the smoke of a Cohiba cigar. "Talk on, my brother. I am very gifted with the ability to multi-task."

Duke stared back at him with a look that said, *I don't like that shit one bit.* But that night he'd let it slide.

Moreno kept a hard stare on Duke as the chick's head rose and fell in his lap. His feet were wide apart on the crimson carpet as her suntanned body rested between his legs.

"Now," Duke said. "We gotta han'le the logistics of the money drops. Antoine, tell us what you know."

Wearing denim overalls with no shirt, Antoine stood and shared everything that Ben had heard in the tunnel when Knight explained how they'd deliver the loot by boat.

"Who gon' be at the vault wit' you?" Duke asked.

"He ain't tol' us yet," Antoine said, "but Crew Q got a meetin' in a couple days. Then I'll know."

"Cool," Duke said. "Shar, you in charge of—"

She was following Moreno's bad example. Her Stud, who never seemed to wear a shirt, was kneeling on the floor in front of her, eating her pussy. Her red patent leather pumps rested on his wide, muscular back, with her knees and skinny calves curved over his shoulders. She'd come in wearing a black dress but now it must have been hoisted up around her waist, because her legs were bare.

Naw, her dress was off entirely, because Baby Blue was sitting next to her, licking all over her titties. Damn they still looked good for her age—high, round, and full—with nipples as excited as a teenager.

"Transportation," she said, opening her eyes. "Here's a list of the vehicles and boats, the drivers and their cell phone numbers, their locations and their projected pick-up times."

Baby Blue turned forward without closing her mouth. She bent down and pulled a folder from the black leather briefcase beside the Stud's hip. Then Baby Blue stood. She was wearing the same kind of crocheted bikini top that she'd worn when Duchess had eaten her pussy so good at Duke's twenty-first birthday party a year ago. The night that Duke had fallen from on top of the world down to Hell in a Motor City minute.

186

Now he wanted to suck on Baby Blue's fat clit to recapture the magic of that night, by putting his mouth where Duchess' lips had been.

On shimmery blue sandals, she strutted forward and handed the folder to Duke. Her matching blue crocheted skirt wrapped around her hips and revealed a thong bikini underneath.

He rested his huge hand on her hip.

"Sorry, Massa Duke," she said, casting a tender gaze down at him. "I don't like dick no more. Yo' girl turnt me out at yo' birfday party. I ain't fucked no dick on my own time since she made me cum like it was a lightnin' storm between my legs."

"Quit clownin'!" Duke said. "Girl, you used to beg me for a beat-down wit' Timbo. An' I saw you suckin' Red's dick in the limo."

"That was work, baby; this pleasure." She smiled then pivoted so that her booty was in his face. Smooth patches of skin peeked out from her round, tight ass under the blue, knitted fabric. She walked back to the couch. Real quick, she let the crocheted skirt fall to the floor. She pulled strings at the side of her thong, so it fell too. Her ass bare, she extended one long leg around Shar's head then put both knees over the back of the couch and over Shar's shoulders. And she ground her pussy into Shar's mouth.

"Da-yum," Duke exclaimed. "She ain't lyin'." Now Shar was hidden by bodies, except for her lower legs and feet over the Stud's shoulders and her hands cupping the bottom of Baby Blue's juicy ass.

But Timbo didn't respond because Duke had business to take care of. And these nymphomaniac muthafuckas were acting like they had all damn decade to make a plan for the heist.

No surprise, then, that Leroy already had a bitch in his lap too.

"Leroy!" Duke shouted. "I need a report on all the preparations you makin' for backstage during The Games."

Leroy's knees twitched. And since he had on a lavender suit that glowed pink in the soft lighting, he looked like a cotton candy muthafucka over there.

He opened his eyes and leaned his head forward from the spot where it had been resting on the back of the couch. "We all set to rig the lubricants. They gon' be burnin' like they got army ants up they pussies an' all ova they dicks. Won't be no victories for Babylon."

Duke nodded. "What about the body oils for the Sexiest Slut and Sexiest Stud contests?"

"Same deal, boss—they skin gon' be bubblin' like pork rinds. Nothin' sexy 'bout that shit."

The disgust that Duke felt inside over all these muthafuckas who couldn't hold they nut long enough to have a meeting only intensified when he checked out B-Boy and Birdie on the long, low coffee table. B-Boy's chubby ass looked like Buddha laying on his back with his big, pale belly bulging up from his open dress shirt that hung over the edges of the table. And that white skeleton on top of him with the bones for an ass, and that spine . . .

Do he think that shit be sexy? Look like that bag o' bones would bruise a brotha . . . or crack if he tried to fuck it too hard.

They were on the table at an angle where Duke could see Birdie's back. Her skinny legs were all bone, with loose skin and knobby knees.

Is she sick? Is that the "waif" look that white girls think is fashionable?

She reminded him of his first baby momma, Milan, starving herself from just-thick-enough down to skin and bones, to look like a fashion model. Duke hated the way her body had felt with bones jutting out this way and that. A sista was supposed to have some cushion, some juicy meat to squeeze and snuggle up to.

Milan's weight loss was all part of the crazy shit that had her sent down to Mexico with his closest boy, Beamer. But she'd been so good at overseeing the Sex Squad. Maybe Duke could bring them back, rescue them from that hellhole that Knight had sent them to.

And Duke was going to bring his kids back to D-town as soon as he got everything straight. And he needed all these sex-addicted muthafuckas to help him do it. Including Moreno's little helpers, that Buddha-bellied cat and his skinny-as-a-bird woman.

Duke watched in disgusted fascination as B-Boy's chubby hands gripped her bony hips and raised her up and down. The bitch probably didn't have any strength of her own.

Damn, Duke remembered that day in the Cleopatra Suite when Duchess had climbed on and taken a ride into a place that left him paralyzed and speechless. Her legs had been like pistons, pumping up and down, slamming down on his dick with relentless force and speed and stamina. Then, after she'd given herself a shuddering orgasm with her fingers working her clit while she fucked him, she'd climbed off and walked away, into the bathroom, without saying a word.

Just left me layin' there like a punked muthafucka.

Nobody had ever fucked Duke like that.

Timbo swelled. He had to get Duchess back. His plan was to wait until the night of The Games. When he had his bank back. And Babylon.

With Knight out of the way forever. Then Duke would make his move to get The Duchess. The idea of blazing his trail back up into the virgin territory that he had plundered made Timbo hard and long, and thick as a log. And he needed to saw it off now, inside the woman who was made for him. The woman he picked right off the TV screen to rule at his side into eternity.

I cain't wait. If I take her now, Knight gon' lose his mind. An' it'll be easier to take him out.

Duke stood. He would go outside where it was quiet, get with his contacts inside Babylon, find out where she was, and go take what was his. Tonight.

And so it is written. And so it is done.

But Reba rushed him. She shoved him down onto the couch and straddled his lap. She was so fast, she yanked off his belt buckle, unzipped his pants, and speared her pussy down on Timbo like she was a sweet, sticky marshmallow trying to get roasted on his fire. The sudden squeeze of her good pussy around his dick relaxed his body and his mind.

He knew where Duchess was. He'd get her. But right now, he wasn't about to let this hot twat go to waste. So he kissed his Reba Sheba and drilled up into her like he was about to strike liquid gold.

Chapter 23

The water was pitch black as Knight pretended his body was dead weight, sinking deeper and deeper into the iciness of the Detroit River. His chest felt like it would explode if he didn't suck down a breath of air. But he couldn't go up to the surface. Because he was dead. Or at least pretending to be dead, for the sake of this exercise.

Ping, in a black scuba suit and flippers, wrapped his arms around Knight and dragged him up toward the light shining from the bottom of the cigarette boat. Ping struggled to pull Knight's 6 feet, 7 inches, and 275 pounds of muscle, bone, and blood.

Nearby, Pong was having no problem pulling the 5-foot, 8-inch, 125-pound mannequin of The Queen. So he deposited her then returned to help Ping pull and lift Knight's limp body.

Finally, the brothers had pulled both Knight and The Queen up into the cigarette boat, and they sped away toward the golden lights of the Ambassador Bridge. They'd take the Detroit River to Lake Erie, where they'd transfer into a bigger boat. Then they'd sail through the Erie Canal to the Atlantic Ocean, then down to the Caribbean. Just like they would do on their wedding night, after everything played out the way that Knight had secretly scripted it, starting with the love scene. And he knew from previous conversations that The Queen would play her role perfectly, so that they could enjoy their final act together in paradise.

Everything was in place—including the decoy bride and groom who would ride away from The Playhouse in the limo and the second decorated wedding yacht. And nobody had a clue, not even The Queen.

Guilt clenched like an angry fist around his chest.

I'm tricking her, but she'll be glad I did.

Chapter 24

Trina Michaels shivered with a mischievous sense of adventure and revenge and spoke with her long-time FBI source inside her office at GNN in Washington. "Not only can I hand-deliver Victoria Winston to you," Trina said, pointing to The Queen's picture on her computer screen, "but I can lead you into the hottest prostitution ring you have to see to believe."

"I'm ready to deal." Rick Reed, a Baltimore native and former classmate from Georgetown, ran a hand over his close-cropped fade. His gold wedding band shone as he straightened his tortoise-shell glasses. In a khaki pantsuit with a white shirt and Burberry plaid tie, he sat with his legs crossed, so that one of his penny loafers almost touched Trina's bare calf. "Sounds like we can both score on this."

"Exactly." Trina scooted her chair closer to his, in front of the TV. "But I need your help."

Rick drew his thick brows together and leaned forward. His glasses magnified his light green eyes that looked bright in contrast to his round, brown face. "I'm all ears."

"Security at Babylon is like Fort Knox," she said. "They've got all these barbarian-looking guards who are armed and dangerous. Men *and* women!"

Rick nodded, letting his gaze roll down the front of Trina's navy blue dress. She had deliberately worn this today because it hugged her body just right, and pushed up her titties into two creamy brown mounds in a way that Rick could not overlook . . . just in case he needed any convincing to help her land the story of the century.

"Now," Trina said, grasping his arm, "the only obstacle I have is their super-tight security. They don't even allow cell phones into the parties. Everyone has to pass through a metal detector, even if you're naked. Can't even hide a tiny camera in there"—she pointed to her crotch—"If you know what I mean."

Rick's serious stare melted into a lusty gaze that focused on her crotch. "So what do you need from me?"

"Well, I want this to be a win-win situation for all of us. You're an ambitious man, with your sights set on advancing to the director's chair at the FBI, right?"

"That's no secret."

"If you ask me, you got robbed last time the chair was open. You deserve it."

"Why . . . thank you. Tell me more."

"Well," Trina said seductively, "I know you've been looking for a high-profile case to thrust you into the headlines. And that would help you get named and confirmed as leader of this venerable institution."

Rick leaned closer. Nodding, he ran a manicured hand over his close-cut beard. "So what do you need from me, Trina?"

"I need Rip Masta Mac."

Rick's eyes became as big as jumbo green olives. Shaking his head, he pulled off his glasses.

"Don't be surprised," Trina said, loving the power of the inside information that her super-skillful investigative reporter skills had raked up from various confidential sources.

Trina thought about The Queen, the way her kissing-fish lips and hot tongue had worked her clit with expert precision. She shifted on the chair, arched her back, and poked out her chest. Oooh, and those girls, Honey and Coco, the way they were doing each other, all that soft, pretty flesh pressing together, sending delightful tingles through their bodies . . . Trina shivered. And that made her nipples harden under the lace of her Victoria's Secret bra.

Rick's gaze fell to her chest.

"I know all about the plea bargain that you so brilliantly crafted with Rip Masta. If he testifies against MixMeister in that deadly embezzlement case that killed three innocent white people and a baby, then you'll grant complete immunity to Rip Masta and his boys. You can imagine that type of story will not garner a lot of support for Rick Reed in the hearts and minds of Congress or middle America."

Rick shook his head. His hands gripped the arms of the chair. "How'd you—"

"A great reporter has her sources," Trina said playfully. She traced his knuckles with her fingertip. "And she knows how to play them. So if you want to keep your little deal with Rip Masta secret, *and* bust wide open on the media as the force behind the capture of Victoria Winston and a raid on the wild sex underworld of Babylon—"

"What do you want?"

"Rip Masta Mac and his crew are friends with Knight and the folks at Babylon," Trina said. "The next big event there is like the sex Olympics. I heard them talking about it when I was in Detroit. It's called The Games."

"Tell me something I don't already know." Rick took her hand and put it on his crotch. A long, hard rod throbbed under the thin khaki.

"I've been there," she moaned, rising up to sit on his lap, without taking her grip off his dick. "I've seen it. Felt it. Now I want you to help me get video inside The Games, before you do the raid. But I can't go."

"Why not?"

"They know me and it sort of ended badly," Trina said. "Rip Masta Mac, however, is one guy they'll be glad to see. And he'll want to go visit his homies in the Motor City to take his mind off his legal troubles."

She stroked his dick in case his mind wasn't grasping all her ideas. "All I need you to do is to promise Rip Masta that if he gets us secret video of The Games, then you'll convince the Federal prosecutors to cut him the sweetest deal ever."

Rick's dick went limp for a minute. "I wanted an exclusive on this. I don't know if—"

She slid to her knees, dropped her face in this lap. She sucked that little spongy-soft link-sausage into her mouth, and slurped on it until it swelled into a fire-roasted jumbo bratwurst. It was like a microphone pointing at her mouth as she pulled away to speak. "Wire Rip Masta and his crew with hidden cameras. He and Knight went to school together and they're still friends. So they'll be able to get past the metal detectors. We get video, they come out, and boom!—you do your raid—story of the century for both of us."

Rick's dick swelled bigger and harder.

Trina stood and lifted up her dress, revealing a navy blue lace garter belt that held up her thigh-high stockings and no panties.

Rick's eyes glazed as he stared at her bald pussy, which was just a pull away from his dick.

Trina thought about taking a slide down on it right then. And when he gripped the sides of her hips to pull her closer, she felt dizzy with lust. But no, for once she would have some control when faced with a big, juicy dick.

"This your reward when we celebrate the fruits of our teamwork. I can write my own ticket as the hottest TV journalist in America, and you'll be director of the FBI. Deal?"

Rick stood, turned her around and bent her over her desk. He quickly rolled on a condom.

His dick slammed up into her love-starved, power-hungry pussy. "Deal," he said with a deep groan. "It's a deal, Miss Michaels."

Chapter 25

The Queen's head throbbed as relentlessly as the driving bass beat blasting through the gym. Here on the second floor of Babylon HQ, just one floor above The Garage, her entire being ached with questions about why the fuck Knight and that Slut had come strutting out of the offices in The Garage in the middle of the day.

Naw, my Knight don't want that ho, does he?

Celeste answered, *Hell no.*

But a hurricane of questions still ripped through her mind as The Queen surveyed the hundreds of beautiful bodies that were fucking in sexercise class on the red floor mats. All around them, even more men and women were pumping and sweating and cycling on silver-and-black weight machines and rows of cardio equipment. Their reflections in the mirrored walls around the huge room created optical illusions that made it feel like even more sexy bodies were flexing and sweating before her.

My world is just one wild frenzy of fucking and sexy bodies waiting in line to get fucked next. How could one man, even one as righteous and love-struck as Knight, stick with one pussy for the rest of his life in the middle of all this? Impossible.

The Queen remembered how Duke had stood right over her here in the gym and fucked two girls at once, slamming Timbo into that center-fold-gorgeous stripper, Chanel, and black-as-licorice Eboni, while The Queen and Honey were doing a clit-to-clit pussy-kiss on the mats. What man or woman could resist the mind-blowing temptation of this?

As many times as she'd seen it, The Queen still marveled every time she walked in during sexercise. On the red floor mats, rows of seventy-two men and women paired off with the chicks on top, facing the dudes' feet. And those Sluts were squatting down on all those big, hard cocks with bionic energy and enthusiasm. The men were lying flat while the women anchored their feet beside the Studs' knees. Then, without holding on to anything, the women rose up, down, up, down, over and over.

"Three minutes!" Noah stood in front of the class with a silver whistle.

The Sluts' pretty, muscular asses slammed down on the dudes' stomachs. Their titties—big, small, firm, floppy—bounced with the force of their thrusting. Tiny beads of sweat rolled between their breasts and down their muscle-toned backs. Some of them glistened with perspiration from head to toe.

The Queen glanced over at Knight as he watched the action. What was he thinking? Did he feel powerful knowing that all this is his? This all-you-can-eat buffet of fresh pussy meat was steaming 'round the clock with any flavor or variety that his appetite craved, so that when he got his fill of her now toasted-bronze white chocolate, he could spice it up with some peach or licorice or cinnamon.

Where's that Bad Bitch who had beat Brian's ass in the restaurant bathroom? I want that confidence back! Is this some whack mind trip being fueled and navigated by pregnancy hormones? I need to find an exit—now!

But watching all that raw booty in action threatened to bring back the barrage of images of Knight and Reba that had been torturing her mind. And it made that horrible feeling—*everybody turned on you eventually*—creep back into her mind like a million leeches, sucking away her faith and trust. If something was really wrong with Knight's health, besides the stress that The Queen believed was stealing his color, his breath, his strength, then what if he had decided to get as much pussy as he could before he died?

That would kill me. If he dies, I'll *die.*

The dizzying image of Knight walking through this fucking field and plucking out the juiciest bitches as his last sexy supper made The Queen's head hurt even worse.

She hardly heard CoCo, standing beside her, ticking off names and events on her clip board. "Sheila and James won the three top events at The Games last year, but"—A tender expression washed over CoCo's face—"Queen, you aw'right? We can take a break if—"

"Let's work." The Queen still wasn't showing any reaction, but she knew Knight was aware that she was all twisted up inside. Because she could hear him telepathically urging her to calm down and believe what he had just explained to her, in the elevator, that what she had just witnessed was all business, and that Reba was an important link to Li'l Tut's takeover plot.

But Duke had HIV. And if Reba was fuckin' Duke, and screwing Knight, then that three-letter death sentence would spray right up into The Queen's heart, soul, and bloodstream too.

And kill our baby.

An overwhelmingly protective urge made her every cell feel like it was exploding with rage. She wanted to march over to Knight right now as he stood beside the superstar Stud named Bam-Bam who was training for The Games. Yeah, The Queen needed to just get it out. She'd scream to that muthafucka that if he wanted her for life, he'd better put on a HAZMAT suit before he even *talked* to rank bitches like Reba.

The tangle of bodies on the mats looked like a field of ripe-for-the-picking asses, titties, and pussies of every shade, flavor, and variety. With the Sluts fucking on top, it was like the pussies were rooted to thick vines—the Studs' dicks, arms, and legs. Just like The Queen was when Knight plucked her off of Duke's dick. As if she had been the choicest berry in the basket.

The mirrors made that gyrating field of temptation feel like it stretched into eternity. It reminded her of that Beatles song that her brother loved called "Strawberry Fields Forever."

Now Knight stood about twenty feet away, touching that Slut, Pebbles, pretty arching back as she and her husband Bam-Bam did lunges. That bitch fucked other men for a living, so being married didn't make her off-limits to Knight either.

Some horrible rage bubbled up so wickedly inside The Queen, it propelled her forward, toward Knight. If he didn't act right, she'd take this rock on her hand, transfer a lot of money out of Babylon accounts and into a private one somewhere far away, and escape the insanity of this morally corrupt world of erotic abandon. She and Knight needed to live, love, and raise their baby far and away, in a safe, normal place.

Suddenly the gym felt as mind-blowingly scary and overwhelming as it had when Duke had brought her here on her first day in the hood. This fuck frenzy had inspired the turning point for her to change from horny virgin to Duke's addicted nympho . . . from frightened captive to willing participant . . . from Victoria to Duchess . . . from fugitive on the Fed's radar to a invisible "thugstress" in a ghetto underworld . . . from white to black.

Did she want all that for the little baby growing in her belly? Hell no. But was Knight crazy to think they could be a family in the middle of all this?

I've had enough. Being pregnant and raising a child in a place like this is just too dangerous.

Her feet stomped over the spongy floor. Her mind went *rat-tat-tat* with the bullet-words that she was about to shoot up at the man she thought was different from all the other lying, cheating muthafuckas of the world. Her chest rose and fell with the kind of overwhelmingly heavy breathing that helped a bitch go off. Her heart pounded.

Daddy's voice boomed through her mind. "*Anger* is only one letter away from *danger.*"

She froze as Daddy's favorite quote by Eleanor Roosevelt washed over her thoughts like a warm sedative.

Pick your battles, Celeste warned. *Give Knight the benefit of the doubt . . . 'cause your little arsenal is a BB gun compared to his mighty battalions.*

The Queen turned her back to him and quickly walked toward the locker-rooms, as if she had to pee urgently. She did, actually. Her stomach was still flat, but her bladder was working overtime; this headache was wicked, her titties felt sensitive and sore like just before her period, and her mind . . . maybe the extra hormones were giving her this paranoid whack attack.

Was this what Knight felt like when he got those panic attacks?—completely out of control of himself? I gotta get a grip.

As she stepped into the locker-room and went to the bathroom, her thoughts reeled at the disastrous outcome she would have created by riddling her beautiful fiancé with the vile words and ideas that had poisoned her mind. They had what everybody else in the world wanted. She had to do any- and everything to protect it from the fatalism of Othello-esque jealousy and paranoia.

Showing anger toward Knight here in the gym with all these witnesses who could be Duke defectors, would be dangerous. Like Reba conniving to trick Knight into thinking she could play spy, when her real goal was to seduce him and oust The Queen. Or rouse some type of gratitude in Knight that would, in her distorted mindset, make him feel obligated to succumb to her seduction. So if Reba saw or heard about an argument between The Queen and Knight, it could fuel her man-stealin' quest.

Plus, The Queen had to keep her cool as a test of wills with Knight. She had seen too many examples of women turning into jealous, suspicious bitches because they claimed to love their man so much. But ultimately their possessiveness had the opposite effect — pushing their man away, right into the conniving arms of the bitches who were trying to hook their men.

"Never let anyone see your anger," Daddy would say. "Never let 'em see you sweat or you'll lose, you can bet."

The Queen took several deep breaths. That fresh oxygen and slow breathing calmed her nerves. Then she walked back out into the gym, where Knight was watching sexercise and talking with Big Moe.

The Queen returned to CoCo, who was checking off names on her clipboard.

"With training like this," CoCo said, "Babylon will win every event in The Games, hands down. Check out Bam-Bam and Pebbles." CoCo nodded toward the muscular couple as they held dumbbells in each hand and did multiple sets of lunges. They both grimaced because that shit hurt when you extended one foot forward then lowered your other knee to the floor over and over.

Lunges were part of The Queen's regimen to help her fuck on top longer. Even though the exercise made her thighs and her booty muscles burn like hell, they raised endurance and the pain threshold so a sista could pump on top forever and a day.

Bam-Bam cast a loving glance at Pebbles as sweat poured down their temples and their pulses throbbed in their neck veins.

CoCo smiled. "Check out the champs. Pebbles and Bam-Bam are the projected winners of the top three events. Longest Fuck, Longest Slut on Top, and Longest One-Knee Stud Fuck."

Now that The Queen had calmed down, her perception of Pebbles and Bam-Bam was different. They looked like a loving couple who was working hard to master their craft.

Just like me and Knight.

The Queen shivered. "Love that."

Yeah, she loved to watch Pebbles and Bam-Bam in action because they reminded her of herself with Knight. And the reason the husband-wife team always won any competition was because they weren't just screwing. Not only did they have tremendous athletic skill, but they were really in love. And that passion helped them perform on stage in the fucking events like no other. Not just performing feats of athletic exoticism, as the Sluts were doing right now as they continued to slam down on all those penises.

This pussy power was what made the Sluts of Babylon the best in the business. A man could lay back and never flex a muscle—and still get the fuck of his life—because these bionic beauties were getting trained like Olympic athletes.

The Queen, who took private lessons with Lee Lee, had built up her endurance so that she could fuck on top all night long. And Knight loved it.

But could a Slut who'd been doing this for years do it even better? Did Reba know tricks that The Queen was unaware of? Could an all-black sista from the hood please an African god like Knight in ways that a half-white chick who was raised in the suburbs would never understand? Did Knight love The Queen for her brains and beauty but still crave a 'round-the-way girl for her raw lust and common black, from-the-hood background?

"Look like you lovin' that shit or you out," Noah shouted down on one of the women who looked like it hurt like hell.

The Slut named Peaches had an orange-brown 'fro pulled back from her peachy, freckled face with rhinestone barrettes. Her dewy face (she couldn't have been older than The Queen's nineteen years) twisted into a scowl. She gripped her quads as if they'd bust open if she didn't stop the pumping motion.

Peaches bit down on her bottom lip in a way that could be construed as an expression of pleasure. And she pumped and pumped some more.

The whistle blew. Noah shouted, "Okay, ladies, on your knees!"

Relief washed over the women's faces. Like gymnasts doing somersaults, the chicks curled their bodies forward, pressing their palms and knees to the mats. Straddling the men's legs at their shins, the women poised their pretty asses in the air. Meanwhile, the men rose up into kneeling positions.

"Love that shit," The Queen said, ogling rows and rows of giant penises, rows of them in every color and all covered with condoms, pointed at all the beautiful, sweat-glossed asses. It looked like the men were about to drill doggie-style.

"On the right!" Noah shouted.

The men lifted their left legs to a 45-degree angle from their bodies, so they were balancing on their right legs only. That made The Queen think of the Golden Labrador Retriever she had while growing up at her family's mansion, Winston Hill. When Mister Brady had to pee, he would raise one leg up toward a tree and balance on the other. That's what she saw now, as a rainbow of testicles hung behind big beige, brown and black dicks.

"Gentlemen, three minutes." Noah blew the whistle.

The men thrust forward in perfect unison and rhythm to the deep bass beat. With tremendous strength and endurance, they banged and bucked and fucked, all while balancing on one knee. Every muscle fiber in their long hamstrings and quads flexed under a sexy sheen of sweat.

The Queen felt dizzy. Her pussy creamed. And all that lust melted away her headache. Maybe it was the pregnancy hormones again, but Celeste felt swollen and wet and heavy, like she had a hot, sixteen-ounce Porterhouse steak rolled up in her thong. She ached for Knight to chew on it, suck the juice out, pummel it with his giant meat-tenderizing hammer.

They'd made love this morning, and Knight had loved how sloppy-wet her pussy stayed these days. If it weren't for the psycho thoughts and sore nipples and headaches, this turbo-charged libido was enough to make a bitch stay pregnant for life.

The stories she'd heard about morning sickness—on top of the paralyzing anxiety about raising an innocent, defenseless baby in this big, bad world that had treated The Queen so horribly—was enough to make her want to get back on the pill, get her tubes tied or get a hysterectomy altogether. That way she'd only have to run the terrifying gauntlet of motherhood once.

Will Baby Prince get the curse? Will it kill his Mama or his Daddy before he even knows our names?

Noah's whistle blew. He shouted, "Switch!"

The men shifted to the opposite knee and fucked away, grunting and sweating.

I need that now.

The Queen shivered with the need to shove her fingers down her pants and rub out the fire that was so hot it would singe her pussy hair if she had any. Damn, it seemed like she couldn't go sixty seconds without craving some fingers or a tongue or a dick to take care of that hot, hungry throb between her legs.

Who wouldn't, in the middle of sexercise? After all, this was the scene of the crime where Duke buttered her up to pop her cherry just hours after meeting her. One look at all those rows and rows of nude bodies practicing sex squats and thrusting, and sweet little virginal Victoria was ripe for his plucking.

She'd been so afraid that by breaking her vow to never lose her virginity or unleash her mixed-race sex curse, that she'd kill herself or Duke in the process. But then while making love for the first time, she'd heard her mother's voice telling her *This is the power—use it to get whatever you want in life— Pussy power.*

And here she was. Loving her life by putting pussy power— hers and all these other women's—to good use. And she could do it for the rest of her life with Knight. Or could she?

The Queen shook her head, wishing her confidence and self-assured thinking would return immediately. She had to look into Knight's sparkling onyx eyes and feel his love and tap into this cool intelligence. That would reset the reading on her mental mechanisms back into the red Bad Bitch zone.

Knight's back was turned to her as he talked with Noah and surveyed the class. But why were his shoulders moving up and down like that? The Queen hurried over the pathway between the cardio machines and the mats. Knight looked up at her reflection in the mirror as she approached.

No!

He looked gray. He was breathing quickly and holding his chest with one hand.

The curse.

She stepped toward him.

"Excuse me, man," Knight said to Noah, who nodded.

The Queen walked him to the men's locker-room. She pushed through the white door. She guided him to a long bench.

As he held his chest and struggled to breath she sat beside him, stroking his back. "Knight, baby, what is wrong?"

He was looking down.

"Knight?"

He turned slightly.

She gasped at the expression in his eyes—fear.

Something is wrong with me, Baby Girl.

What can I do?

Love me. Trust me.

I am. I do.

See me through the wedding and The Games and we'll be all right, Baby Girl.

"Breathe," she whispered. "All the tests turned out normal at the doctor. It's just panic attacks. So attack it back. Say, 'I am a warrior. I am a warrior. I am a warrior.'"

Knight sat up straight. He inhaled deeply, making his broad shoulders rise and fall.

"There you go," she whispered as he gripped her hands in his trembling fingers. "I am a warrior."

The Queen had researched panic attacks a.k.a anxiety attacks on the Internet. Turned out, they could make somebody feel like they were having a heart attack: squeezing chest, struggling to breathe, racing thoughts of doom. Some people fainted. And others rushed to the hospital fearing they were about to have cardiac arrest and drop dead. But it was just a reaction to stress. Or a person allowing stress to take hold of the mind and body like this.

What The Queen didn't understand was how a person like Knight—who meditated and carried himself with cool, calm confidence at all times, and practiced positive affirmations—could allow himself to fall victim to this invisible beast called stress.

Was it PTSD—Post Traumatic Stress Syndrome—sparked by his unjust conviction and even more injurious imprisonment when he was innocent? Knight didn't rape that white girl who had the hots for him; her brothers railroaded him, with the help of the court system, with false accusations that were finally revealed. Yeah—two and a half years after the bars slammed down on Knight's life.

"Knight is a warrior," she whispered in a soft lullaby mantra. Her hand stroked gentle circles on his back. "My Knight baby is an African god warrior." Her mind spun in an effort to make sense of this. A panicky feeling burned in her gut, too. Because what if something was seriously wrong with Knight and the doctor's tests just hadn't found it? What if he were to just mysteriously drop dead? What would she do? Where would she go?

Naw, that ain't an option. I gotta heal him. Now.

"Knight, baby?"

"Yeah, Baby Girl."

"You know that Psalm you love so much?—'Weeping may endure for a night, but joy cometh in the morning'?"

Knight nodded.

"Well, I believe that this, whatever it is, this weeping may endure for my Knight, for a minute, but joy is about to *cumeth* in the morning, in our favorite way." She let out a sexy laugh as she realized her play on words. "But seriously, let's make like the morning is now. The weeping is over. We got each otha, to the infinity. We can't waste another minute feelin' anything less than hype in love and all we got."

Knight's beautiful onyx eyes sparkled back at her. He pulled her into his arms and held her like she was a swaddled infant. With her behind on his lap, he wrapped his arms around her and cupped his giant hands around hers, her cheek resting on his shoulder. "Baby Girl," he whispered softly but happily, "thank you."

She smiled slightly, staring up into the black jewels that were his eyes. "For what?"

"For loving me for me. For letting me let my guard down and show that I ain't perfect. For loving me even more when I hurt."

The tenderness in his glassy eyes made The Queen's throat burn. His face blurred as hot tears stung her eyes. All those ridiculous, paranoid thoughts about Reba dissolved under the intense heat of this karmic connection with her soul mate. All that internal drama she'd just experienced about Knight plucking a new Slut from the luscious fields of Babylon . . . all that dissipated under his loving gaze too.

She squeezed out the tears and stared deep into his eyes. "I love you to the infinity," she whispered, knowing that there would be no life for her without this other half of her soul.

"Love you to the infinity," they said in unison.

But worry still burned deep down in The Queen's gut.

Somethin' ain't right with my Knight I gotta fight to delight him for our wedding night... find a cure that will for sure endure and lure his pure power back into play so we may stay together forever and a day . . . there's no other way if I may say . . . I am The Queen, this is my Knight, and I'm gon' make him right.

Chapter 26

Knight led Jamal into the silent, empty auditorium, which filled the entire first and second floors of The Playhouse. In just a few weeks, it would be packed to capacity for The Games. That was also the time that they would do the multi-million-dollar buyout for Jamal to take charge of Babylon, so Knight could flee into the safety and security of a tropical eternity with his Queen and their Baby Prince.

Manifest Destiny is so close, I can taste the fresh-cut pineapple that I'm gon' feed into my Baby Girl's hungry mouth on the beach . . .

But right now, Knight needed to stop Jamal's second thoughts in their tracks. He also needed to let Jamal know that conspiring with the likes of Raynard "Dickman" Ingalls—who was on Li'l Tut's payroll—was a good way to follow in the bullet-riddled footsteps of a whole lot of dead musical geniuses.

After he knocked some sense back into Jamal's dreadlocked head, Knight still believed that this trusted friend was the only man who could take over the reins of his urban empire in a way that would continue its goodwill endeavors.

"A thousand seats on this level," Knight said as they walked down the purple-carpeted aisle. "Plus, the balconies and the box seats, and we'll have two thousand."

Knight stared hard down into Jamal's eyes. "You hear me, man?—Ten grand a seat, times two thousand people—Do the math. And the other folks payin' five-*K*-a-head to swim, dance, and party in this building during The Games. That's ridiculous bank for one night."

"But you gon' take the admissions money," Jamal said.

"Just this year. Next year it's all yours."

"Dig that," Jamal said. "Yo, dog, if I bail, how come you cain't fin' somebody else to buy Babylon? Like Mr. and Mrs. Marx out west, or even Moreno."

Knight stared down at Jamal, who was framed by the ornate gold figures carved into the balconies. "Jamal, it's not

207

about the money; it's about the principle. I need to know that for the next fifty years, at least, proceeds from Babylon will continue to feed and shelter children in the village I've adopted in the Sudan, and fund college scholarships for twelve graduates of Detroit public schools every year."

Jamal shoved his hands in the pockets of his baggy jeans. "This my beef wit' it—All my bidnesses legit, right?—I'm wonderin' why I wanna take on somethin' that could bring me down?"

Knight's chest squeezed. His mind lurched forward to the moment of transfer, of money and ownership, just minutes before he and The Queen would execute the exit plan. If Jamal reneged at that moment, or didn't show up, or acted wishy-washy, it could jeopardize Knight's entire strategy.

No! I see him the night of The Games, on the yacht, transferring the $25 million into my account, as I give him the keys and papers to take over.

For now, Knight would keep it diplomatic. But if Jamal persisted like this, Knight would have to go ghetto on the young brotha. Yeah, he'd remind that muthafucka where he came from and who *made* his music mogul ass.

"Every detail will be in place for you to take over once I'm gone," Knight said.

"Coo'," Jamal said. "Man, this some hype shit you 'bout to do. Bad as I think I am, I don't know if I could do it. 'Specially if my lady don't have a clue."

Tiny needles of pain shot around Knight's heart—Guilt.

"Yo' dog, you ain't worried yo' lady gon' be so pissed, she gon' kill yo' ass right there on the beach? Like, 'What the fuck you mean, nigga, we ain't goin' back?' Damn, between that an' Duke, no wonder you be lookin' so pale lately."

"No sleep," Knight said coolly. "I been workin' twenty-four/seven. It's a lot of work planning a Houdini act and running an empire at the same time."

Jamal shook his head. "See, I'm worried that runnin' Babylon will jack my music vibe. I don't know, dog. I'm still havin' second thoughts. Gimme a minute to think. I worked so hard to build up what I got—a music business. I ain't no pimp."

"We don't use that term at Babylon; we're far and above that gritty, degrading image for both black men and women. We don't even say prostitute. We provide a much-needed service that creates win-win situations for all parties."

Jamal laughed, making his long dreads shift over his shoulders. "You make it sound so professional."

"It is. The security company is a legitimate front. You know our Barriors and B'Amazons provide protection for your concerts all over the country. Plus sporting events and political gatherings."

Jamal shrugged. "It sound sexy as hell to rule ova Babylon. But music be my numba one—"

"I have directors in place for every city to handle the day-to-day operations. You, your name, and Bang Squad Incorporated will be well insulated from any risk involved in Babylon's main source of revenue."

Jamal nodded. "Dang, dog! You be spittin' some big words dese days. Yo' Queen daddy blood mus' be rubbin' off some white-boy speech lessons."

That "white boy" comment flipped a switch inside Knight's brain from the blue zone labeled DIPLOMATIC into the yellow zone marked PISSED OFF. Knight resented the commonly held belief among too many of his people that speaking correct English meant acting white. He was bilingual—he spoke Ebonics when necessary and proper English when appropriate—and that had nothing to do with his racial allegiance. But that was a debate for Jamal on another day.

Knight put his hand on Jamal's shoulder. "The best thing about this deal is that you'll be the figurehead who makes the most money."

"Yo, dog, say it all like that an' I'm all in." Jamal scanned the wide, shiny pine stage. "Where the judges gon' sit?"

Knight extended his arm over the purple velvet seats. He pointed to the empty space between the stage and the arc of bolted-down chairs. "Up there, at a long table, we'll have security stationed across the front of the stage. And undercover everywhere else."

After a quick tour of the dressing rooms backstage and downstairs, and a glance at where the deejay would spin the tunes for each routine, Knight led Jamal up the stairs to one of the plush box seats overlooking the stage.

"The Queen and I will be here until eleven forty-five," Knight said as they sat on a purple velvet couch in the box closest to the right side of the stage. "You'll be in the next box." Knight pointed to the balcony-like seating area to their left. "At eleven forty-seven, you slip back into these curtains with us, and I hand it all over to you."

"Check," Jamal said. Something in his eyes glinted in a way that kept Knight's suspicion running high. As if Jamal were going through the motions of this conversation with no intention of following through.

Did Jamal think that if his punk-ass disappeared when the deal was to go down that Knight would carry on and "Houdini" himself and The Queen away regardless?

Jamal's eyes looked a million miles away as he said, "An' you got e'rythang set in case it's mutiny in the ranks?"

Knight stared back hard. "Everything is set."

"Yo, dog, what about Duke? Y'all's search an' destroy mission accomplished yet? I don't want no shit—"

"I guarantee," Knight said with a sinister chuckle, "there won't be any."

Jamal stiffened. His eyes grew a little bigger. "Well where that Duke muthafucka at? I want that shit done now. He crazy as hell. I ain't takin' ova, 'less I know e'rythang runnin' smoov."

"We're watching him."

Thanks to Reba, Knight was monitoring Li'l Tut's every move. Knight knew that Moreno, Shar, Raynard, and Leroy were all conspiring with his brother. What he didn't know yet was whether Reba was telling him the truth about what that "motley crew" was actually planning to do. Were they plotting to start their own sex empire? Seize Babylon? Or both?

"What you fin' out?" Jamal asked in a way that pushed Knight's mental mad meter into the red zone marked RENEGADE.

Knight's fist shot out with lightning speed and grabbed the collar of Jamal's white tee, twisted it up against his Adam's apple. Raised that muthafucka an inch or two off the floor and looked down in his eyes with six-gun brutality in his stare. "Jamal, tell me straight up," Knight groaned through tight lips. "Who'd your punk ass come to when you needed bank to start the Bang Squad?"

Jamal's eyes bugged. "You."

Knight twisted his shirt harder and shook him.

"You and Prince and Duke."

"Who gave you the money?"

"You an' Prince. Duke didn't want to—"

"Nice." Knight loosened his grip.

Jamal exhaled with relief.

But just as quickly, Knight snatched him up even higher. The heels of his Air Force One hit the side of a chair. "Who *made* your hip-hoppin' ass?"

"You!" Jamal's voice was high-pitched due to the fact that he was being choked by his shirt. His face bulged and turned red.

"Who has the power to destroy you just as fast?"

"You! You!" His teeth chattered like it was ten degrees below zero outside.

"What you gon' say next time Dickman call?"

"F-f-f-f-f-fuck that muthafucka."

Knight nodded. "And if you talk to him . . ."

"Jamal a dead muthafucka."

Knight threw him down on the aisle.

Jamal thudded on his back. His eyes opened wide, staring up as if he were trying to figure out if he were still alive.

"Jamal," Knight said coolly, knowing that the butt of his gun was protruding from his waistband just past his big silver KNIGHT belt buckle, "Tell me what you're gonna do at eleven forty-five the night of October first on the other side of those curtains." Knight pointed to the purple velvet drapes framing the stage.

Jamal coughed. He grabbed his throat, massaging the red marks.

"Tell me!" Knight's bellow echoed through the auditorium.

"I'ma sign the papers." Jamal coughed. "I'ma give you a fat-ass check. An'—"

Knight raised his brows as if to say, "And?"

"I ain't neva gon' tell nobody nothin' about Manifest Destiny."

Knight stared down. "Remember them magic words for the rest of yo' life—they yo' bulletproof vest as far as I'm concerned." The power pumping through Knight's veins made him feel eight feet tall. His chest was clear. His heart was pumping slowly, calmly.

I am king. An African warrior king who will never be defeated.

Chapter 27

In the dark-paneled office inside The Penthouse at Babylon HQ, Knight huddled in front of his computer with Larry Marx. The California media mogul and his wife were in town to discuss the final details of Manifest Destiny. Now he and Knight were switching accounts to protect Babylon's assets, just in case the Marxes got indicted.

"Julius Mark Anthony, meet Moses Alexander," Larry said as he typed account numbers in the global banking website. "This is switching all your assets into another account that's handled by our company in Sweden. It's untraceable back to Question Marx or Babylon."

Knight patted Larry on the back of his snug-fitting brown sweater that matched his brown linen trousers and polished, lace-up brown and white shoes. "I appreciate all the wisdom over the years, man," Knight said, hoping this money maneuver was the remedy for relieving the tightness in his chest. "You helped me work a miracle."

"I'm about to." Larry said, glanced up with a sparkle in his brown eyes. His curly dark hair shook as he laughed; his suntanned face crinkled, especially around his eyes, where a tiny white strip showed where his sunglasses covered his skin while sailing and golfing. "I cannot wait to see how you pull this off. Takes balls as big as Tokyo to rule Babylon. But this?"

Knight's chest squeezed. "In 'black man' years, my twenty-five is seventy-five—I need to get away."

"I hear you," Larry said. "Me and Prissy have been so worked up over this indictment, we're thinkin' about doing the same thing. Latest word is, the heat's off. But this is a wake-up call. Can never be too careful."

Knight nodded, watching as Larry worked the keyboard to make page after page pop up with seven-figure bank balances.

"All you have to do after The Games is log on with that same password, *Caesar*, and transfer the money from Jamal's account into this new account. All transactions are untraceable. And *voilà*—a lifetime of luxury."

WHITE CHOCOLATE

The proud black man in Knight hated that he needed a white man to help him orchestrate Manifest Destiny. And his escape from it. But that was life in white America. Plus, this man, Larry Marx, had an "honorary brotha card."

*

Knight had met Larry and his wife Priscilla years ago, when Prince was running Babylon. The millionaires had purchased a chain of upscale strip clubs and planned to produce Hollywood movies, documentaries about the sex industry, entertainment websites, and a glitzy, mainstream magazine for couples who wanted to keep their love lives sizzling.

Back then, the Marxes had been in town for a yacht party, when they'd contacted Babylon to provide the sex entertainment as they and their guests sailed the black waters of the Detroit River and Lake St. Clair. They were so impressed with the flawless transactions, the extreme discretion, and the documented health status and performance of all fifty Studs and Sluts, they'd vowed to partner with the Johnson Brothers any way they could to help them build their empire.

"If you ever want to follow the American tradition of Manifest Destiny," Larry Marx had said, "that means moving West and taking what you want—like the white man did when he stole everything west of the Mississippi from the Native Americans—then call us first."

Mr. Marx had christened the deal by offering up his wife, the quintessential California blond, who had bent over, inviting Knight to lay pipe in the foundation of what he viewed as the Taj Mahal of business relationships.

Now here they were, years later, strategizing Knight's exit plan from the biggest, baddest business of its kind in urban America. If it took a white man to help him make it happen, then so be it.

Over the years, even while Knight was locked up, Larry had schooled him on how to succeed in the business world, how to manage money, and how to plan for his future with his family.

*

"Hey man," Knight said, "you a cool cat."

214

"Gotta confess, dude," Larry said, looking up from the computer. "I've been sort of living vicariously through you. Even when you were in jail. I've always had this fascination with black men . . . how strong you are."

"I *know* you ain't about to go gay on me—"

"No, no, not at all. I'm talkin' genetics. The reason black men are so feared is that your sperm can change the color of the white race. It's not about penis size or skill, it's about skin. Making everybody else, a whole race of people, look like you— That's power, man!"

Knight nodded, because Prince had once told him that very same thing.

"Plus," Larry said, "when I first saw you and Prince and Duke, you had this regal quality about you. It shows in the way you walk—like panthers—The way you talk and act like the world had better bow down at your feet, even though from the white world's perspective, you were born, raised, and forever condemned to the gutter."

Knight remembered during their first meeting when Larry jacked his big dick, watching Knight fuck his wife. Was Larry trying to butter him up now so he could fuck The Queen? *Hell naw!*

After all, Larry had said the secret to their long, happy marriage was being open to sex with others. Many others.

Well, Knight and his Queen would be just fine by themselves.

Yet with the click of a button, Larry could jack up Knight's money in a heartbeat. That was too much power for one cat to have. But right now, Knight didn't have a choice.

Knight also remembered early last year, when he'd taken The Queen to visit the Marxes at their oceanside mansion in Santa Barbara to hammer out the deal for Babylon to acquire five cities on the West Coast. That weekend Larry hired several L.A. Babylon Sluts to surround Knight at all times to massage his shoulders, serve him drinks and, of course, pleasure his body. And every custom-ordered Slut had light skin and long hair. (Mrs. Marx had her own male harem of Studs, who were all dark chocolate-brown.)

But if Larry had some kind of vision for tonight, that the two couples would swing for old-times' sake, then Knight was ready to walk away from this high-tech hook-up. He'd figure out how to handle his money some other way. Because The Queen was not a bartering chip in this deal. And that pumped up the pressure in his chest.

*

"You're the boss," Larry said. "You're the boss. And I'm proud of you, dude."

"'Preciate it," Knight said coolly, letting Intuition feel Larry's vibe and visual expression.

He's sincere, Intuition told Knight.

Still, Knight stared hard into Larry's eyes. "Nothin' like trust. Nothin' like trust."

Larry nodded. "Speaking of trust—this dude, Jamal, you really trust him?"

That band of tension squeezed around Knight's chest. "Jamal knows that any deviation from this plan will earn him a lifelong visitor's pass to see Prince at Elmwood Cemetery."

"What's the latest on Duke?"

"He's planning an eleventh-hour heist, but I'm ten steps ahead of him."

"Stay there." Larry stood. "Mission accomplished. Now let's go see what that pretty little Cleopatra of yours is up to."

Knight's heart pounded as he took long strides to the door. He would be down on his Queen faster than Larry could say "Swing."

Chapter 28

The Queen moaned as the woman's long fingernails raked through her long, black hair and massaged her scalp over and over.

"Knight told us you were even more beautiful than you were last year." Mrs. Marx stared at The Queen in the mirrored wall of the dining room in The Penthouse at Babylon. "But you are absolutely breathtaking. You could play Cleopatra in a movie and win an Oscar."

The Queen, sitting in her Louis XIV chair at the head of the table, leaned her head back and looked up into the intrigued blue eyes that were on a thin, upside-down face with bright pink lip gloss. "Thank you. I always loved Egyptian stuff and playing dress-up with my mom. So this—"

The Queen's throat burned so much, stealing her words. This was the first older woman she'd encountered in more than a year. Except for Duke's mother, who'd hated her—until Knight brought her home, and Mrs. Johnson suddenly loved The Queen. Because, as she learned, their mother praised anything Knight did, while in her eyes, Duke could never be as good as his big brother.

Now, Mrs. Marx had to be forty or even older—and she was gorgeous, glamorous, and alarmingly sexy. She was also the first white woman with whom The Queen had a positive interaction, because the time with that traitor Tiffany in the bathroom after the Moreno meeting didn't count.

The housekeeper, Nina, in the customary Babylon uniform for women—the short, wispy, low-cut white dress gathered at the waist with a gold belt, with gold lace-up sandals and upper arm bracelets—pushed through the swinging door to the kitchen and began to clear the table. "Madame Queen," she said with a curtsy that made the tops of her nutmeg-brown breasts jiggle, "I'll serve dessert soon as Master Knight and Mister Marx come back from the office."

"Thank you, Nina," The Queen said, bending her head forward to look into Nina's pretty almond-colored eyes. "You

217

got some French vanilla ice-cream and caramel sauce to go over the pecan pie, right?"

"Yes, ma'am." Nina curtsied again, then piled up dinner plates from the table.

The Queen leaned her head back.

Mrs. Marx, standing behind her chair, cupped a warm hand over The Queen's cheek and stared into her eyes. "You okay, sweetie?—you look sad."

As Nina clinked china and silverware, The Queen squeezed hot tears from her eyes, which dripped down onto Mrs. Marx's wrist. She kept her eyes closed, and loved the sensation of Mrs. Marx's hands stroking her face, from each side of her nose, down to her jaw, over and over.

"I think you need to relax," Mrs. Marx said. "Let's go into the living room."

"I'll bring coffee and dessert out there," Nina said.

As they walked toward the plush all-white couches, Mrs. Marx massaged The Queen's shoulders, exposed by the spaghetti straps of her turquoise, Cleopatra-style dress that flowed down to her ankles, but exposed her legs with a slit from the top of her left thigh.

For some reason, perhaps the affectionate and grateful way Knight had always spoken of the Marxes, The Queen felt extremely comfortable with this woman. She wanted to tap into her wisdom and learn the ways of a married woman that she'd not been able to learn from Mommy.

"Mrs. Marx?"

"Priscilla, please," she said playfully, laying The Queen face down on the couch.

"Priscilla, do you think too much sex can kill a woman or a man?"

"If it can, then Larry and I have nine lives." She laughed, pushing up the Queen's dress to massage her calves. "Or more—why do you ask?"

"MMmmm, that feels good," The Queen whispered as the woman kneaded the flesh of her hamstrings.

All through dinner, The Queen had been getting hornier and hornier as she watched Malibu Barbie, her gorgeous

218

husband, Knight at the table, and then Nina as she strutted in and out to serve lobster, pasta, and salad.

She got the same feeling she'd had when Rip Masta Mac and his harem of hotties had joined them, along with Jamal and CoCo, for dinner last week. They'd barely made it through the lamb chops before Rip Masta put one of his girls in front of him on the table, spread-eagled, and started eating her pussy like it was a pie-eating contest.

That sparked an oral extravaganza around the table, as The Queen had slurped down Knight's dick with wild abandon, and they all ended up on the mattress-style chaises on the outdoor terrace, fucking to the funkiest beats of the Bang Squad and Rip Masta, until the sun rose in an explosion of orange over the Detroit River.

Tonight's dinner had been much more reserved, but the twinkle in Mrs. Marx's blue eyes let her know this guest from the West Coast was saving the best for last.

Now The Queen wished Knight would return from whatever serious conversation he was having with Mr. Marx, so they could cap off the evening with dessert. Because Mrs. Marx's hands were massaging her butt cheeks now, and her pussy was as hot and creamy as the steaming coffee that she could smell brewing in the kitchen.

"Your ass is so round."

"Oooh, squeeze my ass," The Queen whispered. "I *loooove* that." She always could cum extra good when Knight took each cheek in one hand, then squeezed and massaged her ass, while he fucked her.

All of a sudden, something hot and wet pressed into The Queen's booty. It was a pussy. Waxed satin-smooth. Creamy. And steaming hot.

Mrs. Marx ground her clit in sultry circles into the round curve of The Queen's juicylicious booty. Meanwhile, her hands massaged The Queen's bare back.

Celeste screamed, loving this new sensation.

Music began to play. The deep, electric beat of "I'm Cummin' " from the *Dick Chix Mix*, which Nina must have switched in the sound system that boomed through the huge Penthouse.

The Queen, who lay on her right cheek, watched Nina set a silver tray of coffee and pecan pie slices on the coffee table.

Nina then danced alone just a few feet from the couch, raising her little dress just enough to expose the big brown bubbles of her firm, smooth ass, parted by a gold thong. She rolled it back, wound it 'round, and popped it to the rhythm of the music. Then she slowly danced toward them, bending to lick the pink nipples that Mrs. Marx had pulled from her dress. And she pulled her gold thong to the side, hooked her left knee over the arm of the couch, and wound so that her pussy was just inches from The Queen's face.

I'm buried in pussy, and I love it.

Nina danced closer, letting the tip of her clit, which looked like a brown shrimp—a jumbo prawn, poking out of those thick folds of flesh—brush up against The Queen's nose. Then lips.

She stuck out her tongue.

All while Mrs. Marx screamed and shivered and creamed all over The Queen's ass.

The Queen needed Knight right now. She needed Shane to slam up into her hungry pussy and take care of this ache for love.

Just as she wrapped her lips around Nina's clit, she felt his hands on the backs of her knees.

He pulled them apart, pooted up her ass with Mrs. Marx still on it, and rammed Shane into the swollen, slippery jellyfish that Celeste had become.

His dick was like an electric eel, slithering up into her and sending jolts through her every cell. Lightning crackled behind her closed eyelids. She spasmed with the shock of his size and speed, and she shuddered, cumming with one magic stroke.

Chapter 29

Duke took one look into Shar Miller's devious eyes and felt pumped with power. And here inside this white stretch Navigator limousine, Shar looked fine as hell. She sat with Leroy Lewis from Miami, Raynard Ingalls from Chicago, and Red Moreno himself.

"Vegas look good on you, girl," Duke said, glancing over her body. He'd hardly gotten a look at her at the last meeting at the nightclub, when she'd been covered by her Stud and Baby Blue.

Now, Shar wore a skintight black dress that pushed up her big chest and showed off a tattoo that said *SHAR* scrolled across the top of her left tittie. Next to that, her tiny red cell phone poked from between her nutmeg-brown boobs. She had to be damn near forty-five, but her smooth skin proved that black don't crack.

Timbo became as long and hard as a log inside Duke's baggy jeans. "How you gon' look betta wit' age?"

She smiled, glancing at the bare-chested Stud beside her. His brown biceps bulged as she stroked the leg of his jeans. He was holding her steaming coffee cup with one hand and picking a piece of lint off her arm with the other.

"This is my fountain of youth." She glanced at the Stud. "The secret lies in womanly wisdom and a daily regimen of sex. And thank you, Massa Duke. I am so honored to work with you as a partner to put you back in charge of Babylon. We can't let all that business sense you got go to waste."

Duke shrugged, but sat tall. The sound of somebody calling him Massa Duke again made Timbo throb so hard he hurt. "I'm back in full effect."

Moreno flicked his wrist to make his watch fall down from under his crisp white shirtsleeve. How he could even tell time with that blinding sparkle of diamonds was a mystery. And how he could concentrate with Baby Blue sucking his dick was even more baffling.

Duke wanted to see if Moreno's dick looked as waxy as the rest of his skin. That muthafucka looked embalmed—cold,

221

hard, and chemically preserved. Like Prince in his casket. And with that spooky-ass accent, maybe he was some kind of vampire that would live forever until someone drove a stake through his evil-ass heart.

Leroy shifted on the seat. He rested his gold-ringed hand on his crotch and watched Shar in action.

Mixing business with pleasure was always a major no-no for Duke, even at the height of his power with Duchess. His mind was either on one or the other. Sex clouded his judgment, dulled his thoughts, turned him into a weak-ass punk who couldn't think straight.

It was hard enough to look at the top of the crack of Baby Blue's fine ass as she knelt in front of Moreno, her jeans holding that bubble-booty of hers just right. The way her head bobbed on his lap and her mouth made little sucking sounds made Timbo stand up like a tree trunk. And the scent of sex filling the limo didn't help much.

Concentrate, muthafucka. Intoxicants, includin' pussy, done already got you in enough trouble. You clean, now.

Moreno's hazel eyes looked as sharp and alert as he rested his waxy-looking right hand on Baby Blue's head and said, "Duke, my brother, Shar, Leroy, and Raynard, pardon my promptness, but the time is short. We can reminisce once the fortunes are in our respective bank accounts."

Shar sipped her coffee, which seemed to deepen her voice and harden it into a razor-sharp tone. "Massa Duke, your brother seems to have forgotten where he came from. Others on the Board are ready to pluck him out, so we'll just be doing them a favor tonight to expedite the process." She raised her long red fingernails to her mouth, parted her red-painted lips, and poked a nail into the gap between her front teeth. She made a sucking sound like she was disgusted. And she moved her hand like she was trying to pull out a piece of sausage that had gotten caught there during breakfast.

You can take a ho out the ghetto, but you cain't take the ghetto out the ho. Duke smiled, wishing he could offer her a toothpick. But naw, he liked that flava. She looked elegant and business-like, but the bitch was bad as she needed to be. And the hard glint in her eyes as she spoke of Knight reinforced Duke's belief that Shar wasn't about to play pussyfoot and fuck anything up. She was serious as a heart attack.

"Knight's righteous act," she said, taking the coffee cup from the Stud, "strikes the wrong way, when you remember what a ruthless renegade muthafucka he was before he got locked up." She sat with her ankles together so that the pointed tips of her red patent leather boots looked like they could make a brotha cry—either in lust or in pain. Or both.

Duke had already had her like that. But this was strictly business now.

Now this is the kind o' bitch who can help me make stuff happen, yeah.

She already was. Their phone conversations for the past several months had laid the foundation for the coup of the century.

The muthafuckin' heist of the millennium.

If Knight had strutted in like the new sheriff in town, then Duke was about to swoop down on his ass like a global superpower.

"My operations around the world," Moreno said, "will be greatly enhanced by this partnership. I need it to work out to the finest detail tonight." Moreno's tongue flicked over his blood-colored lips. "Your brother has promised me the ultimate delight when my teams win The Games."

Duke stared into Moreno's sleazy eyes. There could be only one thing that could make Moreno glaze over like that.

Dream on, muthafucka. By the time you think you can get wit' her, The Duchess will be mine again. An' I'll kill yo' ass befo' you lay them embalmed-lookin' hands on my goddess.

"It's gon' be wild, fo' sho'," Duke said.

"You'll be glad to know," Shar said with a smooth, deep voice that was nothing like the ghetto-girl twang she'd had while working as a Slut here at Babylon. Her spiky black hair was sophisticated, unlike the too-long red weave she wore with those blue contacts. "That every aspect of Oz is playing out like a well-rehearsed movie; it's almost too perfect." Her dark eyes focused hard on him in a business-like way. They looked into his face without a glimmer of disgust or disdain or pity or any of the other fucked-up attitudes people had been projecting on him since he came back.

But if Magic could live this long with HIV and look that good and still play ball and be the superstar businessman that he was, then The Duke would lick the virus just as tough. He was already putting on some weight and clearing up his skin. He was eating better, sleeping more, and all those HIV drugs were kicking in.

So, in a Motor City minute, Duke would be looking as healthy and strong as his old self that was so fine he seduced his Duchess into his bed within just a few hours. Now, he was a phoenix rising out of the ashes of his own pipe, reinventing himself, bigger and badder than ever.

And Leroy Lewis from Miami was picking up on that. Leroy smiled without showing any reaction to Duke's appearance, and that made Duke feel pumped even bigger and better. "Duke, baby," Leroy said, wringing his gold-ringed hands together, "I been waitin' for this day like I'm still that horny teenager on his first visit to Miss Myra's ho'house. No disrespec', but I cain't stan' that scoundrel who came out yo' momma hoochie befo' yo' sweet ass."

Wearing a lemon yellow suit with matching alligator shoes, silk tie, and a feathered hat in the same color, Leroy looked like the pimp he was. Detroit style. The brotha owned a suit in every color in the rainbow—pastel pinks, lavenders, greens, blues, primary fire-engine red, bright blue, and electric orange. But something about his slicked-back black waves and his aging pretty-boy face made him look like a respectable businessman and not a ridiculous-ass cartoon character that some might see him as.

"We gon' make this happen so big an' bad, we gon' make Babylon look like a back-alley, bootleg."

Shar rolled her eyes. "Right now we need action, not words. I have to warn you, though"—Shar glanced toward the dark-tinted window at the blue Detroit River sparkling in the morning sunshine—"your girl Reba was having serious doubts about this venture. In fact, her absence right now indicates a serious problem. She should be actively participating in every conversation."

Duke ground his teeth. That bitch had better make right and get her act together. He had no place or patience for a snitch or a defector.

Shar added, "I talked some sense back into her, but Duke, you'd be wise to keep an eye on her."

"Already on it," Duke said. "E'rybody in position for tonight? The Barriors and B'Amazons?"

"We've had two drills, both successful," Shar said.

Duke nodded. "And the inside info—you got e'rythang pinpointed, how to take down the dudes wit' the bank?"

Shar nodded down to her phone between her titties. "Just had them on my hotline," she said with a deep laugh, "and we're all set."

"What about Gerard and security?"

Leroy's shoulders shook up and down as he laughed. "We sendin' him the kind o' poontang that'll make him think sweet Jesus done turned into a girl an' come to escort him through the pearly gates."

Raynard "Dickman" Ingalls, wearing a green Pelle Pelle leather jacket covered with rhinestones and benjamins, cracked his knuckles. The twenty-year-old from Chicago was notorious for running a gigolo ring that was thrusting into the upscale market, just as Duchess was doing for Babylon. "I been studyin' the demographic in all the cities we gon' take." He fingered the bill of his cocked-to-the-side baseball hat that matched his jacket. "The Queen ain't got nothin' on what we gon' do." He cracked his knuckles again then flashed a golden grill that had DICKMAN etched in diamonds over his front teeth.

"Coo'," Duke said as he ticked down his mental check-off list for Oz. "What about the Hummers and the drop-off?"

"We've got the schedule and a double backup plan," Shar said. "As soon as The Games officially end at midnight, you and I will meet with Reba and Antoine in the tunnel. Leroy will be in the boat with the crew. We'll target each diver and take their moneybags. Those who may have already reached the boat—"

WHITE CHOCOLATE

"We gon' be pirates like a mug," Duke said with an ecstatic tone. But a tremor rippled through his thin body as the image of his bigger, badder, blacker brother, Knight, came to mind. His heart raced when he remembered Prince's face as he died in his arms.

Even with blood bubbling over his lips, and that horrible gurgle-gasp of life leaving his young body, Prince looked up at Duke with eyes that said, "You ain't neva gon' be nothin' but a punk muthafucka who ain't blessed wit' the smarts that me and Knight got."

Duke shook his head to banish the thought. Knight always looked at him the same way. Especially the night he stole the Duchess and Babylon from Duke. And the night he riddled Duke's already weak body with bullets on the boat.

Duke ground his teeth, loving the strong, powerful feeling of his jaw muscles flexing. He couldn't wait to look down on Knight and make him pay for his lifetime of abuse.

Yeah, pretty soon Knight would be Duke's servant. He might even make big bro' sleep on a cot every night so he could watch Duke make love to his Duchess over and over and over again.

Naw, I ain't a punk no more. I'm The Duke! And I'll be rulin' in a Motor City minute!

He savored the power of his new court here in this limo.

"Yo, Dickman, how y'all's crew handlin' the take-down?"

Raynard cracked his knuckles. "Yo, rock dis—I got a exact map showin' the spot where we gon' get his black ass. My crew flawless. Yo' boy, Knight, gon' be right where you want him in about"—Dickman checked out his watch—"twelve hours."

"Coo', coo'." Duke bit down a smile. By daybreak, he would be back in charge of Babylon. His insides tingled. *With Knight out of the way, the Duchess would be mine when all this shakes down tonight.*

I get my Duchess back.

Timbo jumped and flipped under his jeans. His dick was like an excited fish that couldn't wait to dive into the deepest, warmest, sweetest waters, and frolic for a lifetime.

Chapter 30

Inside The Playhouse, where one of the private suites was transformed into a bridal boudoir and dressing room, The Queen stepped into the sexiest wedding gown she'd ever seen.

"Damn, I feel turned on just looking at myself in this mug," The Queen said with a seductive tone.

"Put *that* into an etiquette book for brides on their wedding day!" CoCo giggled.

Then CoCo said with the kind of prim and proper English that she had used while working for The Queen's father, "Every bride should feel so excited and happy on her wedding day, that her entire genital area should become aroused with a moist, swelling sensation. In addition, her nipples should tingle, and her mouth should pucker slightly, to indicate that she is ready and available to receive her husband's penis on their wedding night so that she can get fucked into a delirious stupor."

"Love it!" The Queen laughed.

CoCo lifted an already-open, dark-green bottle of Cristal from the silver ice bucket on the vanity. She poured a steaming stream into The Queen's crystal flute, then her own.

"Cheers!" CoCo said, as they clinked glasses. "Here's a toast to the sexiest bride marrying the sexiest groom on the sexiest day in Babylon history!"

The Queen raised her crystal champagne flute to her lips and took a long sip. She couldn't wait for the sweet bubbles to dance on her tongue and through her whole body. The cool fluid would relax her tense muscles and erase all thoughts of the high security alert on this stressful-ass day of The Games, Duke on the loose, and all these niggas jockeying for control of Babylon.

"To tell you the truth, girl," The Queen said, "I can't wait to get the fuck outta here and enjoy my honeymoon. I wish they'd just catch Duke and take care of his ass so we can get on with our lives."

"As many Barriors and B'Amazons they got outside this room," CoCo said, "and all the security cameras, you got nothin' to worry about. Knight wouldn't let nothin' happen to you, girl."

The Queen remembered all the terrifying moments over the past month that had made her question whether she wanted to remain in Babylon as a married woman raising a child with Knight. "Sometimes I wonder if I'm in the right place."

"It don't matter where you at." CoCo brushed a loose thread from her pink maid of honor dress. "As long you wit' the man you love. That's how I feel about me an' Jamal. Much as I love Babylon an' his music, I'd drop it all an' live in a barn wit' him if he wanted me to."

The Queen giggled. "Girl, you crazy."

"Money don't buy love or happiness, but love make you happy."

"I'm gonna talk to Knight on our honeymoon about our future," The Queen said. "If I ever surrender my throne, it's yours, CoCo."

CoCo's eyes glowed with appreciation as they filled with silvery tears.

The Queen raised the glass to her lips and took a sip of the sweet, bubbly liquid. *PPpfffffttt!* A golden spray of champagne shot from between The Queen's lips and into the warm beams of sunshine pouring in from high warehouse-style windows and rained on the cream-colored carpet. "Oh, shit!" She slammed the glass down on the vanity. Her other hand instinctively grasped her stomach.

CoCo's eyes widened with alarm. "What's wrong? You got diarrhea? Girl, I didn't think you'd get wedding-day jitters."

"Just a cramp."

The Queen wanted to share the good news for weeks, but Knight insisted that she keep the pregnancy a secret until she was actually showing. Plus, the first three months were the most high-risk time for miscarriage anyway.

"We'll wait until it's safe," he'd been saying for the two weeks since her period was late.

228

The home pregnancy test confirmed what Celeste had already told her, and the doctor down in the clinic had proven it with a blood test.

But The Queen had looked in a book and on the Internet to see what a two-week-old fertilized egg—her and Knight's baby boy—would look like, and that little clump of cells didn't need to be swimming around in Cristal. "Damn!" The Queen exclaimed. "My mind is so fucked up right now, I can't think straight to save my life."

"Don't say that, girl. You know Knight says our words have power. Every bride is whack on her wedding day; it's normal."

"How many brides you know who got armed guards outside their dressing room door?"

CoCo shrugged. "This life in the big city. But you The Queen of Babylon, so be glad about it. Look at you!"

The Queen checked herself out in the mirror. But she didn't really see herself, except for the brilliant sparkle off her QUEEN choker necklace as the sunshine lit up every diamond. It was so bright, it created silver blurs in her eyes as if someone had just snapped her picture with a flash.

From here on out, she would drink only bottled water, juice, and milk. And most of all, she'd keep her head straight so this couldn't happen again.

"You and Knight got what everybody else wants but can't even think about having," CoCo said. "It's too rare. So smile. Celebrate, sweetheart!"

The Queen imagined staring into Knight's eyes at the altar. She believed that the only time she could feel more intoxicated and euphoric than that moment was when she was making love with Knight. Otherwise, the thrill of every little girl's dream coming true, in this most sexy, blingin' way, was so over the top, she felt dizzy.

"Knight's gonna love this dress so much." The Queen giggled. "He'll be at the altar like, 'Uh, 'scuse me, y'all, we got some business to handle.'"

CoCo, who was sipping champagne as The Queen talked, pulled the crystal flute away from her highly glossed lips. She laughed. "Then he'll be like, 'Yo, Rev, move out the way an' lemme jus' drill this fine ass on the altar for a hot minute.'"

The Queen bent down slightly as CoCo adjusted the lace straps of her gown over her shoulders.

"It might be white," CoCo said, "but it ain't innocent."

The Queen grinned and shivered as she looked into the giant, three-paneled mirror set against a wall draped in pink tulle, white roses, and green vines. She pivoted on white satin stiletto slippers, loving how the dress hit every curve just right, and hoisted up her boobs like two golden-brown, buttered muffins served steaming hot out of the oven.

"CoCo, look." The Queen stroked the curve of her chest. Her diamond engagement ring sparkled in the sunshine, and her French manicure with clear, opalescent pink polish matched the dress perfectly. "Looks like the crack of my ass on my chest," she said seductively, running her index fingernail between the pressed-together mounds. "Knight's mouth is gonna water so much from lookin' at my titties, he's gonna drool when he says, 'I do.'"

CoCo sipped more champagne. "Then when the Rev says, 'You may kiss the bride,' Knight will think he said, 'You may lick the bride,' and he'll lean down to slurp on all that pretty skin.

"Girl, you makin' me hot just lookin' at you." Coco made her shoulders shimmy as if she had caught a chill. Then she stood in the mirror and untied her robe. It fell open. In the bright sunlight, CoCo's pussy glistened like a melting chocolate rose.

"Damn, girl!" The Queen made a sucking sound. "Look like you need a bitch to take care o' that."

"Naw. I'm savin' it for Jamal tonight. He like it when my pussy be marinatin' in hot cream all day, then when we fuck, it's like so boilin' hot, he almost cain't stand it."

"Girl, you talk so prim and proper in business, but get you some Cristal and a hot pussy, an' you just as rank as me." The Queen ran her hands down the lace bodice. Embroidered with tiny pink crystals, the body-hugging fabric shimmered as it curved in a perfect hourglass over her breasts, waist, and hips. Right at her thighs, the dress poufed out in an explosion of pale pink tulle, which was also embroidered with tiny white crystals.

"Can you believe I designed this myself?" The Queen said. "It's like a vision just came to me. And the designer was right on point."

Suddenly, The Queen heard Knight speaking in her thoughts, *You were a vision I saw on TV. And the Divine Plan was right on point. Now you're about to be mine for life. Love you to the Infinity, Baby Girl.*

Celeste answered, *I'm your Queen forever.*

The Queen's nipples hardened, and her pussy swelled with heat and cream. It wasn't so much lust for the sexiest man alive; she was aroused by a sensation of pure joy. After all she'd been through, she was finally being rewarded with the most amazing gift—the love of a lifetime.

The Queen gathered her long black hair up into a twist, which she secured on top of her head with two shimmery white chopsticks. Then she turned around to glimpse the back of the dress, which was mostly bare skin. The lace fastened behind her neck, forming a halter top with two strips that stretched down over her shoulder blades to support the backless dress. Framed by a scalloped lace edge, most of her back was bare, all the way down to the crack of her ass.

"Damn!" CoCo zipped the side of the dress from The Queen's hipbone up to her ribcage. "That designer got it fittin' like second skin. And look"—CoCo ran her finger over The Queen's tattoo at the base of her back—"You gon' walk down the aisle and everybody gon' be starin' at your tattoo."

The Queen cast a seductive glance over her shoulder at CoCo. "Love the way you touch me, girl." Then her gaze lowered to the reflection of her tattoo in the mirror. She read the black, Gothic-style letters aloud: "Queen of the Knight— Damn! You won't see this sexy shit in those prissy bridal magazines."

"I bet you'll see a bunch o' hoes copying your style, though. Hey, girl, don't forget about your garter." She pulled it from the vanity, which was covered with make-up that The Queen had just applied. On it also sat a small beaded purse that held The

Queen's pearl-handled pistol. "Here, sit down so I can put it on you."

The Queen sat on the white satin stool in front of the vanity. Fabric rustled as she pulled up her dress.

CoCo, who hadn't fastened her robe, knelt before her. Her tight little body, as she sat on her feet and her upper legs extended forward, was gorgeous. Especially those juicy, cantaloupe titties with nipples so pointed and tight they made The Queen's mouth water. "Does it go on your left or right leg?" CoCo looked from The Queen's satin shoes up to her face for an answer. Her eyes grew large. "Oooh, girl! I never heard of a bride who just said to hell with panties altogether!"

The Queen spread her legs wider and rested her elbows on the vanity behind her. "I get too hot." She cast a seductive stare down at her assistant. She knew CoCo was clean; she'd just been checked the day before, along with Jamal. And The Queen knew for a fact that CoCo wasn't getting with any other girls. "Hot and horny," The Queen said.

In fact, all those pregnancy hormones were keeping her pussy moist at all times, no matter what she was doing. But Knight looked so weak and pale lately, she was afraid to overtax him by demanding dick every hour on the hour.

"Tell me you love to lick my pussy." The Queen moaned in anticipation of CoCo's hot mouth pressing down on all her hot, swollen meat. "Tell me you love it."

CoCo slid her hand between her own legs as she dove forward with an open mouth. She inhaled loudly. "I love to lick this pussy," she whispered, making her hot breath steam onto the top of the bride's clit.

The Queen loved the sensation of CoCo's nipples rubbing against the insides of her thighs.

CoCo stuck out her tongue and licked the tip of The Queen's clit. She loved the sound The Queen made as she moaned.

"Lick that shit like you a little kitten," The Queen whispered. "Suck up all that milk."

CoCo wrapped her lips around her clit.

232

The Queen buckled. "Damn! You do that good. You still gon' lick me off after I'm married?"

CoCo licked faster.

"Speakin' in tongues," The Queen said with a mellow, intoxicated moan. "Love it."

"Damn, girl, all that champagne made me have to pee." CoCo stood up.

"Go 'head. Turn on some music."

CoCo walked toward the living room area. The sexy beat of *Diamond Hearts* blasted from speakers built into the walls around the suite.

The Queen stood and danced in her gown. She grabbed her veil from the mannequin, put it on, and spun in a big blur of white.

Thud!

Pop!

She froze. Her ears strained against the loud music. Those two sounds were unmistakable. And they came from right outside the door, where at least two Barriors were stationed at all times.

Damn, I knew some shit was gonna go down today. The way Knight's been so paranoid. Gotta call him.

She scanned the vanity for her phone. With the push of a button he'd be here. After all, he was dressing on this same floor, in a suite at the opposite end of the long hallways. But where was the phone under all that make-up?

Knight, baby. Trouble.

If ever she needed to use their supernatural vibe to call him, now was the time. She tiptoed to the entrance hall and peeked through the peephole. Nothing. Except an empty hallway with brick walls and wooden doorways lit by cobalt blue sconces.

Where the fuck were the Barriors?

I gotta call Knight.

She spun, holding up her gown. She ran toward the bedroom dressing area. The double doors opened. The Queen's heart raced. The metallic taste of fear burned on her tongue.

Because Reba and Antoine were entering the suite, pushing in a huge armoire.

And not a Barrior or B'Amazon was in sight. Except for the tip of a black boot positioned at the bottom of the doorway. The toe pointed to the ceiling, and the heel rested on the blue carpet, as if he was lying on the floor—shot or dead!

"We got your clothes ready for the honeymoon," Reba said, strutting in wearing a pink spandex bodysuit and matching knee-high boots. Antoine wore a black suit.

The Queen glared at them.

Knight, baby! Help!

Chapter 31

Knight perched on the bed, inhaling deeply. But every breath made those needle sensations in his heart pierce harder. And an aching, burning band of pain extended from the right side of his chest, under his arm, and around his back.

"My body is relaxed," he whispered, yanking at the black bow tie that felt like a noose. He had to whip this heart attack, panic attack, whatever it was, so he could get up to the wedding. His watch said 5:40. So did his cell phone, sitting beside him on the bed, which was supposed to alert him of any security breaches.

5:41.

He unbuttoned his shirt. With one hand, he massaged his chest.

Nineteen more minutes.

"I am strong," he gasped. "My heart is strong." But his heart was hammering against his ribs. His lungs were squeezing, barely taking in air. And his head was spinning.

I am a black warrior. I am strong.

Little white dots of light danced before his eyes. He tried to focus on himself in the mirror facing the bed. But it was like a white squall during a winter storm—big snowflakes blocking his view.

Knight! Knight, baby, help!

Knight's heart pounded harder. Sweat prickled under this starched white shirt.

How long had she been calling for help? His panicky state of mind had been blocking his radar.

"Pong!" Knight called weakly.

The Barrior and his twin, Ping, were waiting in the living room. Jamal, his best man, was dressing in another suite. The plan was for him to come here, then they would all go up to the wedding together.

"Pong!" Knight wheezed. He grabbed his phone. If The Queen was in danger, then it meant that all of Babylon was already in the midst of a serious security breakdown. Knight poised his finger over the single button that would spark Ping and Pong into immediate action, and set off an alarm in the security booth for Gerard to take care of whatever was going down.

Those white lights dancing before his eyes became a blinding flash. Static rang in his ears. And everything went black.

Chapter 32

"Muthafuck me!" Gerard shouted. His fingers raced over buttons and knobs on the console in the security room, where six other men and women concentrated on dozens of video monitors covering three walls.

I gotta get a grip on my problem—my sex addiction—before it gets me killed. Or somebody else, like The Queen. Which would get me killed.

Gerard blocked out the mental pictures of all the pussy he'd been getting, taking, and buying lately. He had to concentrate on the conversation inside The Queen's suite through the sound chip in her necklace. For some reason, the audio monitors that were hooked up to the cameras in that suite had suddenly gone dead. Good thing Knight was so slick he'd had a sound chip installed in The Queen's diamond necklace, so he could keep an ear on his bitch at all times. Gerard had just replaced the chip with an even more powerful one to prepare for today. And The Queen never knew that it was just inside the clasp, right next to her neck.

Damn, I cain't even concentrate when she talkin'.

If she and CoCo weren't talking so freaky, Gerard would have had an easier time focusing on the screens in front of him. And if they hadn't been flashing each other's pussy at each other—as Gerard watched live thanks to the security camera that showed the bedroom of the bridal suite—then he could have looked away long enough to study the other monitors. Then he wouldn't be in this panic. Because he'd just now noticed that the monitors for the hidden security cameras outside The Queen's suite—Room 515—were actually showing Room 415.

"Knight gon' kill me." He tried once more to activate the cameras that would, in orange print across the bottom of the screen, identify the live video as Room 515.

"Whew!" Gerard said, when he read the words on the monitor: Room 515. "She safe." The monitor showed four Barriors standing in the hallway. And the numbers on the door said Room 414. "How the fuck did somebody—"

237

"That's just a short circuit, man." Paul reached over to adjust the knobs in front of Gerard. "Look."

The image of four Barriors in front of Room 515 appeared on the video.

"Dang, I just saw my life flash before my eyes. Knight woulda killed me his damn self if I'da let somethin' happen to The Queen."

"Everybody too doggone tense around here today," Paul said calmly. "I just saw your girl Reba. She so nervous, you'd think it was *her* weddin'."

Gerard went numb. He knew she was up to something. Not for taking the money after their little fun in the Jacuzzi. Or the several other times that she'd sucked his dick like "wifey" never had, even when they was young newlyweds and the bitch was still givin' head.

No, something in Reba's eyes had snitched that she wanted something much more valuable than money. And he didn't like the way she kept blowing her nose, mumbling something about having a head cold that lingered for almost two weeks. But he had let her drop-dead sexiness blind him to looking at why she caused that bad feeling in his gut.

Damn, how could I have been so stupid?

It was the hottest pussy he'd ever had. The way she could sit on top of him and grind her ass down on his stomach while she fucked him. Just thinking about that shit made his whole body feel hot. Those magic moves had the power to make a nigga lose his mind.

Gerard stared at the monitor to make sure it still showed Barriors outside Room 515.

*

In his mind's eye, though, he could see Reba last night, in this security room where Knight prohibited all visitors, whether they were a Slut, a Stud, or a low-ranking Barrior or B'Amazons.

But Gerard and his dumb ass had been thinking with the head between his legs. And he let Reba in. What man wouldn't, when he saw her wearing them little scraps of clothes—a miniskirt and tank top.

Right here in this chair, she had rubbed his dick between her titties till he called out for his momma. Shit, he'd never blown that much cum at once.

But she sucked him so good, musta drawn up old cum. Cum that had been down in them little tubes inside his balls for years. Shit, all those years that wifey went on a boycott from dick suckin'.

Served the old bitch right. Now he was getting even by holding back the dick from her horny ass. And he was getting his from a young sexy thing named Reba. And too many other bitches to name.

For some reason, as bad as wifey treated him, Gerard suddenly found a strong sense of self and power when he was staring down some other chick's pussy. It mighta been revenge or disrespect or self-hatred.

I don't give a fuck. 'Cause it makes me feel good. Every nipple, every cunthole, every crack of an ass. Every damn nasty bit of it.

Gerard didn't care if she was young, old, fat, skinny, pretty, or ugly. She could have a pretty, flower-scented pussy, or a stank fish-stinkin' snatch. His dick got hard as hell if he just thought the word *pussy*. She could have young, perky tits, or saggy empty sacks that hung down her stretch-marked belly button. She could have thighs as big as tree trunks and an ass and stomach so fat you needed a flashlight to find the pussy. If she were flabby and dimpled with cellulite, or smooth and firm as a baby's butt, Gerard would drill down in it, no matter what.

She could have toes that looked pretty with a fresh pink pedicure or gnarly-ass hammertoes that smelled sour. Her skin could be smooth, or it could be covered with oozing sores like that two-dolla ho who sucked his dick the other day on Eight Mile Road. Didn't matter.

That rush, that high of blowin' his nut in a dangerous way, was Gerard's drug of choice. But if he didn't come clean by finally going to one of those Sex Addicts Anonymous meetings he'd heard about, he might as well blow his brains out. Before Knight did it for him if he let something happen to The Queen or all the money up here in Babylon.

*

"Hummer One to Cairo," a Barrior said over the two-way radio. "Hummer One to Cairo."

Gerard pushed a red button on the black two-way box on the console. "Ramses—over."

Static crackled on the line.

"Delivery route clear—over."

"Roger that."

"How it look?" Gerard asked Paul, who was surveying at least a dozen screens that showed about 250 wedding guests at varying stages of arrival. A few still arrived at valet behind the building.

Even though The Playhouse was situated in an old warehouse district, a lot of new construction was going on around it as the city revitalized its waterfront. So Knight had arranged for the guests to arrive in back, pull up near a white tent between the marina and terrace, and walk a red carpet into the building.

"Damn, emcee Sweet got a sexy lady!" Gerard exclaimed as the famous rapper strutted up the red carpet from his white Bentley and into the building.

The woman wore a wispy purple dress with a sequined, low-cut V-neck so low, you could see the tattoo between her belly button and her crotch. The sheer fabric clung to the points of her nipples as if they were hooks.

"Tell me that dress ain't glued to her titties!" Gerard said. "Oooh, an' look at them chicks wit' Rip Masta Mac an' his crew. Damn, he got clearance for all that entourage? Got a whole harem wit' his gangsta ass. They sexy as hell—"

"Negro, you betta pay attention," Paul said sternly. "Distracting a knucklehead wit' pretty pussy the oldest trick in the book if somebody 'bout to pull a scheme out they stank ass."

Gerard stiffened. The smile curling up his lips flattened, and he focused on three elevators full of guests. When the elevators opened onto the rooftop terrace, Barriors and B'Amazons searched the guests' bags and waved metal detector wands over them.

Guns were checked at a special, high-security room.

"All these folks stayin' for The Games," Paul said, "but in a minute, we gon' get a shitload o' new folks tryin' to get a good seat in the auditorium. An' we'll have to get all the guests from the roof down to The Games. This shit betta go smoov."

Gerard punched some buttons to zoom in on the area where the wedding would be in about fifteen minutes. He realized his fingers were trembling. He was nervous. Because he knew something was wrong.

Naw, it's just the aftershock of that Room 515 scare on the video. Chill out, muthafucka.

But that had never happened before. And as many times as they'd done video system checks to prepare for this day, never once had a short circuit or camera mix-up occurred.

Gerard cast a quick glance at Paul, whose profile was serious and focused on the screens.

Can't trust nobody.

Gerard dialed Knight. But it rang and rang.

Knight always answered the phone on one ring, if that. Sometimes it was like he had ESP and he'd just flip open his phone like he knew Gerard was about to call.

Otherwise, if he were busy, Pong would answer to say Knight was occupied. But now, a recording came on to say, "I'm sorry, the customer you are trying to reach is unavailable. Please—"

Gerard punched the END button. "Damn!"

"Now what?" Paul asked impatiently.

"You talk to Knight lately?"

"Naw, but let the man get ready for his weddin'. He 'bout to marry the finest chick in Babylon, so let him be. You know he like to meditate before he do somethin' important anyway."

Chapter 33

Duke's insides felt like fire as he stared down his bride. Her perfect China doll face was much darker now. And her eyes were harder. They radiated the same power and confidence that had made his dick hard and his heart surrender all at once the first time he saw her on TV news reports about her father's suicide scandal.

But now that she'd become The Queen of Babylon, her blow-torch blue eyes burned into him with the kind of power that he used to flex with one glance. A sucking sensation in his chest made him feel like she'd stolen his power, with Knight's help. She was living the glamorous life here at Babylon, eating like a queen, partying like the boss that she was, and fucking her brains out with big bro'.

And my sorry ass been out on the street. I been punked by my own goddess . . . but not for long.

Duke felt frozen in place, even though his insides were melting under her stare. He was paralyzed by the shock of finally seeing her for the first time in a year. He was just a Motor City minute away from usurping the power and the pussy back under his control.

Muthafuck me! She look like she hate me.

And she looked so different from the clueless white girl he'd playfully called Miss Daisy.

Baby Girl done faded all the way to black, an' I wrote this script, from scene one to the happy ending. Now we 'bout to come to the climax of this most wild, whack, give-you-a-heart-attack love story eva.

Her pretty puckered lips looked like she was about to speak. But Duke had already written the dialogue for her in his mind, over and over, every day for the past year.

"Duchess, I'm back," he said as he climbed out of the armoire. "Your Duke is back. We can finally be together. Knight's gone, so you can marry me today, the way it's s'posed to be." He grinned, remembering way back a year and a month ago, when he had prophesized their wedding day by saying, "And so it is written, and so it is done."

242

Now, he felt drunk with excitement that his plan was going so smoothly. They had gotten up here undetected. Took out the guards. Antoine was standing with a rifle by the doors, and Reba had gone to make sure CoCo didn't make it out of the bathroom.

Now all he had to do was make Duchess remember that she loved him. In a Motor City minute those big moonbeam gray-blue eyes would stop flashing with defiance and hatred. They'd soften into that sexy glow that she used to cast on his while they were making love up in their Penthouse. And she'd say his name in that soft, seductive way—and make some erotic rhymes—like she used to do when Timbo was pioneering a freaky path through all that untouched virgin territory.

But right now she looked like a scared cat. Tryin' to look tough and calm, but she couldn't hide the fear in those eyes that were as big as blue Easter eggs. Her mind was spinning a scheme to escape, the way she kept glancing back and forth between him and Antoine's gun at the door.

That pretty pushed-up chest was rising and falling fast as she panted for breath. "Isis! Osiris!" she screamed. "Isis! Osiris!" Her ear-splitting cries set off hot sparks that clawed up Duke's skinny spine and gripped his brain.

"Shut the fuck up!" he shouted. For a split second, he realized how insane he must've looked. Even though he'd gained weight and his skin was clearing up, he wasn't anything like the radiant god he'd been a year ago. And there was no telling what lies Knight had told her to make her hate her first love.

Antoine dashed into the bedroom. "Yo, boss—"

"Get back to the muthafuckin' door," Duke commanded. "I can han'le this bullshit."

"Isis! Osiris!" Duchess screeched even louder. And she dove for a beaded purse on the vanity.

Oh, hell naw.

"I let you live, bitch!" Duke dove toward her as she grabbed the purse. "You woulda been dog meat if I hadn'ta saved you from ghetto hell. Helped you hide from the feds. Gave you love—"

Her pretty manicured fingers grabbed the purse. The beaded fabric showed the outline of a gun.

Duke's giant fingers pried her hands off of it. He snapped open the purse and pulled out the pearl-handled gun. He waved it close to her face, but she did not flinch. "This the thanks I get?" he said with such a deep voice that his throat hurt. "I give you everything and you think you gon' shoot my ass?"

She inched back toward the triple mirrors.

Now he got a 360-degree view of her fine ass—bare back, ass all round and juicy in sparkly pink fabric. Duke stepped closer. He said in a sweet tone, "You think you gon' shoot The Duke on our weddin' day?"

Ooohh, he wanted to kiss her right now. Them pretty pucker lips were all pouty and red, her cheeks were pink, and her titties looked like they were about to pop out of all that tight, sparkly lace.

"Look at you," he whispered, mesmerized by her beauty. With her hair in chopsticks up on her head, he could see the length of her pretty neck that he used to kiss and suck on. *But that necklace.* "Take that shit off yo' neck," he ordered.

The blinding bling of QUEEN made him close his eyes. "That muthafucka got you wearin' a colla like you his dog, bitch. Take the shit off!"

"Isis! Osiris!" she screamed. She bent slightly at the waist as she screamed. And Duke saw in her reflection that something black flashed on her back.

THE QUEEN OF KNIGHT.

"Oh muthafuckin' hell naw!" He grabbed her bare arm. Yanked her like a rag doll. Turned her around. "Get me a knife!" he shouted. "Get me a muthafuckin' knife! I gotta cut that shit off my baby before we can go up to the roof an' get married today."

The image of his bigger, badder brother fucking The Duchess cast a red hue of rage over everything in Duke's sight. A whistly sound rang in his ears. And his heart pounded like a drumbeat that was ticking down one infuriating realization after another.

"We gon' rewind back to when we met an' start ova," Duke groaned close to her pretty face. "You gon' keep doin' jus' what you doin' by runnin' Babylon. Only you gon' report to The Duke. In HQ. And in bed. Startin' now."

Her face snarled up. "You ain't even a shadow of the Duke I used to love. You look like the muthafuckin' night of the living dead."

She glared so hard into his eyes, Duke felt paralyzed. His eyes burned with tears as he whispered, "Duchess, baby, I'm sorry." He pulled the Glock from the waist of his jeans. He held it to her head, just below the big twist of black hair held in place by those pretty chopsticks. "Say anotha word," he said, "an' Knight can take both our bodies to the cemetery on his wedding day."

With his left hand, Duke yanked her arm; his rough fingernails digging into her baby soft skin. Oooh, skin so soft it didn't feel human. All smooth and creamy, no scars or dark spots like too many chicks had all over their arms, backs, legs, and bellies from hard life in the hood; she was fresh, clean meat.

An' I'm 'bout to get anotha taste.

Timbo was so big and hard, he made a tent in the front of Duke's baggy jeans.

But how I'm gon' fuck her when I got her arm in one hand an' my gat in the otha?

Duke released her arm and shoved her at the same time. She kept her balance, though, on those pretty spike-heeled pumps.

Damn, Timbo was swole like a mug. Gotta get 'im out.

Even though he wore a black leather belt with a BABYLON belt buckle, he easily pulled his pants down with a quick yank by his left hand. Wearin' no drawers in anticipation of this occasion, Timbo swayed free like a sideways telephone pole. Duke stepped back to get a good look at his bride. He thrust his hips forward and whispered, "Baby Girl, come get some Timbo."

The gun in his right hand just didn't feel right.

"Now how I'm gon' make love to my Duchess at gunpoint?" he asked softly, looking into her eyes. "Tell me I can put it down."

She smiled. "Duke, you know I missed you. And you know how things shook down; I didn't have a choice when he took over—"

"You didn't have to stay. You coulda found me."

"Nobody knew where you were," she said softly. "All that matters now is that you're back. So, yeah, put the gun down and come get some Duchess."

He looked at the gun in his hand then back at her eyes.

Full o' scheme! Take that pussy now!

Like a football player hunching down for a tackle, he bent at the waist, gun in hand, and grabbed the bottom of her dress. He wrapped an arm around her ankles and pulled forward.

She fell on her ass, and her back hit the floor. So did her head. And her legs spread wide open. That bald, wet pussy smiled back at him. Ooh, it was so pretty surrounded by her dark bronze suntanned thighs and all that wedding dress.

"I'm back in muthafuckin' heaven where I belong." Timbo was like a giant steel arrow pointing at the best pussy he'd ever had. Duke fell to his knees. He just had to crawl closer so he could slam inside her. He grinned, staring into her eyes as she laid there looking at him, over her chest.

"Put the gun down, Duke, baby," she whispered, "an' I'll give you the wedding day pussy that you been dreamin' about for a year—Duke an' Duchess." She softly sang that old-school Ashford and Simpson ballad, "Reunited and it feels so good."

Her lips looked so delicious when she sang that, and the sound of his name floating up off her tongue made him melt inside.

He set down the gun on the carpet.

But a bad-ass bitch look glinted in her eyes.

Whack! Her stiletto heel smashed into his face, piercing a hole in his cheek all the way into his mouth. Hot blood squirted over his tongue and down his throat.

Wham! The other spiked heel slammed into Timbo.

Duke froze. The pain; it was like a red-hot electric knife had just stabbed him in the dick. Couldn't breathe. Couldn't move. Couldn't see nothin', hear nothin'. His head rang like a siren.

"Biiiittttccchhhh," he groaned.

"I'd shut the fuck up if I were you," Duchess said softly. "It's not nice to call names. Especially on my wedding day."

The plan. My people. Who gon' help me now?

Antoine. Reba. Where the fuck are they? All his other folks were under strict orders not to do anything to carry out their plan until they heard from Duke. No word, no action. But how could he lead a coup while laying here with a wounded dick, with the female version of his ruthless-ass brother standing over him?

She was a blur of white, pink, bronze, and black. *Wham! Wham!* She kicked the side of his leg.

He let out a high-pitched whimper like the pit bulls used to do if they lost a fight.

"That's for havin' my sister killed."

Duke wanted to say that that bitch Melanie Winston was about to waste away in a convent anyway. He'd done the Duchess's look-alike sister a favor by sparing her a miserable life without dick. Duchess should've been grateful that his trick had duped those FBI muthafuckas for so long.

His lips moved to let some words out, but he coughed on the blood oozing down his throat. A sound like the horrible one Prince made when he was dying in Duke's arms broke through his blood-wet lips. He wished he would faint from the pain. But he had to see if she'd kicked a hole in his dick. He had to look down or feel down, but didn't know up from sideways or backwards.

Duke did know one thing, however—the cold metal pressing into his sweaty forehead was his own gun, and his Duchess was holding it there.

Chapter 34

The Queen knew Knight or somebody had to bust in here quick. How the fuck could this have happened? Why hadn't the siren blared? All she knew for sure was that she could guarantee that Duke would never hurt her. All she had to do was squeeze down on this metal and put him out of his misery right now. But she did not want a murder on her conscience, even though it was cut-and-dry self-defense.

She remembered Knight citing The Prince Code by saying, "Kill or be killed," in the gun range. Still, faced with the reality of this situation, it seemed a whole lot more complicated.

I definitely don't want to kill my future brother-in-law on my wedding day, but his diseased dick woulda killed me.

The horror of the moment came crashing down on her senses.

Kill or be killed—fuck my conscience! He was about to rape me, infect me, and our baby.

That meant she'd have to kill the muthafucka because Duke would have stolen the only people in her life who mattered—Knight and Baby Prince.

Muthafucka!

Her index finger curved around the hard, cold metal of the trigger. If nobody came, and if CoCo were dead, and Reba and Antoine were about to come in here and kill her too, The Queen would blast away all their evil asses.

Then she'd go get married and get the fuck away from this crazy life in Babylon. Assuming no other crazy shit was breaking loose in the rest of the building.

Knight! Where are you? Knight! Answer me!

"C'mon, girl! Run!" CoCo's shout rang from the hallway. In her white robe, splattered with blood, Coco ran into the bedroom. She snatched her dress off the mannequin and grabbed The Queen's left hand.

"Where's Antoine? And Reba?" The Queen asked, gripping the gun in her right hand.

"Don't worry about—"

The Queen ran, still in her high heels, behind CoCo into the entryway, where, on the wall beside the door, a foot-wide smear of blood trailed down the white wallpaper. It went behind Antoine's head but started back up at the hole over his ear. He sat upright, eyes wide-open.

"What about Reba?" The Queen asked as CoCo opened the door.

"She's takin' a long shower," CoCo gasped as they dashed into the hallway. "The stairs!"

They had to run about a dozen feet to reach the stairwell door.

It flew open.

Several Barriors and B'Amazons, rifles in hand, burst into the hallway.

"We escaped our damn selves," CoCo snapped. "Duke's in there bleeding. And we need to get to the wedding."

One of the soldiers gave orders: "Half of you get Duke. The others, escort The Queen and CoCo to the locker-room in The Playroom."

Knight, baby, are you okay? Knight, answer me!

The Queen had no phone—it was still back on the vanity in the bridal suite—so she'd been calling for Knight on their special supernatural love hotline. But no answer.

Did Duke kill him first?

And since nobody had responded to her screams, or seen the chaos on the hidden video security system, then any of these allegedly loyal Barriors and B'Amazons could be snitches. Duke sympathizers, who wanted to kill her and CoCo and Knight, right now.

The Queen squeezed her grip tighter around the handle of Duke's gun. Part of her thought she should feel scared, but it was so surreal, so adrenaline-charged, she felt like she was in survival auto pilot. And she wasn't going anywhere or doing anything until she saw Knight alive and safe.

Fuck all these people. If security were doing their jobs, then Duke wouldn't have just busted into her room! The Queen sprinted down the hall. Her dress rustled. The chopsticks came loose; she grabbed them with her left hand as her hair tumbled down her shoulders.

"Queen!" CoCo shouted. "Wait for me!"

The thunder of footsteps sounded like the soldiers were following too.

The Queen kept running. Her toes slammed into the sharp points of her life-saving shoes. Finally she came to Suite 501. She turned the doorknob.

The door opened.

"Knight!" she shrieked, "Knight, baby!" But every room was empty.

The digital clock beside the bed said 5:05.

"Let's go!" The Queen grabbed CoCo's hand, and they ran down the hall, Barriors and B'Amazons in tow. Her mind raced as she dashed up three flights of stairs in her heels and wedding dress.

What would Knight do in this situation? If some deadly conspiracy were going on with Duke or someone else, wouldn't they expect her to run straight into Knight's arms?

Trust no one, she heard his voice inside her head. So it didn't matter. If she ran to him and the bad guys at large caught her too, then that was how she wanted to go down—at Knight's side.

Something had to be wrong with Knight right now, or Intuition would have responded to her in their telepathic love connection. She yanked open the door marked rooftop. It led to a covered, glass-walled area beside the elevators. This entrance area faced the beautiful arrangement for the wedding.

But the terrace was packed with people—security, celebrities' assistants, and camera and video crews, ready to capture every joyous moment.

"Shit!" The Queen exclaimed. "Where is he?"

All around her, "Ooohs" and "Aaahs" broke out in every direction. Then The Queen remembered she was in her wedding dress, and she was the star of this show. But she wasn't here to meet and greet right now. And all this would be bullshit if she didn't have the man who made her heart beat.

SEX IN THE HOOD 2

Knight!

A dark pink carpet stretched from beneath her life-saving stilettos over the brick-patterned floor and into the enormous white party tent. Giant white poles, covered with greenery and pink roses, held up the corners and inside lengths of the scalloped tent. Inside, explosions of pink flowers hung from the peaked ceiling. Rows and rows of pink satin-covered chairs held hundreds of beautiful people.

Celebrities. Musicians. Politicians. Pimps. Madames.

But The Queen didn't care about anybody or anything except laying her eyes on her man.

Knight, baby, where are you?

All those people standing in the aisle, she couldn't see the altar, except for the golden backdrop that cast a shimmery sheer over the wide-open view of the blue river and downtown Detroit's skyscrapers.

"Girl, wait," CoCo took her left hand.

The Queen realized she was still holding Duke's gun. She turned toward CoCo, hoisted up her dress, and slipped it into her garter belt.

"Play it cool," CoCo said, pulling her into an elevator.

"I gotta find Knight."

"Everything looks cool and calm up here," CoCo said. "The Barriors are handling the situation downstairs, so don't let anybody see you look flustered."

Trust no one.

The Queen stared hard into CoCo's eyes.

"Girl, don't even think it." CoCo stared back just as hard.

A B'Amazon stepped onto the elevator and nodded at Coco, who let the bloody robe fall. She slipped into her pink dress and said, "Now zip me, girl. We got a wedding to be in."

As soon as they stepped out, Jamal and the Bang Squad, who were set up near the altar, began to play the wedding march.

CoCo kissed The Queen on her cheek. "You come right after me," Coco reminded her.

She nodded as CoCo walked in the soft, late afternoon sunshine toward the tent.

WHITE CHOCOLATE

Someone brushed The Queen's hair while someone else handed her a giant bouquet of pink roses. Another person guided her to the edge of the tent.

A hip-hop version of "Here Comes the Bride" boomed. Everybody turned around with more "oohs" and "aaahs."

The Queen stared straight ahead. She looked down the rose petal-strewn aisle, past the satin ribbons draped on the sides of the chairs, past all the famous faces in the crowd. There, under giant bouquets of pink, purple and white flowers, she should have seen the sexiest man alive.

The reverend was there. So was Jamal.

But Knight was nowhere to be seen.

Chapter 35

A bride wasn't supposed to feel this fucked up on her wedding day. She wasn't supposed to fend off an HIV-positive rapist or kick him in the face and dick or hold a gun to his head. She wasn't supposed to have soldiers with rifles surrounding the pretty white tent where she would say, "I do." And she definitely wasn't supposed to have a gun strapped inside the lace and satin of her garter belt.

No, Alice was not enjoying Ghettoland one bit. She wished she could pass through a secret portal into a Wonderland where she'd feel safe to live, love, and raise a baby with her man who would magically appear. Now.

As she walked slowly on trembling legs up the pink aisle, she hated that all these people were staring at her when she wanted to burst into tears or cuss somebody out or both. She hadn't even brushed her hair on her wedding day.

Neither had CoCo, but she still looked gorgeous up there, grinning back at The Queen, like there was something in this nightmarish day to smile about.

Knight, baby, where are you?

Suddenly, Knight rose from a chair in the front row, next to his mother, who wore a giant pink hat with netting over her face. Like an ebony tower rising in front of all the guests, Knight turned around. His eyes sparkled at her, his sucka lips curled up into a smile that broke out into a grin.

Thank you, God! My baby is okay!

The Queen wanted to run down the aisle and throw herself into his arms. She had to feel the long, firm length and warmth of his body; then she'd know that he was safe and that his heart was beating just fine. They could get married and live happily ever after.

Yeah, right.

It seemed like forever as The Queen walked toward Knight, fighting the bad vibe in her gut. Still wearing no panties, her pussy was sweaty and swollen. The friction of her walk rubbed Celeste, just right, to take a tiny bit of the edge off this awful state of mind.

253

WHITE CHOCOLATE

I want him inside me, now. I want to make love to the infinity with the only one who matters.

Because all these fabulous people didn't matter to The Queen. They had on beautiful dresses and suits. Famous musicians and actors and politicians dotted the crowd. It was as picture-perfect as the celebrity tabloids, daily newspapers, and hip-hop magazines could imagine, yet Knight had issued a ban on all media, for both The Wedding and The Games, even though the who's who of the hip-hop world was here to celebrate her big day.

But they don't care about me.

Not Emcee Sexarella in her rhinestone-studded blue leather dress and her entourage of big-haired beauties. Not Rip Masta Mac and his crew of hardcore gangsta rappers. And not all these other people who were officers and associates of Babylon from across the country. They were just here for the hype factor of the hottest wedding in Babylon history and the sexiest entertainment ever, anywhere, for The Games tonight in the auditorium downstairs at The Playhouse.

Oh, baby, you look like hell.

Hot tears blurred the gray pallor on Knight's face. The closer she got, the harder her heart pounded. Whether it was stress or her curse or panic attacks or PTSD or something worse, she was sure that it would kill him if they didn't get out of here.

He held out his arms as she approached.

Her dress fluffed around her feet as she walked, and her palms got sweaty around the satin-ribboned handle of her bouquet.

Finally, she felt beautiful. Not because it was a gorgeous dress whose price tag could finance the purchase of a small house. No, she felt beautiful because her Knight was staring down with so much love in his eyes. She thought she would faint. If she died right now, she would have experienced more love with him in the past year than some women ever got in a lifetime. It was pure.

And we're perfect together.

SEX IN THE HOOD 2

The Queen hoisted up her dress and ran the last few steps into Knight's arms.

His eyes grew wide as he glimpsed the gun on her thigh. That wasn't part of his security plan for today, but he played it off by embracing her and lifting her up and spinning her around.

They pressed their lips together and kissed long and hard. The audience exploded with cheers.

The reverend playfully cleared his throat, his microphone attached to the collar of his black robe amplifying the sound. Laughter erupted among the guests.

The Queen never wanted to stop breathing health and life into her man. She pressed her face into his neck, feeling his pulse beat against her eyelids.

Yes, he's alive. Alive and well.

"May we begin?" the reverend asked playfully.

"Yes, sir," Knight answered. "Let's do this!"

As The Queen looked up into Knight's onyx eyes and he stared down into hers, they faced each other and gripped hands. Her mind spun with images—Duke laying there bleeding; Antoine shot to death; Reba probably dead in the bathroom thanks to CoCo's quick thinking; the serious security breach that she hoped was handled by now; and who knew what else.

She just wanted to hear the words *husband and wife* so she could stroll off into the sunset with the man of her dreams.

They were close, because the reverend said, "If anyone here has any objection to this union, speak now or forever hold your peace."

A piercing scream made The Queen's gut cramp. All the guests spun around to look.

Blood-covered Reba stumbled onto the pink aisle. "Watch out for Duke!" she screamed.

A shocked gasp rose from the guests.

"Watch out for Duke!" Then she collapsed.

In black, white, and gray fatigues, Barriors and B'Amazons descended on her, plucking her off the carpet and carrying her away.

"Continue, please," Knight said.

Minutes later, the reverend said, "I now pronounce you man and wife. You may kiss your bride."

For a moment, their charmed circle of love made everything around them fade to gray. This was their technicolor dream, live and in color, as they officially became one and three all at once.

But that bliss was shattered when the ear-splitting sirens blared, and B'Amazons and Barriors around the perimeter of the rooftop terrace drew rifles and ushered all the guests to the center of the tent.

Yeah, this was about the most fucked-up wedding day any girl could *never* imagine.

But part of The Queen felt like it didn't even matter. Because her beautiful black Knight was pulling her up against his strong body, and she was burying her face in his neck where his pulsing veins confirmed that he was alive. Now they just had to escape this hell.

Chapter 36

Trina Michaels sat in a surveillance van, watching the outrageous display of gaudy ghetto flamboyance through the eight tiny video cameras hidden on Rip Masta and his fellow thugs. "Imagine a shootout at a wedding, and we have the exclusive video!" she exclaimed to her cameraman, who would leave the van and go inside for more video after the Feds rushed in. "This story gets better by the second!"

In a matter of hours, after Rip Masta would get great video of the sex Olympics, Trina would get the media coup of the decade. The plan was for Federal officers to storm into Babylon and capture Victoria Winston.

The agents were waiting right now in vans parked throughout this riverfront warehouse district where Trina had gotten fucked so good a month ago inside The Playhouse.

"Bye, bye, Miss Queen!" Trina giggled as she watched the live video showing those soldiers calming the frantic wedding crowd. "If you think your day is bad now, just wait!"

This would serve both her and her pet gorilla right for daring to threaten the great investigative journalist Trina Michaels. They would see who'd come out on top.

Me!

"This whole story epitomizes the fact that an obsession with sex in the black community is its downfall," Trina said. "HIV, pregnancy, prostitution—these are all manifestations of the sex addiction that's gripping our inner cities."

The cameraman, who was adjusting knobs on the wall of sound and editing equipment, crinkled his beige face at her and said, "You're a racist witch. Do you have any idea?—"

"As a white male," she snapped, "you have no right to call me racist."

"You're a racist, snobby bitch whose sexual frustrations give you a mega superiority attitude," he said. "You wish you were as wild and free as these folks. At least they don't try to pretend they're something else. Isn't that what the term 'ghetto fabulous' is all about?"

Rat-tat-tat!

257

"Gunfire!" Trina shrieked. "Look at 'em scramble. Nice wedding, Miss Queen. You'd do Martha Stewart and Emily Post proud today."

The cameraman put on a headset that blocked his ears; then he turned back to his equipment. "You got serious issues."

Trina gloated at the screen as The Queen huddled under an arch of pink roses with Knight. "No, I got an award-winning, urban docudrama in the palm of my hands!"

Chapter 37

"Babylon, let's fuck!" screamed the thousand-plus people packing The Auditorium for The Games. They were singing along with the Bang Squad's thunderous theme song for this much anticipated annual event.

It was about to get started, and it couldn't get finished soon enough for Knight.

So we can slip away forever.

As he stood backstage, just inside the huge, heavy, purple velvet curtains, his insides trembled and his chest squeezed almost as horribly as those tense moments during the lockdown after the wedding. The alarm had gone off because Paul had spotted Li'l Tut on the security cameras, limping out of Suite 515 with Dickman's assistance. Then Paul reported to Knight that Li'l Tut was holding his crotch with one hand and pressing a towel to his bleeding cheek with the other.

Now we gotta finish what The Queen started.

The Queen had jacked him up good, but Li'l Tut was still alive and lurking somewhere in this building. Big Moe and a team of Barriors who were searching every inch had explicit instructions to call Knight to come and finally put that muthafucka out of his misery when they found him.

Lightning bolts of stress pains shot through Knight's chest at the thought of Li'l Tut cornering The Queen in her wedding suite, trying to shoot her up with the deadly weapon that his dick had become.

All while I was blacking out down the hall.

Anger and frustration at himself threatened to suck away Knight's breath.

I am a warrior . . . I am a warrior. Manifest Destiny is mine. Just a few more hours.

"Babylon, let's fuck!" The audience thundered with the blasting bass beat as Knight and Jamal stepped onto the stage from opposite sides. At the edge of the shiny pine stage floor, giant glass block letters spelling THE GAMES AT BABYLON glowed cobalt blue. Artificial steam from dry ice cast a sexy-smoky mist around them. The smoke glowed blue and purple,

259

creating an outer-space-fantasy feeling as it wafted over the floor of the stage.

The stage dropped about four feet to the floor, where Barriors stood shoulder to shoulder in ninja black, double-strapped with rifles. In front of them stretched a long table where six celebrity judges sat with laptop computers that would record and tally their scores for each event.

Beyond the judges stretched a rolling sea of blingin' urban style and vibrant energy. Every purple velvet seat in the place showcased sexy chicks and thugged-out dudes and glitzy celebrities and huge athletes and famous musicians and Grammy-winning rappers.

This black-brown-beige sea shimmered with sequined baseball caps, Cartier glasses, leather of every color, gloss-lacquered lips, and every style of denim, designer labels, diamond-studded gold grillz and jewelry, and hairstyles that shot beautiful sprays of braids and dreads and 'fros up toward the ornate gold-painted balconies and chandeliered ceiling.

Knight savored a sense of pride at the beauty of his people, as purple spotlights flashed from the stage, highlighting the mass of people. A haze of ganja smoke cast a surreal cloud over the people as they smiled, laughed, drank, and put in orders to waitresses, who strutted up and down the aisles in white Babylon dresses and lace-up gold sandals.

Knight wished folks could do without the intoxicants, but this whole show was about to offer up the most enticing intoxicant of all—booty.

As he took all this in, Knight's mind reeled with images of how he hoped that the Barriors had caught Li'l Tut by now, and how in just a few hours, with this crowd whipped into a frenzy of fucking here and up in The Playroom, he and The Queen would be well on their way to paradise.

His chest squeezed under his black silk Armani suit, under which he hid four guns.

There's no room for error. If some shit goes down, this is our only chance, or we're stuck.

If somebody had snitched to the Feds and they launched a raid, or if Li'l Tut went kamikaze on the crowd or Knight or

The Queen, and succeeded. Or if Moreno had some double-crossing scheme. Or some other nigga lost his mind in all this pussy and fucking. Or another knucklehead had ideas about stealing the millions of dollars that would be in the vault for admissions, bets, and prize money—then any of the above could toss a monster monkey wrench into this magnificent mix.

And we'd be stuck in the shit. Manifest Destiny would be nothing but a glittering mirage.

Knight sucked down gulps of air to disarm this barrage of worries. He had to enjoy his last night of this outrageous carnal indulgence that made Babylon what it was. In a few days, he'd be able to redefine carnal indulgence one-on-one, tropical style, with The Queen.

"How e'rybody doin'?" Jamal shouted, launching into his rapper posture, holding the mic and taking long, excited steps from one end of the stage to the other. He stopped in front of three enormous white beds that were draped with mosquito netting suspended by huge, black-and-gold striped masks of Cleopatra and Tutankhamen.

Jamal, wearing baggy blue jeans, black Timberland boots, a white tank top that showcased his caramel-brown muscles, and the heavy gold chain with a Bang Squad medallion, held the mic toward the audience.

"Babylon, let's fuck!" they responded with the music.

"Welcome to The *Gaaaaaaa-mes!*" The audience went wild. Jamal held out a hand toward Knight. "Now some o' y'aw' was here las' year when the new sheriff blasted back into D-town, guns blazin'!"

The audience roared.

"All y'aw' know, this the baddest muthafucka eva, rulin' Babylon like a king! Show some love for Knight John*son*!"

Guys in the audience punched their fists in the air and barked. Girls shrieked. Some yanked up their shirts and shook their titties as they cheered.

"Firs', though, y'aw' congratulate the King o' Babylon for gettin' married today."

"Babylon, let's fuck!" the audience screamed.

Jamal worked his hips in a sexy love-grind, which made the girls shimmy their titties once more. "Yeah, but they gon' make love tonight," Jamal said playfully. "There go The Queen, my "poetry-*flow*etry" rappin' sista who's blazin' that shit up the charts!" He pointed up at The Queen in the closest golden box seat balcony overlooking the stage, where she sat with CoCo and Mr. and Mrs. Marx. Honey would join them after the first competition.

Emcee Sexarella, sitting with her girls in the balcony next to The Queen, stood. Tall, curvy, and wearing a transparent gold bodysuit with sequined stars over her nipples and pussy, she screamed, "All hail The Queen, y'aw'!" Her round, brown face sparkled with gold eye make-up. And her high black ponytail, which was long, straight, and silky-looking, flipped over her shoulder as she shouted, "Give it up 'cause she got what all y'aw want—the sexiest dude in Babylon!"

The audience cheered.

The Queen, wearing a pink lace and sequined bustier and pink leather pants that showcased her diamond-studded belly button and tattoos, stood, turned around, and slapped her ass with her left hand, making her wedding ring sparkle in the hazy purple light.

As the audience roared, Ping and Pong stood in ninja black behind her, scanning every direction.

Knight noticed that Rip Masta was turning his whole body at an unnatural angle to look at The Queen.

Keep an eye on Rip Masta, Intuition warned. *Somethin' ain't right with him and his crew.*

The gangsta rappers filled the box next to Sexarella and the one directly across from The Queen. Knight also didn't like that they'd sported saggy jeans with denim jackets and baseball caps to the wedding. They needed to show some respect.

Next to them, all wearing suits, sat Red Moreno and his brothers, plus B-Boy and Birdie in another private balcony box. Nearby, Raynard "Dickman" Ingalls sat with two chicks on his lap beside Shar Miller and Leroy Lewis. Dickman was about to get excused to answer some questions, but that muthafucka didn't know it yet.

Knight smiled up at The Queen, who moved in sultry slow-motion as she puckered, held her shiny French manicure to her lips, making her diamond wedding ring sparkle in the purple light, and blew him a kiss.

"That's love, y'aw'!" Sexarella shouted, rousing a whole new cheer from the audience, especially the women.

"Wooo-weeee!" Jamal exclaimed with a deep, sexual tone. "Sorry, y'aw', you gon' miss the real Games tonight when he an' his bride make it official."

The men barked in unison.

"Wait up, do," Jamal said, "any o' y'aw' who was at the weddin' know ain't no party 'til some shit go down, right?"

The barking men imitated the siren sound.

Knight kept a poker face as those tiny needles of pain surged once more around his pounding heart.

"We outlaws." Jamal grinned at Knight. "So we gotta set the mood, you know. Show we got some juice if a muthafucka try to show out up in here."

People in the audience screamed.

"Yeeee-ah!" Jamal boomed. "Now, let's get this party started wit' the Prettiest Titties contest."

The audience hooped and hollered as thirty women strutted onto the stage. Standing midway between the blue block letters and the beds, they wore thong bikinis and high-heeled sandals in every color. And each had a small sign on her thigh with a black number and team name. Honey stood with them; she was not a Slut, but as Babylon staff, she had the option of joining the team.

Knight bellowed into the microphone, "Behold the prettiest titties in Babylon from coast to coast!"

Jamal read from a list, announcing the women's names, their home cities and the enterprises they represented, including teams sponsored by Babylon, Moreno Incorporated, Question Marx Entertainment, Rip Masta Mac, Thuggalicious, Mob Squad Movies, a group of pro-ballers called Slam Dunk! and Emcee Sexarella.

Jamal announced, "Now our distinguished panel of judges will score these titty queens based on size, shape, firmness, nipples, symmetry, and naturalness."

Knight loved looking at this buffet of female fruits. And these women did represent every kind of nature's candy— brown melons with purple grape-sized nipples, oranges with pink gumdrop tips, plum-colored balloons with raisin clusters, peachy-perky bubbles with Blowpop points, and pomegranate-smooth jugs with sweet little corks on the ends. They were all perfect in their own right; something for every man's taste.

Having sampled every variety and flavor in the fresh market of human temptation, Knight now craved only one flavor. And she was sitting safely up in the balcony, laughing with CoCo as they ogled the contestants. Next to them, Mrs. Marx was sitting on Larry's lap, grinding and, presumably, fucking already.

In the next balcony, Moreno and company were watching intently, as were Shar Miller and Leroy Lewis. But Dickman was being escorted out by the B'Amazons for an intensive Q&A about Li'l Tut's whereabouts.

Knight caught Rip Masta Mac's sneaky glance. Something was definitely not right with that cat. Knight looked at his watch, to which he had affixed his phone so that he could discreetly check for text messages on stage. The screen showed only the time and the symbols for a charged battery and satellite function. No word yet from Big Moe about Li'l Tut.

Knight used his right hand to type a text message into his phone, strapped to his left wrist, to tell Ping to keep an eye on that muthafucka, Rip Masta. Then he looked once more at The Queen.

She pulled her titties out and rubbed seductive circles over her cinnamon-colored nipples. Then she smiled at him playfully and returned her breasts to her bustier.

Shane threatened to raise the front of his pleated pants. He craved the magical moment, in a few hours, when they would make love and consummate this marriage in the hedonistic Babylon.

As The Queen focused on the contestants, so did Knight.

SEX IN THE HOOD 2

What was it about a woman's breasts that made a man lose his mind? Was it that "come-to-momma-for-some-love" symbolism that was burned into every baby boy's mind at birth, when he first suckled his mother's life-giving milk? Was it something he was taught growing up, to worship the size and shape of girls' titties?

Knight loved the squishy-soft, yet warm, firm sensation of The Queen's juicy C-cups. He loved to bury his face in that flawless, creamy skin, breathe in her clean, feminine scent, and lock his lips to the gentle curve on the underside of her breasts. He loved to look at them as they made love or as she stood in the mirror putting on make-up or as they bounced under her shirt as she walked in the offices.

Her breasts were full, round, and plump, with nipples that pointed right at him, like the needle on her body's compass was permanently set in the direction of Knight.

He loved to take them into his mouth when they were soft, twirl his tongue around them, and savor the sensation of them hardening under his lips.

Jamal announced each woman's name, who then stepped forward.

"This here is Zena Drake of Team Thuggalicious."

A girl with huge, silicone torpedoes stepped forward. Small gold hoop earrings dangled from each brown nipple, which contrasted with her butter-pecan complexion. Squatting down on her knees, she flipped her titties up, taking the gold hoops between her teeth, and licked herself like a cat. Her tongue went 'round and 'round her nipples, which glistened with saliva. Then she did a backbend, facing the audience upside down, so that her enormous boobs fell down to the sides of her cheeks. She nuzzled the swollen sacks with her nose and mouth.

The audience went crazy.

Knight glanced up at The Queen. A smile raised the corners of his mouth.

Her eyes glowed with lust as she studied the beauties on stage, including her favorite girl, Honey. She and CoCo were whispering, pointing to the contestants, smiling.

Knight's phone vibrated. A text message flashed: "Got him." Knight nodded to Jamal then slipped backstage.

This time, the king was going to get his hands dirty, to make sure the job was done right.

Chapter 38

It would be an inevitable and unfortunate chain of events, Red Moreno mused as he watched the luscious breasts on stage, *when the Johnson brothers would finally meet their Fate. Soon they would be resting right alongside their despicable brother, Prince. Tonight I will wipe them off the screen so that I may single-handedly rule this underworld by adding it to my global empire.*

Babylon was too large and successful for any black man to own. Moreno had simply gone along with that bogus deal led by that misguided, mixed-up Cleopatra wannabe so that he could legitimately get inside the same building with both brothers at once.

Red glanced at his two brothers as Babylon whores performed fellatio on them. Together they were an international phenomenon. He thought of the Johnson brothers starting with Prince, then Knight, then Duke, always a thorn in the side of Moreno Enterprises, when it came to the lucrative market of inner-city Detroit.

Finally, Red would savor the delight of wiping the remaining two Johnsons off the map. Now, the true showdown would occur, and neither Duke nor Knight would have a chance.

I'll make off with all the money. And Cleopatra will make me a fortune as the exotic superstar in one of my pleasure penthouses in Beijing.

Her half-black beauty and theatrical style would garner thousands from the businessmen who traveled to the sleek city every day from around the world. Plus Red would get to savor her succulence whenever he wanted.

Now, his body tingled from the head he was getting from a black chick he'd picked up in the lobby. In his mind, though, he was fast-forwarding to the moment when Cleopatra would be sucking his *schlong*. She'd have nobody to protect her, and her survival would depend on following the orders of her captors. Just like she'd done, according to B-Boy's account of her life over the past year, when Duke kidnapped her into his urban hell. She'd gone from rich and white to black and poor.

Now she'd go from ghetto fabulous to global fast-lane, courtesy of Red Moreno.

B-Boy had told him all about her real background. By getting her out of the country and relieving her of that federal fugitive status, he'd be doing her a favor. And with his connections, getting past authorities and customs and any other government pests would be done faster than anyone could say, "Kidnapping."

In a short while, Moreno's battalion would be moving in on boats, in trucks, and on foot to bring this building called The Playhouse under siege.

The power, the money, and the pussy will all be mine.

Chapter 39

The Queen thought she'd seen it all, but the way those girls were competing in the Craziest Pussy Tricks event was straight-up mind-blowing. Especially that chick on the Mob Squad Movies team, who was chewing gum and blowing big pink bubbles with her pussy!

"How did she do that?" The Queen gasped.

"She a nasty freak!" CoCo exclaimed playfully, mesmerized by the close-up shots of that bubble-blowing bitch on the two giant video screens on the upper left and upper right of the stage. "She got the smokin' chick beat hands down."

So far they'd watched Sexarella's girl smoke a cigarette with her twat. A Slam Dunk! chick had shot marbles out of her cunt, which she aimed at a hole in the center of a target and made every shot! And a Moreno contestant had made herself orgasm by rubbing her clit with her fingers before squirting cum twelve feet across the stage!

If this shit weren't so wild and crazy, The Queen would have been out of her mind with worry over where the fuck Knight had disappeared to. She knew he and his boys were searching for Duke, and that security was of utmost concern tonight, especially after that crazy shooting at the wedding after the alarm had gone off.

Plus she got the feeling that a whole lot more than she knew was going down right now, and it was about to break wide open in a few hours. Her telepathic love connection with Knight told her so. Along with the very worrisome vibe that something was still terribly wrong with his health. And the stress of this evening could knock him out cold. Or worse.

"Hey, girl," CoCo said, putting her arm around The Queen, "Knight don't lose—eva—so take a deep breath an' enjoy this crazy shit." CoCo pointed to the stage, where a bright green snake was slithering out of a girl's pussy and onto the black skin of her thigh. It came out wet and glistened as it hugged her leg and flicked its tongue toward the audience, which roared.

WHITE CHOCOLATE

The girl's bright green fingernails contrasted with the thick black hair around her pussy as she massaged her red clit. She must've been cumming, too, to push the snake out, because the lips were pulsating around the snake's endless green body, gently easing it out. Ecstasy twisted on the chick's face, which was framed by a huge afro that looked like a black sun rising around her head.

The Queen imagined how the snake, which rules required to be non-poisonous, would feel like a penis stimulating the inside of her pussy while she worked her clit into an awesome orgasm. The Queen shifted on her chair, aching for Knight to make love to her, far and away on their honeymoon.

"*Whaaaaat?*" CoCo exclaimed. "Oh no, she didn't!"

A girl on stage was standing on her head, with her legs doing the splits pointing out sideways. A brass horn was sticking up out of her vagina. And she was playing the Prince song, "Do Me, Baby." She was actually blowing enough air out of her pussy into the mouthpiece to play each note!

The Queen's mouth dropped open as she gawked, wondering what in the world would come next.

Chapter 40

Knight drew one of his four guns before easing open the door to the Champagne Room. That's where, according to Big Moe's second text message, they were holding Li'l Tut with Dickman.

Now, in the silent room, Big Moe sat on the end of the white couch, his eyes wide open, staring forward. Facing him in the plush, cube-shaped chairs, sat two Barriors; two others knelt with their faces touching the carpet.

And they were all dead.

Chapter 41

The intense pain of his cheek and his dick riled Duke into a rabid state of mind. He was on a rampage, and he'd kill and destroy anything in his way. Whether that was Knight or Duchess or anybody else.

I'm gonna take the money then storm the stage and reclaim what's mine—Babylon. And I got some lead for any muthafucka who try to stop me.

Duke charged down the hallway on the third floor. He had to get to the vault before Knight tried any tricks to move the money collected as admissions, bets, and prizes for The Games. Those millions would be a good start.

Later on, Duke would hack into the computer system to access the millions that were his for the taking.

"Man, you shoulda let me stay up there," Duke said as Dickman hurried alongside him. "Coulda knocked off Knight, put that worry outta our minds."

"No time fo' that, dude," Dickman said. "You already done let a bitch take yo' gun an' jack yo' ass today, so I know you ain't right tonight. Let me han'le the security detail—"

Duke spun around and knocked Dickman's leather cap off. "Muthafucka, this my world! You call me *Massa.*"

"I'll call you *crazy*, nigga!"

Duke glared back at his boy. The rage pumping through his thin limbs numbed the pain in his cheek and his dick.

Here I go again. A hot-headed muthafucka who cain't control himself long enough to claim my fortune.

Duke imagined Knight walking up on them during their temper tantrum in the hallway and popping both their stupid asses. Duke spun on his heel and ran toward the vault with Dickman following.

Duke had already called Shar and Leroy to mobilize their crew to physically get the cash. *Fuck Moreno.* Duke had only gone through the motions of including him to get a feel for what that international gangster wanted.

E'rythang. And he's gettin' nothin'.

272

Chapter 42

As Knight text-messaged Ping and Pong about what was going down, so that they'd body-block The Queen at all times, his mind spun with options: He could sound the alarm and put the whole building on lockdown; he could get The Queen and leave now, then flee to the safety of a new life with the millions they already had in his overseas accounts; or he could hunt down Li'l Tut, take him down his damn self, then execute Manifest Destiny the way he'd planned.

Yeah, that's it.

So what if his chest ached. So what if he was breathing hard. So what if Intuition was telling him that he should be worried about much more than Li'l Tut trying to show out tonight. It was time to fight to the death, defy it, and Houdini the hell outta here.

No way in hell was this black warrior going to punk out and run from his own kingdom, until he decided the time was right.

Chapter 43

Baby Blue knew she would be named Sexiest Slut. Didn't matter that she didn't want dick anymore. Didn't matter that she was about to become part of Shar Miller's harem out in Las Vegas. If she get The Queen to eat her pussy the way she did thirteen months ago; The Queen, who could have picked any Slut at Duke's birthday party to entertain her, then Baby Blue knew she had the stuff to impress these judges right now. Starting with her sexiest walk.

She had modeled it after her mother's naturally seductive strut. The strut that all the men in their hood said reminded them of a pregnant alley cat.

Yeah, like this, with my ass pooted out, my toes pointed in, and a slow-motion roll with every step.

That's how she'd walked for Duke way back in the day when he'd hired her to work at Babylon, saving her from life on the streets. Then she'd recruited Reba, her childhood partner in crying alone and being abandoned in the nasty flat while their mothers were out all night working to the brutal beat of their pimp.

No matter how many johns had been bouncing between their legs, or how many times their pimp had humiliated them, Momma and Reba's mother always carried their heads high— like this—and swayed their hips hard—yeah, like this here— making their booty cheeks roll like bouncing basketballs.

The audience exploded.

"Do yo' thang, Double D!" a dude shouted from the front row.

The Queen smiled.

The mesmerizing power of the walk, Baby Blue knew too, was also in the way she worked her face. The way she radiated sex power from her eyes and her glossed, pouty lips. And the way she projected laser beams of attitude that brainwashed and seduced everyone within a mile radius to believe, *Baby Blue is the sexiest bitch around.*

Didn't even matter that she was wearing that skimpy blue leather bikini that Reba had bought her; Baby Blue could've worked this magic in a gray sweatsuit.

I just got it like that.

As she strutted through the ankle-deep mist on the stage, Baby Blue caught glimpses of her audience that affirmed she would win.

Like the basketball star sitting on the end of the second row. His oversized jeans hung around his ankles and the bare legs of the chick who was blowing him as his eyes devoured Baby Blue's sweet stuff on stage.

More proof that she was burning up the stage was Sexarella up there in the balcony. She was sitting on a Stud's lap, grinding like she was about to blow her nut, but staring lustfully down at Baby Blue.

Another hint of triumph was that the chicks in the audience were looking at her like, *Where'd she get all that confidence? And how can I get some? How can I learn how to walk like that?* And even, *I hate bitches like that who can get a guy just by walkin' across the room.*

On top of that, all the judges were staring up, wide-eyed, like they wanted to jump the stage, tackle her onto one of those giant beds, and lick her up, down, and sideways.

Most important, Baby Blue was loving herself. She wasn't doing this to impress anybody else; she was doing this to celebrate herself. How she'd grown up in circumstances that could shred a girl's self-esteem into a million little ribbons and litter the vacant lot that was next to their house in the hood. How she'd become a woman who sold her body to survive, but who never lost her sense of self in the meantime. And how she'd been saving her money all these years, so that when it was time to retire, she could do so without relying on anybody but herself.

The half-million dollars she was about to win in this event would bolster her savings to create a security blanket in case things didn't work out when she lived the glamorous life with Shar Miller in Vegas.

Right now, Baby Blue knew she had all those other gorgeous women beat, "booty down." Because it wasn't about the big hair or the lipgloss or the perfect titties or the pierced belly buttons.

Sexiness is all about attitude and confidence. An' I got boatloads of both . . .

Reba once had it too, but all her evil gold-digging finally caught up with her in the worst way, falling out blood-covered and dead at a wedding! Not just any wedding, but the most important wedding Babylon had ever seen.

Hhmmmph!

Reba had been plotting with Duke so he'd marry her, but Fate had just fucked her up the ass on this one. Everybody knew Duke had HIV, so however Reba had gotten shot today, the shooter was doing her a favor, sparing her from the torture of AIDS.

That's what she and dead-ass Antoine get for bullying me into their plot. All I want is to live my life in peace and do what I love—this.

Baby Blue cast a sexy smile at the roaring audience. She pivoted on a sparkly blue stiletto sandal, poked her juicy ass out toward the judges, wound it just enough, then strutted back to her spot with the other contestants, knowing she was the Sexiest Slut in Babylon and beyond.

Chapter 44

CoCo was about to cum on herself.

Because the whole stage was covered with cocks.

And the one doing the talking was going to give her some tonight and all day tomorrow. But meanwhile, all this other male meat was priming her for the fuck of the year. She couldn't remember the last time she was this turned-on. It was like her pussy was a faucet, soaking her whole crotch in hot water, making a puddle inside the pink leather dress she'd worn to the wedding reception dinner.

"Ladies and gentlemen," Jamal announced, "now it's time for one of the most popular events here at The Games—the Most Perfect Dick contest!"

The audience roared.

CoCo and The Queen pulled out binoculars to check out close-ups of the twenty-five men standing nude on the stage, eye-popping erections pointing out at the audience.

"It's time to announce the five finalists that the judges have chosen." Jamal opened an envelope and called out the names and teams that each man represented.

CoCo wished she could lay spread-eagled on that big bed in the middle of the stage and let those five pull a train on her horny ass. It was just a fantasy, because no way was she going to jeopardize her spot as Jamal's lady. Nope, someday soon she would follow in The Queen's sexy footsteps and become the missus to a very rich man. Maybe CoCo could even take over the daily operations of Babylon when The Queen started having babies.

Damn, Duke almost got me today.

Suddenly the shock of the day came crashing down on CoCo. She had killed two people today in self-defense to save herself and The Queen. How Reba had lived through two bullet wounds long enough to get upstairs to the roof and expire on the wedding aisle was still trippin' her out. And how Duke had snuck into Babylon and bogarted into their suite was even more mind-blowing.

277

It was a good thing CoCo had a gun stashed in the bathrobe pocket, just in case. Why she'd chosen the one with the silencer on it, she didn't know, but if Duke had heard shots when she took out Reba and Antoine, he could've hurt The Queen.

CoCo shook her head to exorcise those haunting, horrible thoughts. She'd been drinking champagne tonight, which had softened her stress. But sex, yes, this was the ultimate escape, the most intense intoxicant, the most decadent distraction.

Yeah, all those delicious dicks down there proved that the world was one big buffet of male meat of every cut, grade, and quality. With chiseled muscles and handsome faces, every one of those Studs was stamped PRIME USDA CHOICE CUT—fresh, clean, disease-free, and succulent to the taste.

CoCo's mouth watered as she examined Contestant Number One through her binoculars. He was redbone, with a dark pink-beige penis shooting out from a nest of auburn-brown 'fro. It was long and thick but sort of pointed at the end. Like the head wasn't much wider than the shaft.

Naw, I need a big ol' head to come knockin' up inside me.

Contestant Number Two was classic chocolate brown with the kind of dick that would make a chick run. It looked like a firehose, wide enough to split a pussy in half, long enough to slam up through her insides, into her throat, and choke a bitch. And he could forget about getting head from a girl. That shit was lockjaw waiting to happen, if she could even get her mouth around that mammoth dickhead!

CoCo stared with freakish fascination. Like that time when she was a kid and her parents took her to the Guinness Book of World Records museum. She'd met the world's tallest woman and just stood there gawking at the seven-footer.

Now, that guy's penis had to be setting some kind of record. Looked like if it weren't hard, it would hang to his knees.

Contestant Number Three shifted slightly, making his caramel-brown dick sway in the misty blue haze of the stage.

Now that's what I'm talkin' about.

It was perfect—long and thick, with just the right proportions. Extending from a soft black pouf that was cut short and trimmed into a neat *V* that did not grow onto his upper thighs, it was a smooth shaft with a slight zig-zag of a vein up the side. It had a big head that looked juicy enough to chew on and featured a hole at the end that stared back at her like an all-seeing eye and winked, *I know you want me.*

"Girl, I would be on that," CoCo whispered to The Queen. "You okay?"

The Queen's eyes shimmered silver in the dim light as tears threatened to drip.

CoCo put her arm around her.

"I'm scared." The Queen sobbed into CoCo's shoulder. "Knight disappeared backstage an hour ago. He won't answer his phone, and Ping and Pong won't let me go find him."

CoCo's heart ached for her best friend. She gripped The Queen's bare shoulders. "Listen, girl, you know Knight won't let nothin' happen to you. Just trust that it's all gonna work out perfect tonight. Say that, *Perfect.*"

The Queen whispered, "Perfect."

"Now," CoCo said, turning The Queen's shoulders so that she had to look down at the stage, "forget your troubles by lookin' at *that* shit. Girl, my pussy is so wet I could cause a tidal wave if I spread my legs."

"I hope Jamal is thirsty tonight," The Queen said, even though her voice was quivery like she was scared shitless. "Give 'im a straw."

CoCo giggled as she focused on Contestant Number Four. Tall and skinny, with copper-brown skin, his uncircumcised dick arched to the left, the foreskin sort of just hanging there.

"Looks like an elephant's trunk," The Queen said, trying to sound playful. "I like Number Five myself."

"Oh yeah! He's definitely your type."

The Queen cocked her neck. "What's my type?"

"Big and black." CoCo giggled. "Like Duke and Knight."

Number Five was iridescent black, bald, and built with muscles just like Knight. His dick was long, thick, and pointed straight ahead, rarin' to go.

"Damn, he does look like Knight," The Queen exclaimed, "but not as good, or as big."

"Ain't many dudes who are 6-7," CoCo said, "but he comes close. An' when he win that money, chicks gon' be all ova tryin' to play that big joystick."

"I think he could be broke as hell an' still get the pussy."

CoCo laughed. "You right."

The Queen burst into tears. "I will just die if something happens to Knight."

"Hush, girl!" CoCo held her. "Don't let none o' these muthafuckas see you cry."

Chapter 45

The Queen had to get a grip on herself. Her mind was a moviestrip of scenes worse than any horror movie. And they were all of Knight laying somewhere in this building, dead at the hands of his brother. The next scene was The Queen finding him, throwing herself on his giant body that was her sanctuary from the wicked world, then figuring out how she could join her soul mate in the blissful infinity of heaven.

It's so fucked up to have this thought pattern. But I can't stop it.

Even with that ridiculously sexy show going on in front of her.

Every contest cranked up the kinkiness a little bit more. And judging by the way a lot of folks down in the audience were already fucking, sucking, and even getting themselves off, the stage was stimulating everybody else the way it was supposed to.

But The Queen wanted to run and scream and find her Knight.

"Ladies and gentlemen," Jamal announced as Studs pushed ten thick futon-style mattresses onto the stage, "it's time for one of the most popular events of The Games—The Longest Fucking Female on Top."

The crowd exploded as ten nude couples walked hand in hand and stopped in front of the mattresses.

Jamal introduced their names and teams as one of the Bang Squad's sexiest songs blasted, featuring The Queen singing the lyrics she had written: "Jiggle jam, slam it, ma'am, yes I am, tryin' to cram, all that ram up in my jiggle jam, bam-bam-bam . . . "

The Queen sang along as Jamal said, "And lastly we have the superstar champs from every year I can remember— Pebbles and Bam-Bam!"

The audience roared.

The Studs laid on the mattresses, which were covered by the blue mist so that it looked like the men were hovering in outer space. Some laid with their toes pointing to the judges;

others positioned themselves so that their heads were closer to the edge of the stage.

"The goal of this event," Jamal said, "is to see which female can keep it pumpin' the longest. Now, ladies"—He smiled at the audience—"you know it hurts like hell in the quadriceps when you do this for even a minute or two, so give your girls some props for all this athletic prowess they 'bout to display."

The chicks in the audience screamed and shrieked.

"Slam on it, girls!" somebody shouted.

That's how The Queen loved to do Knight, with her knees far apart so that her swollen clit protruded from her spread-open crotch. They both liked to look down at it as her bronze, bald pussy lips swallowed his thick, black shaft, in and out, in and out, covering it with her juice that glistened in the candle light.

Now, The Queen saw nothing but Pebbles and Bam-Bam. The husband-wife team was poetry in motion as her muscles, from her poppin'-hard glutes to the firm curves of her hamstrings and quads, to her tight calves, flexed with Olympic power. She was so cut that each individual muscle fiber rippled under her smooth skin. She was squatting, offering the audience a side view of the action as she faced Bam-Bam.

"Oh, shit!" CoCo watched as Pebbles spun like a basketball player dribbling in a circle. "How she do that?"

Suddenly Pebbles was facing Bam-Bam's feet, without missing a beat.

"Twirl on that shit, girl!" someone screamed in the audience. "All night!"

Nine of the women were hammering down on the men like rabbits. That's what Tiffany used to call herself in high school—she and girls who loved to fuck a lot were like rabbits, humping any and everything with a hard-on. Like dogs in heat.

Raw fucking had its place, but Pebbles and Bam-Bam were showing everybody how it was supposed to be done—with smooth, sultry motions—slow, sexy circles of the hips, 'round and 'round as she worked it in and out.

SEX IN THE HOOD 2

Some of the girls looked like they were riding a bull, bucking wildly, bouncing like pogo sticks, hair flying, titties flopping all around, their faces frantic and frenzied.

But Pebbles was mellow, like she had all century to marinate that beefstick up in her self-basting oven. Oiled and opalescent, her muscle-toned shoulders, stomach, and back rolled and poured like liquid, as if the love that she was expressing with her body melted her into a sensuous libation over her lover.

The other girls tickled their titties to tantalize the audience and make their nipples point harder.

Pebbles ran her fingertips over Bam-Bam's thighs. Then she spun around again, staring into his eyes.

He pressed his elbows into the mattress, extending his forearms upward.

She grasped his hands, pressed her palms to his, and laced fingers. Then, while still grinding her hips into him, she leaned down, stuck out her tongue, and licked his face from his chin up to his forehead, then back down to his mouth for a long, sensuous kiss, never missing a beat with her hips.

"Da-yum!" CoCo exclaimed. "I thought me an' Jamal be makin' love, but Pebbles be doin' it!"

Just like me and Knight.

She shot up to her feet.

"Where you goin'?" CoCo asked with an alarmed expression. She gripped The Queen's wrist and said, "I know you ain't gon' miss the pussy-lickin' contest or dick-suckin' event; they're next."

"I gotta find Knight."

If she could get past the human wall of muscle formed by Ping and Pong, who shook their heads, cast somber glares down at her, and pointed for her to put her ass back in her seat—now.

283

Chapter 46

Trina Michaels' pussy was burning with need, and her brain was even more excited. "Can you believe the perversion of this place? The world media is gonna eat this up!"

"You wish that were you up there," her cameraman shot back. "Maybe you wouldn't be such a bitch if you got your pussy pumped on a regular basis."

"That comment constitutes sexual harassment, according to the GNN company handbook. I'm going to report you when we get back to D.C."

The cameraman adjusted dials on the panel of video editing equipment. "Go for it. Because the NAACP, the GNN diversity committee and the black journalists' association are all about to hear about the real Trina Michaels."

She raised her chin, loving the video feeding in live from the eight cameras hidden on Rip Masta Mac and his homies.

The equipment here in the truck was digitally recording the video of the wild sex acts, Victoria Winston, her pimp extraordinaire, Knight Johnson, and all these celebrities taking part in this illegal endeavor.

Later, Trina and her cameraman would send the incriminating video by satellite back to the station in Washington.

And I'll become a superstar.

And her jealous cameraman could do nothing to stop her. Trina raised her chin. "As if the NAACP would support this type of animalistic hedonism. Half those jokers are smoking marijuana, and they're all taking part in an illegal sex ring. Civil rights leaders will praise me for putting an enterprise like this out of business."

The cameraman ignored her as he adjusted the sound on camera three.

Trina loved the idea that she'd have video of the event, thanks to Rip Masta, as well as video taken by the Federal agents when they raided the building. And that was supposed to take place within the hour.

Of course Rip had no idea that hundreds of Federal agents were waiting in nearby vans, helicopters, and boats to interrupt his videotaping tasks. No, he was just a pawn in a game too big for his little mind to get burdened with.

Despite her objections, Trina had surrendered to Rick's demand that his agents also get live video from Rip Masta's hidden cameras.

Trina wanted exclusive access to that video so that Rick couldn't backstab her and give her hard-earned scoop to another reporter at another network. But Rick refused. And without Rick's help, she wouldn't have Rip Masta and his crew videotaping this Babylonian sextravaganza.

Her mouth dropped open as she watched that woman fucking on top of the man. The power of her body and the position of female domination made Trina squeeze her thighs over her soaking wet panties. This was messy work, but she loved it.

Yeah, she and Rick would have a good time reviewing this video together. Because it just kept getting hotter and—

"Hey, what are you doing?" Trina exclaimed. "Why are the screens going black?"

Chapter 47

Duke helped Rip Masta Mac pull off the hidden cameras and wires, while Dickman assisted the rest of the crew in doing the same. It just so happened that Rip, invited to the wedding and Games by Knight, had called Duke earlier that afternoon to find out if his boy was back in action.

Another sign from the Babylon gods that it was time for The Duke to ascend back to the throne; because Duke's offer to make Rip rich in the Babylon underground had sounded much more appealing to his boy than trusting that Fed muthafucka who had promised immunity in exchange for hidden video of the hottest action around.

"Fuck them liars," Rip said, tossing the lipstick-sized camera onto the floor. He stomped on it.

"Work wit' me, man," Duke said. "Disappear off they radar in a Motor City minute."

"Dig that," Rip said, staring at the silver circular handle on the locked vault. "Now, how we gon' get the loot? The Games end in two hours an' they gon' be comin' down here to pay the winners. All cash. Plus I gotta book, 'cause soon as that Rick prick see I directed his home movie to fade to black, he gon' be up in here lookin' fo' me."

Duke playfully raised a fist over Rip's face. "Man, I oughta fuck you up for bringin' heat—"

Dickman grabbed Duke's wrist. "Dude, the vault."

Rip nodded to a slim, beige-skinned brotha with a wild sandy-brown 'fro. "My boy Jimmy, he a locksmith worst nightmare."

Duke led Jimmy to the safe. "Jam on it, my brotha."

Chapter 48

Knight stood in the center of the surveillance room, scanning each monitor for Li'l Tut. Paul and the rest of the security team had just explained how and where they had seen him.

I'ma find him an' kill 'im wit' my own hands.

"Keep zooming in on the crowds," Knight said as B'Amazons studied live feeds from all over the inside and outside of this building. In the auditorium, one camera stayed on The Queen; Knight glanced back at her on that monitor frequently as he scanned the other screens.

"Here go one of the vans," Paul said, zooming an outdoor camera to focus on a black van a block away. He pointed to several other monitors that showed a convoy of vans and a helicopter lurking in the darkness in the warehouse district around The Playhouse. "They got some boats out on the water too."

Icy fingers of worry shot outward along Knight's spine.

They're gonna raid us any minute.

"When they move," Knight said, staring hard into Paul's eyes, "you know it's time for Inferno." Knight had never used the mechanism that would ignite the water in the moat around The Playhouse into a wall of fire.

Modeled after Medieval defense tactics for castles; it worked by emptying huge vats of flammable chemicals into the water, which would then be set on fire. The moat was far enough away from the building that no one would get hurt, but no one could get past it either.

Meanwhile, anyone inside the building could leave via the underground tunnels that led to various buildings in a one-mile radius.

"It's done, Boss Knight," Paul said. "Soon as you give me the sign."

Knight checked out a monitor that showed the rooftop terrace where people lingered at the reception dinner tables. A band played, allowing folks to slow-dance and sip champagne. At the edges of the roof, sniper-trained Barriors and

B'Amazons in black perched with rifles, ready to defend this urban fortress.

Knight had assigned only folks who were veterans of the Persian Gulf War and the Iraq War, and even several older brothas who'd served in Vietnam, for that detail. They weren't scared; their minds were right to execute The Prince Code: *Kill or be killed.*

That's how Knight viewed Li'l Tut. No matter what went down tonight, even if Babylon burned to the ground and had to rise like a triumphant phoenix from the ashes, Li'l Tut would not be part of it.

Knight searched monitors that showed the second floor, where hundreds of people splashed and sexed it up in and around the tropical-style swimming pool and hot tubs. Giant closed-circuit TV screens played The Games at each end of the turquoise playpen.

Gerard sat at the edge of the pool, twisted up under three strippers. One of them was in the water, sucking his dick, while the others gyrated around him.

That pathetic muthafucka will get his due.

"Yeah, Boss," Paul said, "Gerard lost his mind. Abandoned his post and joined the party."

Knight visually scoured the heavily guarded marina where Yacht #1 and Yacht #2 hummed in their slips, while Barriors loaded the cigarette boat and Yacht #2 with all the cash, except for the prize money and bet money for The Games. Together, that amounted to fifteen million.

Knight had left it, because he was not going to jack up Jamal's reputation by absconding with the cash owed to the contestants and participants. The winning contestants would get paid, as would the folks who'd bet on them.

Nope, Knight had taken only the admissions money, which totaled $25 million. And that money, on Yacht #2, was pulling out of the marina right now. His laptop, where he and Jamal would make the transfer, was on Yacht #1. That was also where The Queen would think it was all over.

It will be . . . for a minute.

SEX IN THE HOOD 2

Both yachts were captained by crews from Florida; they had no idea what was about to go down. Knight had paid Larry Marx a ridiculous fee to secure these crews, experienced in the pirate-like world of smuggling everything between the United States and South American countries. They had all the appropriate licenses and paperwork on board to burn through any red tape bullshit that the Coast Guard, Detroit Police marine patrols, or anybody else tried to flex.

Knight watched the Barriors work. They too would be lavishly rewarded for transporting it to a private dock owned by Larry Marx's friend downriver. There, the cigarette boat would deliver Knight and The Queen, and they would board Yacht #2 and sail away forever.

Knight's heart pounded as he thought about Jamal. In just a short while, they would do the deal to exchange ownership of Babylon. That additional $25 million would make Knight attain his target jackpot of $50 million. And that would set him and The Queen up to live like royalty with Baby Prince for the rest of their lives, *if we can get out of here* . . .

He coughed as stress suddenly clenched his chest.

On the lobby level, the Knight look-alike Stud who had competed in the Best Dick event stood with a Latina chick with long black hair and a wedding gown. The decoy couple would walk out through the front doors and get into Hummer One, decorated with a *Just Married* sign. That vehicle would go to the airport as if Knight and The Queen were en route to their honeymoon.

But Knight still had to find Li'l Tut.

Monitors showed the suites on the fifth floor, where all kinds of people were watching The Games on closed circuit TV and holding their own erotic Olympics on beds, chairs, and floors.

Knight looked to the next screens showing the vault. "There he is," Knight said calmly. He tossed back his head and bust out laughing. Because the vault was empty.

The prize and bet money was being protected by a heavily armed battalion of soldiers in a room under the stage dressing rooms. This would be a piece of cake. All Knight had to do was go to the vault room and squash Li'l Tut like a bug.

It ain't gonna be that easy, Intuition said.

Chapter 49

Beat was rock-hard inside Jamal's jeans as he watched the Best Dick Suckin' contest on stage. He couldn't wait to get with CoCo Boo, who looked just as horny as he was up there in the balcony with The Queen.

'Cause good as those chicks givin' head, don't nobody do it as good as my girl.

Despite the sexual excitement of this night, Jamal suddenly felt like he had to take a shit—in his pants. 'Cause he was scared shitless about doing this deal with Knight.

This was hype and everything, but Jamal just didn't know if he wanted to own it. The more he thought about Dickman's offer to go with him and Duke and let Duke be the boss of this illegitimate empire, the more he liked the idea.

Knight was always talking about The Prince Code, keeping his hands clean.

Yeah, I'm a music mogul wit' legit bidness. I gotta keep my hands clean too.

But the image of Knight glaring down at him in the aisle when he'd expressed doubts flashed in his mind.

Jamal squeezed his butt so he wouldn't shit. Then again, how would Knight even know if Jamal let Duke take over? He'd be all the way on an island somewhere, bangin' with The Queen, not worrying about what's going on back at Babylon. All that righteous talk about feeding the kids in Africa and protecting the hood. Shit! Jamal could make sure that still happened. Duke had a heart too. Plus, by dealing with Duke, Jamal would still be showing loyalty and appreciation to the Johnson family for bankrolling his music business. Even though Duke didn't wanted to spring with the cash to make it happen.

Bygones is bygones. I'll do the deal wit' Knight on the boat. I'll come back an' hand it all back over to Duke. Then I can get the fuck on my merry way wit' my CoCo Boo an' my bangin' music business.

Chapter 50

The Queen loved looking at all those beautiful dicks getting licked like lollipops. Especially that Team Thuggalicious chick with the bright pink lips whose cornrowed head and body looked like an old-fashioned water pump, going up and down, up and down, until—

Squirt!

She made that dude cum in a matter of seconds. His dick was like a firehose, shooting white cream longer than it took for her to make him blow.

"They won hands down," CoCo said.

"*Dick* down," The Queen giggled. She had to make herself laugh or she'd cry.

It's gonna be like Armageddon, Celeste said. *The end of the world as you know it.*

The Queen didn't know what, but something beyond even her wildest imagination, which she thought had been stretched to the limits here in Babylon, was about to happen.

Didn't any of those people down in the audience feel it too? They were feeling something, because the main floor looked like a tangle of bodies, writhing, grinding, bobbing, bouncing, all with their faces toward the blue glow of the stage, so they could watch the spectacle of sex.

And the people in the balconies around her, didn't they feel the sinister vibe in the air that was making the hairs on the back of her neck stand up? It was as strong as an electrical current pulsing through the air.

Emcee Sexarella was bent over the balcony rail and getting fucked hard by a Stud who kept slapping her big, round ass.

Moreno was on the phone. His waxy face and scary hazel eyes turned toward her, as if he'd felt her staring. He nodded while talking.

The Queen definitely took it as a bad omen that Brian was here inside Babylon, sitting so close to her, staring at her with hate in his blue eyes.

He'd smiled a few times at Tiffany, who had waved her bony hand at The Queen.

The Queen smiled, wondering if Tiffany knew that this *Bad Bitch* was the reason that punk-ass Brian suddenly had brand-new front teeth. She still didn't understand how Brian hooked up with Moreno, whom she now believed was the same man she'd seen at Brian's and Tiffany's parents' parties—and at Daddy's office a few times. She just wanted to get as far away from his Lucifer-life aura as possible.

Moreno kept staring at her as he put his embalmed-looking hand on the head of the girl who was sucking his dick. As she went up and down, it looked like he was dribbling a basketball. He cast lustful eyes at The Queen, his tongue flickering between his wet lips. When he mouthed, "You're mine," The Queen shivered.

He knew something she didn't know. Only some sinister secret would give him the gall to act so bold on her husband's turf.

Knight, baby, where are you?

The Queen wanted to get up and run and run and run until she found Knight. She would grab his hand and together they would run.

A giant hand gripped her shoulder, and she froze.

It was Pong's. He and his brother were motioning for her and CoCo to follow them. And the expressions on their faces let them know that they weren't escorting the ladies to a champagne toast at the afterparty.

Chapter 51

Moreno was on the phone with his commander, who gave a move-by-move report.

The battalion was charging the tunnel leading from the Detroit River. These young men and women whom he had recruited from ravaged areas of Ireland, Bosnia, Israel, and every inner city in America were trained and ready to kill. They specialized in storming buildings full of people and getting them all under control in a matter of minutes. So that Moreno could get what he wanted and leave just as quickly.

The thunder of their feet echoed up the metal staircases into the first floor, second floor, and third floor of The Playhouse.

Red had a floor plan of the building thanks to Flame down in Mexico. A comrade had interviewed the exiled Stud, who had been delighted to share confidential information about the secret tunnels.

A bit of C4 explosives on the vault and the millions would be his. Then his troops would head up to wherever Knight was hiding. They'd kill him, take Cleopatra, and get to work.

Merging this urban empire with Moreno Enterprises would take work. The transition could get rocky, if they encountered any opposition from the staff. But they were used to being ruled with an iron fist. So it would be only a matter of time before they got used to having a white man call the shots around here.

Red Moreno watched the dick-sucking contest on stage as he calmly gave orders into his cell phone. His troops were about to barge into the vault room; others were seeking out Knight and Cleopatra.

Then Red would have five minutes to extricate the lovely girl from his lap, unite with his commander, and ride away with Cleopatra and twenty-five million dollars.

Chapter 52

"What the fuck!" Paul exclaimed as dozens of white men and women in brown jumpsuits stormed up into The Playhouse from the river tunnel. But they weren't Feds.

Then who the hell were they?

Paul stood in the center of Cairo, watching the monitors. He felt helpless, like all the wild cards he'd never even thought of were being played at once. How could he trump all that by himself? Because even the top-security Barriors and B'Amazons here in Cairo were staring wide-eyed at the monitors.

I need Knight back up here! He didn't say nothin' about this shit goin' down!

But Knight was heading down to the third floor to pounce on Duke, and Ping and Pong were bringing The Queen and CoCo up here.

The show was still going on in the auditorium, thousands of people partying on every floor of this building.

And the Fed vans were starting to move in. The video monitors from the outdoor cameras showed the vans steadily creeping up the street, and the cameras on the roof showed two choppers hovering too close, while Coast Guard boats were bobbing just beyond the marina.

Babylon 'bout to blow!

Paul punched a single button on his console to reach Knight's cell phone. "Answer!" he exclaimed.

If Knight walked up on those white soldiers storming down the third floor hallway, toward the vault . . .

Paul stood in disbelief. The white folks in brown jumpsuits burst into the vault room.

Duke, Dogman, and Rip Masta all drew guns.

Bullets blasted. People in brown dropped.

Pow!

The floor shook. A gray cloud rolled up toward the monitors.

"Somebody blew something up," Paul exclaimed.

And the vault room monitors went black.

295

"There's Duke!" A Barrior pointed to another screen. "In the hallway."

A B'Amazon said, "Here comes Knight!"

A gray dust cloud rolled into the hallway, where people were running, coughing, and blasting guns at each other.

Paul's brain was a tornado. Should I ignite the moat? Put the rooftop snipers on alert? Sound the alarm? How far had The Queen and CoCo made it? Since the auditorium was on the first and second levels, and the vault was on the third floor, were they caught in that chaos? Had the explosion blown through the floor?

No, the music was still blasting in the auditorium; those sex-crazed folks didn't hear or see a thing. On the monitors, they were transfixed on the Longest Fuck contest on stage, where five couples remained in a frenzied fuck-a-thon. And judging by the size of those Studs, and the Energizer Bunny power in their hips, they weren't going to finish anytime soon.

He almost laughed. If this joint was about to blow up, then those Studs were the luckiest dudes in the building—they'd die fuckin'.

Paul felt dizzy. "What the hell should I do right now?"

Chapter 53

Knight had to find The Queen. They had to get out now. He could do without Jamal; he could make do with the twenty-five million he already had.

This is a matter of life and death.

Knight coughed on the gray dust in the dimly lit hallway. He stepped over a white man in brown who was groaning on the floor.

Moreno's people—What fuckin' nerve for that Eurotrash muthafucka to think he could storm my turf and steal my loot!

The Queen. Knight's legs pumped with bionic speed. Holding his breath against the dusty smoke, he ran down the hallway to meet Ping and Pong just as they brought his goddess and CoCo up to Cairo on the ninth floor. He charged into the stairwell, taking the black metal steps three at a time. His heart throbbed with pain as he huffed, finally reaching the eighth floor landing.

One more to go.

He'd get The Queen, tell Paul to ignite the moat, and dash to the boat. As he ran up the final flight, he heard voices. Saw several pairs of black Timberland boots. And pink leather stiletto boots. Two pairs.

His heart stopped, or at least it felt that way.

The Queen was standing there, wide-eyed with fear, as Li'l Tut wrapped his arm around her neck and aimed a gun at Knight. "*Déjà vu*, muthafuckaaaaa!" Li'l Tut teased with a crazed look in his eyes. With that raw wound on his cheek, he looked like Freddy Krueger. His voice echoed off the exposed brick of the stairwell. Then he imitated the twang of a cowboy, "Time for a showdown, sheriff."

Dickman and Rip Masta, plus three of their homies, were all pointing guns at Ping, Pong, and CoCo. The thugs let out deep, sinister laughs.

Knight's chest rose and fell as he tried to catch his breath. He stared his brother in the eye. Then he glanced at The Queen. The terror on her face, and the tremble of her body that in eight months would deliver their baby Prince of Peace riled up something in his soul.

I'll save my family. And not die trying.

Chapter 54

On video monitors, Paul watched the showdown in the stairwell. He mobilized snipers to take out Duke and his crew.

A rifle-carrying battalion of Barriors and B'Amazons was already stomping those crazy folks in brown jumpsuits down in the tunnel, the lower stairwells, and the hallway leading to the already-empty vault.

Whoever had plotted that hare-brained scheme . . .

"Paul." A Barrior pointed to monitors showing the vans full of Federal agents. They were approaching; some of the SWAT-looking officers were piling out in front of the building.

"Inferno!" Paul commanded.

Suddenly all the fear and worry and confusion melted. He knew exactly what he had to do.

The Barrior walked to the red panel and flipped the switch.

Whoosh!

A wall of fire rose up in front of The Playhouse. The SWAT dudes shielded their faces and ran back. It was just like in *The Ten Commandments* when Moses parted the Red Sea long enough for the Israelites to pass to the other side, but as soon as Ramses' soldiers tried to cross the riverbed, the water crashed back on them.

Chapter 55

As Jamal announced the winners of the Longest Fuck contest, the audience screamed and shrieked and even squirted cum up toward the stage. The whole joint was as orgified as any Babylon party was supposed to be.

I'm gon' shit on myself. Right now.

Jamal wanted to know why the fuck his CoCo Boo and The Queen had disappeared during the hottest event of the night. If they were that horny, they coulda done each other right there in the box and let him glance up for a peek. Or they could've waited another twenty or thirty minutes for him and Knight to all get on the boat and get freaky together before the honeymoon lovebirds did their own thing.

Jamal squeezed his butt. *Shit.* Deep down in his trembling gut, he knew the reason the girls were gone was much more serious than them wanting to get their freak on.

Somethin' ain't right.

Duke was supposed to page him but hadn't; Knight was supposed to call him but hadn't.

CoCo would've text-messaged him something nasty to tease him and tell him where she was, and she hadn't.

And why the fuck did the floor shake like that? Even with these superhuman fuck machines on the stage, nothing right could rock the house like that.

Plus, why had that spooky-lookin' Moreno dude and his crew just up and left in a huff . . . while their team was winning too? It didn't make sense.

Now, Jamal still had to oversee all the winners as they collected their cash prizes from that little, guarded room backstage. The Barriors and B'Amazons were delivering the cash to each of them in Babylon's trademark gold treasure chests, and they were getting high security escorts out of the auditorium.

In another room, all the cats who were "blowed" on booze, booty, and blunts were collecting their winnings for the bets they'd placed on each event.

SEX IN THE HOOD 2

Jamal loved the excitement and the eroticism and the enterprising spirit of the night. Naw, he didn't need Duke to run this shit. It was too much responsibility to share with that hothead who was gonna die anyway. Plus, the millions of dollars in the house right now made Beat bang for a hot second.

All this will be mine in a minute . . . if Babylon still standin' long enough for me an' Knight to do the damn deal.

Chapter 56

Knight remembered his favorite scenes in all those wild, wild west movies . . . when the cowboy would draw his guns with lightning speed, blast away his enemies, and make off with the girl. Or the money. Or simply his life.

Right now, as he stared down the defiantly crazy look in Li'l Tut's eyes—and the horrifically terrified expression on The Queen's face—he was about to re-enact one of those scenes with Oscar-worthy talent.

Ping and Pong were so quick, they could do the same in a split second, to take care of Li'l Tut's punks.

Question was, Which gun should he reach for first? The one in the waistband of his pleated black Armani silk pants? The one in the holster under his shoulder? Or the two in his black leather cowboy boots?

With his free hand, Li'l Tut yanked down The Queen's camisole, and her titties popped out.

"Eh, big bro', remember when you took my bitch? She was sittin' naked on my dick at my birthday party, and you just lifted her off like you used to do when we was small—always stealin' my favorite toy for yourself?" Li'l Tut tossed back his head, making his sinister laughter echo up the stairwell.

Knight half-winked at Ping and Pong. It was too subtle for those knuckleheads, Dickman and Rip Masta, to catch. It meant, "Do like I do, when I do it."

The Queen's silver-blue eyes were roiling with a brainstorm as she crossed her arms over her bare breasts. If she still had her gun in her boot, now wouldn't have been the time for her to try to draw it.

Just before Li'l Tut looked back down, Knight cast a look at her saying, "I got ya back, Tinkerbell."

As he held a gun in his left hand, Li'l Tut used his other hand to yank down the zippers on each hip of her pink leather pants. The fabric fell down, exposing her still flat belly, where their baby was growing. Li'l Tut's scarred hand pulled down her hands. He squeezed her breasts, pulling them up to cover her *Cleopatra of the Knight* tattoo. He unbuckled his baggy

302

jeans, let them fall to the floor. His dick, big, hard, and bloody from a nasty gash on the shaft, swung out, and hit her leg.

"Yeah, we gon' do a *déjà vu* moment all the way, big bro'. We gon'—"

Pow!

Yeah, that's how the sheriff rules in this town. Waistband was the closest thing to a wild, wild west hip-holster.

Perfect aim. Perfect shot. Right in the forehead.

Just like Ping and Pong, the sharpshooter muthafuckas that they were. Knocking down Rip Masta, Dickman, and the two other thugs in a flash.

Then, like a giant robot switched into bionic gear, Knight swooped The Queen up in his arms, while Ping picked up CoCo.

The men stepped over the mess on the landing. And headed up to Cairo.

Chapter 57

Trina Michaels could not believe that those ghetto pimps were pulling off this pyrotechnic feat. Her whole story was ruined, thanks to a lying thug named Rip Masta Mac, an incompetent FBI joker named Rick Reed, and a Bonnie and Clyde team who had outsmarted everybody.

"Incredible." Her cameraman gasped as he stood beside her, outside the TV truck, shooting video of the twenty-foot-high wall of fire.

Sure, this would make spectacular story in itself, but it was nothing like what she'd envisioned for her exposé on Babylon and the capture of Victoria Winston. Was she even still inside there? How long would this fire burn?

She dialed Rick on his cell phone. "Have you heard from Rip Masta? Or did he just fuck you up the ass?"

Two helicopters hovered nearby, but they couldn't get anywhere near those flames.

Ping! Pow-pow-pow! Pop-pop-pop!

"Gunfire!" Trina screeched.

"Snipers on the roof," the cameraman said, aiming his camera up where the orange glow of the fire illuminated the black tips of guns aiming down at Federal agents still standing on the streets around the building.

Trina ran back into the unmarked TV truck.

"Shit!" She had dropped her phone. She'd thought she was so smart, orchestrating this story, using her body to get what she thought would be the scoop of the century.

Now, she felt like one stupid, fucked bitch.

Chapter 58

The siren blared as Emcee Sexarella and her crew hurried down the stairwell with mobs of other spectators. An announcement played over and over on the speaker system: "To escape the raid, proceed down the stairs to the underground tunnels. They will take you to a nearby nightclub, a park, and an outdoor concert pavilion. Blend in with the people there for a while. Then discreetly make arrangements to get picked up."

Sexarella's head throbbed. "We all be so fucked up, how we gon' do all that?"

"Better'n gettin' locked up," her Stud said playfully. "Gotta hand it to my man Knight, you know—he laid it out, an' took care o' his peeps in case of emergency."

"What they got us on?" Sexarella took off her high-heeled boots so she could walk faster down these damn stairs.

"PPpfffftt!" a girl laughed. "Prostitution, drugs, gamblin'—"

"Guurrrl, shut the fuck up!" Sexarella said playfully. "Now, where we gon' party at when we get the fuck outta these damn tunnels? Guuurrrlll, I hope it ain't no rats up in here."

Chapter 59

Babylon was burning behind her, or at least so it seemed, with the ring of fire around the building they had just escaped. The *rat-tat-tat* of guns echoed off the fire-lit sky. The screams of people in the stairwells and that deafening siren still rang in her ears.

The Queen was shell-shocked but not surprised.

Every minute for Alice in her sexy Wonderland had gotten more erotic and enticing from the first jump into what she'd thought was a terrifying black hole a year ago.

But suddenly, over the past month, erotic and enticing had nosedived into sinister and scary. So the turn of events today, her wedding day, was just following that trend.

She stared straight ahead at that boat about twenty feet away in the marina behind The Playhouse. That would be her magic carpet ride up and out of this Terrorland.

I can't stand the hand that Fate helped create, got my mate and a date, with a child, it's so wild that we styled a life as a wife, yet the strife like a knife, cuts a hole in my soul, takes a toll on my heart 'til we make a new start . . .

She gripped Knight's hand harder as they ran across the lawn toward the water. CoCo, Jamal, Ping, and Pong clustered close as they sprinted.

The marina lights were out, but the fire cast a bright orange glow over the boats and the black water.

Her lungs ached as she gasped for breath, and her toes throbbed from running down the stairs in stiletto boots.

But I'm alive. Duke didn't get me. Neither did Brian or Moreno or anybody else. And Knight is alive.

Finally, their feet pounded onto the wooden dock. To her right and to her left, the fire ring burned all the way to the water's edge. Knight had never told her about this medieval-looking defense tactic.

As long as it was keeping the bad guys out long enough for them to escape, she didn't care. But what about all those police boats, Coast Guard patrols and who knew what else lurking out on the river?

Trust me, Baby Girl.

Yes, she could hear her Knight speaking again on their supernatural love connection.

The crew on the yacht was pulling in the bumpers and the ropes, ready to speed away as soon as they jumped on board. They stepped onto a plexiglass lip at the back, which was strewn with ropes, boogie boards, and scuba gear. It led to two sets of sliding doors.

Knight hurried them through one door, down into the plush living room area, and the boat took off.

"We're safe," Knight said, breathing hard. He looked pale, dark circles ringing his bloodshot eyes.

If anything had happened to him back there, she would've made like Juliet and followed Romeo to heaven. Hopefully they were on their way to doing that right now. On Earth. She needed a long hug and to make love.

Knight walked to a sleek wooden desk built into the flat-screen TV console. He pulled out his laptop and huddled with Jamal as they typed quickly and spoke softly.

"What the fuck business could you possibly be doing right now?" she demanded.

They ignored her.

So The Queen and CoCo sank into the ultra-suede couches, closing their eyes, catching their breath, and Ping and Pong stood by the door, looking outside.

A deeply tanned crewman dashed in. "Everybody into the phantom room," he ordered, pushing a silver sconce on the wall that made a doorway appear in the beige suede wall. Inside was a windowless room ringed by low, cushioned benches. "The Coast Guard and FBI are boarding."

Chapter 60

Knight balanced over The Queen, kissing her in bed. The sleek, softly-lit master suite was silent except for the soft hum of the engines beneath them as they sped south down the Detroit River toward a better forever.

"Baby Girl," Knight whispered, "I wanted you to wear your wedding gown as I make love to you for the first time as my wife."

Her eyes sparkled and she smiled. Freshly showered with just-washed hair, it cascaded like a black halo all around her head. She wrapped her legs around the backs of his knees and said, "I'd rather wear my birthday suit."

She giggled as Shane throbbed against her thigh. Then she asked, "How did you shoot Duke like that so his blood didn't splatter on me?"

"Baby Girl," Knight said softly, "I want you to push a delete button in your head, starting with anything that happened before this minute. Forget all about today. Everything."

"Then I want you to promise me that you're okay," she said. "You look pale. And something in your eyes . . ."

Knight's heart pounded. The fist of stress was clenching his chest worse than ever. It would go away as soon as they got to the beach. He just had to stop that ringing sound in his head and that fuzzy feeling in his brain. "Baby Girl, you know I've hardly been sleeping, trying to get everything together—"

"There's more to it—Are we still in danger? If the Feds are still looking for us—I mean, I've never heard so many helicopters in my life." She glanced up at the ceiling. The chop of helicopters sounded close. The silvery circles of their spotlights flashed now and again on the closed curtains. "See, you look just as worried as I feel. You're not telling me something, just like you didn't tell me about all that shit today."

Knight pressed his mouth to her moving lips. They stilled. Because there was much more to come that he wasn't about to tell her.

Nope, somewhere between this bed and those double French doors leading out to the little patio and the water, she'd figure it out and help them reach nirvana. She could call it the final test if she wanted to, but then he'd know that she was committed to him forever, no matter what.

Her lips parted. And her tongue, reaching into his mouth, let him know that she'd much rather make love. She reached down and wrapped her hand around Shane. "This is my lifeline," she moaned, stroking his hard-as-diamond dick. "I never want to live without you, Knight."

"You won't ever have to, Baby Girl. Won't ever have to." His mouth wrapped around her open lips, their tongues twirling in a way that made him moan.

But the roar of boats beside them and the beating chop of the helicopter above made Knight's heart pound and ache. His lungs squeezed. Head spun. Limbs felt light and tingly.

Her face blurred.

I'm gonna faint.

"Baby Girl," he whispered weakly. No, he had to make love to his Queen as this happened. He knew she was ready; she was always wet as an ocean. So, just like the first time, this last time, he would make her cum with one stroke, and it would all be over. For both of them.

With the stealth and aim that made him who he was in business and in life and now in bed with his wife, he grasped the backs of her knees, pushed them forward.

"Yeah," she moaned, tickling her fingertips to the sides of his jaw and staring into his eyes.

He thrust Shane into that hot, tight, slippery paradise. Leaned his bare torso over her, and connected his lips to hers. All in a split second.

The way her body went limp and shivery all at once and that soft little moan that surged up from her soul let him know she was cumming with one stroke.

He pulled his lips back just enough to whisper into her mouth, so that the air in his lungs would mix with hers as they took their dying breath. "We're going to heaven together, Baby Girl."

"Oh, yeah," she moaned deeply, sucking on his bottom lip. She was panting, and breathing his air deep down.

His heartbeat was so out of whack, it was making static in his ears. Yeah, his dick felt phenomenal inside his Queen, but every stroke was sapping his energy. The roar in his ears grew louder. Or was that a chopper? Was he hallucinating that voice that said, "Come out with your hands up." Knight's heart was exploding with panic and passion all at once.

Gotta make this so good. The perfect ending to the perfect romance.

He thrust harder; she sucked his breath deeper.

Her eyes were closed, and her body was one with his. Now he was safe. Couldn't go anywhere but to heaven from this luscious launch pad.

Now, I can do it.

He envisioned the tight pink ball of muscle that was his heart. He imagined it never hurting, never making him worry. He imagined it still and peaceful, his spirit floating up with The Queen's soul up to an eternal playground where they could make love for infinity. He closed his eyes and let that fuzzy, roaring sensation, the *numb-tingly* feeling, take over his mind and body.

And suddenly his heart stopped hurting.

Chapter 61

"Knight!" she screamed. Shane was still inside her, hard as a rock, pulsating like he was cumming. "Knight! Wake up!" She pressed her face into his neck, to feel for his pounding pulse. The hot skin against her face was still.

He's dead. And he knew he was gonna die right now.

"Muthafucka!"

The roar of boats around them, those damn choppers overhead, and the rage and horror in her head fueled her body as she ran to the double French doors. She threw them open, barely glimpsing Canada on the right and the smokestacks of downriver factories just south of Detroit. Spotlights from police helicopters cut silver-white lines across the choppy black water.

She did not feel the chill of the September night on her bare skin as she stepped onto the three-foot ledge designed for watersports. It was smooth plexiglass with a lip that went into the water, so folks could swim or scuba dive or hop onto jet skis.

Tonight it would serve a more morbid purpose. She kicked open the gate leading to the black water. From the ledge, she grabbed a boogie board and some rope. She threw them into the room. Then she yanked Knight's arm, to pull him off the bed, but his 275 pounds and 6-foot, 7-inches of African god did not budge. So she pulled harder.

The clock on the nightstand said 3:05 a.m. Someone on the crew had to be awake, driving this boat. But why all the frantic footsteps upstairs? Did they hear her scream?

If they come down here to stop me, I'll shoot.

The Queen laid the rope on the floor under the boogie board. She found superhuman strength to pull Knight off the bed, onto the boogie board. She tied the rope around his chest then dragged him through the doors onto the ledge.

She felt dizzy from all those boats zig-zagging around them, the choppers, the floodlights, and that amplified voice saying, "Come out with your hands up!" She was so glad the crew wasn't coming down here to bother her.

WHITE CHOCOLATE

I told Knight I would do this. I told him.

The Queen positioned his legs so they were already in the water. He was facing up on the boogie board, slippery against the plexiglass. Her whole body trembled as she laid on Knight so she was facing down, pressing her pregnant belly into the warmth of his. With trembling hands, she tied the rope around her waist, fastening it on the small of her back, over her QUEEN OF THE KNIGHT tattoo.

She hummed the theme song to *Romeo and Juliet* as she pressed her ear into the silence of his chest, where his heart should have been beating. Riding him like a surfboard, she pushed her palms into the plexiglass and wrapped her arms around his beautiful, dark-chocolate muscles.

And together, as one, they slipped into the icy black infinity.

Epilogue

The fresh-cut pineapple was sweet and cold on her tongue, but Knight's fingertip was soft and warm as The Queen bit down.

"Gotcha," she giggled as they lay side by side on the plush chaise. The turquoise water stretched to infinity before them as the sun sizzled on their bare backs and asses.

Knight loved how she sucked his finger into her mouth as he flipped her on her back.

"Oooohh, yeah," she moaned, trembling as her pussy pulsated around Shane. "Make me cum with one stroke every time."

"Sssshh, Mommy," he teased, "don't wake Baby Prince."

They glanced over at the white bassinet in the shade of a palm tree. His eyes were closed tightly on his plump, beige face; the gentle ocean breeze jiggled his wild shock of black curls. Knight's whole body tingled with pleasure.

This was Manifest Destiny, live and in color.

He tingled even more with the sexual, emotional, and spiritual thrill of it all. He had all the money he needed in the bank, thanks to Jamal's agreement to buy Babylon and keep it going for the right reasons. His body was relaxed; the chest pains had disappeared the moment they had arrived here on this private island a year ago. All thanks to Ping and Pong, who'd executed the underwater rescue a year ago with perfect precision.

They had plucked him and The Queen from the black depths of the Detroit River, put them on the cigarette boat, then whisked them to Yacht #2, a short distance down the river. Knight didn't die; he merely passed out with relief that they'd made it out of Babylon alive. And once The Queen regained consciousness on Yacht #2, and he'd explained Manifest Destiny, she'd been thrilled to learn that a glorious, safe new future awaited them.

Now Ping and Pong were here on the island, up at the luxurious house just a short walk up the trail from this beach.

Knight's mother was loving her private cottage nearby.

"Make love to me all day," The Queen whispered, "my beautiful African god named Knight."

"Love you to the infinity," he whispered as he thrust gently and stared into her lusty eyes. "Right here in paradise, Baby Girl."

THE END

ON SALE NOW

0-974702-59-5

1-893196-37-2

1-893196-32-1

shoulda, woulda, coulda

from best selling author
La Jill Hunt

1-893196-25-9

DON'T HATE THE PLAYER...
HATE THE GAME

BRANDIE

1-893196-68-2

URBAN BOOKS PRESENTS

AROUND THE WAY GIRLS 3

double trouble

1-893196-52-6

URBAN BOOKS PRESENTS

Little 2
BLACK GIRL LOST

KEITH LEE JOHNSON

1-893196-39-9

Rapper Arrested

Rape Charges Pending

FALLEN

DEBRA CLAYTON

1-893196-42-9

URBAN BOOKS presents

SEX IN THE 2
HOOD

White Chocolate

1-893196-53-4

1-893196-46-1

1-893196-45-3

1-893196-47-X

HIDDEN *intentions*

MEISHA CAMM

1-893196-40-2

URBAN BOOKS
PRESENTS

Make You

LA TONYA Y. WILLIAMS

1-893196-34-8

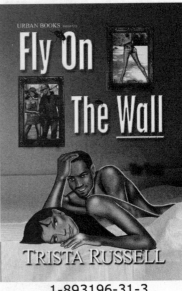

URBAN BOOKS PRESENTS

Fly On The Wall

TRISTA RUSSELL

1-893196-31-3

1-893196-23-2

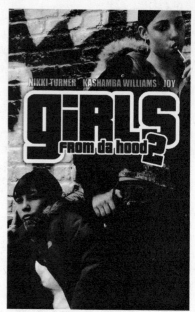

1-893196-28-3

1-893196-22-4

urban books presents

a novel by
Tony Lindsay

1-893196-27-5

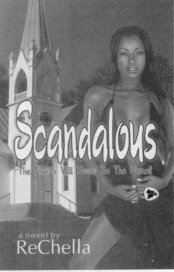

a novel by
ReChella

1-893196-30-5

FAYE THOMPSON

1-893196-53-4

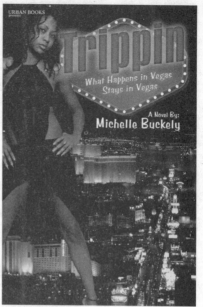

1-893196-49-6

1-893196-41-0

1-893196-33-X

OTHER URBAN BOOKS TITLES

Title	Author	Quantity	Cost
Drama Queen	LaJill Hunt		$14.95
No More Drama	LaJill Hunt		$14.95
Shoulda Woulda Coulda	LaJill Hunt		$14.95
Is It A Crime	Roy Glenn		$14.95
MOB	Roy Glenn		$14.95
Drug Related	Roy Glenn		$14.95
Lovin' You Is Wrong	Alisha Yvonne		$14.95
Bulletproof Soul	Michelle Buckley		$14.95
You Wrong For That	Toschia		$14.95
A Gangster's girl	Chunichi		$14.95
Married To The Game	Chunichi		$14.95
Sex In The Hood	White Chocalate		$14.95
Little Black Girl Lost	Keith Lee Johnson		$14.95
Sister Girls	Angel M. Hunter		$14.95
Driven	KaShamba Williams		$14.95
Street Life	Jihad		$14.95
Baby Girl	Jihad		$14.95
A Thug's Life	Thomas Long		$14.95
Cash Rules	Thomas Long		$14.95
The Womanizers	Dwayne S. Joseph		$14.95
Never Say Never	Dwayne S. Joseph		$14.95

She's Got Issues	Stephanie Johnson		$14.95
Rockin' Robin	Stephanie Johnson		$14.95
Sins Of The Father	Felicia Madlock		$14.95
Back On The Block	Felicia Madlock		$14.95
Chasin' It	Tony Lindsey		$14.95
Street Possession	Tony Lindsey		$14.95
Around The Way Girls	La Jill Hunt		$14.95
Around The Way Girls 2	La Jill Hunt		$14.95
Girls From Da Hood	Nikki Turner		$14.95
Girls from Da Hood 2	Nikki Turner		$14.95
Dirty Money	Ashley JaQuavis		$14.95
Mixed Messages	LaTonya Y. Williams		$14.95
Don't Hate The Player	Brandie		$14.95
Payback	Roy Glenn		$14.95
Scandalous	ReChella		$14.95
Urban Affair	Tony Lindsey		$14.95
Harlem Confidential	Cole Riley		$14.95

Urban Books
10 Brennan Place
Deer Park, NY 11729
Subtotal: _____
Postage:_____ Calculate postage and handling as
follows: Add $2.50 for the first item and $1.25 for each
additional item
Total: _____
Name: _____
Address: _____
City: _____ State: _____ Zip: _____
Telephone: ( ) _____
Type of Payment (Check: ___ Money Order: ___)
All orders must be prepaid by check or money order drawn
on an American bank.
Books may sometimes be out of stock. In that instance,
please select your alternate choices below.

Alternate Choices:

1._____

2._____

PLEASE ALLOW 4-6 WEEKS FOR SHIPPING